Snow White
Turtle Doves

Snow White Turtle Doves

Juliet Bressan

POOLBEG

Published 2008
by Poolbeg Press Ltd
123 Grange Hill, Baldoyle
Dublin 13, Ireland
E-mail: poolbeg@poolbeg.com
www.poolbeg.com

13 5 7 9 10 8 6 4 2

A catalogue record for this book is available from the British Library.

ISBN 978-1-84223-328-3

Typeset by Patricia Hope in Bembo 11.5./14.5

Printed by
CPI Cox & Wyman, Reading, RG1 8EX, UK

About the Author

Juliet Bressan was born in Salford, grew up in Galway and now lives in Dublin where she likes to spend her time drinking coffee, playing the clarinet and hiding from her kids and housework. In between writing novels she works as a physician, medical journalist and TV script advisor.

Acknowledgements

During the researching of this book I talked to Iraqi doctors, American servicemen, and to peace activists from all over the world. I especially wish to express my very deepest gratitude to Dr Salam Ismael, Director of Continuous Medical Education in Iraq, to Dr Michael Ryan and Dr Maire Connolly, and to Frank Corcoran, Ralph Steele and the Iraq Vets, for sharing their various experiences of the Iraq wars with me.

Deepest gratitude to my daughters Jessica Bressan (best writer's assistant ever), and Molly O'Grady Bressan. To Niamh Fitzgerald, Paula Campbell, Gaye Shortland and all at Poolbeg Press for all their kindness, their wisdom and support. To Dara Gantly (for being such a sincere and trustworthy first critic), and to Robert Love of Eireann Publications. To Siobhan Herron (for being an essential first-draft reader and a wonderful friend) and to my lifelong friends Miriam Mc Callum, Jennifer Kelly, and Nicola Kelly for their music, love and inspiration, and for telling me all about The Zone. To the writer Conor Bowman for his encouragement and enthusiasm, to the writer Conor Kostick for superb nights out (and some teaching too), and to the writer Sean Doyle for being such a patient, kind and creative colleague. To Paula Geraghty and Michael

Devoy for ideas, photos and unfailing enthusiasm. To Sam Mc Callum for his absolute perfection. To Kevin and Dermot Homan for their generosity and web-design. To Peter Homan. And to Jacqueline Walters, Edward and Dino Bressan for always being there.

Special thanks to the writer Michelle Jackson without whom it wouldn't have been possible.

Author's Note

The songs that Isabella and Eddie sing can all be found in *Soodlum's Selection of Irish Ballads*, Edited by Pat Conway, Volumes 1 – 4 Copyright 1981 Soodlum Music Co. Ltd. *The Playboy of the Western World* by JM Synge was first published in Dublin in 1907 – I used the 1993 edition published by Dover Publications New York for the various quotes from the performance of the play. The speech that William Cairns makes at Shannon includes a quotation from a letter written by John Millington Synge, the full text of which can be found in *J.M Synge and the Pitfalls of National Consciousness* collected by Paul Murphy Theatre Research International (2003) Cambridge University Press. The Harold Pinter speech quoted in Chapter 29 is an extract from The Nobel Lecture speech (which was broadcast to the public over the Internet). Pinter's visit to Dublin *actually* took place in October of 2005, not December 2006, but I have taken the liberty of very slightly altering the time-table of history for the romantic purposes of this story. I hope that Mr Pinter will forgive this deliberate alteration of the facts, in the spirit of the publication of this book.

For Jessie and Molly

Prologue

They met in primary school age twelve, although Isabella didn't remember it the way that Harry did. But she did remember Mrs Glynn, who wrote in dainty letters on the blackboard, chalk in pink and white and palest blue, and put a tiny circle o instead of a dot on top of letter i. Years later while at university, Isabella would find herself still making the same tiny circle over letter i in all her essays and her lecture notes. She found it gave her a small symbol of her sense of self, that she carried with her through life.

Mrs Glynn divided the class of senior primary into streams: smaller groups paired off in twos and threes according to ability. She explained this carefully to Isabella and to Harry, as she told them that she would be sitting them together by the window from now on, because they were good at Maths and English and History, and would help each other to do better that way. Mrs Glynn knew that children would grow bored unless they could be united in a common purpose, and so she happily exploited their natural instinct for collaboration and unity of intent.

Throughout the year, Isabella Somerfield worked successfully with Harry Waters, who seemed undistracted by her long black curls that trailed the copybooks over which they breathed. He chewed the paint off pencils, and worked out complicated maths for her. She checked his spellings, circled the i's and quizzed him up on rivers, capital cities, history dates, and Irish Verbs.

On a school trip to Lough Bree Forest Park, Isabella and Harry sat side by side, on an itchy bus seat that pricked their legs in shorts, and solemnly shared cheese and tomato sandwiches that were made with thick white toasting bread. Harry's mum, Marion Waters, had given them a bottle of weak Ribena to drink. Marion had watered down the Ribena until it was almost tasteless, just in case Mrs Somerfield, the doctor's wife, would not have allowed them a commercial sugary drink.

The sun was hot and Lough Bree Forest Park was thick and damply shady. In the thick hot breath of the forest, Harry kissed Isabella behind a rotting oak tree, and breathed the sharp fungus smell of the forest through her hair. Her mouth was warm and hard, and salty tasting, and her breath was moist fresh bread, sweet with yeast.

Isabella locked her small neat fingers into his and closed her eyes, and the bees buzzed, and the dragonflies hummed behind them and the forest swished and blinked above them. They kissed for a long, long time, breathing in the dark fungus smell, and they lay side by side in each other's arms, and each in the arms of the earth.

Years later, in an oak-panelled dormitory, to a

background of the snores of twenty other boys, Harry would relive that first kiss over and over again. Even though Isabella had become a distant memory he would still hold his breath, and try to taste her hot hard lips again. He would smell the grease from her hair and feel the grip of her fingers on his hand – which held a bunch of tissues now while the other pumped madly underneath the starched school sheets like a piston. His breath held to asphyxiation, Harry tried to stifle the noise of starched sheets shuddering in the night.

In the middle of her final college year, at the age of twenty-one, Isabella Somerfield would go to England to have an abortion for Harry Waters' child. She would take a bus to the ferry in Dun Laoire and then travel alone with all the cargo lorries and all the family cars to London via Holyhead.

The boat was noisy. Full of lorry drivers, children running up and down, and pensioners wandering blankly in and out of Duty Free. Isabella sat on cold hard red plastic seating in the cafeteria and considered her event. The smell of fried eggs was oily and nauseated her and so she avoided food, smoking John Player Blue instead. Her stomach lurched with sickness on the choppy February sea and so she lit a new cigarette, stubbing out the old one at the same time.

The television fizzling away high up in a corner of the cafeteria was playing the lunchtime news. The year was 1991: Images of Operation Desert Storm, over and over again. Teenage American soldiers wearing helmets were solemnly boarding military aircraft for Iraq. The volume was inaudible against the moan of ferry engines down below. Isabella ignored the television, and watched the freezing dark grey sea spit against the windowpane instead. From the inside of the ferry boat there was no possible view. Just an ugly grey sea spray that masked the glass like a filthy veil.

A singular thought came to her, as she sat smoking on her way across the Irish Sea. *Perhaps there are two kinds of women in the world*, thought Isabella. *Perhaps there is the kind of woman who will do anything to become a mother. And perhaps there is the kind of woman who will do anything to avoid it.*

And so Isabella told herself on that long seaborne trip to London in 1991 that she was probably the second kind of woman: the kind of woman who was not supposed to be a mother. From now on, she and Harry were always going to be alone together. Perhaps that was just the way it was meant to be.

Sinead Skellig, fifteen years later, would also learn that even if she did conceive the child she longed for, to live without Harry was a life that she could not conceive. But while Isabella crossed the Irish Sea, Sinead was boarding a military airplane scheduled to fly her home to Shannon from Iraq. Sinead climbed into the aircraft with her head bent low to avoid the desert heat. She also bent her head to avoid any possibility that her parting view of Iraq might be the sight of guns, or the delegation of khakied soldiers who muttered and spat and chewed cigarettes.

Sinead was very relieved to be getting home. She had no plans for the future, other than to get away from that war. But what she did know then, was that *that war* had already removed her from every real feeling of belonging she had known, and so she flew over sand and seas into a colder, and what would eventually become for her, a far more uneasy world.

Chapter 1

May 2004

Isabella stood, arms crossed lightly in front of her clinging purple polo-neck sweater, at the long wall of windows that overlooked the campus, half-listening to the reading of a Pinter play. She let her gaze blur, over the tops of trees and paths and the open campus of a large suburban university. The small tutorial room was on the tenth floor of a domineering 1960's tower block of glass and concrete.

The top-floor rooms were warm and bright, catching all the delicate rays of sun that are so rarely and lovingly bestowed on Dublin by an otherwise disgruntled sky. In the distance the artificial lake didn't often shimmer or sparkle in the sun. Today, it simply sat there, blue beneath the trees. Cherry blossom was in flower.

"Project a little more. I can't hear you now!" Isabella spoke sharply with her back turned to the small drama group. They were beginning to shuffle their feet and doodle and cough. She had asked two of the first-year drama students to start a reading of *Old Times*.

5

"No acting, no motion, just read through the lines as if it were a radio play. I'll turn my back to you so that I can only hear the voice," she instructed them.

It seemed like a good way to get some work done on a day when her mind was just a sludge of anxiety, self-absorption and dense black mood.

"*Dark,*" began the voice of one of the students.

"*Fat or thin?*" came the reply.

It reminded her immediately of this morning's conversation with Harry, which had ended so unsatisfactorily. So incomplete. Their conversations seemed to be becoming more unsatisfactory by the day. Conversations came and went but nothing was discussed. From day to day, she and Harry talked about each other's lives, asked each other questions, and demanded answers in return, but nothing was agreed.

Every sentence was a non-sequitur. Each question became rhetorical.

"What time did you get home last night?" she'd ask him.

"The meeting we had went very well."

"So who was there?"

"I think the Americans are planning on invading Syria as their next campaign after Iraq."

"Would you like some dinner, then?"

"Nothing on the news . . ."

For Isabella there were whole days, and increasingly many of them now, when she felt as though the entire dialogue of her life might well have been written by somebody else, who could only hear one side of the conversation. It was as if she and Harry had no relationship with one another at all, but they had somehow ended up in the middle of some bizarre party game where you had to make a conversation out of disconnected sentences that were being passed around on bits of paper.

She suddenly remembered a joke that used to make Harry and her snort with laughter when they were twelve in Mrs Glynn's class.

There are two pigs in a bath.

And the first pig says to the second pig:

"Pass the soap."

And the second pig replies:

"What do you think I am? A radio?"

In Pinter's plays the plot *grows out of* the dialogue between the characters, thought Isabella as she watched the sun straining to get out from behind thick clouds. The plot growing out of all the possible dialogues at that moment in Isabella Somerfield's life was becoming increasingly absurd.

The day had started badly. A horrendous row with Harry had left a cloud of gloom over her from the moment she had left the house. She felt wretched, and the familiar lump that rose from her chest to fill her throat was even more powerful than ever. Outside, many floors below, her tiny groups of students walking slowly along the pathways. To and from lectures, to the library, home to digs. Some worried, and some free.

I am free, thought Isabella carefully to herself. I have chosen this life. I have chosen this relationship, chosen this job, chosen this purple outfit. I have even chosen this room to hold my Thursday morning drama group because I like to be up here on top of the building. And yet I keep convincing myself that I am trapped. I feel as though my choices have all been *made* for me. As though everything I do is because of Harry, and everything I *don't* do is because of Harry. But the truth is, none of it is Harry's fault. It's the way I've always wanted it to be, she concluded miserably.

Isabella had always believed herself to be what she described as a deeply *hopeful* person. Harry described her as a pessimistic version of an optimist. Isabella believed that she had the goodness and reliability somewhere within her to make the most of her life. She knew that she was intelligent, caring, and capable of feeling great love, but she did not want to be a pushover. She liked to believe that she had the patience and fortitude to understand and tolerate other people's weaknesses and failings. But she also felt that her undying *tolerance* could sometimes be an easy way of avoiding self-reflection.

Harry, on the other hand, believed utterly in the goodness and virtue of all mankind. He questions nothing, thought Isabella guiltily to herself. He mistrusts nobody. He embraces the world with openness and love, and as a result he benefits personally every time.

"We don't *have* a personal relationship any more, Harry. All you care about is politics!" she had shrieked, when he dropped it on her that he planned to go to Venezuela next year.

"The personal *is* political!" Harry had laughed. "Even love is political, on many levels."

And he did love Isabella. She was quite sure of that. In as much as his love was possible, she tended to add to herself quietly but even then she knew that this qualifier was unfair. Harry did love her, very deeply. But Harry also loved the world.

"I am sick of having to share you with the rest of the *entire world*!" she had yelled. "The *world*, you know, Harry, *the world*, as such, can be a very, very large place!"

"The world is a global village," replied Harry dreamily.

And so Isabella just sat silent, furious and unmoving. The World Social Forum in Venezuela wasn't until next year but it was another plan for Harry to dream up, another series of fund-raisers to organise, another series of public meetings to plan, speakers to book, meetings to go to, articles to write. Another major part of his life that would totally, utterly exclude her.

From time to time, Isabella wondered if she envied Harry. This was not a pleasant thought at all. She did not believe, as it was not in the realms of her belief system, that it was possible to love someone whom one also envied. And yet she felt time and time again as though she was in some way losing, as though she *were* the loser in this relationship – even though at the same time she refused to believe that a relationship was like a *competition* and that one *could* either win or lose. But Harry *is* winning all the time, she thought. Winning friends, winning debates, winning arguments and winning support; and I feel as though I am slipping further and further away.

One of the students stopped the reading, and loudly cleared his throat.

"Sorry, Isabella, but I think it's probably well past one o'clock now."

The sound of ten chairs scraping rapidly off the floor was a sudden ear-splitting climax of relief. Isabella turned around. The students were rapidly shoving papers and books into bags and backpacks.

"Yes. Of course it is. I'm so sorry. Yes. Of course it is." She stepped forward briskly to stand at the front of the group, who were packing books and pencils away and edging hopefully towards the door, and raised her hands to corral them into listening mode.

"Good. Well, now: that was very interesting I think. Wasn't it?" she asked brightly.

Eleven dull, wretched faces looked back at her, grim-faced.

"So," she continued, searching their faces for some sign of forgiveness, "I think you will find this play is probably going to be a bit easier going than the Beckett we were doing last week, won't you? And there are parts of it that are quite funny too. So let's discuss it all a bit more during class next week. And meanwhile, perhaps you could write a short essay, let's say fifteen hundred words, about what you think might be the *underlying theme* of this play? Okay?"

She smiled a fake but bright smile at the sullen faces of the students while they pulled themselves together to leave the room. Oh God, she thought, I am such a dreadful teacher! They will probably kill themselves trying to write this essay over the weekend – when they should be out drinking and smoking and having coffee and making love. They probably hate me now for all of this. Her guilt burnt furiously on her cheeks.

Then again, they could stand up to me, she reminded herself. They could just say: Hey, look here, Isabella, this is rubbish! You couldn't be bothered doing any teaching. You are far too self-obsessed and your boyfriend is clearly getting bored with you. And now you think you can get away with staring out the window for a whole two hours while we read this and then expect us to write an essay about something you are far too lazy to teach us in the first place!

Well, they could say all that, she decided, and began to pack her own small brown leather briefcase with her papers. And so perhaps it is not *entirely* my fault.

Doctor Sinead Skellig sat at her desk alone for a just few more minutes, blowing on her coffee. Her desk was like a sanctuary to her. It was here she wrote to friends, phoned her mother, did her nails, ordered things online. The desk faced towards a wall. Sinead would have liked a view, but the surgery was very small and the only window in the consulting room was frosted, and overlooked a drain.

She glanced up at the clock now: it was just gone five past two. There was really only just enough time for one last quick look at her emails before the patients would start coming in. And so she clicked her mouse and opened up her inbox one more time, just as she had done every single morning for the past two weeks, desperate for a result.

And oh! There it was! At last. Oh, thank God for that! Sinead breathed in deeply, and then let her head sink into her hands, overwhelmed with sheer relief.

Moussa's email: finally sitting in her inbox after weeks of wondering. She paused a happy moment, just looking at it there before she clicked it open, almost triumphantly. But then her breathing slowed, and her heart thumped as she read.

My dearest Sinead,

I write to you quickly and in great fear. We are leaving Baghdad tonight to travel to Fallujah, some doctors and I. We have received short messages from there that the hospital is under siege. My doctors and I have obtained two cars to drive north with medicines and with food. The doctors in Fallujah are starving. One doctor who is a surgeon telephones me tonight and tells me that he has eaten the flowers in the garden around the hospital. I just can't bear to think my colleagues must be suffering so.

The Americans stopped the ambulances leaving the hospital to collect the dead. The doctors tried to leave the hospital in their cars. They tried to save those who died on the streets. But the Americans made them return, leaving many injured to die. Now the hospital has no food, no good clean water, and the medicines are almost gone. Communications are very bad. I have sent two emails to Jon Snow tonight, and I hope that he will understand them. Channel Four News does not always report the full truth but I hope that Jon Snow will try to speak about it on the news in England. I am very lonely here, Sinead. I know I will visit Dublin again. I hope you know it too.

Your old friend
Moussa.

It was horrendous. There was no other word to describe it. But the feeling that she felt most of all was guilt. Tense, uneasy, horrible guilt for Moussa and Baghdad. Oh God, why didn't he get out of that place a long time ago? What on earth was he doing, still living there? But she knew the answer far too well. He was there because it was his home. That was Moussa.

"Talk the talk, then walk the walk too," he'd laugh at her, when she held back from big decisions over patients.

But that kind of risk-taking was just a part of the big macho surgeon thing: it wasn't really dangerous. It was all bravado. "Get it into theatre, and open up! If you don't put your hands into it you put your foot in it!" Moussa used to say. "Not enough time to prep for theatre? Open up the chest in casualty, woman!"

Moussa had seen enough trauma surgery in his time to open up a chest with his two eyes closed. But he sounded frightened now. She held her forehead in her hands, leaning on her desk. *I am so lonely.* That wasn't her friend Moussa talking. It sounded almost as if it could be someone else. The most shocking thing of all though was the thought that Moussa's bullshit confidence might have gone. In his email he sounded almost as if he thought it were his last. *As if he might be saying goodbye.* Sinead sat very still and read it once again. She breathed out slowly, scrutinising every line. The phone rang twice but she ignored it as she printed out the email.

And then she felt tears begin to sting her nose. Tears of utter frustration. She shook her head fiercely to dismiss them.

She glanced up: it was well past two. Pins and needles down her back. She shivered and then standing up she folded Moussa's email printout, and put it in her bag. She gulped her coffee back and paced around the tiny surgery to compose herself. And then she suddenly caught sight of her tense expression in the mirror by the sink. Jesus Christ, I can't start the surgery in a state like this, she thought. She tried to smile instead at her pale reflection in the mirror.

She took her specs off, and bent forward to shake her head around so that her dark blonde hair bounced back when she stood up again. Bit better now, she thought.

I am going to write back to him tonight, she decided.

Her hair looked far too fluffy now. She flattened it down again and tucked it back behind her ears. After work she would read the email properly and decide then what she could do.

She took a deep breath in, glanced at the computer screen and bit her lip. It told her there were already two patients in the waiting room. She sniffed and fixed her glasses one more time and shrugged her shoulders round to ease them out. Okay. It was time to get back to work

Opening the surgery door, she called the first name on the list.

A small neat man with a rather juvenile beard stood up and smiled at her. A warm and generous smile. He looked to be about thirty, and was wearing a grey sweatshirt over faded jeans and carrying a satchel on his shoulder. Sinead held the door open and let him into the consulting room in front of her. Then she noticed that he had a little red and yellow badge pinned on to his satchel: *No War For Oil*. That's a good badge, she thought. He was nice-looking too. He looked intelligent and as if he might be rather fun.

"Take a seat," she said. "I like your badge."

"Thank you. I like your painting in the hall."

Sinead was thrilled that he had noticed it: her painting of a Baghdad street scene, in muted colours – grey, brown, black – that Moussa had given her just before she'd left Iraq; a group of bearded people walking, white-

14

clothed, long and thin. Sinead had hung it in the waiting room so that it was the first thing she saw every morning when she arrived at work. It was her anchor in the world.

She offered him the other chair at right angles to her own. But he moved away and sat on the edge of the couch instead. She had to turn her whole body around in her swivel chair to address him at the back of the room. It was awkward, but she let him sit where he felt comfortable.

"So, what can I do for you today?" she asked, leaning back to look at him.

The young man coughed and wriggled a little as he sat on the edge of the couch. "This is a bit embarrassing," he began with a slightly red-faced smile.

Oh crap, Sinead thought gloomily. Please don't let him show me his arse. He's probably gay and he has piles. She was aware that her face had frozen into an expression of possible disgust, and that her cheeks had pinked up a little, and so she tried to look neutral again as the young man continued. The fact that she wore glasses with dark frames might distract from her expression at a time like this, she hoped.

Sinead's squeamishness was not something she was proud of. She tried to disguise it as much as possible, by suggesting to patients that they themselves might not want to be examined, that it would be much better to have a male colleague look at this. "For you own comfort, you understand?" And could they possibly make an appointment to see Dr Tom Fox on Friday? She cleared her throat and asked the young man whether he would like to wait until Friday when Dr Fox would – but he cut her off mid-sentence.

"Ah, no, not at all. I'm fine with a woman doctor. Thanks a million. No, it's not too embarrassing, actually. I'm sure you're well used to this sort of thing. It's just that I'm in a bit of a hurry to have this seen to. I'm afraid that this is the only free time I've got this week, and so I'd really like to get it seen to right away."

"I see. So, what seems to be the problem?"

"It's my, er, ahem, my dick," he coughed.

Sinead breathed out slowly. "Okay. Well, let's have a look then, shall we?"

Men and their dicks, she thought. *Broken bones, broken hearts. Bring out the broken dicks, why don't you?* She pretended to straighten her glasses as he unzipped his trousers and lay back on the couch.

"It's all right. You can sit up," she offered, trying to sound bright, as she pulled on some rubber gloves.

"Oh. Okay. Thanks."

He swivelled round to sit perched on the edge of the couch again, and plopped it out.

He held it in his hand for her. Thick, round, wobbly and stub-like. Like the stump of a limb, with a pimple at the eye, winking back.

Sinead glanced at it as briefly as she possibly could, and prodded it a bit, and then let it go. Her visible relief was an antidote for his anxious face.

"You have nothing to worry about. It's only a pimple."

She snapped off her rubber gloves, and dropped them in the bin. "Any other spots, or lumps, or discharge? Pain? Itch? Burning?"

He was fiddling with his flies. "No, just this pimple. Is it common? Look, I know that this is probably really stupid, but I thought I'd better get a doctor to have a look at it in case it's contagious. I do feel very foolish about this. But I need to know whether or not I have to tell my girlfriend, and whether or not she should be tested or something . . ." his voice trailed off.

"Don't worry, it's eminently treatable." Sinead turned around again, and smiled at him from her desk. He was still perched anxiously on the edge of the couch. "You should put this ointment on it every day, and it will melt away. But if you're worried about infections, you really ought to go to the clinic and get a proper check-up, because they say that if you think you are at risk of one then you are at risk of another, and so on."

"Because they travel round in packs?"

"Something like that. Yes. That's a good way of putting it, I suppose," she giggled.

"So, I don't need to tell my girlfriend?"

"No – it's not contagious and it will clear up in no time."

"Great. She might think I'd caught it from somebody else, and that would really upset her. I think she feels monogamy is very important. She might think I was being unfaithful, or irresponsible, or something. She takes that kind of thing very seriously. Being faithful, I mean."

"Oh, everybody's faithful, give or take a night or two." Sinead couldn't help a grin.

"Hey! A doctor who likes Leonard Cohen! This must be my lucky day," he beamed back at her.

They looked at each other momentarily.

He is very slightly familiar, Sinead thought. His eyes, there is something familiar about his eyes. They really are rather beautiful. No wonder he's worried about picking up souvenirs of love.

"I'm sorry but I'm not sure whether I recognise you." She cleared her throat. "Have you been to the surgery before?"

"Oh God, no. I'm never sick. My office is just across the river and you were the handiest to come to. I have a meeting later and this is very convenient to the place I'm going."

Sinead handed him the prescription and he stood up. He looked at her, as if there was something else he wanted to say. She held his eyes for just a moment.

Nothing but their breathing.

"I just assumed you must be a Leonard Cohen fan. Because of the quote, you know. It's such a great song, that one, isn't it?"

"I guess it's one that tells the truth."

"Well, thanks. I think you've saved my life – well, not my *life*, of course. That's a gross exaggeration. But, you've saved my relationship anyway. Well, maybe for another week or two. I'd better go." He picked his satchel up. "Thanks again. Doctor. Thank you. Bye."

"Ah, yes. Well, it's thirty-five euros. Pay Dorinda at reception."

She watched him as he left the room.

It was his eyes: she felt there was definitely something about his eyes that she had seen before. And there was something familiar too about the way he moved his head forward slightly when he spoke, and looked up as if he were trying to see over his eyebrows. There is a lovely innocent sincerity about him, she thought. He seems kind. And there's a sort of passionate honesty about him too that I like. He looks like someone you could easily love.

His girlfriend probably gives him a hard time, she told herself, opening up another file.

Chapter 2

When Isabella first met Harry Waters at university, it was at the end of First Year at the History Soc debate.

"I remember sitting right beside you in primary school," he whispered into Isabella's long dark curls, slipping into the seat behind her on the benches.

She recognised his voice before she even turned around. "Harry Waters," she had whispered back.

Harry took her for a pint after the debate; and she took him to her bed that night. They spent the remainder of the year walking round the campus holding hands. They studied in the library in the evenings. They lay kissing on the cricket lawns in summer.

Harry was by no means Isabella's first or only lover. But he was the only man that she would ever spend her life with.

They moved into a flat together in the basement of a large house in Rathmines. The flat was cheap because it had so little natural light during the day the landlord knew the ESB bills would be huge. Isabella and Harry lit candles. They smoked pot in bed together and tasted one another's skin. Harry twirled her curls around his fingertips and smoothed them out again while they talked all night beneath a wine-spilt cover over crumpled sheets. They spent hours in the giant bath together, planning study timetables, revising for exams.

Isabella was a drama student; Harry studied History. He listened to her learn her lines while he soaped her back.

"Do you remember us in Mrs Glynn's class?" Isabella giggled, and she twined her long slim legs around his hairier ones. "I used to do your history tests for you, and you used to do my maths?"

"I only remember that you were *ravishing*," Harry mumbled, lifting up her breasts in his hands and running his tongue around her nipple.

Unlike Harry, Isabella was not an only child, but she had always felt like one. She was the youngest in a family of three older brothers; an *afterthought* was the word her mother with a tight-lipped smile had used to describe the unexpected arrival of a baby in her mid-forties. As a result of Audrey and Jack Somerfields' *afterthought,* Isabella was a full fifteen years younger than her next oldest sibling, and therefore had no real memory of having had a family to grow up with. Her three brothers left for university before she started school, and thereafter she rarely saw them.

Audrey Somerfield had always been a gloomy woman, and following the traumatic delivery of Isabella at the age of forty-five, she became quite permanently depressed. She spent a great deal of Isabella's childhood resting in her bed, and arranged for local women to help out in the house. Jack Somerfield was a country practice GP who had never quite retired, and so even though he was in his late seventies by the time Isabella entered university, he still spent his days working long unfruitful hours, scowling at the patients in a cold and dampening surgery.

As the doctor's wife, Audrey felt that her most important task in life was to answer the telephone in the correct and appropriate manner in the house all day, and tidy up the magazines. If Isabella got in the way and needed someone else to play with Audrey usually sent her around to Ruth's house for the afternoon. Ruth's mother fed them crisps and biscuits and other forbidden things and let them watch TV.

Jack Somerfield couldn't stand the noise of television in the background, even when he was in the surgery at the other end of the house. The Somerfields ate their main meals in the evening in a chilly dining room.

Ruth's mother let Isabella and Ruth lie on their stomachs in front of *Hill Street Blues*, and eat chips and sausages off a tray.

If Isabella's absence from her parents' house was a blessing to her elderly and distracted parents, it was an absolute necessity to Isabella.

Despite the fact that Isabella was to all intents and purposes at the time their only child, Audrey and Jack had not been any lonelier when Isabella finally left the convent school in Dunmallow and went to university. They planned to visit her, they said, as often as was possible while she was in First Year; but somehow or other they never made it up to Dublin.

The three older boys were all married now – two were in America – and there were grandchildren.

"Daddy is still so very busy in the surgery every evening," Audrey would sigh to Isabella on the phone, and Isabella would sigh just as hard to her on the other end of the line. But Isabella's was a sigh of sheer relief. In Dublin at university she was at long last free from the big empty house with its large cold rooms and its constant trail of patients up and down the long tiled corridor to the surgery behind. Throughout her childhood she had never felt as though her house had been a home; it had always been a *practice* first, and a dwelling second.

Home was now with Harry, wrapped in one another's arms, sharing food in bed, bread and mayonnaise instead of meals.

In the mornings they were often late. Isabella skipped tutorials because Harry was between her thighs, loving her too much to go to class. For some reason Harry was slightly better at remembering to set the alarm and getting organised. But Isabella did not compare their grades at all. They were in completely different fields. Harry had always taken life more seriously than her. She was the dreamy one; he was the reader. Isabella would throw back her head of thick black curls and laugh loudly when she was in a group with him. She just loved *being* with him. She loved being *seen* to be with him.

One morning in November of Third Year at university, Isabella's mother rang her very early, much earlier than usual. The sky was still quite dark outside, and it had taken several rings for Isabella to waken up enough to hear the phone, stumble out of bed, find Harry's anorak to keep her warm, and grope around the floor for the receiver.

Jack Somerfield had been found dead, sitting at his desk.

Audrey was hysterical.

Isabella caught the next train down from Heuston Station and helped her mother to lay her father out, and prepare a wake. It was the first time in her life that she had seen someone who was dead, and her father's long thin face was unrecognisable. Jack looked quite mask-like, and the stiffness of his skin had shocked her deeply. All the frown-lines and the folds around his mouth had been released, as if his soul had truly left his body.

Jack's funeral was well attended, solemn, with few tears. Isabella sat beside her mother with the other Somerfields at the top pew of the church, and shook the gloved hands of patients and of neighbours as they filed along.

Harry had to sit with her other friends at the back, but even from that distance his very presence in the church was the only thing that made it tolerable to her.

After the funeral, Isabella introduced Harry Waters as her boyfriend to her mother; Audrey waved a handkerchief across her face and nodded politely to her daughter's lover, another blank face in the queue of mourners that passed by.

And so Isabella wept for her dead father and her pitiful mother only after she'd returned to Rathmines, safe in Harry's arms. He stroked her hair and rocked her in his arms when she woke up crying in the night. He made love to her whenever she broke down.

The following month she missed her period. But she dealt with *that* alone. She wouldn't have troubled Audrey for a moment.

When Audrey Somerfield died in her sleep just five years later, Isabella's guilt was mixed with sheer relief.

Audrey's funeral was sweeter and more uplifting than her husband's. Isabella sang in church with Eddie and Ruth who had been in the college choir with her, and when she left Dunmallow and the big house that her brother Luke was now converting she felt that it was well time to say a firm goodbye. She would miss her parents, naturally; and she would always miss the fact of never really having *had* parents. But she also knew that as an only daughter, she was in many ways quite lucky not to have been left with two very elderly parents in need of nursing care, each as single-minded and as cantankerous as the other.

She returned to her real home, to Harry.

Chapter 3

May 2004

It could be so much worse, Isabella thought. If this were medieval times, I would be told I am a witch. A shrew, incapable of being controlled by a man. She stirred two sugars into her watery coffee, and tried to decide about whether or not to have something to eat as well. Eat now – or later, home alone. Not much of a choice, really. Bad food here, or something even worse from the bottom of a neglected fridge.

Isabella sat alone in the college basement canteen, and stirred and stirred her coffee, soothed by the hum and rattle of conversations and dishes all around. She stirred and thought: about Harry, about her and Harry. The argument that morning had been horrible. She felt guilty, and ashamed.

Harry was upset, and she knew that it was she who had upset him. He is a good and gentle person, she thought, and he does not need to be upset. Not today of all days. And yet I feel that he deserves it. A sudden jolt in her brain, a sharp jab of pain as the reality of her possible meanness rose up like a demon in her throat. She quickly slapped it down.

But he has to feel upset, she revised, if anything is going to change about the way we are. He continues to live in his own world of love and peace and understanding, but his world is crushing and destroying mine. *My world*. She thought for a moment about what she meant by this world.

Her world, the world in which she lived. With Harry sometimes; without Harry often. This world was small, and compact, and it could be, potentially, quite methodically arranged. It was divided into timetabled packages, of events, and occasions, and meetings, and people – but with Harry it was always chaos.

Isabella knew that what she wanted was something that Harry might consider to be in some way rather *wrong*. And it *was* wrong that she wanted to have a plan that was only for her and Harry, and their future, and their life. Harry had a plan to end world poverty. But it didn't occur to him that there might be a single, more important item that she wanted more.

Because I don't, thought Isabella, sipping miserably at her cold coffee. I can't possibly think of one thing that is more important than war, and injustice, and bombings in Iraq. Harry is right. He's the one with the real handle on the world. I know that it is only *my* misery that is causing all of these rows with him. I am trying to hurt him, day after day, because hurting him is the only way that I can make him understand. And yet he still *can't* understand why I need more than he does, why I need to have something else to look forward to, other than anti-globalisation. And I am driving him away.

She felt like crying. But all her head could do was cringe.

She rubbed her forehead with the back of her hand, and sniffed and looked about her at the students crouched around tables nursing cups of coffee. They muttered and gossiped in groups, interrupted by an occasional roar of laughter. They were like the ghosts of hers and Harry's student days. Long coffee breaks. Intense feelings. Deep passions. Afternoons that had been filled with joy.

"Aha! Great. I've found you!" It was Ruth. "Jesus, I've been trying to get in touch with you all day long. Now: please let me get you a coffee and then we can sit down properly and have a yap. Do you want another coffee? Or a cake or something? I'm having a slice of cheesecake. I haven't eaten a single thing all day!"

"Just another coffee, thanks," Isabella smiled.

She was delighted by the arrival of Ruth, and sat back happily to watch her trot over to the food counter to choose a cake. Isabella was actually quite hungry, and hadn't eaten anything yet for lunch. But Ruth would probably come back with something sweet, and she wasn't going to eat a meal that consisted of broken biscuits covered with spray-can cream and jellied cheese.

Isabella, who favoured lentils and brown rice, was a complete stranger to Ruth's daily cake habit. But both women remained slim. And Ruth, who had recently had her first baby, prided herself especially on her protruding collarbones, and tiny buttocks under Levi jeans. One cake a day, Ruth had decided, with no other *real* meals, cannot be a threat to one's torso.

It was Ruth's eternally breathless optimism that made Isabella love her and regard her as her dearest friend. Ruth's undying confidence stretched to an undying generosity of belief in the most outrageous of fantasies in others. And thus, Ruth was the only person Isabella could ever depend upon to confide in about her struggling relationship with Harry – because Ruth would actually listen, take in every self-obsessed detail and digest it. She would churn it about and weave a theory, weave a whole pattern of theories. She would suggest hope, drama, comedy and ideas. Isabella needed hope. She desperately needed ideas.

Isabella's friends Ruth Coppinger and Eddie Mannion had often grumbled before when they were at college that she was spending far too much time with Harry Waters, lying in bed all day avoiding class. In those days, she had just ignored them.

"You want to watch out that you don't get into serious trouble in the exams, Iz – you're always skipping lectures. And then Harry wants you to go drinking with him when you should be in the library," Ruth had warned, when Isabella panicked that her essay on *Shakespeare: Sexuality and Gender* was two weeks overdue. "When it's something that's important to him, like a big student rally, or a speech he has to make, or being president of the student's union and running around meeting faculty staff, you always put him first. You go to all *his* big events. You've got to start putting yourself first sometimes, Iz."

But at the age of twenty-one, Isabella didn't want to hear this kind of thing. She was not a doormat for a man that she adored; that was utter rubbish. She had wondered sometimes in those days if Ruth was slightly envious.

Most women probably were – she was going out with the president of the Students' Union, one of the sexiest men in college, and he obviously adored her. From the outside, perhaps she would have been jealous of herself too.

"I fancied Harry long before you ever did," Eddie Mannion used to grumble. Eddie had been Isabella's boyfriend when they both started off in first year; but Eddie was completely gay, and after two weeks of unsatisfactory kissing and several late-night coffees in Bewleys on Westmorland Street, he confessed his big dilemma. From then on Isabella loved Eddie even more.

"You still fancy Harry, don't you, Eds?" she used to tease him. She didn't think for a moment that Eddie would try to *steal* Harry from her. But a love triangle is a very messy thing, and she wouldn't want Eddie to get hurt.

"Oh God, no, darling. Harry's far too camp for me!"

Eddie lusted after hopelessly heterosexual men who played rugby or studied engineering.

"I'll help you cruise someone at the weekend, Eds," said Isabella. "We'll go to the Parliament again together. I'm much better at picking up gay men than you are."

But Eddie hated the so-called Dublin gay scene.

"I'm barely *out* in college, never mind strutting around town bloody well *asking* to have my head kicked in. No, Isabella," he sighed, "I shall resign myself to the masochism of unrequited love for the remainder of my student days and then fall hopelessly for someone far too young and beautiful to love me back, and end up as an elderly homosexual bachelor, in Venice or somewhere, desperately trying to make sense of my empty but poetic life."

"Oh for God's sake! You're far too theatrical, Eddie. That's why you can't get a man. You'd terrify Shakespeare with your self-importance. You'd terrify Oscar Wilde!"

"Let's go to America together, Iz. After college," Eddie begged her. "Just you and me; and live in Greenwich Village. You could be my fag hag. And I could be happy for a change."

Isabella shook her head. "I'm not going anywhere, you know that. Harry wants to stay on so he can be active in the Students' Union, and in campaigns and stuff. But I'll visit you, if you go."

"Isabella – do you really think you'd be so crazy about Harry if he *weren't* the most popular guy in college?" Eddie asked her. His voice was serious for a change.

Isabella looked at him.

"I mean," he added, "if there weren't a thousand other women, and men – well, one or two of them – who fancied the pants off him, would he still be *as* desirable to you?"

"You make it sound as though I only want him so that no one else can have him! That's ridiculous," said Isabella.

"No, it isn't. I want lots of things, and people, for the same reason. Doesn't mean I'll never want anything else *other than them* though. Oh, it was just a thought!" Eddie shrugged.

Isabella thought that Eddie's assumption was quite wrong; although somewhere undiscovered in her mind she wondered if there was a *tiny* grain of truth in what he'd said. But it made sense that if everyone else loved Harry, that she would be crazy *not* to.

"You're like a grasshopper, Harry. You can't sit still

31

with me for half a minute," Isabella used to complain when she tried to get Harry to stop working the dining hall for half an hour while they ate their lunch. "You are always looking around you all the time to see who else there might there be to sit with. Let's just relax for a moment, and *be* together."

"I'm with you every night in bed," Harry smiled at her. "I like to hang out with other people in college during the day so I can look *forward* to being with you."

And she'd smiled back at him through her long dark trail of curls because she knew that he was telling her the truth.

But that all seemed to be a very different world, compared to now.

Ruth sat down again in front of Isabella, daintily, despite a large tray from which she deposited a plate of cheesecake with bright lurid pink jelly on the top, and two cups of cappuccino.

"Cappo or latte, I can never remember which you prefer. But I thought the lattes looked a bit weak and foamy, so I got these. I hope they're all right. You look tired, sweetheart; your eyes are all puffed up. Aren't you sleeping well? Hey, I saw Harry on telly on the lunchtime news. He was great! You must be so proud of him. How are you?"

"Oh. I don't know. Not good actually. Miserable in fact. We had a fight." Isabella smiled at Ruth and picked her cappuccino up in both her hands.

Ruth was busy arranging plates and napkins in front of her. She looked at Isabella carefully and then took a spoonful of cheesecake from the lurid pink slice.

"That's a pity – what about?" asked Ruth after swallowing first.

"I don't even know!" Isabella shook her head and raised her eyes. "I don't know what we even fight *about* any more," she shrugged. "Ruth, can I ask you something? And please don't laugh." She put down her cup and took a breath. "Am I high maintenance?"

Ruth laughed right out loud.

"Here, have a bit of cheesecake. It's delicious. Oh, look, Isabella, I don't know. I mean, I don't even know what that means. High maintenance. Do you know what it means? Do you?"

"What I mean is, do you think I am too demanding?" Isabella asked. She was frustrated, and spoke quickly. "I mean, do I expect things to happen in a certain way, and then get angry because other people don't see things my way, and do I then take it out on them? I mean, am I intolerant? Because I really don't know which way to turn at the moment. I'm all out of ideas."

She leaned her head in her hands for a moment, and paused.

Ruth said nothing, spooning cheesecake carefully into her mouth, and waited for her to continue.

"It's like this," Isabella began. "Harry and I had an argument this morning. And I think we might be splitting up. And I love him. I really do. And I know he loves me. He is incredibly kind, and funny, and good. He is an amazingly good person. And I know that I can't live without him. But I get so angry with him, and he thinks it's over nothing."

Ruth looked up at her. "Go on. I'm listening."

"And it *is* nothing," Isabella continued. "He does nothing wrong. He is never cruel, or mean, or lazy, or selfish. He is so goddamn good all of the time that I feel angry with him for making *me* feel selfish, or mean, or just not good enough. Because I want to go on holidays. Or go to dinner together or go shopping on a Sunday. Simple stuff. Boring, simple stuff. That's all I want."

"I know." Ruth was absorbed in her cheesecake.

"But for Harry there never *is* a holiday," Isabella carried on. "It always has to be another conference. Or a rally. Or a demonstration. We can never plan to go anywhere together, because Harry is always going with a group of people on a trip to Genoa to close down the World Bank, or some other thing like that. And I don't want to be like this. I really don't."

Ruth nodded as she ate her cheesecake and watched her friend. It didn't matter to her that she had heard the story of Harry and Isabella a thousand times before. She gave the courteous appearance of listening, if not attentively then at least politely, to the story of Harry's inability to be there for Isabella because the world had somehow or other got in the way.

Ruth had an altogether simpler relationship with her architect husband, Bernard. They had met on a sailing holiday and rarely discussed anything deeper than the quality of windproof jackets. It was to this simplicity of detail in their attitude to one another that Ruth attributed their relationship success.

"Ruth," Isabella suddenly asked her, "do you remember when you were furious with Bernard, when he came home with flowers for you when you were pregnant and you had that terrible cold, and you were just motionless and huge in front of the telly trying to get through the afternoon? And he waltzed in and plonked a huge bouquet of flowers on your lap, and then went back to work? And you were furious because you couldn't lift yourself up off the couch, but now you actually *had* to get up and put the flowers in some water?"

Ruth laughed and waved her hands to stop Isabella reminding her of her very hormonal behaviour towards the end of her pregnancy the previous year.

But Isabella continued. "So even though he had been incredibly kind, he hadn't actually done you a *favour*, he'd simply made things *harder* for you? You were angry with him for being *good*."

"Yes, I suppose so." Ruth was cautious.

"Well, I suppose that's the way that I am about Harry. Even though he is incredibly good and kind, he makes *me* feel angry with him. In fact it is his goodness and kindness that I'm angry about. Of course," she stirred her cappuccino around and around, "I would never be angry with Harry for giving *me* flowers, even if I had a broken leg and he made me climb up to the top of a crane in a force-nine wind to collect them. Because he never gives me flowers. It never would occur to him."

"Harry gives you presents. On your birthday. And at Christmas," Ruth said gently.

"Ruth, he gives me books. Don't get me wrong. I love books. I read books. And he spends hours thinking about books, and reading books, and telling *me* what to read. And I know I ought to just like the books he gives me. But do you know what he gave me for my birthday last year? And I'm so ashamed of this because it made me want to cry."

Ruth shook her head, her mouth full of cake crumbs. She dabbed the edges of her small mouth with tissue paper.

"Go on."

"*The State and Revolution*, by Lenin."

Ruth raised her eyebrows briefly to express polite surprise. She wanted to laugh her head off, but her mouth was still full of pink jellied cheesecake, and she wasn't sure if Isabella would think it funny either, and she would rather die than spray biscuit base straight into Isabella's worried, sad little face. She swallowed the mouthful very carefully, and dabbed the corners of her dainty lips again.

"Was it any good?" she eventually asked. She couldn't disguise a massive grin now that the cheesecake was gone.

"I haven't read it."

"Right. Well, maybe that's your problem!" Ruth leaned back in her chair triumphantly and slapped her hands down on the tabletop. "Why *haven't* you read it? Maybe it *is* a fascinating book! Maybe it's the best book you are ever going to read, and Harry would be really impressed and delighted if you read it. And then you could talk about it together. You could lie in bed talking about Lenin and the Bolsheviks, and get all turned on, and have fabulous sex . . ."

"We *do* talk about Lenin and the bloody Bolsheviks!" Isabella snorted with laughter. "We barely ever talk about anything bloody else. And we *do* have fabulous sex." She studied her cappuccino again, for a moment, scooping up and plopping back the foam with a spoon.

"Well, you know, Iz, that's a pretty rare thing, and perhaps you can't complain too much about the other stuff," Ruth said softly.

Isabella looked away again, letting her gaze wander lazily into the distance. Behind the service counter was a long wall of windows through which the tops of trees bobbed and waved like crazy dancers in the wind. It was getting stormy-looking now, and warm, even for late May.

They sat in silence for a while. Ruth took her hand, and patted it gently. Isabella smiled.

"It would be a great name for a rock band though, wouldn't it? Lenin and the Bolsheviks. A punk band maybe?" Isabella smiled.

"Nah. Not a punk bank. It would have to be a rapper. Lenny and the Bolsheviks. Hip hop, rip rap!" Ruth began to solemnly tap out a rhythm out on the tabletop with her fingertips. "Come on. Let's go back to my place and annoy Bernard for the afternoon."

Chapter 4

Sinead sat alone in the surgery after the patients had all left and read Moussa's email once again. The surgery was silent now. Nothing but the background of the squeals and rumbling of the traffic just outside the glass front door. Sinead read it one more time, then shut down the computer, and instead turned to the post which she had only glanced at that morning. She tried to concentrate but it was desperately hard: two blood results. Both normal. Two invitations to a pharmaceutical promotional: both rubbish. A letter from the Irish Medical Organisation about the ballot for the new GP contract: more rubbish. A long over-worded letter from a junior psychiatrist about a recently diagnosed depressive.

Moussa, Oh my God. Poor poor Moussa. What is he going through now?

Sinead let all her letters fall just anywhere on her desk as she pulled them out of envelopes, leaving the torn-up envelopes everywhere among the half-empty coffee cups that grew like fungi in the consulting room. The desk was peppered with her droppings: pharmaceutical give-away pens, paper clips, and the plastic wrappers off syringes. Sinead was never tidy, but she consulted carefully and was deeply grateful for Dorinda's dynamic tidying habit every evening after hours.

She had tried to focus on the mail but it was impossible. She would quit the surgery instead and walk, and try to get her head around what was happening in Iraq. She could write a proper email later on when she had figured out what to say. What she really wanted was to cheer him up. But everything seemed so horrendously complicated. As if the country was in total chaos. Sinead frowned and bit her lip. Moussa's letter was quite terrifying. Iraq was just so far away.

She pulled on her linen jacket, and then pulled it off again, and flung it on her chair. What on earth can I say to him that will make any sense at all in the middle of all this, she asked herself and felt new frustrated tears about to come again, and so she stood quite still a moment while she tried to decide what to do about the jacket.

He wouldn't want her empty futile words of comfort. He would want some common sense. She must send a good email to Moussa tonight that would be useful to him. Which would give him courage. Solidarity, she suddenly thought. Solidarity is what he needs right now.

She decided to leave her jacket in the surgery and get on with having her walk, up to Merrion Square and then back down again by the canal. She walked briskly, short legs dressed in a fitted skirt and chunky heels, her dark blonde head bent, staring at the pavement deep in thought.

Sinead had never been to Fallujah during the time she worked in Iraq in 1990, but she knew about it from the stories Moussa had told her. At that time she had imagined it to be full of parochialism, like a rural town in Ireland, full of eccentric characters in the medical field.

In Baghdad in 1990, Moussa used to spend all day telling stories about all the eccentric surgeons he had known, while he snipped away in theatre or sutured up, or while he waited for Sinead to tell him that the gasses were all right to go ahead and open up.

They had met on a popular Irish-Iraqi exchange programme of surgical training, to staff a private hospital partly owned in those days by an Irish airline. Not many people in Ireland at that time were bothered about what sort of dictatorship Iraq was, and not many of the Irish doctors and nurses out there were too worried about it either. They were getting training in a good teaching hospital in a scheme that was supported by the Irish state. No-one talked in those days about Saddam's regime of terror. Sinead had quickly realised that the Irish doctors, living a cosseted life in a luxurious compound, were quite separate from the lives that the Iraqi people lived.

She knew that her friendship with Moussa was unorthodox and that they were always being watched; perhaps that was what made their friendship all the more important. But none of them had expected there to be a war.

Sinead and Moussa and their friends had all celebrated Christmas only weeks before the bombing came. On New Year's Day of 1991 they were sitting on the rooftop singing songs. The Iraqi newspapers and TV were only reporting victory in reclaiming Kuwait for Iraq.

At Christmas time Baghdad was still full of sunshine; it was a city of mosques and markets, loud coffee shops and children playing. But Sinead and Moussa listened to the BBC World Service and knew that President George Bush had very different plans.

She tried to phone Moussa when she returned to Ireland, but the line kept cutting out and there was an intermittent crackling sound. She knew that it was bugged. They wrote letters to each other instead; Moussa's replies were formal and polite and, Sinead knew, not always in his own words.

But when Sinead acquired an email address it was Moussa who emailed her. At first it had only been an infrequent catch-up note: news of his new-born baby girl, news of his mother's death, news of his promotion to the head of orthopaedic surgery at the Baghdad teaching hospital. And then news that Baghdad was changing utterly, as sanctions crept over the country like a cancer.

Sinead knew the risks Moussa was taking in corresponding. With every email that she received from him she tried to read between the lines of the rather stilted tone in which he wrote. Many of the other doctors that she'd known had left, but Moussa didn't want to go. He had left Baghdad before when things were much less rough, he wrote, and now he felt an obligation to his new orthopaedic wing even though it was now infested with cockroaches. The new wing was unpainted and unsanitary, but it held the only hope of life for all the children with cancers and malformed limbs. Moussa's own daughter Baby Sinead was born in the year 2000.

"We have a millennium baby!" he wrote happily to

Sinead. And she wrote back that she had just started up her own little surgery on Townsend Street.

"Another birth of sorts," she wrote.

"You have decided to specialise now in the diseases of the rich!" Moussa's email joked back to her, when she told him about her private practice.

She reassured him that she also filled repeat prescriptions for the depressives, the Valium addicts and the alcoholic grandmothers who lived in tiny houses in brick backstreets around the city.

From the beginning of the new millennium Doctor Sinead Skellig plunged into her work. Her small glass-fronted surgery was neat, carpeted and modern. She hired Dorinda, her lanky brisk receptionist, and together they did enough work to keep the business ticking over.

By the next year there was only one more email from Baghdad, this time brief and succinct. Moussa's wife Buna had died of cancer just six months after Baby Sinead was born. She had suffered greatly. She'd had no relief of pain. There were no medicines because of sanctions. There was no chemotherapy, no radiotherapy, and the cancer had eaten up her body like a vampire. Moussa asked Sinead to pray for Buna, and to pray for Baby Sinead. He wanted his baby daughter out of Baghdad and so he sent her to live with Buna's sister in Damascus. He plunged himself into his work with a new vigour that defied defeat. His emails to Sinead in Ireland stopped.

Sinead had never wanted to become a GP. It was a career choice of limitations at the end of a very long journey of indecision. After Baghdad, after the evacuation, her only thought was of giving up medicine. As a child

she had been fearless and without any feminine qualms
about the sight of blood, or the smell of flesh that has
been cut or burnt. As a trainee surgeon and anaesthetist
before the war she had barely noticed the smell of
cauterised blood that had caused so many other student
doctors to feel quite faint.

But in Baghdad there had been burns: and they were
the most terrible bomb-blast burns that she had ever seen.
There were bombs that amputated limbs. There were
faces burnt like black cadavers.

After leaving Baghdad in 1991, Sinead didn't ever want
to feel the warm wet slippery feel of human blood on her
glove again or watch a body become limp with gas or hear
the tight scream of a surgical saw again.

She returned to medicine in the form of general
practice because she knew that it was the only job in
which she could pick and choose what she did for her
patients.

"I have lost my nerve," she wrote to Moussa, and she
felt ashamed. But she simply couldn't bring herself to
probe wounds, or lance abscesses, or sometimes even to
syringe ears.

All the gory things could be done in casualty. She would
refer. She would take a male practice partner to do the
invasive male examinations. And she would employ a female
partner once a week to examine female private parts.

She could still inject people: needles held no fear for
her, and she realised with relief that she could busy herself
with vaccinating infants, measuring blood pressures, and
dipping the pale, sterile urine samples of ante-natal pregnant
women.

But she did not have to cut anybody up, or smell burning flesh, or suture limbs that would turn to gangrene, or deliver bomb-shocked babies that would be born dead ever again.

Sinead reached the Pepper Canister Church on Mount Street and turned along the canal. She found a bench to sit on where she could think a while. The sun had just come out, suddenly hot from behind thick cloud. It all seemed so ridiculously peaceful here. She let her eyes glaze over until her vision blurred.

She gazed at the trees on the other side of the canal now, and tried to imagine what was happening in Fallujah: the midnight journey that Moussa had described for her. But in her mind's eye the only thing that she could see was Moussa's face in fear.

She tried to picture the hospital she had known in Baghdad in 1991: the air-conditioned operating theatre; the doctors' res; the nurses' station. Was anything the same? Moussa had told her that the hospital had fallen into disrepair during the sanctions. But now, after this new war, what sort of dreadful conditions were they working in now? She could almost see the expression on poor Moussa's round face, concentrating as he sawed through rotten bone. It was an expression of pure misery.

Sinead shook her head in fury and decided to concentrate instead on all the greenness, the white blossom scattering in the warm wind, and the groups of brown ducks drifting over and back across the canal. She pulled her saved lunchtime crusts from her pocket and threw them to the ducks.

But there were flowers in the gardens of the hospital in Fallujah. Moussa's colleagues had been eating flowers.

I am so lonely, Moussa had written. He is saving lives, thought Sinead. That's what he's doing. He is taking responsibility for rescuing those who are loved by others. He is a man of great love for the world. But what he feels right now is loneliness.

In many ways we are all the same, we doctors, she thought. We seek out solace through good deeds. We learn that attending to the needs of others gains us love from the world. But love from the world is not the same as love from an individual. The love gained through self-sacrifice is certainly quite solid and dependable. It is recordable and rewardable. But it can sit like a stone in the heart.

And then she suddenly remembered that first young man who'd come in to the surgery that afternoon. That very first patient, the smiling brown-eyed floppy-haired young man with the satchel and a badge: *No War For Oil*. A little red and yellow badge.

He had seemed kind. And interesting. A gentle sort of person. That was a good badge he was wearing.

I should have talked to him properly, Sinead thought.

What a pity he was in such a hurry.

Chapter 5

Harry opened the door to the basement flat, and stepped onto a pile of mail in the hall. He grabbed the mail in one hand, and stuffed it into his satchel for reading later. He was dog-tired.

"Iz?" He called loudly, once, then again, and then realised with relief that Isabella was not home.

He shuffled into the kitchen and found a beer left in the fridge. He snapped it open and slugged down a huge mouthful before collapsing on the yellow sofa and flicking on the telly.

Harry switched on to *Channel Four News* and he let his eyes glaze over the footage of severed limbs and gutted buildings following another suicide bombing in Baghdad.

He was exhausted. Exhausted from thinking about Baghdad, which was being bombed while he sat drinking a beer. Exhausted from speaking, and typing, and answering emails, and faxes, and organising the students and activists in the peace campaign. But despite his exhaustion he felt compelled to keep on watching. He could not miss a moment of the history which was currently unfolding.

The beer was cold though. Lovely, Harry thought. Thank God Iz is out. I hope she's doing something nice. Meeting a friend. Having a beer too, with a gang of friends in town. He pictured her laughing over a pint of Guinness in a Dublin city bar, her head bent forward, dark hair hanging down to brush off her beautiful pale face.

He thought about how gorgeous she had looked this morning, after her shower, with her black hair straight, all wet and dishevelled. He had wanted to make love to her quickly before leaving the house: he felt incredibly horny, despite the pressure of a large press conference that day. But then he had also just found that *pimple* while he was having a shower.

And Isabella hadn't seemed in great form. She had just sat stiffly on the bed and pressed her hands together, and said very little.

Harry had rubbed her back with a towel after her shower, and told her happily about his plans to go to the World Social Forum in Venezuela next year. Isabella had listened, but she hadn't said a word.

The anti-war campaign was growing rapidly, Harry told her. It was taking off in a much more radical direction now, and developing a real maturity of ideas. He spoke passionately while he dressed and rubbed his own hair dry. Isabella listened, and said nothing, until he had finished rubbing his own back, and was flicking his overgrown hair out of his eyes.

"Harry, I don't think I can take much more of this."

It had shocked him that her voice had seemed so cold and measured. She stood up to face him, slowly shaking her head.

"All this stuff about Venezuela – what about *our* holiday, Harry? What about that? We were supposed to have a *holiday* together next year. You haven't even bothered to remember. And tonight – what about tonight? You haven't even told me where you're going! I just can't handle it any more!"

She began to pace around the room like a mad thing.

"I feel like I am not a part of your life any more!" she yelled at him. "I feel incredibly alone. I am in a relationship, a very loving relationship, and yet I have never in my life felt more alone!"

She stood in front of him, fists clenched firmly by her sides.

"Oh come on, Iz. Not now. Please don't let's have this conversation now. I have to go out. I've got a huge day on today. Please let's sort this out later."

"What on earth do you want me to say, Harry?" Isabella hissed. "You have someone new to meet every day. You have a hundred thousand people to march with. *You* have a million people who are going to watch you on the lunchtime news today, giving a press conference about your protest against George W Bush. Where does that leave *me*? How on earth can I compete with the international importance of George W Bush? Among the millions of people that you speak to, Harry? What I am asking is, are you even aware of *me*?"

"I could say that you are one in a million," Harry

grinned sheepishly, "but I guess that's not the answer you're looking for."

"Of course that's not the answer I'm looking for!" Isabella roared. "And you know that perfectly well. You talk rubbish! *We* talk rubbish, all the time, Harry. I ask you one question, and you tell me the answer to something else. And nothing changes – no matter how many times I tell you that you are being selfish and only seeing things your own way and trying to suit yourself to avoid having a *relationship* with me! You duck around and avoid me even more. You will probably *never* give me the answer I am looking for!"

She sat down again looking utterly defeated, and played with her frayed dressing-gown cord.

Harry stood still and watched her for a moment. He was puzzled by her remark. *The answer I am looking for.* Was this some kind of bizarre quiz? You never did know with Isabella. *The answer, my friend, is blowing in the wind,* he thought to himself. The answer, of course, depends on what the question was. Isabella had not in fact asked a question. She had made several remarks, which were phrased as questions, but which appeared also to have pre-made conclusions of her own.

Oh, crap, he was going to have to go. It was nearly half past eight now. *Was* Isabella finished? He didn't want to leave her all upset, but if he didn't go now he was going to be late. He waited a bit more to see what she was going to say.

The silence was getting awkward now. He thought he had better say *something*, as she did seem to be waiting for a response.

"Is there any fruit of the forest yoghurt left in the fridge, Iz?"

"Jesus Christ Almighty, Harry! Is that all you can say? This is like living in a fucking Harold Pinter play!" Isabella shrieked, and leaped off the bed to grab him by the hair.

"Ouch! Jesus Christ, Iz, what are you doing?" Harry roared. He bent down to avoid being hurt by her, and she let go, and turned to sob. "It's a theatre of the absurd all right," he growled.

Isabella was crying silently now.

"In any case," Harry rubbed his head, "I thought Harold Pinter was one of your favourite writers. And he's a great anti-war poet too."

Isabella howled with rage, and buried her face in her hands.

"Oh, Iz, please don't cry now. Please, I don't know what it is that you want at the moment, but I think we should stop fighting now, please, darling. Iz. Come on. I've got to go, I've got a press conference to do today. Please give me a hug and let's be friends. Come on, darling. Be my love!"

He put his arms out to pull her head towards him, and stroked her wet hair and hugged her face to his chest, kissing the top of her head. "You smell beautiful." He sniffed the top of her damp head.

Isabella spat on the carpet. She couldn't bear to swallow the tears.

He let her go, and picked up a grey sweatshirt and pulled it over his head. He took his satchel with the red and yellow badge that read *No War For Oil*.

"I've got to go now." He was emotionless now. He felt completely drained. "Wish me luck?"

"Good luck, Harry. But you know, you never need it," she had softly told him, and lay down on her side on the unmade bed again, rolling her knees into her chest.

At the beginning of their second year at university when the whole country was glued to the television to watch the Berlin Wall come down, nineteen-year-old Harry and Isabella had watched the German people dancing on the streets from a smoky Dublin pub surrounded by all their friends. As Harry watched the television in amazement, he began to wonder if for the first time in his life it was becoming possible now to make some sort of sense of the world.

Harry had begun to notice at that time that the world was already changing all around him too, even in Dunmallow, their childhood village on the coast. The Berlin Wall tumbled and the people of Eastern Europe pulled down statues and threw stones along the streets. But even in Dunmallow, Harry noticed that his father started to take on a different tone of voice when he spoke about events and slapped his breakfast newspaper with the back of his hand. The tone was excited, and more confident.

"Will you look at what they're saying about the Russians now! Did you ever think you would see the like!"

His father's newspaper-reading voice was full of life.

Harry did not consider himself while first at university to be political but he could see that the world around him was becoming serious.

"Isn't it desperate what they are saying about the

priests?" his father would say darkly, ruffling the newspaper and peering sternly over spectacles at Harry eating cornflakes by the range.

One summer Sunday, a bishop in County Galway was discovered to have had an illegitimate child. It was in the headline in every newspaper in the shop after Mass, and the country was in hysterics. People could not stop talking about this bishop, and from then on the only thing that people seemed to want to talk about all summer long was that there were women all over Ireland having children with the priests.

Then, in the autumn, back at university, Harry and Isabella went to a debate about the possibility of lifting the ban on divorce. Harry found his thoughts turning to his sunny and devoted childhood, and remembered Mrs Keane, his mother's Lady Help who had bounced him on her knee.

Mrs Keane had always been very holy and against divorce, but when two red-faced policemen came to the house one day and said that Mrs Keane's husband's clothes were found on the edge of the cliffs beside his empty white Fiesta car, Harry, then aged twelve, had felt that something very strange had happened. He knew that Mr Keane was not the type of man who would jump off a wild high cliff, naked in the middle of the night, just to make a hasty end to his life. Mr Keane was a cheerful man. He liked to drink a lot of pints. After the white Fiesta car and the clothes had been found, and the police had called, Mr Keane was never mentioned in the house again, but Harry noticed Mrs Keane's new lightness of step, and the softening of smile when her husband was no more. Some time later, he had noticed Mr Keane's friend, Arthur Bob, who worked above in Wexford town for CIE, had moved his small blue car into the driveway of the little council house. And Mrs Keane and Arthur Bob drove into town together now, and went to Mass and visited the sea. But by then, nobody could remember that there had ever been a Mr Keane.

For years afterwards, Harry had often thought about Mr Keane and the white Fiesta, and that there was something very wrong with a country where a marriage could only end when someone had left his clothes and his Fiesta on the top of a wild high cliff.

So when the divorce debate came up in college that semester, Harry volunteered to speak in favour at a major debate of students, against the Professor of Theology who was campaigning in the other direction.

The Professor of Theology took a belligerent attitude to the nineteen-year-old debating the holy bond of matrimony, and sneered at Harry behind an intellectual smile.

Harry spoke angrily that night about the suffering of women in a loveless marriage. He argued succinctly that marriage was an institution created for the benefit of society; it should not become an unbendable contract for life. "Love," argued Harry in his summing up at the debate, "should be what makes us free." Human beings were far too precious to be denied the right to love whoever they choose, whenever they choose, he declared to the audience. They must be free to love, in order for love to become a force for good.

The students signed a petition for the legalisation of

divorce. Harry was proposed for election, to become the Students' Union President. But his most vivid memory of winning the debate that night was Isabella, glowing with pride for him.

Harry took his new job as SU president very seriously, and started writing newspaper articles, and borrowing library books by Che Guevara, Rosa Luxembourg, and Karl Marx.

"What the devil are you reading now?" his father asked, aghast by the developments in Harry's literary choice.

But then, for Harry Waters – in love with Isabella, in a world that was as exciting as his was about to become – life could not have been more perfect.

Harry sipped his beer slowly now, sucking the fizzy taste in through his front teeth, cold onto his palate as though he were sucking the taste of the day into his mind. It was after ten and Isabella had still not come home. He contented himself with the thought that she had definitely gone to have a drink with Ruth or someone. He was actually quite pleased that she was still out. At least he could now watch *Newsnight* in peace.

He let his mind drift happily away, newsreel after newsreel, and he let himself relax and slouch down deeper into the battered yellow sofa. It was good to get a break from Iz, from all the shouting and the mad demands – for just a while.

Harry scrolled through the videotape in his mind of the events that had made up his day, flipping back and over, checking how he felt.

The row with Iz: painful. The press conference: that was brilliant. The episode at the doctor's: not at all unpleasant actually. She was quite an interesting woman. And he'd got the stuff he needed: that would all be sorted now, thank Christ. He patted his pocket one more time to reassure himself that he had it.

The morning's press conference had really been the highlight of the week though. Harry had been in a dreadful fluster getting there, almost missed a bus, couldn't find the proper change, and realised halfway there that he had cut his face while trying to shave a neat line underneath his chin and had blood splatters on his shirt. The beard idea was too much trouble after all, he had decided. Too fiddly to shave around and underneath.

He inspected the brown blotches on his shirt and decided that he would just ignore them. He would force himself instead to concentrate completely on the task at hand and put the turmoil of this morning back where it belonged. As Harry's bus trundled along Harcourt Street he had flicked through the final notes he'd made in his small notebook for the press conference and began to feel quite happy and relaxed. He bought a cappuccino and an apple on Dawson St, and managed to get himself into the room that they had booked, just a minute before ten.

Chubby reliable Alan Steadman was there already, of course, organising chairs.

"And there he is – not a minute too soon either!" Alan quipped through his thick auburn beard. "No pressure on you, Harry, take your time. Turn up any time you like. No need to help us out setting up the place. Fiona has at least ten arms on her body."

55

"I'm really sorry, lads." Harry downed the last of his cappuccino and took his seat at the table by Fiona. "It's just been one of those weirder-than-weird mornings." He sat down to read his scribbled notes, furious with himself for being late again.

All his life Harry had been well able to organise himself. So what the hell was happening to him these last few months? The constant rows with Isabella were wrecking his head completely. It was as if the whole relationship was just eating into his ability to get his act together any more.

Fiona Kennedy who was so short-sighted that she couldn't see what the bloodstains on his shirt were, asked him, "Have you spilt your dinner down your front?"

"Shaving incident."

"Goes with all the posters anyway." Alan had finished decorating the wall behind them and stood back to admire the posters with the blood-splashed slogans: STOP THE WAR. SAY NO TO SHANNON WARPLANES.

"Hold some papers up in front of your shirt when people look at you. Nobody will notice," Fiona suggested kindly.

The journalists had already started mooching in, clumsy with their cameras, lighting and equipment. Fiona ushered them around while Harry checked his final notes. Alan was leaping up and down to make sure the other speakers were all lined up and knew what they were going to say. There was a silent tension gathering in the room. The dull low-pitched voices of cameramen lining up, the clicking of tape recorders, the intermittent rumbling of buses just outside.

"All right then, everyone!" Alan called, and then realised that he ought to use the microphone that they had arranged. The journalists from the TV and radio stations had perched their own mikes up for their recordings like a flock of little birds along the tabletop. Alan tapped his microphone for attention. *Whoof* went the microphone, and Fiona jumped. Harry smiled at her.

"Thank you all very much for coming here today," Alan began. "As you know, this press conference has been called by the Stop The War campaign which is a coalition from the colleges, the churches, the political parties and the social justice groups, to call for a national demonstration at Shannon Airport next month against the state visit of George W Bush."

Harry breathed rapidly while Alan talked. He scanned the room to check the faces, to see what the expressions were like. It was impossible not to feel nervous, not knowing what kind of treatment they were going to get from the press today. Most of the mainstream media was still quite uncritical of the war. Several leading journalists had even written articles supporting the invasion, and many of the papers were arguing that the peace campaigners were supporters of the old Saddam regime. Harry swallowed hard. They had a tough day ahead of them now to convince the media that the Bush protest was important. And then the questioning began, and the cameras clicked and flashed.

The first few questions were really rather dull. Things about numbers of people on the demonstration, what the police arrangements would be on the day, the kind of people who were involved in the campaign. It seemed like very routine stuff to go into a newspaper article, Harry worried – at this rate, it was all going to look more like a laundry list than a political debate. What if the journalists were bored *already*, Harry wondered. If the media attention drifted *away* from the Shannon issue now, it could be very hard to drag them back. Everything depended on getting a big turnout on the day, and in order to get a big turnout in Shannon, they desperately needed big media to be interested. If the papers and TV were going to ignore them, they were really sunk.

But Harry needn't have worried about any media boredom. As soon as the first few housekeeping questions were out of the way, the opinion-column writers started asking questions.

"What about the *violent* element of the anti-war campaign? Why don't you tell us something more about that?"

"Are the anti-war activists planning any more damage to American warplanes?" asked a burly moustached journalist from *Today FM*.

Harry had spotted the fifty-year-old nurse who had hit the nose of an American jet at Shannon airport and was due to be tried for it, sitting wide-awake now in the audience. He knew that she was perfectly capable of mounting her own defence, but he thought he'd better take that question on himself. He could see the other journalists pricking up their ears and poising their pens to make sure they quoted his reply.

"We are proud of all peace activists," Harry began and cleared his throat. "And although direct action is not a form of protest which is open to all of us, we acknowledge that those who choose direct action do so in good faith and with honourable intent."

The cameras flashed, and reporters started scribbling. It was tough convincing anyone that they could *defend* the damage to an American warplane; and yet, he had to give it some kind of historical context. Direct action – think Martin Luther King, Harry suggested to the journalists, when they asked him exactly what he meant. There was a small smile from most of them; it was a simple sort of reply. But he felt okay about it.

Fiona Kennedy, who was chairing, pointed to another journalist.

"How many do *you* expect on the demonstration, Michael? From your own party – the Greens?"

Michael Bennett, the Green Party representative nodded to Fiona to indicate that he'd like the microphone.

"Well," he began in his mild meandering style, "we had over a hundred thousand in Dublin on February fifteenth."

It was a soft enough reply, Harry thought. But Michael Bennett wasn't going to be too pushy about estimating a crowd, he knew. The papers were obsessive about numbers, and it was fatal to predict and get it wrong.

Fiona couldn't see much through her coke-bottle glasses, so Harry poked her to show her that Maggie Hennelly from the *Sunday Times* was trying to get in.

"Many people in the Shannon region will be very angry with your movement," said Maggie, "saying that you're going to take jobs away from the airport. What do you say to them?"

Fiona Kennedy turned and looked across to Harry, to

see if he wanted her to answer. The jobs issue at Shannon was a sticking point for many journalists, but Fiona was from the South West of Ireland, and felt this issue was very close to her. *Put the West of Ireland under pressure.* Harry nodded at her to take the question.

"We have spent a good deal of time in the Shannon airport area, speaking to the local people," began Fiona in her West Cork accent. She gesticulated with her biro as she spoke. Her sharp grey eyes were steel behind her glasses. "The Irish people are very compassionate and peace-loving. We don't believe that the people of the Shannon region should be bullied into supporting an illegal war for oil."

Maggie Hennelly nodded slowly at Fiona, and scribbled in her pad. The other journalists seemed happy enough with this response, and Fiona felt quite proud of what she'd said. Through her thick glasses, she didn't see that Maggie had winked at her just before she spoke, and then afterwards at Harry; but she would have loved it if she had.

"What about Saddam Hussein's regime of terror?" someone from the front row asked. Harry recognised him as a well-known TV reporter. "Surely now that Saddam is out of power you will agree that the invasion has been a success?"

"We agree with you that Saddam Hussein's regime was a regime of terror. But the people of Iraq have already suffered far too much under that regime and under sanctions. This is an illegal war that has no mandate, and it will only increase the risk of terror in Iraq," Harry replied. He nodded at the journalist, who looked dissatisfied.

"Senator Cairns, how do you answer the accusation

that you are anti-American in your association with the protestors at Shannon?"

William Cairns, a tall, portly Labour party senator, who was a successful playwright in his time, was sitting next to Harry.

Cairns was developing a belief in the twilight of his career that the only way to get anything done in politics any more was to seize the bull by the horns and let rip. He decided to take the question of anti-Americanism full on and with relish. William Cairns took the microphone from the chair and looked head on into the television cameras.

"If it is to become anti-American," he began in a low-pitched voice, "to oppose an illegal war, to acknowledge the will of the United Nations and to preserve the neutrality of our nation, then indeed, I do, as you suggest, sir, stand as charged. If it is to become anti-American to oppose the torture of untried suspects in Guantanamo Bay, against all the conventions internationally agreed of the treatment of prisoners of war, and against all the international legal agreements that guarantee *any* civility in the world, then I do, sir, in your eyes, sir, stand as charged. But if you believe for a single instance that I will bend or bow to your McCarthyist bullying, your fumble-in-the-greasy-till conservatism, your fawning false republicanism and your mealy-mouthed sobriquets, then, sir, you are very much mistaken. I do wish to advance the cause of peace and justice and liberty for all. *But liberty was never bombed into a people under occupation, by the lies of a foreign army!*"

William Cairns boomed, and the microphones jumped on the table.

"The American nation was built on liberty. But liberty is the *opposite* of occupation!" he went on, while Fiona tactfully moved the microphones several inches from his range. "This war in Iraq is *illegal*, and *immoral*, and *wrong*. And our government betrays all its citizens by assisting in it!"

The air in the small conference room was suddenly quite still. They could hear the traffic whining just outside, and the breeze flapped in the blinds that covered up the open windows. But William Cairns had silenced everything and everyone in the room into what Harry would later on in a fit of giggles describe to Alan as "an atmosphere of shock and awe".

Cairns returned the mike to Fiona as if it were a chalice, and winked at her.

The journalist who had asked Cairns the question pretended to be making some more notes and curled his thick moustache around while he frowned over what he had written, bending his head to avoid Cairn's penetrating stare.

Harry was trying hard not to smile too obviously in front of all the cameras. This was all becoming pretty *savage* now, he decided. But at least they were being listened to.

"Any other questions for the panellists?" said Fiona in a gentle voice.

The journalists sat in silence. A few more photographers flashed, and cameras wove around them for TV, but it seemed as though Cairns had simply wrapped it up. There was no more to be said. They had their story, and it was as if William Cairns had put out the kind of vibe that would put anybody off questioning him about it now.

Harry turned to Cairns. "That was just great, Bill!" he breathed. "Thank you. Thank you so much for coming."

"Good God, Harry. What the fuck else would I be doing?" Cairns snorted, and slapped Harry on the back. "Bloody media hacks. Look at them all sneaking back to their lairs now to type up petty-minded pseudo-opinion. None of these idiots are worth talking to, Harry – except Maggie there, of course." He winked again and nodded in her direction.

Small mop-headed Maggie Hennelly from the *Sunday Times* had lingered on to catch a few extra details and was still scribbling on a pad. Alan and Fiona were sitting at the desk with her happily filling her in. Maggie giggled as she wrote, and flirted with chubby, red-faced Alan while he tried to answer her questions with sincerity. The fact that the top three of the buttons of her tomato-coloured blouse had opened, revealing a blushing freckled cleavage that dragged Alan's eyes away as soon as Maggie's would allow it, was making this task difficult.

"Come for a coffee with us, Maggie?" suggested Fiona.

The room was empty now that all the cameramen and journalists had gone. Harry and Michael Bennett had moved to start the clearing up, hauling chairs across the floor and re-stacking them in a corner. William Cairns had repaired to the bar where he was chatting up a very pretty camera girl from TV3.

"I'd dearly love to," sighed Maggie (making Alan blush again as her long breath stretched her gaping blouse another inch), "but I've got to put this to bed quickly enough tonight, and there's a big science conference on tomorrow that I've got to cover so I'll be flat out all weekend over that. Maybe another time though? You lot must have lots of time for coffee!" She nudged Alan gently but with enough pressure to arouse him into believing that he had been groped.

Alan shook his head and laughed a high-pitched nervous laugh. Fiona rolled her eyes.

"You know nothing, Maggie!" Fiona's Cork accent was as strong as her Coke-bottle lenses. "We've got another two thousand posters to put up, and public meetings to organise around the country to build numbers for this thing. And Harry goes on the *Late Night Show* on Saturday. Did you know that, Maggie? On a panel with two other peace campaigners, to talk about the Bush protest? They want to do a special on it."

"Congratulations, Harry!" Maggie was genuinely pleased. "That sounds really great. Who are the others with you on the panel?"

"Oh, one of them is a nun from Nicaragua who supported the Sandinistas; interesting woman." Harry spoke over his shoulder as he peeled the posters from the walls. "And the other is Jeremy Manning, the academic who founded *Campaign for a Nuclear Free Ireland*."

Fiona and Alan gathered up the sellotape and rolled-up posters in their arms and walked to the door.

"Aren't you coming back to the office to us, Harry?" Fiona mumbled through a roll of sellotape that she clamped between her teeth.

"Oh, I'll see you later. I've got to meet someone." He

felt his face pink up hotly. He wanted to get to a doctor just as soon as he could.

"A new supporter for the campaign?"

"Ah – no. It's just a personal thing. It's nothing really. I'll see you both tomorrow." He turned away from them to fiddle with a box of thumbtacks that they'd left behind.

Fiona removed the sellotape from her mouth with the two remaining fingers that were not grasping onto stationary, pens and posters. "Be on time tomorrow, please Harry. It's the Ocean Wave hotel at eight. Have you prepared your talk at all?"

"I'll be writing it on the train." He gave her a guilty smile. He was desperately behind the work. Hopefully he could get some time alone tonight if he could get the house to himself. Isabella *had* said something about going out.

"You big eejit!" Fiona laughed, and kicked the door of the conference room closed behind them.

And so that evening Harry sat in silence, alone for the first time that day in the small dark flat, while the television flickered quietly. Isabella *would* have been proud of him today, he thought. She probably didn't get to see them on TV, but she would get to read it in the papers tomorrow.

He patted his trousers pocket, the package rustling again, and realised it was probably a damn good thing he and Isabella had not made love that morning. He would get the other thing sorted out tomorrow. He flicked the television off, and prepared himself for his long evening ahead, of phone calls, details, writing up his talk, building for the demonstration.

Sinead switched her television on in her large Donnybrook apartment and sat down for the nine o'clock news with a giant glass of cool white wine.

She'd had a much longer day than she'd anticipated. Several of the patients had taken up far too much of her time. She had been caught up in phone-calls, answering queries from the hospital, hunting down lab results and missed appointments. As a result she still had a lot to sort out after she came back from her walk. Dorinda had been scolding her for keeping her back late, and then the traffic had been hell. She was quite exhausted now and all she wanted to do was veg out in front of some TV. But she still hadn't got around to thinking about what on earth she was going to write back to Moussa.

She sniffed her rather floral wine, and took a very grateful gulp. The first news story was about Iraq as usual. Another suicide mission there, and one American soldier and twenty-five Iraqis had died. Desperate, she thought. But then the story switched very rapidly to the plans for George W Bush to visit Ireland the next month.

Sinead watched a rather stilted studio interview with an American diplomat, who was arguing that the Irish people should be welcoming the Bush visit, not protesting. The newsreader was nodding cheerfully. She swigged another gulp of wine in fury. It was almost unbearable just to watch. Ugh! She snorted in angry disbelief and was beginning to think about changing the channel, when she caught a glimpse of a man who looked familiar, sitting underneath a large banner that read in block black letters with blood-red splashes in the background: STOP THE WAR. SAY NO TO SHANNON WARPLANES.

A peace campaign was organising a demonstration against President Bush's visit next month to Ireland. This was good. This was very good. Sinead sat up, and grabbed her wine bottle to pour herself another glass in excitement. Another demonstration. Thank God *somebody* is doing something about refuelling in Shannon. She glued herself to the report.

Sinead sipped the cold white wine, tasting it to and fro through her front teeth, and slowly began to realise that she *did* recognise the man who was sitting beneath the banner.

And this time he had his trousers on!

But she recognised quite clearly the same slow gentle eyes. The overgrown hair. The beginnings of a rather scrappy beard. The same voice, only on TV he seemed to be *much* more confident than he'd been in the surgery with her. The little sound-bites they'd recorded sounded quite measured really. He comes across as pretty knowledgeable, and serious enough, but with just the tiniest amount of mischief.

That's him, she thought. *Harry Waters!* He's involved in this big protest they are planning for George W. Bush. He's a political activist. No wonder I thought there was something different about him.

And I have his phone number, and his address.

Sinead sat back and sprawled across her sofa letting her mind drift pleasantly away from all the rest of the news.

She felt extremely happy now. Tomorrow she was going to be able to do something that would really make a difference. Tomorrow she would know exactly what to say to Moussa.

Chapter 6

The air inside the operating theatre was thick with sweat. From underneath his cotton surgical hat a river ran down Moussa's forehead.

"Let me dab you."

He turned to face his friend Ali the anaesthetist, allowing him to wipe his face again.

"Have we no more blood?" he asked him.

Ali shook his head.

"Haven't we any other fluids?" Moussa looked at the anaesthetist again, and at the suction container.

It was filling, still.

The child's tiny body open to the world.

He wiped his gloved hands once again on the sterile drape. There weren't any more packets of gloves to change them if they got too slippery.

"Doctor Moussa, we have no refrigerators going," he heard the theatre nurse telling him in exasperation. "We have no air conditioniong. Just look at us! We're doing open abdominal surgery without an EEC machine, without saturation monitors . . . " She rolled her head from side to side.

Moussa sighed at her. "I know. I'm sorry. This child . . ." He tutted and shook his head again, searching through the ruptured spleen for more bleeding vessels, checking for remaining shrapnel. "All right. Enough damage here. Ali, I'm taking out the spleen," he told the anaesthetist.

Ali grunted.

"Suture?" Moussa turned back to the nurse again. "Let's just tie off this splenic artery and keep the child alive."

Inside his cotton mask Moussa could smell his own breath; he was dehydrated. But the tap water was undrinkable now since a sewage pipe had been hit by mortar and flooded the river with raw sewage. Bottled water was difficult to find now too, although there was Coca Cola in the hospital canteen. But Moussa swore he'd never touch another drop again since his last filling fell out. He had called his dentist, Dr Raja, an ex-classmate who taught at the Dental Hospital; but Dr Raja, it seemed, had disappeared. Someone had told him afterwards that Raja had been wanted by the Administration. Moussa took the news with his accustomed silence.

He poked his tongue into the small hole in the side of his tooth now while he worked, shrugging his right shoulder up to wipe his forehead with his upper arm every few minutes, clamping blood vessels, tying off their pale stalks.

Doctor Ali was listening to the child's heart rate with a stethoscope; without an EEC machine it was the best that they could do.

He pressed the child's fingernails once again, checking for perfusion.

"Oxygen?" Moussa wiped again.

Ali shook his head. "The heart rate is over a hundred now. We can't really go on like this, Moussa. We should let it go now."

"Have we any blood at all left?" Moussa begged the nurse again. "Even some saline? Anything to keep the volume up?"

The nurse stared at him solemnly. "Doctor Moussa. Some of these casualties are too badly injured. The triage system is going to have to work better."

Ali shook his head again and muttered at Moussa. "Suture up, man, and get out of there. Let's give him a chance and say our prayers for him."

"*Allahu Akbar,* God is great," the nurse added.

"God has left this hospital a long time ago," Moussa mumbled behind his green cotton disguise, hoping that no-one would really hear him.

The blessings of a cotton mask are uncountable when living in a country full of spies, he would have once privately joked to Sinead. But most of Moussa's comments in theatre seemed to go unnoticed now.

"Can I have one more suture to tie off this splenic artery again? It's just very minimally tied . . . I can't just leave it like this, still oozing."

The nurse shook her head. "We have no more, doctor. That was the last one that I have here. You know we have no more supplies. We don't have enough syringes any more either. You need to just close up the skin."

Moussa looked around in desperation. Three tired, angry, sweltering faces looked at one another.

"We can only do our best," he heard Ali saying.

He looked at the child's open abdomen once again, but the cavity was oozing rapidly now.

"We have to suture it off again or he will exsanguinate!" Moussa looked around at the chaotic theatre; at the two dead bodies on trolleys by the doorway; at the filthy window covered in brown dust. There must be something . . .

"Ali, cut a thin ribbon from this latex glove!" he told him.

"From around your wrist?"

"It's a rubber band. I'll band off the artery and we will pray that the latex will hold and that the child will not develop an abcess! And we can cover him with antibiotics . . . " But he saw the nurse's face again. "All right, sister, I know. We haven't enough antibiotics. Well, look here. And here. We'll just tie this," he worked rapidly now, impatience taking over from despair, "and this, and this. Great. Elastic band surgery; and we are going to tie the skin, yes, sister?"

"I told you, we have no more sutures left. We are trying to make what we have last . . . "

"*Then get me some cotton thread!*" Moussa almost screamed at her.

Ali touched Moussa lightly on the shoulder. "I'll see what I can do. We'll find something; I'll go and see if they've got anything left downstairs; we can always use some more staples if we can find them."

Outside, in the dense midday air, the sound of helicopter gunfire once again.

Moussa sat down on the stool. "I need to take a break,"

he told the nurse. "I have been awake all night. We all need to sit down and have a glass of tea."

My Dearest Moussa,

I do hope that you will receive this reply. I am terrified by your news, so terrified you can't imagine. But I know that you are very courageous, Moussa, and so I want you to know that I am thinking of you all day every day. I am sure that your work is quite terrible in Fallujah. But you are a wonderful surgeon, Moussa, you will be able to save lives and every life is precious when so many people are dying so young.

I feel very helpless as I read your letter. I feel guilty, because I sit in a warm and safe doctor's surgery in a peaceful country with more medicines then I know how to use. I will send you any medicines you want me to, Moussa, and I will organise other doctors to do the same. But I know you will know what is the right thing to do. There is probably no point in sending medicines if they won't be allowed into the country.

Moussa, today I decided to join the peace movement here in Ireland. There is a group working full time on it, printing out leaflets, posters, putting up a website. So, if Jon Snow doesn't answer your emails, or forgets to mention the truth about what is really happening in Fallujah, our website will at least be out there, in cyberspace if nothing else!

Do you ever start to believe that life has become so sick, and strange, and so terrible that it mustn't actually be true? That this is all a crazy dream, dreamt up by some madman and we are all just characters in his deranged head? But then, I think we all know who the madmen really are.

What a terrible perversion of the old friendship between Ireland and Iraq!

Dearest Moussa, please remember that the people here are with you and we are protesting at what is happening to your country. I know that is the only thing I can do now.

I will write again very soon.

I wonder if the CIA will intercept this email, and you'll be arrested by the Americans for subversion? What an irony that would be for the new Iraq!

Yikes!

Your very loving friend,
Sinead X

Chapter 7

Harry Waters was a revolutionary.

"A revolutionary *what*?" his bewildered mother asked, wiping her red hands on her apron. With her only son now twenty-one and just about to start his final year of university, Marion Waters was beginning to worry rather desperately about him. She stared at Harry as she stood by the sink full of steaming sprouts straining in a colander for lunch, billows of steam condensing on the steel-paned window in front of the rolling garden. More steam rose from the electric kettle on the boil and from the huge pan of potatoes cooking slowly.

Marion loved his passionate idealism. She was extremely proud of his political interests. But she was worried that he didn't seem to be heading for anything that could lead to the remotest possibility of him having a job. Harry seemed to be becoming so impossibly dreamy.

"A revolutionary er, writer, Harry? A revolutionary artist? A revolutionary businessman?"

"A revolutionary activist," explained Harry importantly, and he savoured each word as it emptied from his mouth into the large moist kitchen. He gave a small bashful shrug and smiled happily at his worried mother.

Marion Waters was a large, awkward woman. She seemed even larger, even more awkward to Harry now as she stood staring at him while he sat on a chair drinking beer in the family kitchen.

Marion wiped her hands again and continued to stare at Harry as he sat smiling.

"Well," she eventually replied, "is that so? I see. A revolutionary activist. I see. Well, that sounds great, Harry. Great, it is. It really is. A revolutionary activist, is it? Like, um, like Michael Collins, is it?"

Harry smiled and giggled slightly. "Well, no, not exactly, Mum. I suppose James Connolly would be a more likely role model, for me at least. I want to become politically active in building a better society for all of us, in Ireland and throughout the world. The world in which we live is a very unequal place. Every three seconds a child dies of hunger, Mum, and not because of any fault of their own. The richest twenty percent of people own eighty percent of all the wealth in the world. And people are taught that there is nothing they can do about it. People in Vietnamese sweatshops are told to be grateful. Black people in South Africa were told not to resist apartheid. But it took a revolution to end slavery. It took revolutionaries to win women the right to vote. And so, it's going to take a revolution to end world poverty too."

Harry enjoyed making this speech. He loved explaining ideas to people, as if he was giving them a great gift. The gift of truth, of belief in oneself, and in the greatness of all humanity.

What Harry felt that summer sitting in the kitchen with his mum, was that ever since his earliest childhood he had been searching for something he *belonged* to, and that now he'd found it.

Harry was an only child. The family were comfortably off. There was no other difficult sibling to balance his parents' naked adoration from the day that he was born. But there had been other shadows in Harry's sun-filled world.

On his first day of school, Harry had queued with twenty-five other small grey four-year-olds in line to enter their classroom behind Sister Treasa. Harry carefully took in the uniformity of greyness, and the small grey faces all around. At playtime he watched the playground carefully to see which of the groups of grey children he might want to hang around with. There was one large red-haired freckled child whose playtime activity was mostly to yell and laugh at a small isolated boy with a runny nose. The other children liked to giggle and join in, and when the large boy yelled, they mimicked and repeated all he said. Harry listened to the content of the yelling. It made no sense whatsoever. *Your mother's a knacker, your father's a pimp, you got a piebald for Christmas, you were born in a ditch!*

Harry wondered what the small isolated boy had done to deserve this kind of disgust. He studied the tall redhead and wondered how *he* seemed to have come to hold that kind of power.

Harry also noticed that the large redhead seemed to be

the slowest at reading out aloud. And the large redhead often missed his spelling words when Sister Treasa walked around the classroom and called out words to be spelt by children named at random: a game which she called Spelling Bee. Sister Treasa was quick and snappy, and made the game seem serious and important.

"Niamh O Rourke, spell Happy."

"H-A-P-P-Y, Sister!"

"Still in! Good woman, Niamh. Sean Heaney, spell Mammy."

"M-A-M-M-Y."

"Still in, take a bow, sir, take a bow. Charles Mongan now, spell coat."

"K-O-T."

"Out of the race, Charles, out of the race. Down you sit, child, down you sit. Now, Jennifer Kelly, spell snack."

"S-N-A-C-K, Sister. "

"Great girl yourself, Jennifer! And another round we go."

Harry knew that Charles Mongan could not remember the spellings of words, and therefore could not be Sister Treasa's favourite child. But he also noticed that Charles Mongan was the child that spent a great deal of time deciding where people had to stand in the playground.

And so, when other five-year-olds hung primary reds and blues and yellow-haired pictures of each other on the walls for open day, Harry's portraits of his school friends were of sad stick figures, in brown and black and grey.

Charles Mongan had taken control of who got to enter the bicycle shed during lunch break. And he had assumed for himself the task of inspecting lunch boxes each day, to make sure that the content was acceptable. Apples were sissy, and must be discarded. Cheese in the sandwiches was okay as long as it was processed. Sweets were good. The more the better. Jam, acceptable. Children who brought dangerous items like corned beef or fruitcake ran the risk of having their lunch flung around the classroom, or out of the window into the yard where the seagulls swooped.

Harry understood, from day one, that the wisest thing to do was to eat one's lunch in secret on the way to school.

Harry hadn't eaten a lunch at school in over two years. He decided it was time to talk to the small and isolated boy. He had hidden his corned beef sandwich in his pencil case for after school, and then approached the small isolated boy on the way home, and offered half the sandwich, which the boy crammed into his mouth wordlessly. Harry talked to the boy for ten minutes up the hill that left Dunmallow, and discovered that the boy was not an idiot at all, as was the dominant theory of the day. He was not an evil child, a freak of nature, or a poxy bollocks, as was the widespread reputation of his character. He was an ordinary and sorrowful child, who certainly was not capable of the intense evil that had been attributed to him by the freckled red-haired powerful Charles Mongan.

As Harry held back near the crest of the hill where the gateway to his own house was and let the small boy walk on ahead, he came to the realisation that the boy was hated and despised by Charles, and by Charles' large group of admirers, solely because he *could* be.

Harry went home that day and wrote an essay.

Some boys are small. Some boys are big. Big boys hate small boys. And small boys hav to go home and they hav to crie. But I no small boys are just as good as the big ones. I want the small boys to hav a gang on the big boys and we can get them.

Sister Treasa showed the essay to Marion and Tony Waters, on open day, coupled with the grey, black and brown portraits of Harry's classmates. The Waters read the essay, and examined the paintings. They looked quizzically at Sister Treasa. Marion was not quite sure what it was that the nun was so concerned about. The paintings were gloomy, but not incompetent. The expression of sadness, in the portraits of children in a playground was rare – but not unreasonable. Tony thought the drawings to be accurate, the colours masculine, and the sentiment of the essay to be, although dull, at least reasonably well spelt.

"Harry seems to be a very dark child – emotionally," Sister Treasa confided in a low voice.

"Ah!" said his father. "I see. Well, he is not distracted by frivolity. Yes, I do agree with you, Sister. I am proud to say that Harry does indeed take life quite seriously indeed."

And so Harry continued to paint in black and brown and grey, and to examine his rather isolated life in all its darkest expression, which gave him, if not comfort, then the solace of a spirit of truthfulness in all regards.

As Harry prepared for his Leaving Cert Exams, his father and the headmaster of the school thought his son might go into the law, technology or medicine. His father even suggested that he enter the Bank. He would guarantee that Harry would have a job for life. But Harry ignored his father's pleas for business studies and science.

Commerce was an alien to him. He mistrusted all authorities that held power.

The same year that Harry left his boarding school, Marion Waters decided that she would go back to work as a nurse again, and applied to sit the Back To Nursing examination. Harry called it the *Back To The Future Examination*, and excitedly scrutinised his mother's books on Anatomy, Microbiology and Wound Management In The Home. By the time Harry was getting ready to leave home completely and go to university, Marion had begun a part-time job as night nurse in a small hospital. She drove a newer car now, and had slimmed down into neater, shorter skirts, which she alternated with dark-coloured leggings, sweatshirts, and denim jeans.

Harry knew the world had changed completely when he came home from college one weekend to find his mother standing in her coat in the middle of the kitchen after Mass, announcing that she was going to canvass for Senator Mary Robinson to be the President of Ireland.

"Canvassing, is it, Marion?" asked Tony Waters in a high, nervous voice, his eyebrows up on stilts. Marion put her handbag down solidly on the table, and looked her husband in the eye. She wasn't going to put up with another foolish sexist word from that parish priest again as long as she lived. So, canvassing it is.

"Yes, Tony. I am going to canvass."

Harry couldn't wait to get home from college every weekend that semester, to help his mother fold and lick a thousand envelopes with literature for radical feminist Mary Robinson. He and Marion drove for miles in the small Toyota car into the villages and down the lanes, and knocked on doors, and asked people to vote for Labour.

"Mary Robinson for President, the women's rights campaigner!"

"Mary Robinson, is it? The abortion campaigner? And you the bank manager's wife?" the farmers sneered, and chuckled at the literature.

Marion Waters drew herself up tall to her full height of five foot ten and a half and announced that a better deal was long overdue for all the women of Ireland, and she was not going to stand about all day listening to people's prejudices; she had canvassing to be done.

Afterwards, when President Mary Robinson won the election, Marion Waters danced around the kitchen with Harry and Isabella, and they laughed until they cried.

And after the election, Marion Waters went back to attending the Tidy Towns Committee meetings once a month, and weeding the flowerbeds and baking scones for Harry's father's tea. But she did so with a straight tall back, and laughed lewdly now at witty comedy shows on Channel Four.

And at the end of that year, instead of hovering around a turkey in the cold dark dining room of Harry's childhood, Tony Waters took his wife on holidays to Lanzarote for the Christmas.

The year was 1990. The last decade of the millennium.

It was the year that Sinead Skellig took her first post-graduate surgical training post and moved from Ireland to Iraq.

It was the year that Isabella's father Jack Somerfield died sitting at his desk.

And Harry held Isabella in his arms, in a basement in Rathmines, and vowed that they would always be in love.

Chapter 8

June 2004

"How come you and Harry never talked about having children?"

Isabella and Ruth sat in Ruth's large sunny kitchen peeling carrots at the long scrubbed pine table. Isabella peeled slowly as they talked, letting long curling orange strips fall into a small colander, laying each bald carrot aside on a wooden chopping board for Ruth. Ruth sliced each one slowly into diagonal oval strips, which were destined to join the broccoli they had sliced. With the mushrooms, the ginger, the chopped garlic and the peas, they arranged the stir-fry ingredients onto a series of plates like the haphazard elements of a still life.

June had become a hot, rainy month, with long light-filled evenings that Isabella was attempting to fill with occupation. Harry was campaigning night after night now, up and down the country. The Bush visit was just two weeks away. Harry left the flat at eight o'clock every morning and was out 'til all hours almost every night.

The nights he spent at home were filled with phone calls, speaking to the other organisers of Stop The War, preparing statements for the press as events unfolded.

Cooking with Ruth was a perfectly decent way to pass the time, decided Isabella. Term had ended. She had failed to get the only part she had auditioned for since spring, and was therefore at a very loose end. She wanted to be a help to Ruth, who was a lazy cook, avoiding culinary efforts as often as was possible. Ruth's husband Bernard usually ate out.

"I was just thinking," Ruth continued, "that maybe if you'd had a baby then it might have brought the two of you together again. You were such a great couple once – you would have made great parents. Didn't you ever even think about it?"

"Me and Harry, make great parents? Oh Ruth, you've got to be kidding!" Isabella laughed abruptly and then popped a piece of carrot in her mouth and began to chew it noisily.

Ruth's son Roly crawled around underneath the table, picking up odd pieces of chopped vegetable that they had dropped. He alternated between sitting solemnly chewing on his finds, and attempting to poke them up his nose.

"Oh Roly! Please don't do that, you silly banana!" Ruth snatched the child up from the floor and prised the small stick of carrot, that Roly had chewed into a small penetrative shape, from his chubby salivated fingers. She put it into her own mouth to eat.

"Now *that* is probably the reason why I will never have children!" gasped Isabella with a laugh.

"What?"

"That! Salivated leftovers. Ruth, how can you put something that has not only been on the floor but also up your child's nose, into your own mouth to eat? Are you mad?"

"Oh, God, sorry. I didn't notice. You are right. Roly, you are revolting and I am going to take you outside. Immediately. Look, Iz – what do you say we forget about this bloody chopping for a while and grab two glasses of nice wine and sit out in the garden and talk this whole Harry thing through, outdoors? It's lovely outside, getting really warm now. There's a bottle of white in the fridge. Come on – you open it, and I'll get Roly something to do."

Ruth busied herself with dusting down the baby and kissing him better after having had his face briskly wiped, and took him outside to the small rear garden on her hip.

Isabella brought the wine and glasses, and went to sit beside her on the wooden bench that Bernard had once built. It was early evening and the sun was long and warm. Isabella closed her eyes and leaned back to soak up the comfort of its heat. She didn't know how to answer Ruth's question about why she and Harry had never talked about having children: at least, she knew what the answer *was*, but she wasn't sure if she could tell Ruth everything.

"I did have a sort of pregnancy. Once. A long long time ago."

Isabella swirled her wine around in her glass, and then sat up and sniffed it. She glanced sideways at Ruth to check her reaction.

"Just a little one," she continued, as Ruth had not

reacted at all yet. "And I was only just a few weeks gone. I got caught: I suppose that's what you would call it."

She looked down again, gazing solidly at the ground.

Ruth sat in complete silence. She wasn't sure whether or not to touch Isabella. Her first instinct was to hold her hand. But Isabella was holding a glass of wine in both of hers. And she was sitting tightly on the bench with her arms clenched by her sides, and her face turned down towards her lap.

Ruth said nothing for a while, and then asked in a very quiet voice: "Was that with Harry, Iz?"

"Yes, it was with Harry. It was in the beginning, when we only had just met. Just after my dad died. I got a real shock. You know."

She stopped and said no more. She felt her face begin to redden. There was a tiny niggling fear at the back of her mind that Ruth might in some small way judge her. And she couldn't bear it if Ruth judged her. Ruth said nothing. They both watched Roly, sitting heavily in his sandpit, push a toy car up and down.

"So – what happened?"

Isabella said nothing for a moment. Then she glanced at Ruth before dropping her gaze again. "I didn't have it," she said. "It was all so sudden. I was far too young. It was well over ten years ago – more even, thirteen years, I think. Things were very different then. I was in college. I was really young. My dad just died. You know how religious my mother was." She felt her face burn hot and she kept on staring at the ground while she spoke. "I didn't have *any* money. I couldn't possibly have had a baby."

"What exactly happened to you, Iz?" Ruth asked.

"I went to England." Isabella felt her voice beginning to choke up. She took a long deep drink of wine. She knew why it was so hard to tell the truth. She was just so terrified of being judged by it.

"I stayed with Vivienne from school," she continued in a small voice. "Remember her? She was living in a flat in South Ken. She was the only person I knew in England that I could trust. You couldn't have told anybody in those days. It was a long time ago, and I was afraid that I would be caught and get arrested or something. I was terrified in fact."

"Oh Isabella! Oh darling, why did you never tell *me*?"

"I don't know, really. I suppose at some level, even though you are my best friend, I suppose I was afraid. And I didn't want to upset you. It would have put you in a position that perhaps you mightn't have wanted to be in. I thought you would be better off not knowing." Isabella looked up at her friend. "Actually, Ruth," she finally admitted, "I just couldn't tell anyone. Anyone at all."

"You poor lonely lamb," murmured Ruth, and took her hand. "Roly!" she shrieked. She leaped up from the bench, and seized the child once again, this time scooping a mouthful of sand from his gummy wet mouth.

Isabella was relieved by the distraction. She didn't want Ruth to notice that for an instant her eyes were filling up. She tossed her head and took another long drink of her wine instead.

"Poor me? I'm fine for God's sake!" Isabella laughed out loud at her friend's exasperation. It was easier to make a joke now than to start to cry. "You do nothing all day except jump up and down rescuing your son from his own misfortune. I got away lightly!"

Ruth sat down again with Roly on her lap. "You know you don't mean that, Iz." She bounced the gurgling baby and made faces to distract him from the unpleasant experience of having had his mouth evacuated of sand.

"No, I know. You're right," said Isabella. "Of course I don't mean that. The thing is though, Ruth, that I think, actually, most of the time, that you and Bernard are just extremely lucky. Roly is a darling little boy."

"But haven't you ever wondered what would have happened if you had *had* the baby?"

"No, because I didn't want to have the baby. I know perfectly well what would have happened. I would have had to quit college for a start."

"Oh come on! You can't possibly know that!"

"Oh, I do know," Isabella said hollowly. "I know exactly what would have happened. Believe me. You have no idea what my mother was like back then. And Harry wouldn't have had the first clue about babies. He would have absolutely no interest. Oh, he would have had a mild interest in whether or not the child might become a future Che Guevara or something, but he wouldn't have changed a nappy to save his life. I would have been stuck raising a kid all on my own and Harry would be away in a hack, living happily ever after."

"Are you saying you had the abortion to hold onto Harry? Because if you are, then that's just bizarre. And I don't believe you. You aren't like that."

"Of course I'm not saying that," Isabella was frustrated. "It's just that Harry had nothing to do with it. Actually, he doesn't even know, to be honest. I had the abortion for myself. I couldn't have done anything else."

She hated the way this conversation was going. She had never wanted to discuss this event with *anyone*, not even Ruth, and yet here she was *having* to explain how she felt about something that she didn't even understand herself.

"You never told Harry that you were pregnant?" Ruth whispered.

"No. It happened all so suddenly. And so I kept it a secret – it was far easier that way. I didn't tell anybody, except for a woman I'd heard about in the Gender Studies department who gave me a phone number I could ring in London. But it was all so clandestine, and so I didn't tell anyone I knew because I thought I would upset people. I thought I would upset Harry. It would have been too difficult for him to *have* to know. He was so . . . oh, I don't know, *busy* at the time."

"So were you."

"Yes, but Harry is, well, Harry is Harry. You know. Places to go, people to meet. He wanted to be SU president. It would have been too much of a –a – *challenge* for him to have to deal with that kind of problem. I didn't want him to have to get involved."

"So, you dealt with it alone?"

"Don't most women?"

"I don't know. I don't know anyone else . . ."

"I mean in general. Don't women deal with most *things* alone?"

Ruth wasn't sure what the answer was to this one. She didn't really agree with Isabella at all because she found that in her neat and simple life, Bernard dealt with some things like money, paying the bills and sorting out the car. And she dealt with – well, she wrote her PhD on the social relevance of medieval art forms, and she looked after Roly. It all made perfect sense.

But she knew that it would be tactless in the extreme to start to compare her own life with Isabella's now. And she felt slightly annoyed by Isabella's self-assuredness about certain subjects, when she seemed to fall to pieces trying to manage the most ordinary things: like having a relationship.

"I guess that maybe men and women deal with things *differently*," Ruth eventually replied. "But people who have kids *can* have a life."

"Oh Ruth, I know. Please don't be hurt. Of course they do. I didn't mean that. You have a fabulous life. I was nineteen," she lied, and then felt immediately foolish again. Ruth would easily spot that she had been older at the time. "And you were thirty when you had Roly," she continued. "You are married. And you have a wonderful husband."

"He's all right."

"He's a babe, Ruth. Bernard's gorgeous. And you *suit* the whole motherhood thing, you always did."

"And what on earth makes you think that you don't?"

Isabella shook her head and looked at Roly who had been put down on the grass again and was fiddling with a plastic ball. She rolled her head against the back of the bench to take in as much as possible of the evening sun and closed her eyes. The warmth was heaven on her face. If only this sunshine could last forever.

"Ruth, the thing is," she said in a low voice with her eyes closed against the sun, "I just don't think about having children because it's not something I *can* think about." She sat up again and turned to Ruth. "Look at my lifestyle for example. Occasional theatre work when I can get it. Never knowing where the next pay cheque is coming from." She stood up and began to pace around the lawn in front of Ruth. "I haven't even got a proper job yet. Nothing secure, or reliable in any way. Teaching part-time six months of the year. *If* they give me something."

She stopped pacing and began deadheading the rose bush, flinging dying buds into the bushes.

"I suppose I just feel that it would all be . . . just impossible. And that's just the way it is. But you know, Ruth, the thing is that I don't really even want to try to think that *it could be for me*. All the family stuff." Isabella tossed dead heads into the air. "Like you have. I suppose I think that I don't have the *resources* for it. Because I guess I could have had a baby at that time, and I didn't want to. So there must be a reason for all of it. If I am going to be a mother, I really, really don't want to be a *bad* one. You've got all this, this lovely garden . . ." She began to pace again.

"It's tiny!" interrupted Ruth.

"It's lovely, Ruth. And the house is lovely." She stopped and looked at Ruth full square in the face. "And you have money, and time because you work from home, and so you can enjoy Roly, and Bernard enjoys you, and it all works out. And it's great, Ruth, it really is. But for Harry and me it will never be like this. For a start, I'm the only one who brings in any sort of a wage. And even then that's pretty unreliable. Harry only does voluntary work and political campaigning, and writes the odd newspaper article for peanuts. And although his parents are always willing to help us out, and they are very kind, I'm the only one who brings in any real money. We live in a basement, and we couldn't bring a kid into all that. A child needs a garden, and a nursery and all sorts of things. I'm being practical here."

"You could move."

"Yes, we could, and I've often thought about it, but that would involve planning. And planning is just something that Harry and I are never ever going to do. In any case, why are you pestering me about this? Why is it of any interest to you, whether or not I have kids?" She felt herself becoming angry now, and hated herself for it. Why was Ruth trying to make her feel so *guilty* about everything?

"How can you be just so sure? Have you ever even talked about it?"

"Oh, for God's sake!" Isabella rolled her eyes. "No, we haven't talked about it. We never bloody talk about anything! But we don't need to talk about this one. I know that he doesn't want it, or even to think about it, because I know where all his interests lie. In politics, in activism, in protests, in organising people. In climbing up lampposts to stop racism, or going to Shannon airport to stop the war! Not in raising a kid, in *the privacy of the family* as Harry might put it!"

"Wow! So even though you've never talked about it, you know instinctively that in *this* relationship, you are never going to have kids. End of story."

"And what's wrong with that?" Isabella was furious. She hated being made to become so defensive.

"Oh, no, nothing's wrong with it. It's great, Iz, honestly, it really is. You know what you want, you both want the same thing, and you don't even have to talk about it. You and Harry know exactly what the other is thinking, without even having to ask. It's fantastic, Iz. Honest it is. Good for you."

Isabella picked her wineglass up from the grass, and sat back down on the bench again. That wasn't what she had meant at all. She gazed down at her lap, cradling her wineglass in her hands, and wondered what more there was to say. Ruth was a good friend. She wasn't angry with her. She was angry with herself.

"The thing is, Ruth," Isabella said quietly now, "I'm not sure any more that it is all that good for me, this relationship. What if I do change my mind about having kids? Which I probably won't. But you said it, when you said that I know instinctively what will or will not happen. I know exactly what it will be like for the rest of my *life*, if I stay with Harry now, because nothing ever changes. We met when we were students. And now, we are both in our thirties, but we are still living like students. Still completely out of pocket. And still living from day to day – and I don't mind. I really don't. I'm not a snob. I don't care what people think. I don't care about having dinner parties, or having a garden lawn to mow, or bloody home improvements to arrange."

Isabella picked up a ball that had strayed over to her feet and squatted down to hand it back to Roly. She knelt down on the grass beside him and let him crawl into her lap, where she sat quietly a moment, stroking his hair while he gurgled and tried to fit the ball into his grinning mouth.

"That's all the other women in my department ever talk about, you know, Ruth. Home improvements. They are forever knocking down walls, and having granite kitchens put in. And I don't care because we've always been 'bohemian' and we like it that way; we like the freedom that we have. I can take a theatre part if I get one, or not, if I don't feel like it. And Harry gets to do what he wants to do and what he does best, and I can teach, when I get the work, and it's fine. Really, it is absolutely fine. But sometimes, not very often, just sometimes, I get scared. I get scared, Ruth, because Harry will never change, and he will never plan anything that is not a campaign, or a protest, or a demonstration. He will never plan anything which is just about *us*. And I get scared, because the truth is that I might, eventually, want something different."

As Roly crawled away again Isabella got up from the grass and picked the bottle up to pour herself and Ruth another glass of wine. "And, because of that, Harry and I will never move on. We will still be renting a flat in our eighties. Still poor. Still . . ."

"Still what? You could be having the greatest time – pair of geriatrics in a bed-sit." Ruth grinned at her. "Don't knock it, Iz! You'll suit the lifestyle."

"Still lonely, Ruth. That's what I was going to say. Still with Harry, still here, and still alone."

They were silent for a moment.

"I offered to be a surrogate for a lesbian couple that we were friends with, once," said Ruth.

"Jesus, Ruth, you did not! You and Bernard? I don't believe it. So, what happened? Why didn't you go ahead with it?"

"Oh. They didn't want to have a baby."

Ruth and Isabella collapsed in laughter.

Chapter 9

The first summer after graduation, Harry went to Israel. Isabella couldn't face her mother in Dunmallow and so decided that she would spend some time with Eddie in America after all. Eddie wanted to start off in Cape Cod Massachusetts, to get a nice suntan, and then work his way on down to Greenwich Village. Isabella and Eddie had become closer now that Ruth had met an architecture graduate and was planning marriage in the autumn.

"You'll go back and marry Harry too, by the end of summer," Eddie told Isabella gloomily, while they lay on the beach planning what to wear for Ruth's wedding.

"I don't think Harry is the marrying kind, Ed, and I'm not sure if I am either," she said, thinking of her parents long-suffering union. "Marriage is a bourgeois institution, as Harry might say," she grinned.

"Isabella, darling, if you *are* going to end up in an institution, the very least that you can do is to make sure that it's a *bourgeois* one," said Eddie from behind dark glasses.

While Isabella and Eddie spent the summer on the Cape, Harry travelled East with another history student called Basil, who was obsessed with the Holocaust and had made it his dream to spend some time on a kibbutz. Harry thought that a kibbutz might be a good experience of practical socialism.

"Think of me with every orange that you pick," Isabella warned him. But even then she didn't feel too threatened by the thought of strapping farm girls, with steadfast Jewish mothers breathing down their necks.

She had Eddie to look after her; and besides, she and Harry would be back in college in no time. He had enrolled again for post-grad, and they had kept their flat on in Rathmines. She would have to save quite hard for the entire summer, but then once she got back to Dublin she would start to get some theatre work, and maybe do some tutoring in another school.

Basil and Harry travelled by train to the south of Italy, and then through a complicated arrangement of boats and buses they managed to reach Israel, where Basil had a contact through a Jewish American post grad.

But the kibbutz thing never happened. Harry and Basil drifted apart when Basil met a blonde American, and Harry lost his passport, his wallet, and some of his clothes one night in a spectacularly drunken episode in Jaffa.

He made it as far as East Jerusalem, but without the means to travel home he found himself lodging temporarily with a Palestinian family of four girls, whose father was a schoolteacher and whose mother was a nurse.

Harry managed to have each of the four girls of the household fall desperately in love with him, much to the terror of their father. He was also beginning to feel an inescapable *amour* for their middle-aged but very elegant mother.

One night the mother of the family he was staying with came home with her Hijab torn off her head, her face covered in bruises and her beautiful brown cheekbones streaked with tears. Through the mumble of her sobs, Harry understood that she and two other women had been pistol-whipped at a checkpoint by soldiers on their way home from work. The nurse, the mother of four beautiful daughters, wept for what to Harry seemed like hours at her husband's side. Eventually she admitted that she had spent the day at work trying to save the life of two small children who'd been shot at in broad daylight for throwing stones at the police, and she had taken it out on the checkpoint soldiers. She had shouted at them and called them names when they made her stand and wait for an hour to get past. And now, in her humiliation she had paid the price.

Harry sat in the small study where he was staying and listened in horror to the mother weeping in the *liwan*, and thought of his own mother, another nurse, studying her *Back To The Future* exams last year in Ireland. That night he felt for the first time that he had begun to understand something much, much deeper about the world.

He returned to Isabella and to Ireland at the end of that summer spiritually much harder but more seriously determined than ever. He knew that winning a divorce referendum in Ireland and being the Student's Union

President would be a very small victory in a world that was being torn apart by war. He understood that his task was not just to change the small things in his own student world: it was to change the world around him. And that his task should immediately begin.

That autumn, as a post-grad and the president of the SU, Harry started going to most of his public events without Isabella. She was busy anyway, with the theatre group in college, trying to do a Masters, and spent most of her evenings learning lines for tiny theatre parts whenever she could get one. Harry felt it was important that they had a life apart sometimes. And Isabella didn't want to be the clingy type. She tried to organise a different sort of social scene for herself. She went to experimental theatre groups with Ruth. They bought a chocolate cake from Marks and Spencers to eat while they watched *Reservoir Dogs* and *Strictly Ballroom* at the Savoy. They had both joined the college choir (Harry was, despite his early days of piano tuition, quite unmusical) and they still went to the Choral Festival in Cork each year, and sang in solemn services at Christmas time.

But Harry was becoming busier and busier. He started writing articles in history journals, and was planning to stay on in college and do more research. And due to his increasing popularity as Students' Union President, he got invited everywhere.

Harry liked to be a good guest at a party, and to get there early to help out with preparation. He liked to give the host a dig out, before anyone arrived. He was also usually the last to leave.

"I've had such a wonderful time, I seem to have forgotten to go home," he would giggle when he eventually wandered out the door, blurry-eyed with drink.

And sometimes, away from Isabella, at the beginning of a cold pale morning light, Harry would find himself inexcusably in another woman's arms. He would apologetically stumble away, go home to his sleepy, love-filled bed, and fold himself back into Isabella's naked skin again. Harry did not commit these mild encounters to his memory. When he and Isabella kissed and touched each other, no other woman had existed. He would breathe in Isabella's same sour smell, and taste her saltiness, and make sure everything was right.

Chapter 10

June 2004

"What's she like then?"

"What's who like?"

"Your girlfriend."

"My girlfriend?"

"Mmm."

It was cosy in the pub now that the evening was unfolding after such a busy day. The street stall had gone really well, despite their being eventually rained off. There were loads of Americans in town, which was fantastic. The campaigners were getting a very hard time in the media now from politicians who kept arguing that American tourists would stop coming to Ireland if the people were protesting against Bush. *The American multinationals will pull out*, all the newspapers were threatening.

Harry knew how to argue against these points, but it was still personally very gratifying to see the very same Americans queuing at the stall to sign the petition against the visit of their own President.

The only problem was that the American tourists wanted to *buy* all the anti-Bush posters. The posters were very attractive: a picture of George W Bush trampling over the globe carrying the stars and stripes, with the slogan *Stop The Bush Agenda!* The Americans were *begging* Harry and Sinead to be allowed to buy their posters. Harry didn't have the heart to say no, although the stocks were running very low as the council kept taking down the posters every night. Sinead thought they should charge the Americans for the posters, perhaps a tenner each. Harry wouldn't hear of it. He was giving them all away for free.

"We're going to start running very short of posters," he had eventually admitted to Sinead. "You were right – we shouldn't have been giving them away all evening. I think I got a bit carried away."

Sinead and Harry sat side by side now at a small wooden table underneath one of the windows in Chaplin's bar. Chaplin's was pretty empty for a Thursday evening. A barman watched a football match while he slowly polished glasses. There was just one old man in a heavy overcoat sitting at the bar, falling-apart eyes over another whiskey chaser, and a group of damp tourists in the other corner in expensive anoraks, quietly drinking Guinness.

It was still daylight bright outside, that magical cold night-time northern summer brightness, and although well past nine o'clock, the sky was sharp and clean, a Virgin Mary blue behind the blackness of the buildings and the trees that wouldn't darken for at least another hour.

He hasn't answered my question, thought Sinead, looking sideways again at him. She wondered if he was being deliberately evasive now, or just forgetful.

She had a right to be genuinely curious about the elusive Isabella, she thought, about whom Fiona and Alan often spoke, but never Harry. He did briefly mention her from time to time, but only in passing.

Where are the pamphlets we wrote about the lies about weapons of mass destruction?

I'll ring Isabella and see if I've left them at home.

What time is it? Are we going to miss the news?

I'll ring Isabella and see if she will tape it.

Sinead pushed one of the pints of Guinness she had bought towards Harry and took a dainty sip from the top of hers.

"Thank you, doctor. Cheers!" said Harry and took a massive gulp from his glass. "Thirsty. Mmm." He took another long deep drink. "Lovely." He glanced at Sinead. "What's my girlfriend like? Why do you ask?"

God, was that question a rhetorical one, thought Sinead, as she watched Harry lick his white moustache away. Why do I ask? Because I need to know.

Because . . .

The real reason was because she was very deeply worried that Isabella might be very pretty. Or very clever. Or both. Or that she might just have a beautifully warm personality that Harry couldn't help but love forever. Or, any of a number of other terrifying reasons.

Sinead had heard Isabella mentioned several times by Alan and Fiona, but hardly ever by Harry. She knew that she was an actor and that she spoke in a soft, quiet, low-toned voice, and was very polite to her on the phone. Isabella didn't ring the office often, and only, it seemed, when Harry was away.

Sinead didn't see Harry's lack of interest in speaking about Isabella as a positive thing. Rather, she worried that he must be hiding something. Like her amazing beauty that he was keeping as a secret from Sinead in case she died of jealousy when she found out. Or, perhaps he deliberately avoided speaking about Isabella because he actually found Sinead attractive. But this scenario would be even worse, because so far she had found a certain amount of solace in the idea that Harry might be unobtainable.

But his keeping silent on the significant other in his life worried her even more than if he had talked about her non-stop. Because if it meant that Harry was (as he very much appeared to be) taking a love interest in her, Sinead, then the possibility of a challenging rival was a potential emotional turmoil that she was not sure that she could face.

"I'm asking you what she's like," she explained, "because I've never met her. Because I've got to know you pretty well, during the past few weeks. And we have been up and down the country campaigning, and we have been out God knows how many nights postering and leafleting in Dublin. And yet I've never met her. You never seem to bring her out or invite her to any of the meetings, or things. Even when we had a party there last week for Fiona's birthday after the thing we did in Belfast, you didn't even invite her to that. So," she smiled at him, "I was wondering, why don't you bring her out of doors?" She knew she was being pushy. But she was actually beginning to enjoy seeing him under pressure. "Your turn," she nudged him, moving in a little closer.

"Well . . ."

Sinead realised that he probably wanted to change the subject, but that didn't quench her curiosity. It only made it worse.

"It's not that I don't *bring her out,*" he finally conceded.

Sinead was surprised that he'd answered the question with such gravity.

She felt as soon as she saw his guilty expression that she ought to withdraw. Perhaps Isabella was some sort of crazy who ought to be locked in the attic.

"Oh, Harry, no, I'm only joking!" she laid her hand on his forearm. She really ought to drop it now.

Harry suddenly seemed to appreciate the intimacy of the moment. He turned to face Sinead. "No, I know what you mean." He paused and looked down at his pint. "It's just that Isabella doesn't like doing this sort of thing. She's an actress, you know. She's very arty and talented, and she does a bit of teaching too, for drama students. But she . . ." He paused, and slowed his pace down, thinking carefully about the words he chose. "She is very um, well, *emotional,* I suppose. Yes, that's what she is." He looked at Sinead. "And she is sensitive. And intense. And deep. And she has her own things to do too. Writing things, poetry, and – and learning lines and so on. She is a little bit different to us."

Sinead listened carefully, drinking it all in. *Different to us.* "I see," she said eventually.

It was hard to know what to say next. Harry was

smiling his slightly drunken smile at her. His leg felt hot against her thigh, and it pressed hard against her as he reached out for his pint. She was beginning to feel buzzy; in between her legs it tingled.

"Well, she sounds really interesting." She took a breath. "I suppose . . . I suppose the reason I'm asking is that I thought I might like to meet her. You know, when you like someone, you usually look forward to meeting their partner, because . . . you . . . you assume that you are going to like them too."

Sinead chose to drop the remark carefully and to land it delicately, with all the precision of a dragonfly landing on a flower.

"Mmm. Right. Of course." Harry looked at her with a very mischievous grin.

Drop the subject. Oh God, just drop it now, thought Sinead.

Harry swallowed the last of his Guinness. "Another pint for you, doctor?"

She still hadn't finished hers and she placed a hand over the top of the pint and shook her head. "No thanks, but I'll get you one." Harry could drink like a fish. Her frequent hangovers since she'd met him were making her increasingly wary about trying to keep up. She patted Harry's hand. "Back in just a minute." She walked over to the bar and clambered up to sit on a high stool while she waited to be served.

Harry watched her languidly. He felt tremendously happy, just watching her there, stretching out his legs in faded jeans. The campaign was going really well. He was really very impressed with Sinead. She was sharp, courageous and witty. He cast his mind back to the day he had walked into her office, one sunny afternoon three or four weeks ago.

She had been the perfect doctor too. Kind, without being particularly fussy. Mildly disinterested, but very supportive and polite. The next day, when he was up to his eyes on the phone to the Labour party trying to get them to toughen up their line on Shannon, she had walked into the office – and he could still picture every detail of the way she had appeared that day. A small, dark-blonde woman, with black rimmed glasses that made her look rather like a solemn, bookish child. He had liked her from the moment she arrived. She fitted in perfectly. She was very serious, but at the same time had a rather bizarre sense of fun.

She was older than him too. Harry wasn't sure, but he thought she must be sort of thirty-five, although it was hard to tell as she dressed quite youthfully in a denim skirt, a T-shirt and knee-high low-heeled boots. Although she was not slim she walked gracefully. She had very tiny hands and feet.

Harry noticed now, as he watched her at the bar, that she was really quite voluptuous from behind. Her blue-skirted bottom was generously shaped, with rounded knees below. Cute, is how he would describe her. Not beautiful. Her face was quirky-looking with eyes that sloped down in a funny way, and a fairly square chin. But he liked her big wide smile, and the way she punctuated her conversations with suddenly solemn expressions and then burst into howls of laughter.

She was taking the work very seriously too, Harry

thought, which was brilliant because things were really coming together now. Sinead had marvellous patience, and fantastic organisational skills. She sat beside Harry for the first few days and learnt the running of the office, surfing the international newspapers everyday to seek out information that they needed; putting together stories for the website and the newsletter which was mail-shot fortnightly, phoning politicians and senators, asking them to condemn the Shannon refuelling.

And Sinead was fantastic on the phone. Harry found the lobbying the hardest part of the whole campaign. He hated cold calling. He hated speaking to politicians whose views he utterly despised, in the hope that he would find common ground with them on Shannon. He found it hard to trust politicians, and felt unsure, and then demoralised, when after half an hour's deep polemic, some *nobody* senator from a remote constituency decided that although he agreed with everything that Harry had to say, he would not support the anti-Bush campaign, so, sorry about that. Harry wanted to slam down the phone, and yell a stream of obscenities when he came up against political fence-sitting. But Sinead seemed to be able to take these misfires in her stride. She spoke calmly and encouragingly to people. She said she understood perfectly when they felt unable to help. And she was warm and quite persuasive without being pushy. She understood when people felt they needed more information. She usually suggested meeting politicians for a coffee, which Harry knew was a good strategy, as politicians love to sit around bars being seen. He was learning from her all the time. She had also suggested that they organise a writers' group to oppose the war. She wanted to contact artists and have an anti-war art exhibition. She wanted to organise singers and musicians and have an anti-war concert.

Sinead was really very special.

Chapter 11

"Isabella. Hi! It's Eddie here. Eddie Mannion."

She almost had to stop and think. *Eddie Mannion!*

"Eddie! Oh my God! This is a fantastic surprise! How lovely to hear from you! Aren't you in America?"

"Of course I am. And loving every minute of it. How are *you*?"

"Oh, me. Great. Fantastic actually. Fine. I'm doing fine. I mean, not a lot of work at the moment, but it's a small place. You know, Dublin. And I tend to do a lot of other things too, of course. Teaching still, a bit, in college. And . . . things. And Harry, oh, Harry's doing loads. He's organising –"

"Hey, Iz, look, I'm really sorry to cut you short but I'd better cut right to the chase. I'm actually ringing you to offer you a bit of work. It's a *big* piece of work actually. In fact, I think it could be absolutely *huge*. I'm directing a *Playboy of the Western World* with a fantastic little company here in the fall, and it's going to be a great production.

We've got a fantastic cast, really young, energetic, and a good budget too, so we're going to get the set right, get some music in, have a really *really* good show. And I want you to do Pegeen Mike. We have one or two other Irish actors, but some of the accents are just too dodgy for words. Pegeen's accent has got to be perfect. The guy who's playing Widow Quinn is fine. Lovely young queen I know for years. Really *good* in fact. But I want you to be Pegeen, Iz. I always told you you'd be perfect for the role. You are so feminine, and with your jet-black hair you're a pure West of Ireland romantic heroine. And you could do your lovely Mayonnaise accent —"

Isabella broke into his dreamy monologue by laughing right out loud. Her excitement was uncontainable. "Eddie Mannion, you're a lunatic! Are you joking? Is this for real?"

"Of course it's for real!" he retorted. "Isabella, it's going to be *fantastic*. We start rehearsals in a fortnight, and we need *you* to make your mind up pronto. Please say yes, otherwise Pegeen will have a Brooklyn accent and I will have to *kill* myself rather than face the shame to literature. Say yes, Iz, and I'll get you over on a plane on Monday."

"Monday. Oh, God, Eddie, this is all too sudden. I can't make up my mind that quickly. I really need more time. I need to have a think. I need to have a huge think! But I will ring you back. I promise I will. I'm going to have to ring you back. Tomorrow morning. Oh no, tomorrow evening would be better. Same time, all right, Eds? But I'm thinking yes, definitely, maybe, I'm really thinking that I hope it's going to be yes. Okay?"

"Okay. I'll be waiting!"

"Bye, Eds."

"Bye, love."

She replaced the receiver and stood motionless in the hall, listening to the traffic swish outside.

The street was wet after the downpour, and it was turning darker now. She had got drenched coming home from Ruth's on her bicycle and her hair was sticky from her sweat and rain.

Isabella suddenly caught sight of her startled expression in the mirror above the phone; her small pointed pale face, anointed with trails of hair that draped in wet clumps like squashed Medusa's snakes. She stared at her reflection for a moment, and then burst out into peals of laughter. How ridiculous I look. How mad and crazy and ridiculous I look now. And how absolutely brilliant too.

She walked slowly away from the phone still smiling, shivered, and decided to run an enormously deep bath. This was a time for luxurious self-indulgence, she felt. She was feeling quite cold now from her soaked-through clothing. She would make a cup of tea to drink in the bath, she decided, and went into the kitchen first to make it.

The tiny kitchenette was at the end of the hallway and opened into both the hall and the main sitting area, which Isabella thought was probably a major fire hazard. But then, she always had consoled herself, she and Harry had always liked to live just ever so slightly on the edge.

There were cups and plates piled up like road-traffic accidents all over the draining board, across the cooker top, and in the overflowing sink. Due to the warm weather all that week, the beginnings of a rather revolting stink seemed to be emanating from the bin. Isabella opened up the cupboard door underneath the cluttered sink, and confirmed that indeed the bin was stinking. She remembered a half-empty tin of sardines that she had tossed inside the bin last weekend. Or was the tin half full? Either way, the sardines were a definite health risk now. She picked the plastic bag out of the bin, bulging with rotting banana skins, coffee grounds and eggshells. Several bits of detritus fell over the sides of the over-full bag: a rain of tiny orange peels, the cork from a forgotten wine bottle that bounced along the floor. Isabella let whatever had fallen lie on the grubby lino floor and dreamily tied the top of bin-bag into a small knot. She left it over by the wall and proceeded to rinse one of the least filthy cups she could find to make herself a cup of tea.

The kettle was slow to boil; she had overfilled it. She decided to run the taps for her bath while she waited for the kettle and returned to the bathroom just behind the kitchenette, off the middle of the hall. There was a bottle of Radox on the corner of the tub, and so she sat down on the edge of it to pour the Radox into the pounding water, watching the mass of bubbles rise like lava. She let the water run, and peeled her wet skirt off, and pulled the damp and sweaty vest over her head and dropped it on the floor. Pulling her underwear off she dropped it too, and then wandered slowly, naked, into the kitchenette to make her tea, thinking hard and fast.

Eddie Mannion – what a lovely lovely surprise! She thought the last time she had seen Eddie was when he'd come back from America for Ruth's wedding just after college. She missed Eddie terribly. And then she remembered that he had been back in Ireland once, around the time of her MA graduation, and they had spent a lovely evening giggling over a long boozy dinner at a Persian restaurant in town.

Eddie had become very Americanised now, and in the nicest possible way. He was sharp and witty, long-limbed and hand-wavy, and completely garrulous, which had attracted him into a large artistic group of friends and networks. And now, in America, he was very much out, and although not necessarily particularly proud, because he really couldn't be bothered quite frankly, he was at the very least homosexually very assertive.

Eddie was producing plays off Broadway now. They were small runs of mostly Anglo-Irish drama. The choice of material had taken Isabella completely by surprise when she read the brief messages that he scrawled on his regular Christmas cards. Eddie, when at university, had utterly despised all of Synge, O'Casey, Friel and more or less anybody who had written a play in which the characters had no opportunity to cross-dress. He was simply and utterly in love with Shakespeare, and spent hours cross-dressing before parties, choosing to attend as one gender-obscure character or another as the season took him.

He attended the legal society debates dressed as Portia. In the University Outreach School's Drama programme he insisted on being Rosalind, despite his six-foot-odd height and rather masculine jaw. But he managed to produce a fairly sexy female voice, and brought a beguilingly male femininity to the role that fascinated the schoolboy audience. Eddie liked to think that he could challenge their sexual stereotyping out of them in one mesmerising performance, and wipe away several thousand years of sexual repression, homophobia, and transgender stigmatisation in one magnificent afternoon.

He had swept away to New York as soon as possible after graduation, and kept in touch with Isabella through an occasional Christmas card with *Happy Holidays* written on it, or a (usually vulgar) gay St Patrick's Day card. On the back of the envelope there was always a new address: a street that was numbered, not named, and a postcode, not a neighbourhood. Eddie's life had a numeric dimension which Isabella found impossible to picture now. He had disappeared into the network of numbered streets and coded corners of Manhattan. The city had sucked him into its matrix of late-night bars and jazz clubs, cross-dressing and saunas, and Isabella's memory of him had become dim, as his stature grew and spread and embraced the city of New York.

Greenwich Village. Chelsea. Lower East Side. These were Eddie's dramas now.

He had phoned her once after 9/11 to say that he was phoning everyone he had ever known in case they thought he was dead, or in case they were dead, or in case the world was about to end and therefore there should be at least a few million answering-machine messages lying around for the future generations by which to remember our once magnificent generation. Isabella and Harry had been out, and Eddie hadn't left a number to ring back. And in any case the New York phone lines were completely jammed. But it was good to hear his voice.

And he sounded happy now. Isabella wasn't sure, after the Twin Towers bombing, how someone like Eddie would have taken on the prospect of a war. He was desperately apolitical, and known to reduce everything to a series of twittering jokes instantly. Despite Harry's attempts to force him to be serious about important matters of world affairs, Eddie used to have them both in stitches within minutes. She had wondered, after his last rather hysterical phone call, if he was the only person in New York who was, in some bizarre and twisted way, seeing something *funny* in the tragedy of the Twin Towers. Could that be even remotely possible?

As it turned out, Eddie had been very much disturbed by the clouds of smoke, the overwhelming grief and the death which fell like a blanket of evil upon his treasured city. He took a sharp, almost hairpin turn to the left – and became politically aware. He stopped partying so hard. He stopped taking ecstasy. He stopped taking lovers who were young and nubile, and he stopped taking advantage of older, wealthy but naively gay men. He settled down in a committed relationship with Rob, who was black, neurotic, stunningly beautiful, and a concert violin player. They bought a tiny coop quite near Stuyvesant Park and East Fourteenth St. It was just about large enough to swing an undemanding cat.

In a most remarkable turn, Eddie stopped one day outside the doors of St Patrick's cathedral, and decided to go inside out of the beginnings of a light snow. It was early morning on February fifteenth. He was in Midtown on his way to demonstrate against the promised invasion of Iraq, which was to take place just one month later, in his name, and in the name of all those who had died in the Twin Towers.

Manhattan was freezing cold and emptied of all its traffic in preparation for the march. But the streets were full of people. The people poured out from every street and subway station, walking quickly and purposefully towards the United Nations to assemble with their groups. There were banners and placards everywhere. Trades unions, women's groups, African-American groups, Vietnam Vets in wheelchairs, Iraq vets, lesbians, vegetarians, all muffled up beyond recognition, eyes peeking out from under thick woollen hats, like Afghan women in their burkkhas.

Eddie was perhaps encouraged more by the horribly cold weather than by a sudden religious epiphany. But he decided to enter the cathedral anyway, and genuflected as he did, a movement that came awkwardly to him after over fifteen years of religious denunciation. He refrained from dipping his ski-gloved hand in the font, but sat down cautiously near the back and listened to the prayers and incantations that were almost burnt into his brain, they were so familiar from childhood. *The Lord be with you and also with you. We lift up our hands. We raise them up to the Lord.*

The choir began a hymn that Eddie knew from school. Years of Jesuit childhood came flooding back. Dirty-minded priests. Giggling grey schoolboys in grey shorts on hard kneelers with runny noses. Incense. Pain. He stood up quickly, genuflected, and turned around to leave the church. He walked away from the cathedral, quicker in the sudden coldness after the warm indoors, comforted by what he had reviewed, redeemed by his affirmation that he still had something good and strong, that he still, and always would believe in.

Eddie Mannion believed in himself.

Two days later the skies darkened, and then froze, and Manhattan was barricaded in by thick walls of snow. The city was paralysed with cold. Traffic stopped. Shops closed. Human life abandoned and went home. Eddie lay in bed, watching the weather channel on TV, sprawled out on his Ralph Loren comforter with the heating on full blast. He watched the entire east coast metamorphose into an ice age. He watched children digging family cars out of the snow. Bewildered pensioners shovelling themselves out of their own houses. Eddie lay in bed all morning eating toast while cheerful weather girls repeated themselves over and over again on his giant TV screen.

It's a big freeze-up for Manhattan today. We are snowed right in Down-town. Here in Midtown it's a real white-out!

And then the airports closed. The bridges and the tunnels closed. The subway past the tunnels was shut down. Manhattan was frozen in a time capsule. There was no work being done. No restaurants opened, no street vendors sold, and the buses and taxis dwindled to a skeleton crew. The rest of the world stayed away – reabsorbed into their own private worlds. And Manhattan was left alone.

Eventually, when the barricades of snow had cocooned the city into a silent network of snow corridors, and the long whitened streets were like grim catacombs of ice, Eddie decided to go out. He wrapped himself up like a body-bag, and struggled to get a few blocks up the avenue. It was desperately cold, and Eddie realised after taking almost five minutes to just cross the road, in the thick early midday blizzard that darkened the sky to a twilight, that it was going to be very difficult to go anywhere that day.

He slipped into the subway station out of the icy gale, and caught a train to the Strand bookshop. It was a struggle to get across the road again, and the Strand, when he finally got to it, seemed damp and chilly and unwelcoming. Eddie spent a half-hour browsing in the basement, scrutinised a shelf of Transgender Literature, and then spotted a bargain bin of dozens and dozens of copies of a book called *Night And Day*, by Virginia Woolf, all going for a dollar each. He picked one up, bought it, and decided to go for coffee.

Over the road, a coffee shop looked warm and steamy. Eddie was beginning to feel the effect of wet trouser bottoms and a very cold nose, and so he ordered a large mocha, and sat as far away from the door as possible, to read his book. But he didn't feel like reading now. He simply wanted to stare into space, to take in the feeling of Manhattan under silent snow, to listen to the conversations of snow-brave Greenwich Villagers who sat in ones and twos, sipping herbal tea, taking life as it came. He spent as long as was possible doing just that, and then noticed that across the road a cinema was playing *The Hours*, the new film based on *Mrs Dalloway*, also a book by Virginia Woolf! How much more perfect, thought Eddie, on a day of enforced solitude in New York, to watch *The Hours*, than to be pretending to be reading *Night And Day*.

And so he bought a ticket and a bottle of still water, and found that the theatre was packed. Eddie took a seat right in the middle on the end of a row, and had to get up and down several times to let other people in, but he didn't mind. Everyone was overdressed. Woolly hats and gloves and scarves and coats were folded into piles at people's feet.

Everyone was warmth, and white-teethed smiles, and friendly remarks. It was as if the only people left in Manhattan in the snow had all decided to reach out to each other and come together while the rest of the world had ceased to exist. The population had divided into two. There were those with families, and homes in the suburbs, whose lives that had only ever touched Manhattan in their alienated world of work. The city was not a living organism to them – it was a factory. But the snow had now excluded them from that place. They were banished as if forever.

The island of Manhattan had been emptied out. It was adrift, an island of snow floating off to sea. It was as if the only people who remained were here in this cinema; the singles, the small groups of friends, the ones and twos. They smiled and nodded to each other, to acknowledge that they were the only people that were left after the ice age, comrades in the snow.

A war is about to begin, thought Eddie. This togetherness – this isolation – this shutting down of a city, and this feeling of *survival,* all braving the hostile streets to come together on an afternoon when the ferocity of snow has forced an end to the rest of the world.

This is what war feels like.

He watched the film in tears. He cried silently and alone in the crowded cinema, not minding in the least that tears visibly rolled down his cheeks and onto his pale grey cashmere scarf. He didn't mind that he was crying in front of people, because nothing like that mattered any more. A war was about to begin. And the people of Manhattan were watching a movie about the consolation of death.

Eddie decided that he definitely did not believe in war. He did not believe in God. But he would believe in humanity from now on.

Isabella opened up the small, under-counter fridge, and found a scant amount of milk in a suspicious-looking carton. She sniffed it, and then tossed it down the sink in disgust. A cup of herbal tea would do. She poured boiled water over a stringed tea bag of Wild Peppermint, and carefully, because she was naked, carried the cup back into the bathroom where her now-full bath foamed like a giant witches' brew.

The water was just perfect. Isabella lay very still under all the foam and water for more than an hour, staring at the tiles in front of her, sipping occasionally at her mint tea. There was no window in the tiny bathroom, which was in the middle of the hallway, so that it was really just a cupboard rather than a room, with a jerkily sliding door, and it had the dimensions of a cupboard too. It housed the bath, there was no sink, and there was a toilet but the sliding door tended to get in the way of that, so both she and Harry tended to pee with the sliding door open most of the time. She had closed the door now however as she wanted the long low privacy of her foamed cocoon in which to hide and work out some ideas.

It was wonderful that Eddie Mannion was producing Synge. Eddie must have really changed. Changed utterly. But then, so does everybody. We start off at the age of eighteen thinking that we know who we are. Ten years later we suddenly come up against this Stop sign. Everything looks different now. Eddie producing Synge. Me teaching Pinter. Harry protesting against George W Bush. The world has changed us. *And now we are all defining our lives by other people who have changed the world.*

Isabella remembered a conversation that she and Eddie had had about Synge, way back at the beginning of the first year, in the canteen over a can of Sprite and a muffin and brown toast. Eddie had despised John Millington Synge then.

"All that blarney, God–awful blarney!" he had scowled. "Synge is bullshit!" He rolled his eyes and leaned his long skinny body back in a chair and feigned a sudden death by boredom. Isabella had laughed heartily, but she still felt slightly hurt by his dismissiveness. She became irritated when she tried to make him take her seriously again, and tried to make the *Playboy* seem more interesting to Eddie's mock corpse, whose eyes were closed, and whose face was turned well away.

"Think of it as an allegory, as if it were a Greek myth or something. The woman, Pegeen Mike, is a symbol of Ireland," she explained. "Of a country. The playboy, Christie, is the revolution. He kills his own father, or so the people think, and at first they admire him for it. But then, the makeup of the new relationships between the people and the land is realised. The people discover that the destruction of the old regime would change their lives completely. The dead father rises again and appeals to the people, to follow him and to punish those who overthrew the old regime. So the people turn against the revolution, and return to their old, familiar ways. In the final scene, they realise their mistake but they are too cowardly and too motivated by their own greed, to really want to change the world. And so they lose the playboy who escapes with his father."

Eddie had faked a long loud snore.

But now, Eddie Mannion was producing *Playboy*, in his theatre company in Manhattan. And Isabella was about to become Pegeen Mike.

Wow, she thought. *What on earth will Harry think?*

Chapter 12

It was Saturday evening. Harry was exhausted, but he had pushed himself all day, wound as tightly as a knot. The *Late Night Show* could be a deal-breaker, he thought to himself as he tapped about on the grubby office keyboard hoping that the presenter Paul Cranny would be decent to them. Cut, Copy and Paste, he swept his mouse across the screen. We really need to win this argument tonight. Everything for the Bush demonstration will hinge on this bloody television show. Almost everything.

Harry rarely got stage fright any more. But all day he had been strung with a much higher tension than usual. He had felt irritable. He had spent the day in the office avoiding conversation, making changes to the website, and working on a long article he was writing for an American leftist publication. He wanted no distractions, and turned his face to the computer resolutely to block out interruptions.

Sinead watched him carefully from the corner where

she folded leaflets, noticing every time he pushed his ink-stained fingers through his hair. He could do with a good haircut, she thought. That overgrown thatch will look wretched on TV. She folded her leaflets, organising them carefully into piles, avoiding eye contact with Harry. She waited for evening to come.

Harry leaned back in his chair to stare out of the window for a moment at the darkening street below. It was ten o'clock. Their car was due at half-past. He thought about having another coffee now, but Sinead had been running out and back for coffee for him all day. He couldn't ask her again. He looked around the office for her and saw her still bent in her corner by the door, ticking something on a list. She was wearing her black-rimmed glasses, which made her chubby, round face look rounder. More childlike.

"Hey!" he called over to her and she turned.

"Hey, yourself," she replied.

He beamed at her.

"You look happier," she remarked.

"I am. I've got loads done today. And I'm really looking forward to tonight." He preferred to keep any nerves to himself. "This show is going to be good. I've got a really good feeling about it."

"That's great, Harry. You should be really proud of yourself. Are you feeling confident about what you are going to say?"

"Pretty much. I'm convinced the majority of the audience will be sympathetic to us." He stifled a yawn. "Sinead, that car will be here to collect us soon. We should pack up here and get ready."

"I'll get you a coffee from across the road, and you can take a break before we go out."

He smiled gratefully. A twinge of guilt, but mostly satisfaction. "You are an angel to me, Sinead."

To her horror Sinead felt her blood rise up through her neck into her face where it would rage like a boiler. She hastily got up to leave the room, but he grabbed her hand as she walked past his desk to fetch her handbag from the corner.

"Thanks. No, I really mean it." He held her hand, looking up right into her eyes. "I mean, for all the support, and for being so, well, so absolutely bloody lovely all this week."

She tried to smile at him, but her face was like plaster. "It's too hot in here," she mumbled, and lurched out of the room. She had to get out of the building and breathe in some of the cooler night-time air.

Harry rubbed his eyes, and decided to shut down the computer. He lit a cigarette, and opened out the window. Traffic was screaming from the quays, and the air was gently warm and sticky with sharp fumes.

I like Sinead, he told himself happily. He felt surprised by his admission, but also rather pleased to have discovered it. Is this a minor crush? Harry wasn't sure if he had ever experienced a minor crush before. He simply knew that he always felt very happy to see Sinead. She was peaceful. Solemn. Sincere. Measured. She listened carefully. Giggly when mildly drunk, but otherwise very strong and sensitive. *Is* it a crush, he wondered, to be thinking about another woman's attributes? Or to be excited when she is around? He smiled to himself, watching the buses nose into place, and the last of the evening's shoppers cross the Ha'penny Bridge.

I just like her a lot. It's just nice, it feels nice, to be in the process of liking someone a lot.

He sat down again, waiting for her to bring up his tenth cup of takeaway cappuccino that day.

Sinead and Alan had audience tickets for the show, while Harry was on the panel, so they would have to split up in to different studio areas once they got inside the television building.

The office phone had rung all day. Alan had fielded calls, quietly talking through ideas with jittery supporters.

Alan was taking it all very seriously, Harry thought, and lit another cigarette.

He had originally tried to argue that Alan was over-estimating the importance of this one television show. But Alan was convinced that the appearance of the peace campaigners on the *Late Night Show* could make or break the big demonstration and so Harry was quite prepared to believe him. He had huge respect for any of Alan's ideas. Already they had come up against many obstacles in their building for the day. The American Ambassador had hotly condemned the march against President Bush. Criticism from the American embassy was causing acute embarrass-ment to the Irish Government. Harry had argued succinctly against the suppression of freedom of expression during an interview on the lunchtime news, but he was coming under pressure from a number of politicians who had until now been supportive of the demonstration.

Harry dragged long and hard at the cigarette. The peace campaign was full of contradictions, he thought. They had huge support: in the church, among schoolchildren, among women. All day long people dropped into the office offering support, signing the petition, taking posters for workplaces, wanting to give leaflets round their neighbourhoods. But there were huge enemies too.

There was the Dublin City Council, who sent a team of litter wardens out every night to remove every single poster that Harry, Sinead, Alan and Fiona were hanging up every night on every lamppost that was available. It was infuriating them, but they kept the posters going up regardless, and the council kept on taking them all down again.

"They're probably selling them to the Americans for a tenner each, just like you suggested we do," Harry had grumbled.

Sinead had grinned and replied that maybe next time they should think about a different strategy.

She is so calm and unshakable, thought Harry. She knows how to deal with any problem, gently and effectively. Is this part of being a doctor, he wondered. She must be used to coping with crises and emergencies. Or maybe she's just good at getting a plan together quickly.

She touched his elbow. "Coffee, Harry."

He smiled at her. "Thank you so much. You really are an angel."

"We'd better drink this quickly," she replied lightly. "They'll be here in a minute for us. Alan, here's a coffee for you. Are you ready to go? Shall we start packing up things? I'll put the answering message on here. Alan, did that fax go to the *Sunday Times* yet, or shall I resend it?"

"Leave it – it's too late now." Alan climbed into his

large leather jacket and took a big swig from the paper coffee cup. Foam decorated his beard.

Sinead, giggling, dabbed it off with a paper napkin. "That's better. Now you look quite gorgeous too."

It was quite dark by the time they got to the TV studio. Sinead and Alan were taken to the audience area, and Harry was ordered straight to make-up. Sinead took Harry's hand just before they parted in the hallway, and squeezed it tight.

"Hey," she said in a low, almost whispering voice. "Listen to me, Harry. You're going to knock 'em dead. You've got all the arguments. And you know that we are right. If you get any aggro, any tough questions, or bullshit right-wing McCarthyism, you just say to yourself – *bring it on!*" She made a fist in the air.

Harry watched her small frame trot away through automatic glass doors with Alan. She is lovely, he thought. Kind and sweet. The sweetest person I have ever met. He felt incredibly lucky that night. This is going to go brilliantly, he said to himself.

Harry was told to sit in front of a long line of mirrors illuminated with bright lights to have his make-up done. The girl who did the make-up was from Mayo. Just like Sinead, Harry thought. He asked if she knew that there was a peace campaign group in Castlebar now, and would she be interested in joining it when she went home? The girl politely told him that she rarely left Dublin any more, but that she might tell her mother about the group if she got a chance. Harry didn't spot her roll her eyes in the mirror at the make-up woman next to them.

He looked around the room to see what else was

happening. It was a long room, with a wall of mirrors surrounded by light bulbs on one side. A line-up of make-up artists powdered and painted, and hair-driers roared over low toned conversations. Harry was anxious to see what sort of people the other panellists might be. There was an elderly lady next to him, who was making a tremendous fuss about not having make-up put on her rather whiskery face, and Harry suspected that she might be the Sandinista nun. He decided that he rather liked the look of her – short grey hair, black ferocious eyebrows, and a mouth as sharp as a blade.

After make-up he was escorted to the dark, low-ceilinged green room, to sit on long low sofas. There was bottled water to sip. Harry glanced around again at the group.

"Well, I suggest we all introduce ourselves to each other," he began with a smile.

Sister Mary Immaculata of the order of the Everlasting Saviour, as she had been previously known, but who now tended to introduce herself as Molly, was indeed the feisty woman with the ferocious black eyebrows who preferred to wear no make-up. She was tall and masculine, and looked to Harry to be about seventy-odd years old, and she wore a pair of navy slacks with grey and navy runners underneath, a grey sweatshirt on top with a small white collar poking out above the neckline. Her face was strong and mannish, with a Frida Kahlo moustache to match her ferocious eyebrows. But her eyes were soft and wise. Harry decided that he liked her very much.

On the long green squashy sofa opposite her sat a small and delicate-looking man. This was Jeremy Manning, the retired professor and historian and founder of the *Campaign for a Nuclear Free Ireland*. Professor Manning looked tired. His eyes were watery, and his skin loose. He drank a cup of tea from a rattley cup and saucer as Harry and Sister Molly talked, and he said very little. Harry wasn't sure if he should try to include the professor in the conversation. He didn't want to be rude, and he was fascinated by what the professor might say. But the man looked sad, disinterested and distracted, and so Harry followed Molly's example and left him alone.

"Time to take your seats on the set, now, folks."

A woman with a clipboard led them down a long series of dark and concrete corridors and into a large damp-smelling television studio. It was absolutely freezing there, and ugly too.

"Nothing is ever as jolly as it looks on TV, is it?" Sister Molly murmured to Harry as they looked around them. The studio seemed to be all scaffolding and lights, and cameras roved around like dinosaurs on wheels. The audience was already there, on uncomfortable-looking tiered seating doing clap-testing for the sound check. A small woman held up signs, one after the other, with *Clap, Laugh* and *OOOOH* written on them, and the audience were responding appropriately, laughing happily to one another.

Someone was steering each of the panellists in turn to the soft seating area in view of all the cameras.

"That's great, folks, come this way now, come this way. Now, Harry, I want you to sit in the centre, so as to balance out the other two. Sister Immaculata next to Paul Cranny please, thanks a million, that's great, that's just fantastic. Professor, you are over here. Make sure you have plenty of water please, everybody – pour a glass now so that we don't have too much noise of water pouring during camera. Now, we're going to pin this small mike onto your clothing here, so that you can be heard, and when you have the mike pinned on we will do a quick sound check to make sure that everything is working, before we go on live. So, Harry, first, I'm going to ask you a question about yourself, and we'll record your answer and make sure that it sounds all right. So: Harry, tell me who you are and where you come from." She nodded at him sharply.

It was the most difficult question she could have asked him. Harry was used to making long important speeches; he was not used to giving anyone a one-sentence reply. He sat and stared at the impatient sound assistant and froze into a beetroot-panicked face.

"Harry, tap your mike for me, please – *ouch!* – yes, that certainly is open all right. Harry, just answer the question please, quickly, say anything, we have to get this sound check done, and we are rolling live in two minutes now, so, *go!*"

"Erhmm," began Harry, who had just spotted Sinead and Alan waving at him madly from the back row of the audience. "My name is Harry Waters and I am twelve years old . . ." he began and then stopped as he saw the astonished face of Sister Immaculata looking at him, black crazy eyebrows up like two sails in a wind.

"Fine Harry, fine, thanks, sounds okay. Now, Professor Manning, can you go please? Just tell me what your name is and where you come from."

Sister Immaculata turned to Harry and whispered,

"You don't have to lie that much about your age, Harry dearest!"

Harry giggled. "I don't know why I said that. I guess this all just feels a bit like school again."

Sister Immaculata, otherwise known as Molly, nodded with a knowing look.

The professor cleared his throat and began in a wobbly weak voice: "My name is Jeremy Manning, and I am the founder of the Campaign for a Nuclear Free Ireland."

"Lovely, that's live, that's fine. Good man. Just have a little drink of water there, Professor, and try to project your voice a little bit, thanks a million. Sister? Your turn – very quickly now. Who you are and where do you come from."

"George W Bush is guilty of war crimes in Iraq, and so is Tony Blair," replied Sister Mary Immaculata of the Order of the Everlasting Saviour and folded her hands on her lap and sat bolt upright as she stared down the cameramen and production staff.

Harry turned in amazement at her and issued a small gasp of laughter and surprise.

She turned to face him. "They are, you know, Harry. They *are* guilty of war crimes. I know that history will record it as such, one day."

"Oh, I quite agree, Sister," Harry replied happily. He was beginning to enjoy this now.

They were counted in to the live broadcast, and Paul Cranny was on his feet. He paced about the studio, speaking into the cameras as they followed him up and down the set, in and out of the audience probing their ideas about the peace campaign, provoking their responses.

Cranny was well known for his controversial views and tough interviewing style. Alan said that Cranny's strategy was to torture interviewees until they confessed. Harry suspected that Cranny was extremely politically motivated himself. This was part of the reason that Harry had been so loath to do the *Late Night Show* and had had to be argued into it by Alan, who took a much more pragmatic view. "It's publicity, Harry, that's all it is, and at this stage we need every ounce of it that we can get."

But Cranny was making no effort to disguise his irascibility tonight. He thrust the microphone into the faces of the terrified-looking students and housewives who had packed out the audience and his stance was provocative and almost rude as he went around assessing ideas and points of view.

"This war is all about oil. It is not about weapons of mass destruction. We have been told a lie," pleaded one young student, stammering her words, nervous to be interrogated on live television but at the same time desperate to have her viewpoint heard.

"Yes, of course this war is about oil," Cranny barked, "but oil is very important. You may think that you are above going to war for oil, but how do you think our cars are run?"

He turned to the next audience member, a middle-aged woman with a fat and sweating face. She was anxious to participate. Paul Cranny asked her if she supported the peace campaigners who were on the panel here tonight.

"Well," began the lady, shyly, as the cameras focussed on her hot red face. "I am looking forward to hearing what they say. But I don't agree with everything they're doing. I wouldn't like to see anyone lose their job here because of a protest against George Bush. The American multinationals have always been very good to the Irish. And I think that Iraq is a lot better off now that Saddam is gone. So that's all I have to say."

Cranny took the microphone away from her, and nodded.

"You, sir!" He pointed to an elderly man in the row behind. "Are you for or against this anti-American so-called peace protest?"

"I just wanted to point out that the United Nations were not in favour of this war."

"Everybody knows that. Not a useful point." Cranny dismissed him, leaving him with his mouth open in mid-sentence, and moved rapidly away to the other side of the room. He continued to pick the audience here and there, and built up what he considered to be a representation of public opinion with which he could challenge the panel.

Harry was unphased. If anything he was stimulated now by the clearly hostile agenda of Paul Cranny, who was living up to his reputation and beyond it.

"What do you think of your man?" he whispered to Sister Immaculata but she was motioned by one sound technician to stay quiet and so he never got to hear her reply.

But Sister Molly made her feelings clear to the audience and the live viewers when she was the first to speak from the panel.

"I was a young nun when I went to Central America," she began, and she addressed Paul Cranny straight on, ignoring the audience and the four cameras that wheeled and weaved around her as she talked, "and I was politically very naïve. When the Contra Coup came, thousands of people were killed in the most terrible bloodshed you can imagine. I want to see an end to suffering everywhere, and I see the suffering of women and children in Iraq and Afghanistan now and I will do whatever I can do in my small way to fight against that."

The applause from the audience was reverential. Harry was delighted. He loved Sister Molly. He felt extremely excited about the way the show was going now.

Paul Cranny took a few more points from the audience, which were of a more subdued nature, thanks to the rather overwhelmed reaction that most of the audience had had to Sister Immaculata's straightforward homely style. A lot of the focus of the audience was on the amount of money that was being spent on security for the Bush protest. The other question that kept coming up was whether or not the war was worth it, to end the Saddam regime.

Jeremy Manning got to speak next. He answered the questions that Paul Cranny put to him quite simply, and with a mild, delicate manner.

"I am simply old enough to be able to remember, fortunately or unfortunately I am not sure which, the experiences I have had of two world wars, and most importantly in relation to this one, of Vietnam too. I am old enough to remember the First World War. My father was killed in that war. He volunteered from Ireland when I was only two years old so my mother lost a husband and I was just a little boy who lost my dad. I don't remember my father, but I do remember all the lies that were told to my generation about the war, that it would end all wars.

It did no such thing!" His voice suddenly boomed, and everyone in the studio jumped.

Professor Manning, despite his clearly very elderly body, had a most impressive mind. He raised one long bony finger at Paul Cranny, and continued. His voice was steady now.

"I grew up in London. I shall never forget the experience of the Blitz. And nor will this generation of poor Iraqi children ever forget their experience, which they feel tonight, of being bombed. Because it is a terrifying ordeal for any child. Any mother who has had to hold a terrified and crying child to her breast and listen as bombs fall all around her will not forget this terror either."

The atmosphere in the studio was becoming tense. Paul Cranny leapt up and strode the stacked seating for a few more opinions from the audience, before turning his attention to Harry.

"Harry Waters, you are a well-known left-wing activist, who jumps on every anti-establishment bandwagon that there is." He smiled at Harry but Harry glared solidly back. "And now you are in the thick of organising this anti-American protest, a protest that has never taken place in Ireland before. A protest against the President of the United States. A man to whom many would say the Irish owe a debt of gratitude for his courageous work with the Northern Ireland Peace Process. In fact, many people feel that there would never have been peace in Northern Ireland if it hadn't been for the President of the United States. Surely you realise that that this anti-American protest will very seriously jeopardise our own delicate political balance in Northern Ireland?"

Harry looked at Cranny full square in the eyes, and then turned away to face the camera. His argument was far too important to waste on Cranny. Paul Cranny was wide-awake to all sides of the argument. The people he really needed to convince were in their sitting rooms at home.

"The peace process in Northern Ireland," began Harry in a careful voice, "is not benefiting from Bush and Blair's invasion of Iraq. The Blair government is now removing resources from the people of Northern Ireland that should be going into hospitals and schools and public services and diverting them into military hardware, bombs and guns. But if the Northern Ireland experience tells us anything, it is that military occupation leads only to revenge. And so I agree with Professor Manning, that the occupation of Iraq will lead to more atrocities in the West. Not less." He turned to face Paul Cranny now as he continued. "But on the subject of anti-Americanism. You see, nobody feels insulted by this jibe. We know that many of the American people stand in solidarity with us. What you need to know, Paul, is how big the peace movement in America is growing."

Cranny turned back to the audience again, and asked how many people were aware that there was an anti-war campaign in America. Very few hands were being raised. But Harry still felt proud. He could see the faces of the audience listening carefully. Cranny is no fool, he thought, taking a sip of his water. He will turn around soon enough as this war pans out and public opinion turns massively against it. The media will eventually jump the fence and pretend they were against the Iraq war all along.

Paul Cranny was winding up the show. "Let's have a quick look at our phone-in poll. We asked you the question, viewers at home, at the start of the show, to dial in your answers to the following poll question: are you in favour of the protest against the visit by the President of the United States of America to this country next week? Yes or No. And we have calculated your answers and can we see the result please? Yes, well, there it is. Seventy percent in favour of, twenty percent against, and ten percent unknown. Well. It seems as though you have been able to convince the audience for this time." He looked at the panel with a tight smile on his lips.

Harry was absolutely thrilled.

The media would back off now, he thought. If the protest was that popular, the media would have to leave them alone. They couldn't keep hounding them and throwing out the same McCarthyisms. The politicians would have to back down too.

"Let's see a show of hands from the audience." Cranny craned his head, and tried to do an instant head-count of hands that were for and against the Bush visit. "Much less support from our studio audience, I see – well, just very slightly over fifty percent in favour of the protesters, but only just, I would have thought. And anything could change closer to the day," he ended ominously.

What an idiot, thought Harry. He could easily see that well over half the audience had their hands up against the Bush visit. Cranny is fooling nobody, Harry thought.

As the music played to signal the ending of the show, Cranny nodded briefly to the panellists, and then stalked off the set to his dressing rooms followed by a flurry of assistants who handed him bottled water, removed his microphone and wiped his forehead for him. Harry stood up, completely relieved that it was all over now and turned to shake the hands of Professor Manning and of Molly.

"Good man yourself, Harry," growled Sister Molly warmly, "and I am thoroughly looking forward to seeing you at the Shannon protest."

Harry felt quite high. The relief that the show was over was making him feel light-headed. He stood up very tall, thrusting his chest out, and scanned the audience to try to catch sight of Alan and Sinead. But he couldn't see them anywhere. He was dying to see what they would think, especially Sinead. The audience were being ushered down from their seating in a regimental fashion. Harry wandered over to the studio exit area, and decided to wait for the others there.

We were brilliant, he thought to himself. We are really getting somewhere. He tried examining the expressions of audience members as they shuffled out of the studio. There were one or two grim-faced, stoical expressions. But the general mood of the audience was of excitement. People were quite animated, discussing all the issues raised. Harry felt delighted – he could see that the level of consciousness was bubbling up, that debates were arising, that people were talking and wanting to know more, to make their own minds up. He felt himself positively glow.

He decided to stand back for a moment as the audience filed by, not sure whether to leave in the middle of the crowd, or to try to find Alan and Sinead first. People shuffled by.

The studio was emptying out. Cameras were being wheeled away, and equipment being unfolded. He stood with his hands in his pockets and waited some more.

In the noisy emptying of the studio he suddenly began to feel quite small and lost and quite alone.

And then her arms grasped round him tightly, and he gave a quick yelp of surprise.

"Oh, well done, Harry, well done!"

Sinead's low voice tickled the back of his neck, as she hugged his waist. He giggled. He turned around to return her hug, and knocked her glasses sideways. Sinead broke away to fix them back into place, and they stood apart again, away from one another awkwardly.

Alan slapped him on the shoulder. "That went well, mate. Really well. And all the other speakers were great too. It went even better than we could have imagined." Alan grinned behind his fox-fur beard.

Somebody was ushering them aside into a long corridor that led them to a large reception room, where they were serving drinks. Harry, Alan and Sinead each took a glass of rather sharp red wine and some ham sandwiches, and stood aside to take in the atmosphere. The room was dimly lit. There was a long sleek bar with mirrored walls and lighting on the drinks behind, and all sorts of television people were propping the bar up slugging back free drinks. There were waiters circulating trays of food and wine and crisps, and the air was thick with smoke.

Harry and Alan turned to one another and began to discuss the politics of the evening. Would they have made an impact on the numbers who might now attend the protest? Would some of the more reluctant politicians perhaps become more supportive now?

Sinead stood slightly apart from them now and sipped her wine and looked around her for a while as Harry and Alan talked. She felt suddenly rather small and undiscovered.

She had liked the look of Professor Jeremy Manning. What a fascinating man. And Molly the Sandinista nun – what an amazing woman she was. But both had gone as soon as the programme ended. Tucked up in bed already, probably, thought Sinead, and stifled a small yawn.

It was well after midnight. The room was ringing with laughter and high noise. Journalists and familiar TV faces all around her. Next to the long shiny black bar she spotted Maggie Hennelly from the *Sunday Times*. Maggie's flaming red hair was down around her bare evening shoulders now instead of in her usual loose chignon, and her tiny heart-shaped freckled face was laughing uproariously at something Paul Cranny was saying to her. What the hell is she doing here *again*? thought Sinead. She's a newspaper journalist. She doesn't even work in television. And she's at every bloody thing where Harry speaks.

Maggie was deep in conversation with Cranny, who had to stoop to speak to her directly. But that won't stop her coming over here to flirt with Harry as soon as she's spotted him, thought Sinead. She half wondered if she should go over to Maggie Hennelly herself and start to lionise her, which might keep her away from Harry. But that wouldn't work either. Maggie seemed to have an electronic homing device for Harry Waters. She'll be at his side by the end of the evening no matter what I do. Giggling, and talking politics, and dropping hints about what the major politicians really think, and what other newspaper editors *really* think about the war. Giving him her precious inside information. Hateful woman, thought Sinead.

She suddenly realised that she was very tired. They had all worked so hard all week to get to this point. Tomorrow is Sunday. On Monday Harry is going to Shannon again to speak on local radio and to go around the housing estates again with Alan. And I'll be back in the surgery. We have another street stall on all week, so it will be full on every evening after work. And then Saturday is the demo.

She was beginning to sense a horribly unwelcome sense of anticlimax, before the climax had even begun. What happens then, after the Bush demonstration, she wondered. Where do we go from here? She glanced about her, taking in the earnest expressions of TV staff. Self-important journalists, bossy opinion-makers, drunken TV presenters pretending to be intellectuals. What a very strange world I'm entering, she thought to herself. Harry seemed to fit right in. He seemed to be able to flit from street politics to liberal media hacks, to celebrity, and back again without a flicker of visible effort. Aside from her rural companions of childhood and the eclectic mixture at her convent boarding school, Sinead was unaccustomed to anything other than medical company. Dull tweed-jacketed GPs with portly wives, smooth-faced surgeons and blue-suited drug reps – these were her usual society. And now she was mixing with the media, courting political opinion, measuring out her life in opinion polls.

She thought about all the reasons she had got here in

the first place. As she stood in this luxurious television bar with a glass of warm red wine, listening to the gales of laughter, watching the bright-jewelled hands wave and the long blonde manes flick like thoroughbred horses, she thought about something far more important to her. It was the very reason she was in this place: Moussa.

Here we are, sipping wine, trying to impress the over-fed over-paid media – and where is Moussa now? Oh God, what a horrid contrast our two lives have come to make! He's probably still in Fallujah now.

The siege had ended and a ceasefire was declared, but she knew that he would have wanted to help the other surgeons with the work that piled up after the attack. There would be dozens of amputations to care for. There would be hundreds of post-mortems to perform.

"Are you okay, Sinead?" Alan had noticed her distracted and strained expression. "Do you want me to take you home?"

"I'm fine!" she replied brightly, and turned to face him, forcing herself to smile. "I'm going to have another glass of wine. Anybody else want one?"

Chapter 13

Moussa woke up suddenly to the whack-whack-whacking noise of a Black Hawk helicopter. He sat up in fright and then sighed at the darkness, and lay staring at the ceiling, barely breathing, waiting for the helicopter noise to cease. But then he noticed that the ceiling fan was on. Electricty again!

Great.

Moussa, wide awake now, leaped out of bed, less bothered by the thunder of the helicopter now and more excited at the prospect of the chance to do his laundry.

He padded happily down the hallway from his bedroom to the bathroom, had a pee, and padded down the wide staircase past the living room to the laundry area. A light that he must have left on before the last power cut flickered in the downstairs sittingroom like a little welcoming sign, and through the large sitting-room window Moussa noticed other lights popping on, one by one across the street.

Neighbours all awake, catching up with whatever they had needed to do before last evening's power cut.

He pictured all the neighbours pottering rapidly around their houses just like him, a sudden flurry of activity in the middle of the night. Putting laundry on, boiling tea, ironing shirts, channel surfing for some news, sending emails, doing whatever it takes to get through until the next power cut. Moussa smiled at the thought of his neighbourhood now all awake in the middle of the night, bustling with sudden domesticity.

The house was a low two-storey beige stucco villa that had belonged to his family; but Moussa lived alone now. He spent very little time there any more, as the hospital had lost so many staff. There had been a spate of disappearances. Doctors and scientists had been assassinated, he had heard, or had been kidnapped or imprisoned. Moussa rarely slept at night. He was either kept awake by nightmares of being buried under rubble, kidnappings and beheadings, or blasted into wakefulness by gunfire or helicopters. Either that, or the suffocating heat would wake him like a vice around his throat, signaling that the electricity had gone off again.

He stuffed the washing machine with his socks and T-shirts, towels and jeans and then stood back to watch it tumble into life. Excited at the prospect of a cool drink from a refrigerator that had also sprung back to action, he padded back down to the kitchen, opened up the fridge, and stood a moment in front of the open door, allowing the slightly stale but cool air to hum around him. In the welcoming glow of its pale yellow light, Moussa stood a moment to enjoy the shelves of cucumbers, cheese and cartons of orange juice. He took a carton of the juice and poured a large cold glass, deciding that he would take it up to his favourite place on the rooftop, and watch the neighbourhood wake up.

Even though the electricity had come back on again, he always liked to sit out on the roof at night. Taking a candle with him (he didn't like to use the rooftop lighting any more), he climbed up the tight little staircase to the roof, and sat on his favourite battered seat up there, underneath a wash of stars. It was an extraordinarily beautiful night tonight. The helicopters had thuttered off into the distance and he rested his glass on his lap, watching the city sky and the velvet night around him.

In the garden of the house next door, his neighbour Abu Rasheed was up and about. Moussa watched him for a moment, feeling rather like a spy from his rooftop while his neighbour stood alone in his garden smoking a cigarette. He suddenly realised how much he missed Abu Rasheed and his wife; he hardly got to see them any more even though they only lived next door. Abu and Umm Rasheed had been such good friends for so long: and they still were, weren't they?

Moussa had often been into their garden to spend an evening with them cooking fish on the barbeque. They had celebrated the Futoor together with their families. He had celebrated with them for the Eid.

Now Abu Rasheed seemed to spend a lot of time anxiously poking around his back garden on his own. It suddenly struck Moussa that he hadn't seen Umm Rasheed or their three daughters, or Umm Rasheed's mother and sister either, for quite some time.

"Salam Alaykum!" Moussa called down from the rooftop to Abu Rasheed. But Abu Rasheed jumped and looked around him, terrified.

Moussa realised that he probably couldn't hear where the voice was coming from. He took his glass back down the tiny staircase to the house again, and went out into his own back garden and approached the fence.

"Salam Alaykum, Abu Rasheed," Moussa spoke more quietly over the fence to his neighbour.

"Moussa!" Abu Rasheed's voice was hoarse, but he looked pleased to see him. He cleared his throat.

"I thought I'd come down and have a cigarette with you." Moussa opened the gate in between their gardens and joined his neighbour.

The two men sat side by side, perched on the edge of the dried-up fountain. Abu Rasheed had been so proud of that fountain when it was in full swing; a blaze of tinkling jewels in the summertime. Now it sat dry and motionless like a ghost, the once-glamourous marble basin filled with leaves.

"This strange midnight lifestyle," Moussa smiled at Abu Rasheed who offered him a cigarette. "How are your wife and children these days, Abu?" he asked, indicating the lights that had popped on in Abu Rasheed's house.

"Ahah! What a question! My daughters are very unhappy," Abu Rasheed smiled guiltily, flicking a match away into the scrub of the once-elegant garden. "They are fed up with being indoors all day. And the eldest two have had to drop out of university, so they are pretty fed up about that. Boredom, I suppose, is their main problem.

And Rasheed who graduated last year is still out of work like me."

Moussa nodded, smoking in the silence.

Abu Rasheed had once been such a busy, bustling father and husband, whizzing off every morning in a suit to his job as a computer programmer. But since he had lost his job, the whole household must have gone into a decline.

"And is your wife well?"

"We are all struggling really, Moussa," Abu Rasheed shrugged. "The women are either battling to keep the house going in between the power cuts, or they are at each other's throats because they can't go out. I am thinking that we should think about moving away – but my mother-in-law is digging in her heels. It isn't easy."

"Where would you go?"

"If I had my way? Jordan, Syria, Dubai – wherever we can go, actually. I have a PhD in computer science and I am a qualified architect!" Abu Rasheed laughed hollowly. "But they say the borders with Jordan and Syria are packed with cars. And the roads are too dangerous now with all the kidnappings. It's either kidnappings, bombings, extremists or drugs, but there's always something to be afraid of."

Moussa made a sucking noise with his teeth to convey sympathy. He put his tongue into his toothhole again, feeling its rough crater scrape against the soft pad of his mouth.

He looked around briefly at the blackness of the garden. A windless night. But more noise was coming from another helicopter overhead.

"Did I tell you that my friend the dentist disappeared?" Moussa spoke quietly, nudging Abu Rasheed.

Abu Rasheed looked quickly at him, his face alarmed. "You know, Moussa," he dropped his voice to a whisper, "I heard the CPA are looking to recruit architects and engineers to rebuild the bridges and new ministries . . ."

Abu Rasheed and Moussa looked over their shoulders once again. The garden was quite empty. Nothing but a solitary tree behind them, dust-covered palms reaching up into the sky like giant shoulders heaving in melancholy.

Moussa said nothing. He ground the stub of his cigarette into the ground beside him.

"I am so desperate for work," Abu Rasheed went on. "But if I were to look to the CPA for employment, I am afraid I would become a target for the militias. And that is far too big a price to pay. Look at what happened to that police recruitment station last week. It's sectarian violence I am afraid of now."

"You know, in Ireland they have a saying for that kind of situation," Moussa smiled at him. "They say that it is as if you are being trapped in between a rock and a hard place."

Abu Rasheed smiled. "How is your little daughter, Moussa?"

"Little Sinead is five years old now, Abu. And she is well."

"Sheen-ayed," Abu Rasheed mouthed. "I always mean to ask you – where did you get that special name?"

"From a surgeon who worked with us when the Irish were here before the Gulf War."

"You know, Moussa, you should go to Syria to be with her."

Moussa nodded and frowned. "I know. I will go soon. I just have to do some more work here. We have so many children injured, and there are very few doctors left. It's difficult – and you know I'm not a quitter."

Abu Rasheed shook his head and tutted. "You are working far too hard. And I am not working at all. Everyone in Iraq is either unemployed or is dying from overwork!"

Moussa grinned, and clapped his neighbour on the back.

"Abu Rasheed, why don't we go up to my house? The air conditioning is on and we can drink a glass of tea and have some thing to eat. Look, the dawn is nearly breaking. We can speak properly up there. I have some goat's cheese, nice and fresh as I refrigerated it yesterday for a full three hours, and cucumber and what about a glass of Irish Whisky, too? And Baklava!"

Abu Rasheed laughed. "I would love to, Moussa. But you know I don't touch alcohol! In any case, I'll stay here if you don't mind. I won't leave the women alone in the house 'til daylight."

His voice was drowned out by the thunder of the helicopter once again. The light in Moussa's laundry room fluttered out like a dying little ghost. The neighbourhood returned to darkness.

"Oh, no!" Moussa groaned. "There go my socks again!"

Chapter 14

The air was very cool outside and Sinead shivered slightly as they walked away from the television building, and pulled her cardigan around herself more tightly. Harry was being very giggly now. They had each had several glasses of the wine, and Sinead had stumbled going down the steps of the TV building, so that Harry had to grasp her by the waist. They walked along a tree-lined driveway to the road, talking rubbish all the way. Harry was incredibly happy.

"How are we going to get home? Are the buses still running?" asked Sinead, knowing that they weren't. Her words were slightly slurred, but Harry didn't notice.

"Mmm. I don't know. What time is it? We could walk. Or try to get a cab. Where are you going now?"

"Home. But I live just around the corner. We could go to my place and I could ring you a cab."

"Mmm . . . " He wrapped his arms around her. "That would be perfect."

Sinead's apartment had a long comfortable sitting room with a long low sofa that was a perfect pearl white, in front of a large television screen. Tall wide-leaved plants decorated the window ledge, and the floor was scattered everywhere with books and DVDs and newspapers. But it was all spotlessly clean, and homely. Harry sat down on the pearl-white sofa and looked around him. Sinead had lots of paintings on her walls, of Eastern themes. There were pictures of mosques, and desert camels, and an Arabic market scene. Over the wall behind the television was an effigy of a Muslim woman with her eyes closed, sculpted out of leather in faded brown and blue.

"Sinead, have you been to the Middle East?" Harry called to her.

Sinead came out of the small kitchen with two glasses of champagne and a bottle tucked underneath her arm.

"Wow, this is a nice treat," grinned Harry. He sprawled out on the sofa, and stretched his legs towards her.

She handed him a glass, and they clinked. "Cheers. I thought we ought to celebrate." She took a swig herself, before putting the bottle down on the floor. "You were asking me about the Middle East. I used to live in Baghdad."

He stared at her while she patted cushions, trying to organise somewhere to sit down.

"No! Really? No kidding? When? How come you never told me until now?"

She sat on the sofa at the opposite end to Harry so that she could turn to face him.

"I suppose I didn't tell you because I don't talk about it much. People don't know how to judge you now, if you tell them that you were in Iraq. I rarely ever talk about it to anybody. It was a very strange time. Well, not all of the time. The first few months were wonderful. When I went out there, in 1990, it was before Saddam Hussein invaded Kuwait."

" Before the first Gulf War?"

"Yes. I had a job there that I loved. I was in surgical training. And we had some lovely friends. One friend in particular, and he's still in touch. And he's under terrible pressure now. I write to him every day. I send him emails."

"And does he write back?" Harry was wide-eyed.

"Sometimes he does. They have a lot of power cuts. I don't know how many of my emails he gets, and I don't know if he reads them all or what he's doing now. I haven't heard from him for a week. And then I get upset. But I know he'll write again when he gets a chance. He was caught up in the siege in Fallujah recently." She looked up at Harry and paused to take a sip of her champagne. "He has had such a terrible life really, living under Saddam, trying to have a career in Baghdad during all the sanctions. And he lost his wife – she died of cancer, and they had a little girl that they called Sinead."

"He called his daughter after you?" Harry took Sinead's hand and looked at it, stroking the backs of her fingers.

"Yes. We ... liked each other quite a lot. I mean, it was all a very long time ago. Almost fourteen years; when I was very young."

"You are still very young," he said.

"Oh, I know," she smiled, "but then I was just out of college. It was my first job really. I was training then to be a surgeon. And so I went to work in Baghdad for six months. With my husband."

"You have a *husband*?"

"Well, I had. Derek. He was a surgeon too. We met in college, went out for two years, the perfect couple. Both top of the class, both wanted to be surgeons. We were going to do a six months' job in Baghdad, and then go to Australia. Everybody wanted to go to Baghdad or Australia in those days. We had jobs lined up on a training scheme in New South Wales. It was a perfect plan. Only it turned out to be very imperfect." She put her wineglass down. "Iraq invaded Kuwait. We never thought that *that* would happen. And then there was a lot of talk about what America would do next."

"What do you mean?"

"Well," she frowned, "at first we didn't really think that they would bomb Baghdad. We thought they would bomb some part of the desert, just to show they had some muscle, and back off. Saddam Hussein was so powerful then. Every room in the hospital had to have a picture of him. It was quite frightening when you think about it. Even though our lives were good, for the Iraqis there it was a real police state – a bit like living in East Germany with the Stasi everywhere, I suppose."

"Spying on people?"

"Yes. Sort of. There was this Russian guy who'd had a heart attack in our hospital, and he got fed up being stuck in hospital in Iraq and having to look at the picture of Saddam all day, so he asked if they could take it down. I'd say it was only twenty minutes before the police were on to him, letting him know what kind of trouble he was in.

I suppose, in the face of a regime like that, you can see why some people in the West were saying that bombing the place didn't seem like such a bad idea."

Harry nodded.

"Then we all got caught up in it, and we weren't sure if we were going to be evacuated or what would happen. Derek is very laid back. He is a big, tough, macho surgical type, but when we realised that there was going to be a war, Derek decided to leave straightaway. Virtually all of the other ex-pats had left anyway. Derek didn't feel any responsibility to the people who would get killed, or injured, even though he was a doctor. He didn't feel any responsibility towards our colleagues, who would be left behind to work on the bomb victims. But I couldn't go."

Sinead swirled her champagne around for a minute in the tall glass. They sat silently for a while. "Don't you just love Veuve Cliquot?" she eventually said.

Harry laughed. "I've never had it before. But, yes, I do love it. It's delicious. Tell me the rest of the story. Please, Sinead." His voice was low and tender.

She poured out some more wine for each of them, and raised her glass again. "Cheers! So Derek went. He went to Australia, just like we had planned, and took up the surgical job there, and lived happily ever after. But I didn't go. The worst night was when they hit an air-raid shelter on February the thirteenth. It was during the Eid. I'll never forget those burns, Harry." She shivered.

"Are you getting cold?"

" No. Well, just a bit."

He took his jacket off and moved over to wrap it around her shoulders. She looked up at him.

"Go on," he said.

"There were children with sixty, seventy per cent burns coming in to the ICU – they lived for a few hours or a few days, and then died horribly, full of infection everywhere. There was a woman who lost both her legs when a wall fell on her, and then got an overwhelming infection and a pelvic abscess and eventually died, but not before a huge amount of surgery." She shook her head, and shivered again. "There was one grandfather who had a huge chest injury and we actually opened up the chest in casualty and tried to repair the heart – but of course he died. I was the one who had to break the news to his wife, but she couldn't stop screaming at me, and I couldn't bear it."

"So is that when you came back?"

She nodded. "I had to come back to Ireland then. I was too shell-shocked, I guess. So the United Nations evacuated me. I didn't care where I was going. I just wanted to go to bed forever, and not wake up again. I didn't belong in the world. It wasn't a world I recognised. It was a foreign place, a rabbit hole, a parallel universe. It was as if I had just discovered that the human race was all a big bad story, and the whole thing was just a cruel joke in somebody else's head. Moussa called this thing existentialism – but that was just his sense of humour. He had always been a bit whacky. But I genuinely believed that I was the only person who existed, and the only thing that mattered or was possible to experience were my own feelings, thoughts, sensations, and all the other people, events, and everything, were just a weird illusion. I hardly spoke to anyone for six months. More, maybe. My mother must have thought I'd really cracked up. But she was so good. She just looked after me like a baby." She looked at Harry again. "I think that what I felt about the world at the end of that time is that the only experiences we ever have that matter are the experiences of other humans. Relationships, conversations, work, entertainment. Everything that makes our lives happen is just a network of reactions to other people. And so, if you stop reacting to the other people – what becomes of your life? Do you even have a life?"

"Surely you will have a life, even if it is a life of isolation?"

"I don't think so. Because I think that this is a sort of theory of relativity. I believe that we only *live* because we have relationships with other people. All of our experiences are defined by the ways in which we are controlled by, or relate to others. Even if those other people are on the television, or in a book, or whatever. We simply don't exist as individuals. We don't have ideas, unless those ideas exist in relation to the ideas in other people's heads. I can't even say that I like champagne, unless I have some sort of relative notion as to whether or not you like champagne too. Do you see what I mean?"

"Oh, clear as mud!" Harry laughed at her, and then took her hands in his again. "And so," he looked at her intently, "do you, are you prepared, to accept the real existence of other people now? I mean, do I exist here, now? After all that stuff?"

"Yes. Of course you do. It was just something I experienced at the time. I got better. I had to come to terms with the world. Things changed. And Derek met somebody else. That jolted my head back into place again, which was a good thing too. I decided that I would leave Mayo, and move to Dublin. I didn't know anybody here. It would be a new start. I couldn't stand any more of the squinting windows in Castlebar. I wanted the anonymity of the city."

"And I'm very glad that you did," Harry said. His voice was hoarse. He reached out and took her face in both his hands, and turning it towards him kissed her.

Hungrily.

Her bed was huge, and soft, the covers rustling with feathers and crisp ironing. In the darkness and the moonlight of an unshielded window he undressed her clumsily. Buttons pulled. Underwear tangled. She kissed his face and held his head in her hands and kissed his eyes, his mouth. He kissed her throat. She loved the groaning sound he made, and his lips trembled when he tasted her fat nipples, each in turn. She gasped with unconcealed delight when he tasted her below. She held her breath. He licked her reverentially, slowly tasting every drop of her until she came right in his mouth. She pulled his head up with her hands, and he let her lift him up inside her and she watched his face above hers, long eyelashes and his eyes closed, holding on to himself, until she gripped his buttocks urging him to ride her harder and to ride her faster until it swept over her again like a giant wave, burning up her face, her body and her legs. Harry groaned into her throat, inside her in a long deep jerk.

He lay in sweat, heavily on her neck, and slept.

Chapter 15

Harry was unrousable. Sinead had woken early. She was unused to sleeping other than alone, and so the warm muscular body beside her had stirred and woken her shortly after dawn. She lay watching the skies brighten and the sun began to shine, and when its light became too bright she went to the large patio window, wrapping Harry's shirt around her, and pulled the blinds. Creeping back into the bed, she woke him up and he pulled her soft smooth body back towards him, burying his face in the nape of her neck.

She took his hand and pressed it to her breast, loving him as she turned her back to him, urging him to slide inside her now again. Harry came quickly and aloud into her sticky wet behind. She held his hand around her, letting him softly fall away. It was over swiftly but it was perfect.

He slept a little more, and then woke suddenly as if in shock.

"What time is it?"

"After ten o'clock. I didn't want to wake you. You looked so tired." She touched his hair and stroked his face.

"I have to ring Isabella."

She took her hand away.

"The phone is in the sitting room."

She lay quite still as he sat upright, rubbing his puffy eyes awake, and she watched him grope around himself for the shirt she had discarded, his jeans and belt. He stood up, naked, and she watched his small stocky body as he fumbled for underpants underneath the feather quilt. His penis bobbed and waved. His legs were shorter undressed than in jeans. Chunky hairy thighs, firm buttocks and slim hips. Sinead closed her eyes and lay back down. This was too much now. The nightmare was only about to begin.

Harry, in the sitting room, was phoning Isabella.

She heard him speak in a gruff hoarse voice. Something about staying overnight because it was easier than getting a taxi at that hour. Guilt in his voice. Solemn. Low-toned. She hated it.

She hated the very thought that another woman was listening to that same voice, the voice that she could now hear speaking, in her sitting room, in her flat. Another woman who had a genuine claim on Harry. Who was important enough to him that she needed to be phoned in the morning after their love. To be apologised to. Another woman whose feelings were important to Harry. More important to him than Sinead's.

She lay silently and breathlessly, trying to listen to the voice, but it mumbled, and then it said no more.

Harry returned to the bedroom, and sitting on the side of the bed, said in a low voice to her, "I've got to go."

"What did you say to Isabella?"

"She wasn't there. I left a message."

"Aah."

"I told her I had to stay the night with someone because I couldn't get a taxi. That's all I said."

"Will she believe you?"

"I don't know."

He was putting on his shoes.

"How will you get home now?"

"Er – bus, I guess. What number do I get from here?"

"Any of them," she told him, flatly. The sun had gone out of her life again. The room seemed cold. Empty everywhere. "Across the road in front of the newsagent's. They all go into town."

"Thanks. I've got to go." He bent to kiss her, but she felt almost nothing now. She watched him cross the room. He was just a stranger. He looked back at her from the bedroom door, to say goodbye. *Please just go, Harry – don't make me have to look at you any more.* It was an agony.

"Thanks. Sinead, you were . . . lovely." He was almost shy. He stood for a moment and they watched each other, saying nothing. "Thanks for such a lovely evening. And night. I . . . I don't know what to say."

"Goodbye, Harry."

"See you during the week?"

"Of course you will." She couldn't smile. She didn't even try.

He left the bedroom door wide open, and she heard the hall door click.

Chapter 16

Isabella had watched the *Late Night Show* alone, surrounded by her luggage. She sat on the battered yellow sofa, while her two battered suitcases and one rucksack sat on the floor, and watched Harry and the anti-war panel holding court. She had cupped her small face in her hands, resting her elbows on her knees, holding on to every word. Harry was just brilliant. Cool, precise, intelligent, and full of charm. She felt excited for him. Incredibly proud. She could sense the mood of the studio audience as it grew while Paul Cranny had provoked and probed.

Isabella had a ticket to America. She had cashed in her savings, two thousand euros, and had bought a three-hundred euro ticket for a plane that was leaving in a matter of hours. And Harry didn't even know. She had not been given a chance to tell him. Every day and every night since her phone call from Eddie just over a week ago, Isabella had thought about nothing except whether or not to accept Eddie's offer, and take up the role in

New York, leaving Harry, not knowing when she might return.

It was a nightmare decision to have to make. But Harry simply wasn't around. He was out all day every day, returning late at night, unable for conversation, disinterested in any topic other than the campaign. She waited up for him, night after night, but somehow couldn't bring herself to broach the subject when he came in droopy-eyed at all hours.

How would one begin? She tried to work it out for herself. Harry would be horrified. He was busy. He was tired. It was late. It was too late and too early. It was simply not possible to horrify Harry, with a tale about a job in America and going to live at Eddie Mannion's place for an indefinite period, at this point in time. Horrification was simply not an option.

And so she had simply chewed her thoughts over to herself, while Harry busied himself with street stalls, and phone calls and television shows. Isabella spent the week walking around the city streets, sitting in the coffee shops, standing in front of shelves of travel books about New York, examining all their Statue Of Liberty and Brooklyn Bridge-photographed covers, never picking one up to look inside. She had taken a bus to the Phoenix Park and walked the whole length of the park and back again, briskly marching in the summer air, asking herself over and over and over again: *What is it that is actually keeping me here?*

Tearing herself away from Harry would be like cutting her own umbilical cord. They had lived together for over thirteen years. She did not know what it was like to be without him. Despite all her frustration, anger, and bitterness, her rage at Harry's indifference, her jealousy, her pain, she did not know how to leave. She could not even bring herself to discuss the possibility of leaving. It was as if she needed to admit to herself that she had in some way let everything go wrong. Having the conversation about the possibility of leaving, asking Harry's opinion, considering his feelings – all of this would lead to a situation whereby she would have to admit something that she had not yet admitted even to herself: that she did not love him any more. And Harry was impossible not to love.

She had watched him on the *Late Night Show*, speaking slowly in front of the cameras, looking around him to include the faces of the others in the debate, facing Cranny squarely and with dignity. She studied all of his hand gestures, as familiar to herself as the back of her own hand. He is so *at home*, she thought, in the company of thousands. He is simply made to be one of a multitude. A leader of others, I suppose. But I can't follow him any more. I hate what he has made of me.

Isabella had felt sick with nerves, as she continued to sit on the yellow sofa, and waited for Harry to come home. There would be drinks after the show, she knew. But he would be home any minute now. It was almost one o'clock in the morning. She would have to tell him sometime that she was going to go.

She had decided to place the suitcases around the room in an obvious and most visible arrangement, so that they would be the first things Harry would see when he came into the room. They would force her to confess. Harry would walk in, tired, pleased with the television debate, and would immediately see Isabella's strategic arrangement of suitcases on the living-room floor. He would ask, straightaway, *why are they out there?* And she would have to reply.

Isabella paced around the room as she rehearsed what she would have to say. She would tell him that she had thought long and hard about whether or not to take up Eddie's offer. She would tell him that it was the hardest decision that she had ever had to make. She would carefully explain that she wasn't going to go for long. It was just a break. Harry would be fine because he was terribly busy with the campaign anyway. She would phone his mother from America and make sure that Harry really was okay. She was going to take up a job that was really important to her, and to see a bit of the world. It was a great career opportunity. It was important for her to be with Eddie again. She had really missed her friends since college – Ruth was so absorbed with family life, and she felt that she needed to meet some new people now. Harry would be fine – she would phone and write to him and keep in touch. But she felt that it was time for her to leave the flat, to leave Harry for a while, and to move away. It was something that she knew she had to do.

She would say all this with love and with kindness in her heart. She thought that Harry would most probably start to cry. He would be angry. He would be hurt. He would be desperately hurt. He would beg her to stay. This is why she'd had to buy the ticket first. Otherwise she would feel she couldn't go. She would take one look at Harry's deep brown eyes filling up with tears, and she would want to stay forever. She would promise herself again, to an impossible situation, to the stifling, throat-strangling misery of neglect, of unrequited love, of affection undetermined.

She could not commit herself forever to a life half-lived, to a promise never kept, to a love she could not feel. Her ticket was a voyage into the dark. But the dark was a place in which she felt perhaps she now belonged.

At ten o'clock on Sunday morning, Isabella Somerfield stood in the doorway as she left her flat, and turned around to view the shabby sitting room once more. She stood for one last moment to let her memory scan the room. She studied the piles of newspapers, the yellow sofa, and the empty coffee cups, the wallpaper, the photographs, the clock, as if to memorise them one by one; every item she and Harry had ever shared. Then she lifted both her cases out into the hall, to where the front door opened out into the world.

At five past ten, Harry Waters left a message on an answering machine that no-one else but he would ever hear.

At half past ten on Sunday morning, Sinead Skellig made herself a cup of tea. She sat down at the cluttered kitchen table, and wrote a long email to Moussa on her laptop, without knowing if he would ever read it.

At ten thirty-five that Sunday morning, Marion Waters felt a sudden impulse to phone her son. She had taped the *Late Night Show* while at work the night before, and went to rewind and eject the tape now, in her dressing gown, carrying a cup of tea. She had planned to watch the TV show as soon as she got home, but felt exhausted and now she only longed for sleep. However, something made her feel that she ought to phone Harry now, just to make sure he was alright.

Marion felt an uncanny sense that Harry needed her – as if he might be in some way vulnerable at that moment. In trouble of some sorts. She wanted to say hello, and goodnight because she was going to bed after her night shift, and to let him know she would watch the show properly later on that day. Marion let the video recorder run and whirr through the tape to rewind, and sat down on the edge of the small blue armchair to telephone her son. She felt anxious now to speak to Harry, or to Isabella, suddenly realising that she hadn't spoken to either of them that week as she had been so tired from doing nights, and it was Harry's big night last night on the television show, and a big week for them both now with the Bush visit coming up.

The telephone rang, over, and over, and over again, but there was no reply. Marion left a small message on the answering machine, and went to bed.

At half-past ten on Sunday morning, in Castlebar, County Mayo, Ursula Skellig following her usual morning routine of cat, bird-table and watering can, sat in her dressing gown and wellies on a high stool at her kitchen counter with a mug of coffee in her hand, and contemplated the beauty of her garden.

The kitchen window faced east, and sunshine filled the kitchen fondly, wrapping itself around pots and jars and over the large scrubbed pine table, sending sparkles from the taps. Ursula bathed herself in its warmth and light, and felt inordinately happy. She felt deeply at peace as she gazed onto her lush summer garden, full of life, watching small coloured tits peck at her neat peanut feeder and splash about in their birdbath. She admired her early roses beginning to twine around the edge of the small trellis that she had attached to the side of the shed, and thought: *how beautiful the world is today*. How absolutely perfect too.

She felt so peaceful and so perfectly satisfied with the world at that particular moment, that it occurred to her that there must be something wrong. Life is not this perfect, she thought. It simply can't be. Something somewhere must be happening to hurt somebody – or many. And knowing that seems to make the beauty all the more acute. How can there be such beauty and such peace in the world, when there is also so much horror?

Ursula decided to phone her daughter Sinead above in Dublin, who must be feeling very busy at the moment with all the campaigning and the work that she was also doing in the surgery. She would let her know how wonderful the garden was today. Perhaps Sinead would come down for a weekend when she was not too busy, later on in the summer. Ursula picked her mobile phone out of her handbag to call Sinead, as she didn't want to leave this perfect view of her beautiful garden – she wanted to talk to Sinead while also soaking it all in. She wanted to tell Sinead about it and to let her know that there really is beauty somewhere in the world. She let the phone ring several times, but it was engaged, engaged, engaged.

She's probably sending one of her emails, thought

Ursula, putting back the phone. She's always been so good to that poor doctor over in Iraq.

At midnight in the orthopaedic wing of the Mother and Child Hospital in Baghdad, Moussa took a coffee break and sat alone in the doctors' mess just to listen to the quiet. He sipped a black, sweet, sticky cup of coffee, perching on the edge of a shabby black leather sofa with his knees apart, balancing his coffee cup carefully in his hands so as not to spot his crisp white coat. He sipped and sat for a while and then, putting down the coffee on the floor, pulled the folded pathology report out of his trouser pocket again, and spread it out upon his knee.

Moussa sat and read, and read again, for the fiftieth time, the pathologist's report.

At half past two on Sunday afternoon, twenty-five thousand feet above Shannon airport, Isabella accepted a large gin and tonic from the air hostess, and watched the mass of clouds beneath her, grey and silver-fringed above the earth. How does it feel to be aboard a plane that is about to crash, into a tower block, deliberately driven into a fire of steel to die, Isabella wondered placidly to herself. She glanced at the passenger next to her, asleep beneath his seatbelt. Does one hold the hand of the person next to one when one is about to die? Does one cry, or pray, or hold one's breath and wait for life to end? And will anyone ever board an aeroplane again without wondering just that?

Harry Waters sat alone in his empty flat and listened to the answering machine. One message from himself. And one from Mum. He cringed to hear his guilty voice, gruff with late-night drinking, and erased it immediately. He listened to the other one from Marion, and noted that she seemed a bit concerned. He played it over once again, and then wiped it out as well, until there was nothing left in the flat but himself and the single sheet of paper that contained a farewell note from Isabella, complete with tiny circles above all the letter i's.

Chapter 17

Sinead woke every morning to the thought of Harry. She slept alone in her large, clean bed and felt the place where he had slept, willing him to be there. Their lovemaking returned to her head over and over again, and when she thought about it she imagined she could feel him going inside of her again, or feel his head between her legs, or smell his musky skin.

During the days before the Shannon demonstration she had hardly got to see him. He was rarely in the campaign office now, and Sinead was busy too, trying to catch up with her paperwork and keep the surgery ticking over. She helped out on a couple of street stalls in the final days before Shannon, but the leaflets and the pamphlets that they sold were a secondary consideration now. She was on a knife-edge of anticipation in case Harry should arrive and join them on the stall. Or in case he might be at the office when they got there to dump the table and the posters back. Or in case he might phone her during the day to ask her if she would come to Belfast, or Waterford, or Galway with him to speak to another group, or to help him get something ready for the radio, or give an interview to the press. But she only got to see him once, briefly, for about five minutes when she popped into the campaign office at lunchtime one day.

She had to visit the office, because, she decided, she had to send a new email to Moussa that day, and her own office email was not working at the moment. There was something wrong with the computer and she had organised for Dorinda to get it fixed; but, meanwhile, she would have to get to a computer during her lunch hour and send the email then because Moussa was clearly waiting for a reply. Harry was usually in the office around lunchtime. He would be busy, getting something ready for the afternoon at short notice, doing everything just in time. But at least she would get to see him. She absolutely had to see him.

Fiona was alone in the office, deeply absorbed in something at a desk.

"Hi, Fiona!"

Fiona looked up and smiled briefly, and carried on with what she was doing at the computer.

Sinead tried again. "Hi, Fiona, how are you?"

Fiona squinted through her thick glasses, and then recognised her. "Jesus, Sinead, I'm as blind as a fecking bat!"

He isn't here, Sinead thought, and she felt her heart fall. Oh God, he isn't here.

She felt awkward and unable to speak. The room seemed empty, and purposeless. She couldn't ask Fiona where he was. That would be so obvious of course. But if she didn't ask . . . well, if she didn't ask, then she would never know. And the whole trip down here would be futile. There was silence for a moment.

"You okay, Sinead? Can I get you anything?" Fiona glanced up again. "Sorry, I'm up to my eyes here trying to get this thing sorted out."

"Is Harry away then? No one helping you?" Sinead tried a joke.

"He's just popped out for cigarettes." Fiona smiled at her and put her head back down again. "He'll be back in a minute. Can I do something?"

"I need to send an email and my computer's on the blink. I wonder if you could do me a huge favour and let me use your one. I'm sorry to intrude." She felt her face burn up. "It will only take a minute."

"No problem. Just let me shut this down."

Sinead took Fiona's seat, and began to type a letter quickly to Moussa. She felt incredibly guilty using Moussa as an excuse, just to try to get to see Harry like this. It all seemed quite ridiculous now. She was simply making a fool of herself. She typed miserably and as quickly as she could. I'd better just get out of here now, she thought. I have to get back to work. This is just pure madness. I'm getting out of here. I'm gone.

Fiona was deeply distracted again in a pile of photocopying. Sinead thanked her and walked slowly as she left the building, plodding down the stairs. She opened out the heavy Georgian hallway door that wailed to her on its stiff hinges and then just as she turned round to face into the noisy street again Harry stood in front of her, on the pavement with a packet of John Player Blue in his hand. He looked surprised and very pleased.

"Sinead! Hey!"

Sinead felt her stomach leap. He was smiling, but there was an uneasiness between them. She wasn't sure what to say to him, or do. She stood quite still, apart from him on the steps, with her arms straight by her sides. She couldn't touch him, or reach out to him. He wasn't hers to touch.

But he looked at her as if she was still his.

"I was going to call you," he said to her.

She paused a moment. "So, why didn't you?"

She was surprised at her own bold reply. But she would have to be direct. She didn't have much time to waste.

"I didn't know what to say."

"Aah."

"How are you?"

"I'm fine. How are you?"

"I'm good. Busy. You know," he laughed a little, "lots to do."

"I suppose you're up to your eyes."

"Yes. Well, it's only a few days now. Saturday, in fact. Of course, you know that. We're just organising the final numbers for the buses. You'll be there?"

"For God's sake, Harry. Of course I will!"

"So." Harry looked at her intently.

She couldn't stand the silence. She wanted to take him in her arms, and cradle his head, and tell him that she had missed him, oh how much! She stood stiffly an arm's length from him and waited for him to speak. Normally, she would have filled these silences with funny remarks or with animated chatter. But now she had to hear what he would say. She didn't want to waste any more time between them, talking about nothing.

"So . . . ahem . . . what about *us?*" he asked her tentatively.

His face was soft, and earnest. She had never loved him more.

"Do you think there *is* an *us*?"

"Do you want there to be?" he asked.

"Do you?"

"I wanted to phone you," Harry said, again.

"But you didn't."

"I know. I should have. Like I said, I just didn't know what to say."

She nodded at him. She would have to go soon. But it couldn't stop right now.

"Look." She felt despair. "Do you have time for a cup of coffee?"

"I was just about to suggest that." His face was naked with relief.

"Come on," she smiled at him. "Let's go to that pub on the corner there. That way we can have a little more time."

The bar was a long cool tiled-floored traditional Dublin pub, where students tended to hang out during the day. Harry and Sinead sat towards the back, in a darkened corner where they would not be seen. It's bizarre, thought Sinead. Before last Saturday we would have been seen sitting together in public no problem at all. Even with our arms around each other, flirting with each other. And I'm sure that other people noticed what was going on between us.

But now that we have officially slept together it's become a secret. Now I'm something that he wants to hide.

But she didn't want people to know that she had slept with Harry either. Part of this was the thought that it might occur to them that she was only Harry's groupie. And of course, there was Isabella to consider.

"Do you want a coffee?" Harry asked her from the bar. "I'm having just a coffee."

She shook her head. "Sparking mineral water," she replied.

Harry pulled his hand from his pocket and took out fifty cents.

"Er, I'm a bit short at the moment." He looked hopefully at her.

"Don't worry about it." Sinead handed him a tenner.

The fact that Harry never had any money and she always had to pay for drinks for him didn't bother her at all. She would have given him all the money in the world right now, just to have five more minutes in a pub with him.

He brought the drinks over and sat beside her, and carefully looked at her again. He examined her face and, grinning rather foolishly, said "I must say, Sinead. You really do look very pretty today."

It all sounded so ridiculously formal. Almost rehearsed. But it was spontaneous Harry. She wanted to leap with joy, and hug him, and tell him how happy he had made her now. She smiled and looked down at her hands with mock shyness.

"Thank you," she said softly, and looked up, beaming at him.

She had worn a pale stone-coloured suit to work today, which her mother had always told her was a great colour for a blonde. Sinead didn't really like neutral colours but she always tried to wear dull clothes for the office so as not to attract too much attention from male patients. But today she had worn the stone-coloured suit with a white T-shirt underneath, and she had taken off the jacket now, so that the shape of her breasts was clear to Harry. She knew that his eyes gazed over at them, and she loved him all the more.

They sat side by side on the padded bench at the back of the bar, not touching, watching one another's faces and hands for a while, as if there was in invisible force between them that attracted them but also held them physically apart. If he had touched her now she would probably have exploded.

"Sinead. I wanted to tell you that I really enjoyed *that,* the other night," he said gruffly. "I haven't been able to stop thinking about it."

"Really?" She was beginning to feel overwhelmed.

"I have to confess," his voice dropped several tones, "I have been fantasising about it." He giggled slightly.

"Me too," she grinned.

"Really?" Harry was amazed. He looked excited by this.

Sinead laughed out loud. "You see, Harry. We really are very good together."

"Yes, we are."

"So. What do you want to happen now?"

There was a silence. She sipped her mineral water and watched his face again.

"I just don't know," he sighed. "It's very complicated now."

"With Isabella?" She hated even to pronounce the name.

"Well. Yes. It's just that . . . I'm just not . . . all that free, you see. Isabella isn't the kind of person who would . . . *forgive* something like that."

"You love her very much," Sinead said evenly.

She had to say it now. It would be easier in the long run if she spoke her worst fears to him out loud.

"Yes. I do. I do love her very much."

Sinead was nodding her head in agreement. She nodded slowly, keeping her face quite still. She tried to maintain a look of understanding, while keeping all her options open for a different outcome. What she really felt like doing was closing her eyes and getting up and walking away again, into a car, under a bus, under a train, anything never to have to come back to hear him say these words again. But she sat still, and watched the bubbles in her glass, listening carefully to what he had to say.

"I suppose that, at another time, in another place, you and I would have had . . . a relationship?" He checked her face.

Sinead nodded slowly, listening to him, this time slightly more encouragingly.

"And it would have been . . . ah!" He stopped in mid sentence, letting the image of unending sex with Sinead fill his mind. She saw his eyes glaze over and his pupils dilate at the thought of her in bed with him again. She smiled mischievously at him.

"It could have been quite wonderful, Harry," she said softly.

"Oh God, yes!" his voice was hoarser now. "And I would like to do it all again," he added, innocently.

She detected a slightly pleading tone. "You would?"

"Oh yes. I can't stop thinking about it. About making love with you. I would love to spend another night with you. As soon as this bloody demonstration is over and we can get back to normal again, and all the work calms down."

"The work never will calm down, Harry," she said. At this stage, she just wanted to keep it realistic. She couldn't bear any more false hopes.

"That's probably true."

"What about Isabella?"

"I don't know. Like I said, it's complicated. I've known her all my life."

"Well, the way I see it, we have three choices," Sinead began, in her measured, scientific way. She held up her hands and made three little shapes in the air, to demonstrate the three choices that they had, as if they were three little blocks of matter.

"One, you could leave Isabella. And we could get together. And have a fantastic life, happily ever after. And that might work. And, it might not. We might be terrible in a relationship together. We might hate one other. Or, it could be the greatest love that we could ever know. But we'll never know until we give it a try. And I think it's certainly worth trying."

"I would have wanted nothing more than that, at one time," began Harry, "but, I don't know if I can start a new relationship at this time. I'm so busy with the campaign. I really do want to sleep with you again. I really want that very much. But I don't think we could . . . it's Isabella really. I would never want to hurt her that amount."

"Then you are right not to get involved with me," she said calmly. "So, there's the second option. Which is that you and I forget about last Saturday night and Sunday morning, and tell nobody about it, and put it all behind us, and live with all the people we are with for the rest of our lives, never knowing how good it might have been to be together, and never knowing what it might have been like to be with someone that you really love. And Isabella will never know, and she never will be hurt because you and I will take this to our *graves.*"

Harry raised his eyebrows. It sounded very dramatic, and he wasn't sure that he was ready for that kind of finality.

Sinead waited for him to react. He paused for a while, and then asked, gently:

"You said that there was a third way?"

"The third way is, that we do carry on seeing one another, and having sex, and loving one another, but we don't tell Isabella. And we make sure that she never finds out. That way, nobody gets hurt. But we don't have to spend the rest of our lives wondering what might have been. We get to find the answer."

Harry stared at her. "Now that," he suggested with a guilty smile, "would be the best of all possible worlds."

"It's called having your cake and eating it, Harry," she lightly replied. "But you will have to think very carefully about this. You've got much more to lose than I have."

Her mobile phone rang from inside her bag.

"I've got to go." She rummaged while it rang. "Hello?"

It was Dorinda to remind her that it was two o'clock, and there were people in the waiting room already.

"I've got to go," she said again.

She walked him back to his office door and they stood a moment on the steps together. They couldn't even kiss goodbye.

"So, I'll call you. Yeah?" he said.

The wind blew her hair around her face, into her mouth, sticking to her lips, and she paused to take it out again before she spoke.

"Of course you will," she replied.

Chapter 18

At five o'clock next Saturday morning, Sinead was wide-awake. She watched the alarm clock on the table beside her for a while and then eventually got up at a quarter to six to make a cup of tea. It was a bright soft morning on the street outside and she could see the park was misty from her window. She sipped strong milky tea, and stood for a while at the long wide kitchen window, watching the tree-lined avenue below. There was very little traffic on the road that early. Just the occasional swish of a taxi beetling back into town from the outer suburbs, or a bus wheezing at the stop across the road.

Sinead felt extremely calm about today, simply because she had spent so much time thinking about it for so many weeks now that it had already been played over and over again like a dress rehearsal in her mind. The only unknown element in the performance would be the unknown quality of Harry's love for her.

She had checked her phone a thousand times for

missed phone calls or messages from him, and checked her text lists over and over almost every hour; but he hadn't been in touch. She had sent him one short text. Harry had made a brief television appearance and she had watched him with a burning face as he briefed journalists about the final details of the march, and made a plea to all people who stand for peace to support the Shannon demonstration.

The vast majority of the news for the past two days had been about the build-up of security arrangements at the Shannon Airport. The other major issue that rocked the media that week was the lack of access that journalists were getting to the Presidential summit, full stop. Shannon Airport and the whole of County Clare was full of secret policemen now, the media speculated. Millions had been poured into the CIA. It wasn't the democratically elected Irish government any more, people were commenting in the media – it was the FBI who were running the country now.

Harry had been interviewed for what seemed to be only five or ten seconds, and it was played at the end of a long discussion about whether or not the press might be able to get any way near the summit, how long the summit might last, whether or not the President would be able to solve all the problems in Northern Ireland in his twenty-four-hour Shannon whistle stop. Sinead watched all the reporting but it only made her feel more angry, and she thought about the last message she had got from Moussa only just a week ago. It had been a message full of terror and of pain, but also full of huge hopes for the Shannon peace march.

But her heart had leapt when Harry made a brief

appearance at the end of the report, and she sat for a long time watching the weather report and all the adverts, and the start of *Friends*, before she decided that she would send him a quick text.

Good luck tomorrow thinking of you lots of love Sinead.

Instantly she regretted it. Six hours later, when she had received no reply at all, she utterly regretted it.

At six o'clock on Saturday morning, after finishing her early cup of tea Sinead got back into bed to rest for a while. She snoozed a little and then remembered that the bus for Shannon was actually due to leave at eight, and so clambered out of bed and found a pair of jeans, a cashmere hoodie and a blue T-shirt, and pulled on striped blue and grey socks and Converse shoes. It was still quite cold this morning, and she might be cold again tonight; but then again it could be hot all day on the bus; and it might rain. She didn't want to bring an anorak, but she hadn't paid the slightest bit of attention to the weather forecast last night after Harry and the *News*. She sat a moment on the bedside and looked down at her feet in their navy blue and white Converse and wondered if she ought to ring her mother now. Ursula knew the national weather forecast as if it was her own personal horoscope report. She watched the weather and the skies like a Druidic soothsayer, and was always ten steps ahead of every caterpillar, slug and greenfly that the West of Ireland climate might bring into her garden.

Sinead looked at the clock again and thought that her mother would most likely be awake, as it was almost after seven now. There was a tight toss-up between being comfortably on time for the bus but still unsure, and late but happy because she had got to speak to Ursula before she left. She picked her mobile up from her bedside table, and speed-dialled Castlebar. Ursula was wide awake.

"Ah, for God's sake, don't be worrying about the weather, lovie! You've enough to think about. The weather will be fine!"

Cool at first, with sunny spells, and scattered showers later on tonight, just like every West of Ireland summer's day, but by night Sinead would be safely back on board the bus and getting home again. Ursula would be glued to the radio all day out the back, to listen for the news of the march. And how is Moussa? Ah, God love him. Ursula would be down in Shannon herself too, only it was a long way up and down in one day in a bus, and there would be no one there today to mind the dog. Brownie is saying hello – she's wagging her tail.

"Take good care, lovie. Mind yourself. Say hello to that President Bush from me!"

Sinead smiled as she pressed the call away, threw her phone into her handbag and flung her hoodie over her arm. She bounced down the stairs of the apartment block instead of waiting for the lift, and stepped outside onto the noisy morning street. She hailed a taxi passing by, and it swept into the forecourt just in front of her block like a bird swooping for a catch.

"Liberty Hall!" she told the driver, and sat back while he drove and she watched the rest of the world go by. A million people fast asleep had just become awake in rooms in buildings by her side, as she sped through traffic lights and swung along the quays.

The quays beside Liberty Hall were absolutely buzzing with reporters and cameras and TV stations, at the unusual hour of eight on a Saturday morning. The sight was quite astonishing. The journalists were at a very loose end, because they had been excluded from going anywhere near the actual summit, so every major international TV station seemed to be here outside the glass trade union tower. It was exhilarating.

Sinead's taxi couldn't get anywhere near the crowds of media and people gathering on the pavements and spilling out onto the road in front of buses, cars and taxis waiting patiently for them to walk towards the Shannon buses. She got out of the taxi just past O'Connell Bridge and decided that she would walk along the quays. There were over thirty buses lined up in a bedraggled queue to bring the demonstrators down to Shannon, and they were filling very fast.

Sinead got nearer, and pressed her way into the crowd, looking for familiar faces. She spotted Alan. He was balancing his bulky frame on the edge of the pavement and consulting a clipboard. He seemed to be organising small groups of people into individual busses. And oh! Just over there Fiona was giving an interview to BBC News. Oh my God! Sinead thought. This is going to be so much bigger than I could have possibly imagined!

She had brought a small cotton banner with her that her mother Ursula had sewn, with perfect red embroidery and decorated with the letters: *DOCTORS AGAINST THE WAR*. She checked her handbag now to make sure that it was still folded there since they had dutifully hung it on the wall at a public meeting two weeks ago. People were jostling and pushing one another to get into specific buses with their friends.

Sinead searched desperately for him through the crowds. There were men and women, old and young, in formal clothes and scruffy ones, all sorts of people standing around in little groups, sipping coffees out of paper cups, and squinting into the sun which by now had risen perfectly over the Liffey and the port and was washing down into the city in a flood of mellow light.

But she couldn't find Harry anywhere. She looked at all the little groups of people that she could see, and tried to crane her neck over and around the crowds. She craned up at people who were looking out of the windows of the buses that now towered above her, filling up with strangers, every one. And Harry wasn't there. He wasn't anywhere that she could see. Of course, he must be somewhere in the crowd. Or on a bus. Or, perhaps he had gone down already, separately. There were far too many possibilities.

She began to realise that she would have to pick a bus and just find a seat and get on it and travel up and down to Shannon without Harry, perhaps with complete strangers, and the thought of it suddenly drained her as if all her joy had just run out of her, and her legs became heavy and she wanted to lie down again. She turned to the bus beside her, and realising that she would have to just get on board and go, she clambered up the steps reluctantly.

"Sinead!"

A hoarse voice behind her.

And it was him. He was there. Everything was going to be all right.

"Are you travelling on this bus?"

She stared at him standing looking up at her. He looked quite tired, and clearly just out of bed, but excited, and was clean shaven for a change, and had a just-scrubbed look about his hair and skin. And he had cut his hair – the long curling soft brown locks were gone, and his hair was militarily short and rather spiked. As usual, he hadn't dressed for television, she noticed, despite the gangs of cameras and photographers who clicked and roved around with fuzzy mikes. He was wearing his favourite grey sweatshirt with the hood, and faded jeans, and wore a red Palestinian kaffiya around his neck that probably covered up the now-yellow love bite she had given him.

Sinead nodded, saying nothing, looking down from the top of the steps at him standing on the pavement down below.

"Good," he said. "Will you get a list of names on board when you've got started, and contact details for after the demonstration, and so on? And, will you tell the driver that we are taking a ten-minute toilet break in Port Laois. Okay?"

He waved at her and he was gone.

One full week of waiting and daydreaming, and hoping and imagining over and over again. And that was it. Nothing more than that to say.

Sinead took a pen and notebook out of her bag, and tore out a page to make a list as she had been instructed. She made her way along the bus, stooping or bending on one knee, to ask each person to give their contact details. She chatted briefly with some of the demonstrators, to see where they had come from, and what they thought about today, and passed a few remarks about the Bush visit. She moved mechanically through the bus, and her lips spoke numbly, her head nodded rhythmically and her pen wrote briskly, but her mind had left her body now. Her mind whirled around and around, and spun, and spun and spun. Out of her control it went, and quietly out of the window of the bus and off into the clouds and floated far, far away.

Eventually she found her seat, and they were off, and she watched the glass tower of Liberty Hall slip by, as the bus swung over Custom House Bridge and trundled down the quays out of Dublin and towards the West. She had wanted to hang her little white cotton banner on the windows of the bus, her *DOCTORS AGAINST THE WAR* cotton slip that Ursula had painstakingly embroidered, so that everyone who watched the convoy of buses going by would see it. But that all seemed almost foolish now. Or did it?

Sinead suddenly felt rather angry with herself.

This trip to Shannon had nothing to do with Harry really, she thought. Well, nothing to do with him and *her*. It was about the Bush summit. It was to do with refuelling at Shannon Airport. It was to do with war in Iraq, and the Irish Government's support of it. It was to do with a country under occupation. A country that she loved. And most of all, it was to do with Moussa. God, I am such an idiot. Sinead began to smile. She traced her finger in her breath on the window, and watched the motorway go by. Commuter towns. Factories. Fields. And cows. She rummaged in her bag, retrieved the folded white cotton embroidered banner, and placed it on her lap.

"Have you any idea how we could hang this on the window?" Sinead smiled at the elderly lady sitting reading poetry next to her.

Eventually they hung it up with someone else's chewing

gum, which was fairly disgusting, but sticky anyway. The cotton banner obscured the view. But that was all right too. Now everyone would know that there were doctors who were against the war. Somehow, perhaps, some television camera might film it as they arrived in Shannon. And somehow, maybe if you stretch your imagination very far, Sinead thought, Moussa might get to see it via satellite in Baghdad.

The journey was over three hours long, and after two she nodded off, and then she woke to find the bus was pulling into a large shopping centre car park, in what appeared to be the middle of nowhere. Shannon town and the airport were blocked off. None of the demonstrators' buses were allowed anywhere near the summit areas, explained the police who stopped and searched the buses. The army and police had blocked the roads. They were all going to park here, in this out-of-town shopping mall, and wait for the demonstrators to come back.

Sinead listened with the other demonstrators on the bus, and sat for a while, waiting to see what was happening. The car park was filling up now, with buses from the North, and some had come over from Scotland and from Wales. It was all looking very exciting. She decided to get down off the bus and take a look around.

To one side of the car park a large area had been corralled off, which was reserved for the media. Every major news station of the world was there. They had each erected a little tent-like structure, like a desert caravan, and in each little broadcast tent unit there was a camera crew, filming their reporter, saying to the world that there was nothing to report today from Shannon.

The Bush summit was in progress. They had heard the helicopters overhead, which signalled the President's arrival on Irish soil. But the press and media were excluded, so there was nothing they could report. The reporters all talked solemnly into cameras as Sinead walked by, watching what was happening under each little tent. But the reporters looked frustrated and the camera crews looked bored.

Just behind the area where the TV stations were broadcasting, a big McDonalds restaurant was all closed up and barricaded by tanks and armoured cars to keep the demonstrators out.

"Freedom fries, anyone?" Alan stood behind her grinning through his beard.

Sinead giggled. "How are we going to organise the demonstration with all this?" she asked him.

Alan explained that they were just waiting for the last few buses to arrive from Belfast and the North. Then they would assemble in a long march, with their banners and flags raised high, and just march slowly as far as the police and the army and the FBI would let them go.

"We are banned from Shannon Airport, and the Castle," Alan told her. "So, we are going to march around the town, and then up that hill and towards the Castle where Bush and Bertie are in session, and just go as far as we are allowed. And then, I guess, sing a few songs, make a few speeches, whatever. See what happens. Some of the anarchists want to storm the fields or something – but my guess is that unless they want to be shot on sight, they might change their minds when they see the security," he grinned.

Sinead moved away with him to join the mass of people

who were gathering in line now, banners tugging, flags blowing in the wind. She felt incredibly happy. It didn't matter that the gathering was not going to be able to get anywhere near the airport – what mattered was that the people had come. This tiny island, on the edge of Europe, and all these people had come in buses and cars and made their way across the sea because it mattered. She took a long flag with a rainbow on it from a young man with facial piercings and very holey jeans, and held it right up high. A *Sky News* cameraman walked by, filming her and everyone else as he roved along the queue. *CNN* filmed them from the other side. The media were interviewing demonstrators, filming banners, and photographing slogans painted on cardboard, snapping children who were still in prams.

And then she spotted Harry deep in conversation with a familiar redhead. Oh for God's sake, Sinead groaned. Maggie Hennelly, of course. Can she ever stay away? she snorted to herself. But it didn't spoil her happiness. Not even when she saw the mischief in Maggie's eyes while she organised Harry to pose smiling underneath a banner for a photo for her paper. It didn't spoil it much, at least.

The march took off and at first they marched so slowly, at an absolute snail's pace Sinead thought, for what seemed like hours. They walked around the town, singing *Power To The People*, and *We Shall Overcome*. There was a samba band at the front, which made things quite jumbled from a musical point of view, but it all blended in easily enough as the march stretched out and wound its way around the streets, and through estates and blocks of flats, and the people waved, and leaned out of windows from above, and clapped, and stared at them as they sang.

And then eventually the demonstration left the town and began to trudge its way up the hill towards the Castle. Sinead sang and chanted, and hoped that some of the filming would be shown on RTÉ and that her mother might get to see some of it. She wanted Ursula to be there. She wanted Moussa to be there. She wanted Harry to be anywhere else in the whole wide world than where she could see him right now, at the front of the march, giggling with Maggie Hennelly, who was wearing a tight white T-shirt with a padded bra, her anorak tied around her waist, chatting animatedly with him and William Cairns.

The hill was long and steep, and so Sinead put her hoodie in her bag, and marched in her T-shirt, as the sun was growing warm. She sang every one of the songs and chants, and felt the light wind ruffle in her hair, and breathed in deep the country smell of cow dung and wet hay.

All we are saying is give peace a chance!
All we are saying is give peace a chance!

She had spotted Sister Molly from the *Late Night Show* stalking up the road with a stick in one hand and a banner in the other, a determined look fixed on her rather fierce, masculine face. Sinead waved at her and Sister Molly nodded and gave her a proud V-sign back.

And then suddenly they were stopped. A barricade of armoured cars was parked solidly at a crossroads, and they could not proceed. That was as far as they were permitted to march – there was no more they could do. The demonstrators at the front of the march sat down and began to chant: *"We shall not, we shall not be moved!"*

The police were masked in riot gear.

"Robocops," murmured Alan at Sinead's side.

People down the back of the demonstration couldn't see what was ahead, and became impatient now. There was jostling and catcalling at the police. Alan was telling people to shush and urging them to sit down instead. There was some confusion, and Sinead sat down dutifully, cross-legged on the road.

Eventually the movement to sit down was far too strong, and so they all sat, carefully avoiding cow-pats on the road, and took out sandwiches and drinks. One lady had a flask. Another sliced an apple tart and shared it round. Sinead took a slice, and smiled gratefully at the lady. "Delish," she told her warmly

They sang some more songs and chants now,

"Bertie Bertie Bush's Man! Blood! Blood! On your hands!" and *"War! What is it good for? Absolutely nothing!"*

Harry was lining all the speakers up to address the crowd, and there was fiddling around choosing one of several scratchy megaphones. Professor Jeremy Manning was the first to make a very crackly speech. He'd had to be driven up behind the march because it was so long, and had only been able to walk a few hundred yards to the front. The crowd whistled him in applause.

Harry made a very short speech, and then William Cairns made a very long one, which the crowd adored. Sinead hung on to every word – Cairns was such a beautiful orator, she thought. He ended his speech with a quote that Sinead didn't recognise, but she listened carefully trying to memorise every word.

"When I think about what motivates our fine

Taoiseach, to wine and dine with the world's most brutal warmonger for the sake of a few photo-opportunities, I am reminded of something that John Millington Synge wrote in a letter to his friend when he returned to Ireland: *'There are sides of all that western life, the groggy-patriot publican-general shop-man, who is married to the priest's half-sister and is second cousin once removed of the dispensary doctor, that are horrible and awful. I sometimes wish to God I hadn't a soul and then I could give myself up to putting those lads on the stage. God, wouldn't they hop!'"*

The crowd roared with laughter. Cairns went on with the Synge quote.

"'In a way it is all heartrending, in one place the people are starving but wonderfully attractive and charming and in another place where things are going well one has a rampant double-chinned vulgarity I haven't seen the like of!'"

The crowd whistled in applause. Sinead and Alan laughed out loud.

"Bertie, Taoiseach," concluded Cairns, "your double-chinned vulgarity is certainly something that we haven't seen the like of! But as you dine tonight with war criminals, feasting as you do like two pigs at the trough, remember one thing: *that you can never wipe the blood of the children of Iraq from your plump hands!"*

The demonstrators whooped in delight.

It was turning colder, as the sun clouded over, and people were getting stiff from standing around, and sitting cross-legged on the ground. The protesters sang a few more jeers at the police, and then turned and marched, much more briskly now, back down again, towards the car-park where they had parked.

It was almost seven when they got there, and the skies were getting bright again, and it was beginning to warm up. Some of the buses loaded up straight away, but the Dublin buses had been hired all night, and so the drivers weren't planning to get back until after midnight.

"Plenty of time for a pint, Sinead," Alan grinned.

At the pub beside the shopping mall, Sinead slipped quietly around to see if she could find him. The lounge of the bar was beginning to fill very rapidly with happy, hungry demonstrators. There were flags, and banners folded up, and bags, and rucksacks, and coats, and jackets piled up in corners and on tables and stools everywhere. The bar staff looked alarmed. They weren't in the slightest bit prepared for an onslaught of five thousand people. But most of the travellers were going on home now anyway, and although the bar room filled quite rapidly, it settled down again into a busy and excited hum of noise. Packets of crisps were spilt open and shared, sandwiches handed over people's heads. Sinead drank two pints of Heineken in quick succession and sat down in a corner with a group of people who had come down from Galway.

She found herself sitting next to a young, thin, studious-looking man called Frank, who shared his peanuts with her. Sinead smiled and pretended to listen while Frank talked about the politics of Turkey, about the war in Afghanistan and about the price of oil. She nodded and picked up peanuts and made agreeable noises while she let her mind run free.

She thought about the day, and how it had all panned out in the end. Plenty of press attention – you couldn't disagree. But to President Bush, would it make the slightest bit of difference? The real purpose of her being there, she reminded herself, was to be able to do something for Moussa. She had wanted to be able to tell him that she was trying to help.

Oh God, thought Sinead, it's all just too hard. If I were Moussa, in that hellhole that Iraq has become, then it *would* mean so much to know that we are here today, all marching and talking to the press and singing and drinking pints in County Clare. He knows what Ireland is about. He understands what people here are like.

He would be sitting here too, she mused, if only there hadn't been a war in 1991, and sanctions, and then 9/11 after that. He would be drinking a pint of Guinness and pretending that he liked it. He would be laughing his head off now with someone, or perhaps with me, because he was always laughing just like that. I wonder if he laughs at all now?

She wasn't sure what Frank was saying any more, but he did appear to be asking her a question because he had stopped and was waiting for her to say something with an expectant look on his face.

"Ah, well, ahem, Frank, look, could I just go up and get another pint first? It's just that I'd just like to have a proper think before I answer that one. That's a really tough question to answer straight up without thinking about it for a while, you see." She smiled at Frank who looked extremely surprised.

"I was only asking her what part of Dublin she lives in," said Frank in wonder to the rest of the group from Galway, while Sinead slid away over towards the bar.

The bar was a hot and sweaty place, and the barmen

could hardly keep up with the crowd. They were pulling pints, and taking orders, and counting change, and slopping beer, and opening bottles and flipping lids all at the same time. Sinead shouted in her order and waited for her third beer, smiling at a fat old man who sat on a stool beside her. *I'm completely pissed,* she suddenly realised. She hadn't eaten much today, apart from a tiny piece of apple pie and then a few of Frank's peanuts, and the alcohol had flown from her empty stomach straight like a mainline to her brain.

And then suddenly there was Harry.

Sinead looked at his too-familiar face, with its new haircut, and her face broke open with unconcealed joy.

"Sinead!" He was delighted.

She let him slide in, close to her, and listened to his analysis of the day. Harry was excited. He was clearly very proud. And she was full of beer now, and felt as though she was witty and amusing, and chatted easily to him. Harry was quite tipsy too. She bought them both another round of beers, and they began to giggle. Harry started telling her about one of the anarchists who had wanted to storm the line of riot police.

"He hopped over a stone wall, into a field, and started running away from the crowd, screaming at the cops, and yelling '*War pigs! War pigs!*' And the cops were there in full riot gear, with their dogs straining on the leash. And this guy is yelling at them and jumping up and down, and shouting political slogans, all on his own, in a T-shirt, in a field in the middle of County Clare, and there are helicopters overhead, and the army are parked all around him. And I just kept thinking: what on earth does he think he's going to be able to *do* in there, on his own, against a hundred riot police, the army with their tanks, and a pack of dogs? And I'm standing on the wall myself, with a megaphone, shouting, '*Brian, get out of the field! Will you get out of the field, Brian? Please, Brian, just get out of the field!*' And he's dancing up and down screaming '*Warmonger!*', and '*War Pig!*' and so on, in his *T-shirt!*"

Harry went off into hoots of laughter again, and as he bent his head to laugh Sinead bent hers, and their heads touched off one another. She quickly looked into his eyes and held his gaze there for as long as she possibly could. She wouldn't let him get away tonight. He held her eyes with his. He couldn't possibly look away.

"What happened eventually?" she asked him over the rim of her beer glass.

"Oh. He got out of the field. Of course. He had to. He would have been eaten by the dogs!" Harry giggled again.

Sinead let him press against her, as someone pushed them on their way forward to get to the bar. They were squeezed aside into a corner now, and people who pushed past to get their drinks had pressed them further and further into one another. She could smell the food he had just eaten, and feel the heat off his legs as they eased against hers. Her body touched him softly.

"Sinead," he sighed.

He was pretty drunk now. She didn't care. She only wanted him more.

"Sinead." He lowered his voice and hiccoughed. He sighed again. She waited.

"Sinead. That time – with you. When we were . . . together?"

"Yes?"

"I just wanted to tell you that I haven't stopped thinking about it."

"Me neither," she said.

"*Really*?" He looked genuinely surprised. He sighed again, and burped. Sinead ignored that.

"Sinead, I'd really like to kiss you now," he breathed.

"Let's go outside," she muttered, tomato-faced with joy. He took her hand.

They had to fight their way out of the pub as it was packed around the doorway now. On a ledge outside the back door he pulled her by the hand, into his body, and she pressed herself against him. His eyes were closed and so she kept hers open. She wanted to see that she was with Harry. She knew that they were being watched. But it was too late now. Harry pulled at her and ran his hands around her waist and underneath her clothes.

At first she felt mortified, because of the small group of people that she knew were watching them. They looked away, and watched, and smirked, and looked away again. But Harry was oblivious. He plunged his hands into her jeans. Sinead pulled back in shock; but when she saw his face again, she gave right in.

She took his hand and led him with her away from the back door of the pub where anyone could watch them, and so they stumbled and walked and stopped and kissed and stopped and pulled each other to a place away from everyone, across the grass, behind a tree where they were sure, more or less, that they could not be seen.

Harry leaned her back against something that she thought might have been a dustbin, or a barrel, or perhaps it was a wall, she didn't know. It was difficult, and her trousers around her ankles were like a leg restraint. She kicked one of the trouser legs away, and opened her plump legs and slid her thighs around and over him, straddling him there. He spread his hands underneath her legs, to lift her up, her thighs around him.

"Sinead!" Harry moaned, his face buried in her breasts. "Is it safe? To go inside?"

She knew exactly what he meant. "Yes," she mumbled. "I mean no. Just don't worry about it, Harry. I can sort it out," and she gasped because he was inside her now.

"Are you sure?" he groaned again.

"Of course I am," she whispered to his face. "I am a doctor, don't forget."

His face creased up.

They held each other for a while. Harry rapidly growing soft, and Sinead rapidly growing cold, her bottom bared to the cool night air until they broke apart feeling clumsy and unattractive now, bare legs with underpants down. They had to bend down to get dressed up again, and Sinead tried to make a joke but it all felt kind of awkward now.

Harry said very little, and in the silence as they fastened belts and buttoned shirts; they suddenly heard a very loud cough and sounds of heavy movement right behind them. Sinead caught Harry's frozen face, and they looked at each other, terrified. Then they heard the cough again, and much more noises.

Sinead watched the bushes carefully, to see if she could figure where the cough came from. She reached out to touch Harry's arm to make him still. Out of the back of the two bushes, right behind the spot where Harry had screwed her up against a wall, rose two soldiers' helmets with twigs stuck on, and underneath were two very solemn, emotionless, blacked-out faces, emerging from their hiding place like creatures from the underworld, dressed in camouflage fatigues, slowly revealing themselves, machine guns held akimbo.

"Oh – my – God!" Sinead whispered, in horror. Her face was raw with shame.

"Oh, Holy Fuck!" Harry giggled.

Chapter 19

New York was like an oven. Isabella couldn't get used to the hot damp air, and the sunless cloudy streets. And the buildings were like fridges on the inside. It was like a permanent feeling of being parboiled. She tried to see some sights and walk around as much as possible, but she felt exhausted by the heat and her jet lag seemed to last for days.

She had found the small off-Broadway theatre where they were due to start rehearsals, and spent a day or two trying to acclimatise herself with the area around Times Square. Isabella loved the sudden anonymity of the city. She ducked in and out of the shade of buildings, and crossed the hectic streets, enjoying the feeling of being lost in a busy purposeful crowd.

One day, almost a week after arriving in Manhattan, she was walking down Broadway through Times Square in the late morning when she looked up and read on the neon ticker tape that wound around and around One Times Square with Breaking News:

ANGRY DEMONSTRATIONS GREET PRESIDENT
BUSH ON OFFICIAL STATE VISIT TO IRELAND.
THOUSANDS PROTEST AGAINST THE PRESIDENT.
STATE VISIT CUT SHORT.

Oh, well done, Harry, said Isabella to herself, and felt grateful tears come to her eyes. *Well done, my darling boy!*

Playboy stage rehearsals were due to start the following week, and Eddie was excited. He pranced around the stage, pulling actors this way and that to set the scene correctly. Isabella threw herself into her part with intensity. She loved the part of Pegeen Mike and adored the language of the play. The other actors were enjoying it too and Isabella almost forgot about Harry on several occasions, when the theatre company went to a nearby Irish bar after rehearsals and laughed for hours about nothing in particular.

Eddie was very protective of Isabella and tended to treat her like a mini movie star, which suited her perfectly. He made sure that the other actors allowed her a lot of scope with the role, and bought her watery American coffee and French toast to eat in the morning before they went to work.

For Isabella, being spoilt by Eddie was delightful. She wound herself up emotionally into being Pegeen Mike on stage and so it would have been quite difficult to relax without the doting she was getting from Eddie and Rob at home. Even though she had to share their tiny flat which was cramped enough, sleeping on a pullout bed in Rob's little music room, they made her feel as though she had always lived there. In the evenings she often stayed out late now with Eddie and with Rob in cafes and in bookshops that never really seemed to close. She went to cooling midnight shows at the Angelica. New York's stifling hot summer allowed one to live outdoors all night, which suited Isabella perfectly as the last thing she could have tolerated would have been long lonely nights spent inside the tiny flat.

Eddie and Rob had discovered a rooftop swimming pool at the Gansevoort Hotel in the Meatpacking District off 14th Street. Eddie had worked hard through an old theatre friend who was now a major TV star to get them into this exclusive club. So Eddie and Isabella had a bolthole in Manhattan from the burning streets below. They lazed in the rooftop pool on hot afternoons after rehearsals. Afterwards, when the pool got busier with hotel residents, they would go across the road to eat in a large upmarket restaurant called *The Diner* on 9th Avenue. Isabella ordered beer, while Eddie and Rob drank margaritas.

"Babes, your blood pressure will be rocketing," grumbled Eddie, when Rob insisted on extra salt around the rim of his pale green drink. Eddie drank his margaritas salt-free – which Rob said turned it into an absolutely pointless cocktail. Isabella sipped her beer and laughed at the two of them because they never seemed to stop fighting over everything.

Eddie ordered steak, and sometimes chicken or baby back ribs in a thick brown sauce. He was on a high protein diet, he explained with a sigh to Isabella. Nothing carbohydrate after six o'clock. Rob, who worked out much more diligently, ordered fries and mashed potato with aplomb. Eddie groaned when plates of fries arrived, and then stole them in handfuls off Rob's plate. Isabella scoured the menu, trying to find something she might like. "There's nothing here I really want" she'd explain. Rob and Eddie would roll their eyes and grumble until eventually she would agree to order Cobb Salad. Or Tuna Melt, depending on the weather. On the cooler days, she could just about manage to order something that was called a melt.

Even though Isabella made a huge fuss over food, she was not pleased that Eddie worried all the time about his weight and tended to watch what other people were eating far too carefully. It was as if he thought that as long as everyone else was on a diet too, then everything was all right. But if other people had the audacity to be carefree with their food, it really did upset him. If he was eating carelessly, then it didn't matter. He just didn't want to be the only one who worried about getting fat.

"Don't tell me that you're still a vegetarian," Eddie grumbled.

Isabella shrugged and picked the chicken and the bacon out of her Cobb salad. It was going to be impossible to remain a vegetarian for much longer in New York, she decided. They ate out all the time. She found New York menus difficult to navigate. There would be nothing for her to eat if she tried to stick to vegetarianism, she told Eddie. And besides, she felt that she was entitled to change her ideas about some foods. She didn't want to have to worry about nutrition all the time. There are only so many meals of lentils and brown rice that she could tolerate in a single lifetime in any case, she told him. And she was fed up of being the odd one out.

"I hate having to feel that I'm being difficult," she grumbled, as she stole a French fry from Rob's plate and dipped it into Eddie's rib sauce. "I don't want to have to be all noble about what I have for dinner any more."

"Didn't you used to smoke, too?" Eddie wanted her to have some sort of vice. "You were this weird hippy smoking vegetarian." Eddie waved his hands around, imitating her smoking as he remembered.

"We all did," Isabella burst out laughing and almost choked on her Arugula. "You smoked like a chimney, Eddie Mannion. Everybody smoked in those days. Me, you; Harry still smokes. We didn't eat in those days," she added for Rob's benefit. "We just smoked packets of cigarettes for lunch."

"Well, thank God you gave it up before you came to New York, or you'd be suffering now," Rob said happily.

"They're going to ban it in Ireland next year too," said Isabella.

"Oh God, I can't believe it. The Irish are giving up smoking. I blame the Americans," moaned Eddie, reaching out to Rob's plate to snatch another handful of cold fries.

Eddie was desperate for Isabella to *hook up*, as he called it, with someone in New York. He was convinced that it was essential that she got over Harry, and got stuck into someone else.

"You can't have the same boyfriend all your life and expect to get away with it," he instructed her. "It's outrageous. And you can't spend your time in New York like an everlasting nun, for God's sake. You've got to get back *out there* again."

Out there sounded to Isabella like an uncomfortable, cold, and unwelcoming place. Eddie had tried to introduce her to all the suitable men he could find, from the theatre company, or from around the theatre circles, but Isabella knew that they were all closet gays. They were all far too polite. Far too neatly dressed. All the rest of the men in the company seemed to admire Eddie far too much in any case.

Isabella's co-lead, who was playing Christie Mahon, was particularly beautiful.

"Oh, I told you before – he's as gay as Christmas," said Eddie cheerfully, when Isabella asked him about Christy. "I met him in a sauna, and I insisted that he take the part. He's just adorable, isn't he? Fabulous altogether!"

Isabella was relieved to discover that there was absolutely no point in her developing a crush on Christy Mahon. She would find it infinitely easier to play a romantic role with a gay man, she told herself.

Eddie wanted to take Isabella jogging in the park on Sundays and insisted that she cruise eligible bachelors that he selected from a bench with her sitting at his side. Isabella had never jogged in the whole of her life, and she wasn't going to start now. But she enjoyed walking for a while in the hot, shady park, while Eddie jogged up and down ferociously, his head becoming hard-boiled in the heat. After jogging, while they rested on a bench, Eddie made eyes at passers-by on Isabella's behalf; a tactic which Isabella felt was ridiculous and bound to fail.

"I'm hardly going to pick up a man in the park with my gay boyfriend trying to do the flirting for me," she observed.

"Darling, stop being so picky. You are just being ungrateful!" Eddie snapped at her.

Eddie tried to take her shopping, to get herself some New York clothes.

"It's too hot to go shopping," she complained.

"That's nonsense, sweetheart. The shops are the only place in Manhattan where it isn't too hot. Come to the Gap, in Chelsea. Please. Just one shop. And I'll take you to a movie afterwards, if you just buy one thing. One tiny thing. A T-shirt, even?"

"I'm just not ready yet," she explained.

Eddie was convinced that her long sundresses, and batik prints, and flat leather sandals with purple braid around the toes, were not the sort of thing that would pull a suitable man.

"I like my clothes," insisted Isabella. "I'm not going to change the way I look. There's nothing here that suits me. Back off, Eddie Mannion."

Eddie sighed, and admitted that he was somewhere near defeat. He would take her to the movie anyway. It was the only way to cool down. They went to see *Super Size Me* at the Angelica, and ate giant packs of popcorn in an ice-cold cinema.

That night she found she couldn't sleep. It was noisy, it was hot, and she felt itchy and creased-up in her tight sofa bed. But most of all she missed Harry. At first, after arriving in Manhattan she had relished her new empty bed. She had slept like a baby, feeling free to sleep and dream and roll around her bed for the first time in years. But the emptiness was becoming stranger now. She listened to the silence of the room, against the roar of air-conditioning vents outside.

There were cars and taxis and people making noises.

And her silent indoors was a lonely place. She realised, in her empty room, that she missed the small whimper noises Harry used to make, that woke her up like punctuation in her shallow sleep. She missed the sharp tug of the bedclothes, when he roved and wriggled in their lumpy bed. She missed his thick bony knees, prickled with hairs. She didn't miss his snores, but they were rare, and gentle like a child's nasal wheeze.

She thought about calling him now. Not one phone call to him since she had arrived several weeks ago, even to just ask him about the demonstration. She hadn't wanted to have to hear his voice in case it made her cry. If he really wanted to speak to her he would be able to track her down to Eddie's house. But she had written him a note that told him not to ring, and begged him not to write. She had wanted to cut off all the ties.

Isabella had felt, on that early bright cold Irish morning, waiting desperately for him to come home before her taxi arrived, that if he did not come home, that if she could not speak to him to tell him where she was going to now, that he should never know. She wanted him to feel some pain without her. But now, suddenly, in the middle of a hot New York night, the thought of hurting Harry horrified her. She let her tears spill down and soak the pillow, while she lay on the hard edge of her sofa bed, watching the window where the night was still quite black and airless.

In the middle of the New York night, what time is it in Ireland, she wondered muzzily. Four o'clock here in Manhattan — or nearly that. Five hours ahead? Or is it seven? He won't be in, either way. She lay back down again, and closed her eyes.

If it is only four hours ahead, he could be in. It could be only just a quarter to eight. He will be getting up now. Or . . . maybe not. What if he wasn't in the flat at all when she rang?

She sat back up glumly on the edge of the sofa bed, and let her head fall into her hands. Her long black curls fell over her hands and she rubbed her fingers against her hot scalp, as if to rub away the pain. The steel edging of the pullout arrangement dug like a pike into her leg, but she let it hurt her anyway. She wanted it to hurt. It was easier now to feel a physical pain, than not to feel anything but the blurred swollen-brained agony she had felt intermittently since leaving Dublin; since before . . . before what? She still didn't know what had happened that night. Maybe now she would never know.

And she couldn't ring him now. Because if he wasn't there, and it *was* eight o'clock in the morning, then she would know everything.

She rolled onto her side again; knees curled to her chest, and stared at the moonlit window. Sleep was hours away.

Chapter 20

"Sweetie, you look drained. Gorgeous, but completely drained. Here, have another coffee. Have one of these plums; they are divine. Have a chocolate croissant – *le pain au chocolat*. Rob brought them earlier. He's gone jogging, the preposterous swine. At this hour! I want to go jogging too, but I can't motivate myself to move. And if I put on any more weight I'll have to kill myself."

Isabella glanced up over her *New York Times* at Eddie's muscular flat tummy. In his boxer shorts and nothing else his golden-brown tanned limbs undulated like a mermaid in the waves. Eddie skipped around the tiny kitchen, flicking on the gas and making pinging noises with the microwave. Isabella smiled to herself. Her head hurt from lack of sleep, but the coffee was strong and hot and Eddie's endless energy was forcing her to comply.

New York was full of energy, all the time. Nobody stood still. Mornings began before the dawn had broken; days raced at breakneck speed through cups of coffee and rehearsal space and meetings and conferences and lunches and more coffee and jogging and yoga and cocktails and then clubs. She was doing her best, and although not coming anyway near to keeping up with Eddie and his manic effervescence, she felt that she was living a faster pace than she had ever done in her life.

Saturday morning was a lie-in until eight at least, for Eddie and Rob. Isabella, whose bedroom was right next to the living room, normally had to be up and about before the two men were out of their noisy and often communal shower. She was therefore thoroughly enjoying herself now, slouching lazily in her pyjamas on a stool beside the bar that divided Eddie's kitchen from the sitting area.

Isabella cradled a large mug of coffee in her hands, and watched Eddie munch his Danish pastry and drop crumbs everywhere, reading two newspapers at the same time while keeping up a stream of conversation.

Eddie hasn't changed a bit really since college, she thought as she watched him spill and wipe and spread jam sloppily. He was even more giggly and temperamental, even more distractible and self-absorbed. Today they were going to go up town to Fifth Avenue to watch the Gay Pride demonstration.

"It isn't a *demonstration,* you know, you European liberal pinko!" Eddie squawked. "It's a *parade.* You're in America now, Pegeen."

Isabella wasn't sure what she should wear. Eddie had suggested a baseball cap and baggy trousers with an ill-fitting pink T-shirt.

"You're far too thin to be a lesbian," he grumbled, as Isabella threw the ill-fitting T-shirt away, and pulled on one of her Indian cotton stringed tank tops instead.

Rob was taking part in the parade with a group from an Aids project where he did voluntary work in Harlem. He was wearing a T-shirt that said LOVE+ on the front, and HIV+ on the back. The project volunteers were going to throw condoms out to the crowd from the back of a truck. Rob had decided that they should add in something slightly more entertaining, so he had got a small jazz group that he occasionally gigged with called the Overnight Express to play New Orleans jazz as the brightly coloured condoms flew by.

"Ghastly name for a band, isn't it?" Eddie giggled. "Sounds like a desperate motel sandwich-vending machine or something."

Isabella thought that Rob was great to get up on the back of a truck and play the violin in front of all the crowds of Fifth Avenue and the whole of New York City, no matter what the band was called.

"*Rob* isn't HIV positive? Is he?" she suddenly thought to ask, while Eddie cheered and screamed when the Overnight Express with its swinging hail of fruity condoms sailed on by. The thought had never occurred to her until now. But it was an obvious consideration. Oh God, how awful that would be for Rob!

"Nah!" Eddie waved madly to a seven-foot-tall drag queen in shocking pink, blowing kisses from the parade. "Rob's health is good. He's just a great big fat do-gooder, that's all. But he got involved in that volunteer project for poor gay boys from the black lands when his partner died several years ago. He's fabulous really, Rob is." Eddie turned to Isabella, pulling a sad face.

"I had no idea that his partner had died," she said. "Oh, poor Rob. That's so awful for him."

"Tragic. Utterly."

They watched a motorcade of vintage cars go by, driven by elderly men, who raised a huge cheer from the crowd.

"The Stonewall Veterans!" Eddie shrieked, and wolf-whistled loudly while the crowd roared with approval. "Now those are some brave men." He raised his hands up high so that the veterans could see that he was clapping.

"Yes, Rob is a widower," he carried on to Isabella, craning his long neck at the same time. "It was tragic what happened to David, of course. I never met him. He died a good few years ago. But Rob has shown me pictures of him. He was much older than Rob is, you know. And white, too. He was just this nice old white guy that Rob knew from the Juilliard. He's got me now, of course," Eddie grinned at Isabella, "and he's a very lucky man!"

"You love him very much, don't you?"

"Oh God, sweetie. I would die for him," Eddie sighed passionately, rolling up his eyes.

"Don't do that, you ape!" She slapped his arm. "Your eyes will stick"

"Yikes! Look at that! Dykes on Bikes. *Providence and Mercy, spare us all, Pegeen!* Will you look at the mother on the Harley! *That'd be a queer kind to bring into a decent quiet household with the likes of Pegeen Mike!* I'm surprised it's still upright – you'd have thought she would have flattened it by now. How do they tolerate all that leather in the heat?"

"And the helmets – and the goggles," said Isabella in amazement.

"Would you look at the face of that one with the whip on her? I'll slap the freckles off your hairy arse, missus!"

growled Eddie in a thick *Playboy of the Western World* accent, as a very large leather-clad lady snarled by, cracking a long whip at the crowd, which squealed with delight.

"Are you sure that that's not a man?"

"Christ no, sweetie. All the men are much more feminine than that!"

Isabella thought a lot later on that night about what Eddie had said about Rob at the Gay Pride march. *I would die for him.* She wasn't sure if Eddie was really serious, but it was a serious thing to say. People did die for one another. David, Rob's first partner, had died for love – *the love that dares not speak its name*. Eddie might be joking about his dying for Rob, but there was a love there between them that Isabella knew would outlive life. And when life is over, perhaps that is when that kind of love dies: but what if the love dies first? She had loved Harry once, as if her life depended on it. And now?

I wouldn't die for him, Isabella thought, as she lay awake that night in the overheated flat, staring at the over-familiar ceiling fan. That was why I left. I wouldn't give my life for him. I wouldn't share his cause. It wasn't that she had not wholeheartedly believed in Harry's cause. But to give a whole life to something that one can't ever really hold in one's hand? To feel the truth of what one believes, even for a moment in your hand – Harry lived for that. But she – she needed something else to live for. Something . . . that was hers. Something passionate. Theatre, art, literature, these were Isabella's loves, but were they ever going to be her *passions*? And if one feels a passion for a belief, a cause, a mere idea, would one also have to be prepared to die for it? Is loving a *person* the same as loving an idea?

Isabella had thought until now that most likely it was not. But she could see the same passion in Eddie that she had known in Harry. The same undying belief in theatre and the arts, that Harry had held in *his* heart for politics and protest. And Eddie's love for Rob – that was a passionate adoration too. *I would die for him,* Eddie had said to her, tongue in cheek, but none the less she knew that in her wildest moments she would never have admitted half as much about her love for Harry.

What does it really mean: love? Isabella wondered, as the clock ticked on towards three in the morning and she remained awake, awake, awake. Does it really mean to say that I would die for someone: or something? A cause, a country, a lover – do people really feel these passions, or are they just ill-thought-out beliefs?

And if you love someone enough to die for them, does that mean that you would lay down your life so that they can live: or does it mean that without them, you would rather you were dead?

Isabella turned her face to the wall again, and waited, waited just for sleep to come.

By the beginning of August, rehearsals for the *Playboy* had become intense. Eddie worked the cast to the bone. They were due to open in September, and the weather was ridiculously hot. The cast worked diligently, but everyone was in need of a break to get out of the city heat. Eddie had decided that they should all take four days off to visit the seaside.

"It isn't Inis Meain," Eddie warned them, "but everyone must get to a beach or be near the seaside during the four-day break. Smell the sea. Walk along the beach at midnight. Remember, it's the same Atlantic Ocean. Wave hello to Ireland!"

He was an absolute fantasist, Isabella thought. She was intrigued by Eddie's new obsessive attention to Synge and to the lyrical language of the play, to the nuances of the Mayo dialect. She had perfected a rather mad-eyed West of Ireland stare for her character of Pegeen Mike, which Eddie loved and so he encouraged her to use it frequently outside of rehearsals, to try it out on people for effect.

The stare was a deliberate look of suspicion mixed with an urge for adventure. It was a look, said Eddie, of a woman whose mind is bubbling with sexual frustration, dampened by sexual repression and guilt, and fired with despair. She tried it out regularly on the bus on Broadway, at the driver as she handed him her coins, but he just stared straight ahead at the road and told her in a mechanical voice to slide the coins into the tray please ma'am. She tried it out on the lady in the drug store underneath their flat who Eddie said looked as though she'd had a lobotomy. The lobotomy lady didn't blink an eyelid. So Isabella tried the stare out on the manager of the drug store. The store manager got the store detective to follow her around next time she came in. Isabella began to feel that the stare was *getting somewhere* now.

On the phone to Ruth on Sunday morning she attempted to explain the stare and the effect it was having on the play, and on her own feelings about the part, to the accompaniment of Roly's happy squeals as he banged his toys along the floor.

"God, the play sounds mighty altogether!" bubbled

Ruth. "Give me that fire truck, Roly, you're making too much noise! What did Eddie say? Oh Jesus, Roly, all right, take the fire truck back for God's sake! Just try not to rev it over here near Mummy. By the door, yes, good boy, over there. And when are you going to go to the beach again? No, Roly! Not over Mummy's foot. Fuck's sake, Isabella, I can hardly hear a word you're saying!"

Isabella wanted to tell Ruth other things about New York. About the hole in her heart that she felt without Harry. About her fear, her utter terror, that Harry might be hers no more. And that, despite the fact that she had walked away so easily, she thought about nothing except whether or not she should go back. It was as if she had jumped a sinking ship without a life belt and was now having to swim desperately to land. But the desert island that she swam to was an unknown territory. There might be nobody ashore. She might have to live alone forever. To have remained aboard a sinking ship would have been to live in full knowledge that one would almost inevitably have to die. But there is always the very slim possibility of some sort of fantasy rescue, before the ship disappears completely beneath the sea. To jump off, and hit out for dry land, in deep cold hostile water, could have been just a bit too brave.

From time to time, Isabella congratulated herself for having had the courage to pack up and walk away. It was the nobler thing to do; she was quite sure of that. Every now and then she stood in front of the full-length mirror that Rob and Eddie had screwed onto the walls to make the corridor seem less pokey, and looked at her reflection in her clothes, to see what sort of woman she had now become.

What is it that I have, Christy Mahon, to make me fitting entertainment for the like of you, that has such poet's talking and such bravery of heart?

The face that looked back at her was still quite wistful; her effect was unsure.

She ran her fingers through her dark curls of hair, and swept it up, around her head, behind her neck, or in a twisted knot. She sucked her cheeks right in, and then puffed them right back out again. She curled her lips. She examined her flat figure, from the front, the side, and from behind, and lifted up her skirts to see her legs. She held her skirt at mid-thigh height, and imagined herself going out like that in a bum-clinging mini, or a pair of shorts. In Ireland, her legs would have looked too bony. She would have felt as though she still looked like a child. Here in America, sixty-year-old women have legs like children, thought Isabella. Heck, I need to get some clothes.

Eddie was desperately impatient to get to the seaside that weekend. He had hired a Chevrolet car to take them to Cape Cod for the mandatory seaside break. Rob complained that Cape Cod was a ridiculous distance to drive in high summer for a three-day jaunt, but Eddie refused to listen, and revved the engine loudly just outside the flat until they both came down.

Isabella had, after a lot of to-ing and fro-ing in between the shops, bought herself a pair of green khaki shorts, with a sharp white halter-neck bikini top and gold flip-flops. Eddie wolf-whistled as she folded herself into the seat beside him.

"Gorgeous legs, babes! Mmm!" He ran his hand along the inside of her thigh, and she slapped it off, squealing in delight. Rob tut-tutted in the back, and went to sleep as soon as they hit Queens. Eddie and Isabella sang Irish ballads, just to get into what they imagined might be the spirit of the *Playboy of the Western World*.

Some say the devil is dead, the devil is dead, the devil is dead
Some say the devil is dead and buried in Killarney
More say he rose again, more say he rose again,
More say he rose again and joined the British army!
squawked Eddie, in falsetto voice.

Isabella decided to tone it down a little, as they glided through the forests of New England.

"Oh Danny Boy the pipes the pipes are calling
From glen to glen and down the mountain side
The summers in and all the flowers are dying
Tis you tis you . . ."

But she choked and couldn't sing the rest. It suddenly seemed to be the saddest song that she had ever heard.

"Who writes this stuff?" she sniffed. "All these bloody emigration songs and songs of unrequited love. What are they – torture material for the bewildered?"

"Tis you tis you, must leave, and I must bide," squeaked Eddie, in the same range as Isabella, putting out his hand to hold hers as he drove.

"But come ye back!" came Rob's deep baritone from the back seat of the car.

"Oh Rob! You know the words to 'Danny Boy'? Oh, gorgeous! Sing up, please!" Isabella sighed with relief.

And so they sang together
But come ye back when summer's in the meadow
And all the valley's hushed as white as snow
Tis I'll be there, in sunshine or in shadow
Oh, Danny Boy, oh Danny Boy, I love you so!

"Rob, your voice is just so beautiful!" Isabella was crying properly now.

"Don't ruin the upholstery, sweetheart!" scolded Eddie, handing her a packet of tissues from the glove box. "This rental is costing me a fortune."

It seemed to take all day to get to the Cape and Isabella felt quite exhausted by the time they got there. They had a pizza in a roadside restaurant and Isabella had a beer, although the others weren't drinking alcohol at all. Eddie was off the drink until opening night. He felt on edge with hangovers, he explained, and wanted to keep his belly down for all the photographs too. Rob was driving now, but was looking forward to a bottle of wine with Isabella later on the porch, or after a quick midnight swim on the beach. They said very little at the restaurant, and munched hot pizza, each absorbed in their own thoughts.

Isabella thought about her lines for Pegeen Mike.

I'll be burning candles from this day out to the miracles of God that have brought you from the south today, and I, with all my gowns bought ready, the way that I can wed you, and not wait at all. And myself, a girl, was tempted often to go sailing the seas till I'd marry a Jew-man, with ten kegs of gold, and I not knowing at all there was the like of you drawing nearer, like the stars of God.

She had tried not to see Harry's face when she spoke her lines of love and longing and desire.

Rob thought about the gay bar that he had cruised last summer and wondered if Eddie would be on for that again, and whether or not Isabella would feel left out.

Eddie thought about the boy from the bar that he'd had at the rented beach house two summers ago, and wondered if he might be still around.

They wiped their mouths, and smiled at one another.

"Great. Let's go!" Rob picked the car keys off the table.

The weekend on the Cape was not much fun for Isabella. Rob and Eddie were out all night every night and so they slept all morning, rising at around two o'clock to fool around the kitchen in their boxer shorts and then wrestle each other back to bed, or onto the beach where they collapsed onto the sand to sleep like the dead. On a very windy beach, Isabella tried to read a book, *The Hours*, which Eddie had recommended, but it was desperately tragic.

The women in it were plagued with pathos; a bit like Pegeen Mike, thought Isabella. Caught in an impossible pain, pining all their lives away. Wishing that they could be something, loving men they couldn't have, and having to live with being nothing. In the end, the only woman who had any *real* life committed suicide.

Is this just some universal truth about all women? She wondered, putting down her book, defeated by the hot wind. The idea was horrifying. I often felt like nothing when I was with Harry in the last few years, she thought. I felt so small, so insignificant, and so totally invisible beside him. But I knew it wasn't true – I knew I wasn't insignificant at all. I am a person. I have friends. I have a life. But it never seemed to matter much, to him. It was just that *he* didn't need *my* life, to make his own complete. Oh God, how very foolish I have been!

"Ruth, do you think that I've always tried to live my life through Harry's?" she implored next Sunday morning, trying to ignore Roly's gurgles this time on the phone. Thankfully, Ruth's household was more serene today.

"I think . . ." her friend began. She paused.

Isabella waited for the rest.

Back in her kitchen in Dublin, Ruth was thinking that this was important to get right, as she watched Roly beginning to look bored again. All the way over in America, and she still can't get this man out of her life. And he's seeing someone else. She even knows that. He is still in love with anti-globalisation. And he has the personality of a teenager. And she knows that too. She knows all the flaws, and she knows all the facts. But still she won't move on. Ruth felt that she had to say the right thing now for Isabella to come to sense. And if Isabella couldn't come to sense by now, then she would never change.

"I think," said Ruth, handing Roly a bar of very expensive organic French chocolate from the top shelf that she was keeping for a treat. "I think, Isabella, that all your life you have wanted to *own* Harry, and you have wanted him so much that you couldn't see how wrong that was."

"What do you mean *wrong*?" Isabella felt her cheeks begin to burn with sudden anger; but she had asked Ruth for her advice. And she needed to hear the truth.

"No, that's not … look; I don't mean that you were *wrong* for Harry. Or that he was wrong for you. But I think that you always felt that Harry was a … possession that you had to mind. You had to guard him with all your life. It was as if you had been bequeathed him in a will, or won him as a prize or something. You had found your special task for all your life was to protect him, and to keep him safe. And you always did protect him, Iz, no matter what he did."

"I loved him; that's what you do when you love someone," Isabella heard her own voice say. But she knew how pathetic it sounded.

"What I think that I am trying to say is that you *encouraged* him to feel that you would always hold his hand, no matter what," said Ruth. "And that is a great way to love someone. Don't get me wrong, it really is. But it isn't *true*. It's a cover-up. It's almost what you could call a sham. It's not real love, just to hide the truth from someone. Adoration isn't what we want."

"Ruth, that is just so unfair..." Isabella began, but then she bit her lip and stopped again. "I'm sorry, Ruth. I rang you. I do need to hear this. I need to know exactly what you think. I mean it."

"I guess we all want to know the truth about ourselves, but it's not often the truth that we were hoping for," said Ruth.

Isabella laughed a small defeated laugh. But she could tell, even over the phone, by the tone in Ruth's voice that she smiling too. She missed her friend desperately.

"Hey, say something horribly truthful about me, and then we're even," Ruth suggested.

"Your baby is adorable but undisciplined," giggled Isabella. "And you are a terrible cook."

"All right. But I was thinking of something that I *don't* already know. But at least it's a duce now. Look, Iz; I reckon that the person who will love you most in life has got to be the one who tells you who you really are. You loved Harry – and I know that you still do. But you love the idea of Harry more than the reality. You love the popular guy, who's winning all the games, who never lets himself get down, or cries, or falls apart. Who trips, but never falls. That's the guy you want. But that is a public image of Harry Waters that he's created."

"That makes me seem so shallow!" Isabella moaned. But still she needed to hear more.

"Of course you love his image – but it isn't a real, feeling, hurting, mistake-making person that you love. He's a warrior, a hero, and a celebrity. You want to own him, the way that you might own a nice watch. But it's only nice when no-one else can have it."

"I feel as though you think that I'm the one who's being selfish."

"No, I never said that, Iz. Look, Harry is a special guy. But, he isn't *just* for you. He can't be put into a box, and minded like a prize. It's time you found yourself another toy."

Isabella took a long deep breath. "You're right," she said, and sighed. "I know you are. I just wish it wasn't all so hard."

Chapter 21

Sinead knew in the darkness of her heart that Harry did not love her. In the darkness of her heart she knew that he craved her – but his duty was to Isabella. Whenever she had asked him about, or mentioned Isabella in any way, he had clammed up into a series of muttering excuses. Sinead concluded that he could not leave her; that he was trapped in an unequal relationship, based on a loyalty of affection, habit, and of naïve trust.

She knew that he desired her, Sinead, in a way that could never have been repeated with another woman. The passion she had felt was a gasping, terrified passion, a desire that overwhelmed her, and she sensed that she also was irresistable to him. But that was where it ended.

There was a stumbling block for Harry: a lifetime of fidelity, of sorts, to a woman with whom he had already built a life. Disabling and then attempting to rebuild one's life all over, for a man like Harry, Sinead knew was a challenge he was not prepared to consider.

It wasn't cowardice as such, that lead him to paralysis on the subject of Isabella, she felt. It was a much more ordinary fear, a childlike trepidation of a territory unknown. In the security blanket of habitual affection, Harry clung to the idea that his love for Isabella was uncomplicated, perhaps for her unsatisfactory, but nevertheless unequivocal.

Sinead had asked him several times where Isabella had gone: and yet each time he had dodged a truthful answer, suggesting a variety of possibilities. That she was busy, out of town, not interested in going on protests. He seemed disinterested in Sinead's dissatisfaction, and gave the impression that he was dismissing it as feminine jealousy which made her feel worse.

For Sinead, the mere idea of beginning a new and whole relationship with a younger, much more economically and socially unstable man, would normally have been a decision she would have had to think very long and hard about. But in this situation it was a decision that Harry appeared unwilling to let her make.

After they returned from Shannon, she had met him once, at the bookshop in the Jervis Centre, but she was in a hurry and they had not had time to talk.

"Very busy," he had smiled, and looked happy when she had asked him how he was.

She felt infuriated. She was doubly busy, running her medical practice: but he seemed to believe that his work was clearly much more *worthy*.

"I can't talk. I've got to go. You ought to ring me sometime," she had said, but her voice did not sound like her own. She felt it flat and toneless. She wanted to slap him.

"I will," he had replied, with a nervous smile.

But in a moment she could tell it was a lie.

There was a part of her that didn't want to tell him what she knew. She felt that it was the one small thing she had, that he did not; the only piece in the jigsaw that might put an end to all the games, and give him something real that he would have to deal with. And yet she also felt that he had no right to know.

It was as if what was happening in her body was her own creation, entirely separate from his being. She ran her hands around her hips, and felt her breasts engorged, and touched herself where he had touched her, remembering that he had been there once.

Eventually he rang her: a husky smoked-out voice early on a Friday morning, interrupting her surgery on her mobile phone.

"Can you help set up a students' meeting in Trinity College next Tuesday night? We are trying to get a teach-in going."

Half of her wanted to scream at him: but the other half was the one that had answered the phone.

Of course she would. Seven o'clock. Looking forward to it. See you there.

He didn't notice that her breasts had swelled. Of course not. And even if he had, she knew he would have been too polite to ask. The crowd of students that he'd organised were charming. She actually enjoyed the perversity of the situation, the dark backroom meeting in a fungus-smelling pub, damp-stained seating, infested with fruit flies. There was something rather brave about it all.

She had two glasses of red wine: why the hell not? She

needed to pluck up the courage, and she would have to say it to him tonight. She might never get the chance otherwise again. There would be one chance to say what she knew she had to say, and then to wait with agonising breath for his response. And then it would be over. For good or bad. At this point, she felt, after two thickly-scented glasses of Shiraz, that the situation would be good. Harry was treating her with great affection, in the smelly fly-infested pub.

"Sinead is a *doctor*," he told her students, and she enjoyed hugely that he was proud to know her.

He had offered her a lift home, which was perfect: perhaps that was partly why she had drunk all the wine. Vulnerable and tipsy: was there any other way to be around Harry Waters, she wondered, as he lead her out to his little navy-blue car. Harry drove very slowly ("I am a late learner," he told Sinead) and stopped painstakingly at every amber traffic light. She glowed with joy to be with him, and the opportunity that she would have to talk to him about it all. Harry chattered on about the student group and so she listened politely, waiting for her time.

Eventually they were silent.

"I miss you," she began.

Silence.

"Why did you say that?" he asked. " Sinead, what did you mean by that?"

It was over. She knew it then. There was nothing, he felt nothing for her.

"Oh, just forget about it, Harry. It doesn't matter."

" No. Tell me why you said you missed me"

"Please forget about it, Harry." She turned to stare out of the window. Nothing mattered now.

"Did you say that you missed me because you and I were starting something together, and you wanted it to continue?"

"Yes," she said, "and that has been very painful for me."

It was out there. She had said the worst; and he couldn't make her feel lower than she did now, ever again. She would triumph in her own mind simply because of her courage in laying out all of her most humble and unrequited affection for him. She hadn't begged, she had merely stated a fact.

"Sinead, why didn't you say so, if you were finding it so painful?"

"Because that's not what people say. They don't say, 'Oh, this is very painful for me.' They keep a dignified silence in these cases."

"But if only I'd known . . . "

"If only what, Harry? What would you have done about it? You wouldn't have left Isabella for me. You love her far too much." The words were agony to speak, but she spoke them anyway. Like a loose tooth that nags all day, she had forced herself to probe and poke at her most painful fears so that she could explore them fully. Once explored, they could hold no power over her.

"You have loved Isabella all your life," she continued. "You've only just met me. You aren't going to risk destroying something that you know, that is so familiar to you, so cosy, so dependable, so reliable, to risk a relationship with a woman like me, even if it is more exciting, more sexy, more adventurous. Even if you and I could have had the greatest love that we'd have ever known. You don't want to risk anything to find that out. And I respect that.

I just hope that one day we don't regret what we have lost."

"The thing is, Sinead, that part of me wanted it to continue. With you. There is a part of me that wants you very badly. It's just that I couldn't . . . It's just all too complicated."

Oh, if only you knew, she thought. How complicated it could have become. And yet she couldn't bring herself to tell him now. She probably never would.

"Yes. Of course it was. Unrequited love is always complicated. So why complicate yourself, Harry? Make life easy for yourself. And I'm sure that you'll be very happy."

"Sinead . . . I don't know what to say"

They were silent once again. The indicator ticked, the car rumbled along streets, but neither of them spoke.

And then they were at her street. He stopped the car carefully in front of her apartment block.

She turned to him and smiled. "You know, Trotsky had an affair with Frida Kahlo, when he was married."

He looked at her wearily. "Sinead, why are you telling me this? Is it supposed to have some sort of meaning for our situation?"

"Well, Trotsky had a very passionate affair with Frida. He adored her. But when his wife found out, she was devastated. And Trotsky didn't want to hurt her. So he went back to his wife, and abandoned Frida."

"And what's the moral of that story?"

"Oh, God, Harry, I don't know! The guy got assasinated, didn't he?" she laughed and shrugged her shoulders.

Harry laughed. But there was something unfinished in

the air. She found the handle of the car door before she kissed him briefly on the cheek.

"Goodnight, Harry." She got out, closed the car door behind her and walked quickly, almost ran away.

It was Fiona who told her about Alan's birthday party.

"Alan is only thirty?" Sinead immediately tried to suppress her surprise. "I mean, he seems so, um – *mature.*"

"Jesus, how old did you think he was?" Fiona's Cork accent always seemed to come out stronger when she was indignant. "Well, I suppose he looks older with the beard. And he's kind of fat. So will you be there? They are going to show a film first. It's a documentary Harry got from South America about a coup d'etat or something: typical of Harry of course, can't just organise a party. It has to be a fund-raiser and consciousness-raiser as well. So there will be the film and then a few drinks after and then a party back at Alan's. DJ, decks and all."

Sinead knew that she would have to go. After the last conversation that she'd had with Harry, she had to face him one more time, to show that she could be there, in the same room, the same company, and not need him any more.

That was one motivation for going. But the more she thought about what might happen at Alan's party, the more her mind envisaged the other possibility. The possibility of Harry gazing at her across a room: Harry holding her eyes with his, the way he always had done, and she would know that, after a long night's drinking, he would desire her more than she had ever been desired before.

On the one hand, she could just about pre-construct a party in which she and Harry mixed and mingled, merged and circulated, and then went home to their separate houses with no raw aching misery that would begin the following day and last for weeks; no gut-wrenching agony of inexplicable rejection; no haphazard, drunken, rapturous tortured lovemaking having taken place. But it was a very thinly held vague notion: and it was much more strongly replaced by the fantasy that Harry would indeed look at her with the same desire and lust in his eyes that they had always held, and would beg her to sleep with him, and would then disappear again into a merry crowd leaving her bankrupt of emotion.

Which sort of party she *wanted* to go to could potentially have been her choice. She was capable of maturity, even if Harry, after several beers, was not. But she also knew quite clearly now that she and Harry were no more. He had chosen Isabella: the elusive, invisible Isabella, whom she was never going to meet. But the fact that Harry was inobtainable now to Sinead, by his own admission, made her expectations for the sort of party it was going to be, even more irresistible.

Sinead went to the hairdresser's after work. She bought a sapphire-blue empire dress with a halter neck that showed her bare brown shoulders off. Instead of her usual chunky wedges she found a pair of kitten heels that she'd bought last year for someone's wedding. The dress was tight now over her swollen breasts, emphasising her even more voluptuous shape. She stood in front of the bathroom mirror, twirling around to admire her sleek shining hair. She felt that she could face Harry with conviction.

At the pub, Alan was alone, fussing around the video. Everybody else was still in the bar.

"I'll give you a hand," she offered.

It was easier than walking into that bar alone.

"Jesus, you look great!" Alan beamed at her through his fox-fur beard.

"Oh happy birthday, Alan! I almost forgot."

She had bought him a book of essays by Arundhati Roy.

In the darkened lounge after the film, Sinead watched Harry over the rim of her Ballygowan while she tried to have a conversation with some of Alan's friends. Harry sat chatting with a different group at the next little table to Sinead. They were each trapped in separate little worlds of party people: each embedded in their separate conversations about nothing. He nodded at her occasionally, as if he seemed to be attempting, across the barricades, to include her in his conversation.

Sinead suddenly realised, as she sipped her drink and watched the room and chatted politely at her table that she didn't want to have to keep trying any more. She smiled politely when Harry caught her eyes. But she did not penetrate his gaze as she would have done before.

And Maggie Hennelly was there, of course, over by the bar. Maggie was flitting in and out and all around the room, laughing merrily at everything. She waved over at Sinead, a great big friendly wave.

Sinead wound her way around a maze of stools and tables to the bar. Sometimes being alone is easier when you don't have to engage in earnest conversations, she decided, ordering a gin and tonic. Just one would be no harm.

"I love your dress!"

Fiona stood beside her waving a tenner at the barman.

Sinead looked around the room. "I feel completely *over*dressed," she confided.

Fiona laughed. "Don't be crazy, girl. You look fantastic. It's the rest of us are scruffs."

"And I love your *shoes!*" Maggie Hennelly was wearing a tight white sleeveless vest with the usual welcoming plunge, over low-cut jeans. "I just wish I could wear high heels," she beamed at Sinead.

What a *load* of bullshit that is, thought Sinead. "Well, I wear heels because I guess I'm just not tall enough without them!" She laughed heartily with Maggie, but it wasn't really all that funny. She was beginning to feel quite fuzzy after just one drink. "Would you like a drink, Mags?" Her determination was to be dignified.

She bought another round for all of them, and then got into a reasonably jolly conversation with Maggie and Fiona. The party was moving on now to Alan's house and people were buying beers and ordering taxis. Sinead bought a six-pack over the counter for the party, and in the confusion of people trying to decide who would go into which taxi she found herself linking arms with two men who taught at Alan's school.

"Sinead's coming back to Alan's place with us!" One of the two men, Dave, was looking very pleased, and he grabbed Sinead around the waist to squeeze her out the door. She stumbled in her kitten heels, and both men clutched onto her to stop her falling, all three of them giggling inanely as they hailed a taxi.

"Why aren't your girlfriends coming with you?" Sinead asked them.

"The girls aren't really into the kind of parties Alan does," Dave mumbled darkly into her hair. "Gorgeous dress by the way." His lips brushed her bare shoulder. Sinead giggled and let him nestle into her. "Where are we going?" She couldn't see a thing. She'd deliberatly left her glasses at home and had no idea which route the taxi was taking.

"Mmm . . . don't care . . .do you?" Dave reached around to squeeze her breasts, and hiccoughed into her hair in the back seat of the taxi. "Whoops! Sorry 'bout that. Sinead, you're gorgeous."

"Give me a break!" Sinead nudged him away with the shoulder that he'd been nuzzling. But she was enjoying the attention.

Alan's house was a neat redbrick terraced Victorian, with a long narrow corridor that stepped down into a modern kitchen with a bathroom off the back. Outside the kitchen door in a patio yard people smoked ferociously underneath a big umbrella, sheltering from light midnight rain.

Sinead opened one of her beers and poked around, in and out of the yard to see who was there (Harry wasn't, not yet anyway), and then inspected the tiny kitchen (not in there either). She waited ten minutes to use the bathroom but then Alan swept out of it suddenly, taking two other people with him.

"Hey! We've been waiting ages!" Sinead complained loudly. The other people in the kitchen stared at her. "Well? Haven't we?" she asked them. "That's really mean, isn't it? All three of them jumping the toilet queue like that. Isn't it?" She knew that she was being shrill. She couldn't help it. It was like a panic.

"It's Alan's house," mumbled one girl. She looked completely drunk so Sinead looked at another man who was waiting for the bathroom.

"Don't *you* think that was mean? All three of them going in together?"

He looked embarassed for her. "I don't think they are exactly taking a piss in there together," he muttered, looking around him to avoid her glare.

"What?"

"Well, my guess is that they are using the *mirror,* rather than the toilet, in there together. *You know?*"

She went to look for another bathroom. But there wasn't one. Upstairs someone was having sex underneath a pile of coats.

In the kitchen she leaned against the sink to drink a beer and attempted a conversation with a nurse that she'd met once before

But Christina the nurse smiled lazily at her and her eyelids drooped. "Mmmm. Yeah. Absolutely. Big time."

Christina was oblivious to everything Sinead had said to her, nodding her big fuzzy head like a doggy in a car.

"I'll be right back." Sinead touched Christina's arm politely. Christina nodded and her doggy's eyes drooped like a lizard.

Sinead went to sit on the staircase on her own. She closed her eyes and let her head rest in her hands, leaning on her knees. She'd come all the way out here, in the vain ridiculous hope of being with Harry once again. And now she was stuck, out on the other side of town in a neighbourhood she didn't recognise, quite unsuitably drunk and all alone, in an unnavigable house that was full of strangers who were stoned.

Harry wasn't here, and even if he had been, Sinead wasn't sure if she was up to his unavailability any more. It was all just too hard now. She felt too tired for all of it. That was all. She wasn't being ridiculous. She was just an adult who should be somewhere else: it was nothing more than that.

"You okay, Sinead?" It was Maggie Hennelly.

Maggie sat down beside her on the stairs, and they moved over and back to let people past them up and down, in a gentle symbiosis.

Sinead looked down at her feet in kitten heels.

"I just don't think I fit in here any more, Mags. There's a line of people doing cocaine in the bathroom back there," she smiled. "And I can't talk to anyone here: they are either stoned, or I don't know them, or I don't know what to talk to them about. And I feel so *old*, all of a sudden. I'm just too tired for all of this."

Maggie took her hand. "You're not old, Sinead. You're beautiful. But I do know exactly what you mean. We both feel that we don't fit in here, don't we? So, let's do something that'll get the party going."

For an awful moment Sinead thought that Maggie was going to suggest they leave together and go somewhere else, just the two of them.

"Do you want to do some ecstasy?" Maggie whispered.

Sinead stared at her. Why the hell not? she thought. Go for it. Go for it big time, as Christina might have said. She nodded at Maggie, and exchanged a mischievous smile.

Maggie took her by the hand into the breakfast room, and left her on a couch while she brought her a glass of water from the kitchen. "Cheers, sister!" Maggie passed her a small tablet, winked at her, and then went off to find another drink.

Sinead downed the ecstasy and sat, watching people passing by, not minding her solitude in the slightest. Everything was perfect now. She was going to have a good time here. Nothing bad was happening. She felt just the same. She'd had a good few beers, so that was all it was. Nothing big or special. People passing by. Harry, over on an armchair now – oh, so he'd turned up after all. Buried in between two younger women: who were they? She didn't know. Were they Harry's frends or Alan's, or just two strangers who'd walked in to pour themselves all over Harry? Did she care?

Of course she cared. It was infuriating. But that was Harry. Giggling, two girls sitting on his lap, or sliding off the arms of the big chair or something, chattering and laughing, two women showering him with admiration.

Sinead sat, and watched the world go by.

A good-looking man curled up on the sofa beside her and started talking to her. He was charming and she would have liked to carry on the conversation, but *that* was when it happened. *Whoosh* and the room expanded, the music burst into a thousand decibels, filling her ears with an incredible sound as if it was coming out of her own head into the world.

Sinead gazed around her. The room had become so huge, and all the people standing around her were huge too: giant people, walking all around like statues in a movie. She turned to face the man who was chatting her up, and smiled a big thick smile at him.

"I think I see where you are going," he said. "I reckon I'll just leave you alone so."

"That would be good," Sinead nodded at him. Poor chap, she thought. I'm being so rude. But she couldn't speak. Her mouth was paralysed. Her brain didn't operate it any more.

"Have some chewing gum," Maggie was beside her again with a pint of water.

Sinead stared at her and gasped. "You look so beautiful, Maggie!"

"Stand up!" Maggie pulled her. "Look around you."

"The room looks so small now." She looked at the other people who were milling around the kitchen. "Look how small it is. Look how big I am!" Sinead gaped. Maggie stroked her shoulders. Sinead looked down at Maggie's pale freckled hand, and took it lovingly. She gently squeezed the other girl's beautiful white dainty hand.

"Come and dance!" Maggie led her into the room next door.

It was the most wonderful music in all the world. The room flowed with music, like a great river of heavenly sounds, *pouring redemption for me*, she thought, remembering a poem that she'd read in school. Alan waved at her and she danced over to him. Her body swayed around him in a blissful trance.

She had become the most beautiful dancer in the world. She was a goddess. Alan came over and ran his hands over her body, caressing her hips and bottom, squeezing her breasts as he kissed her on the lips. She kissed his wet beard back and his lips were soft, so soft they were almost soggy. She tasted them with her tongue.

"Sinead, you look so gorgeous tonight," Alan mumbled, squeezing her bottom again with both hands.

"You do look great, Sinead." Harry danced beside her. "That dress is great on you."

But she was beautiful. She danced as if she were a star.

"Harry!" Sinead breathed into his face, and stroked it with her hands. She touched his eyebrows and caressed his lips. "Isn't Maggie the most beautiful woman that you've ever seen?"

Maggie looked surprised. "Thank you, Sinead. That's a beautiful thing to say."

"But you are," Sinead touched her cheek. "You are so beautiful. You must know you are. You must know that every man desires you. Don't they, Harry? Doesn't every man want to be with her? Don't you Harry? Don't you want Maggie?" She touched Maggie's glowing velvet skin. It was so soft she wanted to lay her face against it.

"Maggie is beautiful," Harry said, "but she's a bit too thin."

"Oh, I'll promise to eat more, Harry!" Maggie laughed with sarcasm more than humour.

Sinead took Maggie's face in her two hands. "I think you are the most beautiful woman here tonight. And if I were Harry I would want to be with you."

Maggie squeezed Sinead's hand and stroked her shoulders. They danced together.

Harry disappeared.

Sinead danced for hours, all alone. She danced in the little room in Alan's house as if she were a beautiful angel ascending into heaven. No woman had ever danced as beautifully as she did that night. She danced while others watched and smiled. And she smiled back, and wound her arms around her head and swayed and let her body speak of beauty, lust and sex and joy, and all the sorrow that she had ever felt. There was no more sorrow now. All the pain had vanished, and in its place she had become a dancer who spoke of purity and love.

And then she suddenly had to stop. She looked around her and realised that it was morning. She was exhausted now.

The music was still playing, and she could hear it outside on the street as she looked up and down to get her bearings. It was broad daylight, well after eight.

She had turned to walk away from Alan's house when she heard Harry's voice, hoarse with cigarettes behind her.

"Sinead! Wait up!" He was stumbling towards her.

"Harry, I'm going home."

"Please don't. Don't go home. Come back inside."

She hesitated. But she couldn't go back in again. Inside there were other girls, other women, people to contend with. Inside was an unknown quantity. It was safer to say goodbye out here, and go, and be the one who got to leave.

"I've got to go. It's too late – it's too early! We've been up all night. I've got to go to work tomorrow, and I need to get some sleep."

"You looked so great tonight."

She put her arms around him, and kissed his mouth. "I've really got to go, Harry." She kissed and kissed him. Over and over. Just one more. Just one more kiss. Just one more.

He solemnly kissed her back, and then she noticed that his eyes were drooping, and he was full of drink.

He's been drinking all night long, she thought. And I've been doing E. What on earth are we up to, the two of us? This is crazy stuff. I have to get out of here or it will never end.

She gently pulled away.

"Please, Sinead. Just let me put my hand up your skirt?"

"Harry! Are you crazy? We're on the street!" she hissed at him. "It's broad daylight. Have you got no shame?"

And then she laughed. Harry was completely drunk.

"Oh, God!" He looked around him. "So we are. I hadn't noticed. Whoops! Sorry about that." He squeezed her bottom instead with both hands, and groaned, burying his face into her cleavage.

"Harry!" Sinead pushed him gently off her. "I've got to go home now. I'm exhausted." She kissed him one more time, deeply on the mouth, enjoying his unending passion for her, tasting him in her mouth for just one more time.

It really was the last kiss she would ever give him.

"Now I really have to go."

"Thanks for boosting my ego, " he said.

"What on earth do you mean by that?'

"You know what I mean." His eyes were sorrowful. "You think I don't need reassurance. But I'm just like you. I need reassurance all the time. Just like you do."

"Oh, Harry. You don't need anybody to boost your ego for you."

She turned away.

"Do you know where you are going to?"

"I'll find out."

"Sinead. You're very precious."

She turned around. "Goodbye, Harry." She blew a kiss, and turned again to walk away.

"Sinead – you look so beautiful!"

But she was waving at a taxi. She turned again to Harry just before getting in.

She looked at him, just standing there. He was still awfully cute, even when he was completely drunk like that. But she knew then, for the first time, and with the deepest sense of relief, that she could live the rest her life without him now.

Chapter 22

In the week before the *Playboy's* opening night, Isabella took a bus downtown to see Ground Zero. In the balmy mid-September heat, the crater of the Twin Towers swept like a gap-toothed smile before her: a concrete hollow in the gums of old Manhattan. Isabella stood at the viewing platform, and watched bulldozers buzzing up and down like electric toys. She felt like a bizarre voyeur, watching through a security fence, as though spying on a prison. Except that the site that she viewed was actually a graveyard.

The re-construction site is a *reincarnation*, Isabella thought. All around her the traffic and the everyday noises of New York screamed. There was no atmosphere of peace.

She turned to examine the faces in the photographs on the notice board and read the prayers and messages of the bereaved, and inspected the memoriae. The messages were heart-breaking.

There was just one other person there, browsing all the public notices, reading everything intently as if memorising for an exam. Isabella couldn't help noticing him out of the corner of one eye, as he carefully and methodically read every single public notice, and studied the messages of condolence as if they were written to him personally. He was a tall black man, with neat short hair. He wore a pair of mirrored sunglasses, and was holding a black baseball cap in one hand. There was a clean, freshly folded look about his clothing: his smooth beige chinos, navy blue soft shoes, and pinstriped polo shirt, tucked in over a very flat tummy.

Unlike most of Eddie's friends whose smooth flat tummies and Michelangelo arms sang of a lifetime of protein shakes and the gym, there was something very *natural* about this man's slimness, and his lithe, supple build. Even as he stood still, he was like a swift, cautious animal. A cheetah. A gazelle.

He turned round to face her suddenly, and she jumped in fright.

"Aaaahhh! You scared me!" Isabella laughed.

"My sincere apologies."

Americans are so polite. "That's all right."

He smiled. "Looks bigger than you expect it to, doesn't it?" He waved his head to indicate the viewing area, and the chasm that plunged into the earth a thousand feet below.

Isabella turned to look away and said vaguely, half to herself, and half by way of a reply, "I don't know really. I don't think I know what I expected."

"I guess I expected it to be more *tragic,* somehow."

Isabella thought about this for a moment. More tragic.

The way that he had said it, it was a beautiful word. And a lot of Americans might have said, *Don't it,* rather than *doesn't it*, she thought. *Doesn't it* sounded strangely formal from an American. Almost foreign. She looked sideways at the handsome stranger now again.

"Yes. So did I. I expected it to be much quieter. More like a war cemetery. Less like a building site."

"A building site with tourism."

"And that's the strange part. It's only two years ago, since the buildings were right here, but it feels as though it's been like this forever."

"An accident waiting to happen?"

"Do you believe that?"

He laughed. "Do you?"

"God, I don't know." She looked away again and thought about it.

"I don't believe conspiracy theories," she eventually said. "But I have to confess I don't believe a lot of what we've been told about all this . . ." She stopped, stuck now for words. It was difficult to speak about *all this*. She was having the first real conversation she had had about the war, with an American, since arriving here. "This *situation*," she finally concluded.

"This, specifically?" he waved his hand again. "Or . . . ?"

Isabella looked away again. "I'm not American," she replied quietly. She was being cautious now. "But I am against the war. And, this was such a terrible thing to happen to any country too. But now I just want it all to stop. And watching this here today just makes me feel even worse about Iraq, Afghanistan, and all of that. I hope you don't support President Bush?"

She looked at him, feeling awkward now for having *mentioned the war.* But it was impossible to think of anything else. The Presidential elections were only weeks away. New York was full of democrats canvassing on the streets. The TV stations were broadcasting nothing but smear rumours about Kerry's record, polls, predictions and commentary. Most American's *didn't* like to talk about the war, she had noticed that all right. But some things can't be left unsaid.

"I've just come back from Iraq."

He pronounced it Eye-Rack.

Isabella said nothing. She suddenly felt very lost and quite alone. The tall man was behind his mirrored sunglasses, and he had just been to Eye Rack, and she didn't know what for, and now she had done the unthinkable in America and criticised the war.

"How come you are here, today, looking at all this?"

"Same as you, I guess. Curious. I wanted to pay my respects to the dead. Wanted to see what a couple of pilots can do with a couple of commercial airplanes on a nice September morning, that can start up a war like the one I've just been in."

"In Iraq?"

"That's right." He paused. "But I'm home now"

"I see," said Isabella.

"Sope Jordan."

He removed his mirrored glasses, to reveal one very large, deep and beautiful brown eye. The right one. Where the other eye might have been there was a fastened socket, a buttoned-up fold of puffy-looking skin, with a few lashes growing out of it like spikes. She tried very hard to pin her gaze onto the good eye, rather than the puffed-up folds on the left side of his face. It was very difficult, realised Isabella, to look at a person in the *eye*, rather than in the *eyes*. She felt lopsided and uncomfortable, as if she had lost a part of her sight herself.

He put out his hand to her, and she placed her tiny white one in his large brown one and they shook, and smiled at one other.

"Isabella Somerfield."

"Beautiful."

She blushed.

"Pardon my appearance." He grinned at her.

"Is it a . . . war wound?"

"Something like that. It's better with the glasses on, I know."

"It's nice to see your face though," she smiled at him. "Um, did you say your name is *Soap*?" She tried hard to maintain a serious expression as she asked him this. Americans did tend to have names that sometimes sounded more like household objects, or verbs, than real people. She thought of other Americans she'd met: Chip, Parker, Porter, Skate. Rob had brought home a friend last night called Skip. He hadn't been amused when Eddie told him that in Ireland skip was what they called a giant trashcan.

But Soap – that was one set of parents with a sense of humour, she decided.

"It's S–O–P–E. It's a nickname," he shrugged. "But, hey, it's what's stuck. My parents called me Jack. But I've been called Sope ever since school. It's a long story."

"I've got plenty of time."

She couldn't believe what she had just said. Here, standing at the site of the Twin Towers, telling a complete stranger who only had one eye in his head that she had plenty of time to spend with him. *Jesus Christ, what am I doing at all?* she thought. But after her last phone call to Ruth she'd promised to quit moping over Harry. And Eddie hadn't stopped nagging at her yet. So. Nothing ventured.

"You hungry?" Sope asked.

"Starving!" she beamed at him.

"In that case," he told her, "I know a great hot-dog stand."

Until now, she had avoided the New York Subway altogether. Unlike subways in London and Paris where she had been before, New York's stations were like big dungeons underground, with their dim lighting, steel girders and sinister platforms on both sides of the tracks. The passing trains sent hot gusts of air up to the streets above that felt like dragons' breath. There was a feeling of being in a grave as soon as one went underground. There were dark shadows everywhere, and a menacing feeling to it all. The steel pillars that propped up the roof obscured the views along the platforms and turned the place into a sort of maze. And she had never been able to get on the right train, going in the right direction, and stopping at the right stops. But Sope seemed to know exactly what he was doing. And in the middle of the mid-September working day, their carriage as they rolled through Brooklyn was almost empty.

"Where do you live – in New York?"

"No. Just passing through. But I got family here, up town and in the Bronx, and I just like this train ride out to Brooklyn. I find it therapeutic by the sea. What about your story? What are *you* doing in New York?"

Isabella sighed. "Lots of reasons really. Mainly work. I'm in a play. We are opening this week, as a matter of fact. And I'm the leading role. Pegeen Mike, in the *Playboy of the Western World*. You should come," she smiled.

"The Playboy of the *what*? That sounds like . . . er . . ." Sope shook his head, and tut-tutted.

She laughed. "It's got nothing at all to do with Huge Heffner, if that's what you're thinking. It's a very famous Irish play about a woman who falls for a man that she thinks is a hero because he tells her that he killed his father. But when it turns out that his father is still alive, all the villagers turn on him, and so does she. And so she drives him away, and then regrets it immediately because she's lost the only man she ever loved."

"And then?"

"And that's the end of the play, I'm afraid" Isabella laughed. "It's − I suppose it's a bit symbolic really. Revolution and patriarchy, conservativism and rebellion, and − oh, all sorts of things like that. The idiocy of rural life, the evil of gossip, the myth of fidelity, the curse of misplaced loyalty, honesty, heroism, patriotism, morality − all that kind of stuff . . ." She waved her hand round in the air and let her voice trail off.

Sope laughed at her miming. "Patriotism, heroism, and morality? That sounds like heavy shit. And you're the heroine?"

"Yes, I am. Only she's an unfortunate heroine, because she comes to a tragic end. Do you believe in patriotism?"

"I believe that it can come to a very tragic end."

"Tell me all about Iraq."

They were over ground now, and chugging past the back yards of the flat-built Brooklyn suburbs.

"Do you really want to know? It's not nice stuff."

She lowered her voice. "Is that where you lost your eye?"

"Well, I didn't pluck it out. I might be a bit crazy after all the wars, but King Oedipus I ain't."

Isabella smiled. "I'm sorry. But I can't help being curious. You must know a lot that we don't know, about the war. I mean, the people who just sit at home and watch TV and read about it in the papers. I told you I'm against it. But you must have a very different point of view to me. I'm a European. Don't you? See it differently, I mean?"

Sope looked out of the window at the porches and verandas, at the small suburban gardens, the children's toys and barbeques in back yards.

"What do you know about America?" he asked.

Isabella looked out the window too, at the backs of people's houses.

"I sometimes think that America looks . . . well, almost *humble* sometimes. I mean, compared to Europe. Which is ridiculous, I know. But the people here seem to be so much humbler now than when I came over here before. And that's something that I never expected I would find."

"The people who live backed onto railroad tracks are rarely in the upper class," Sope smiled.

"Yeah, I know." She watched the backs of houses and apartment buildings again, noticing the small differences in people's yards. The accumulation of junk in one. The painstakingly tended garden in another. The peeling window frames, next door to spotless painted porches. The shiny brand-new cars, the broken down and rusting ones.

"I love my country, Isabella," Sope stared at the gardens and the houses with her, "but my country sure doesn't love me"

"Why did you join the army?"

"'Cause that's what black people do to get to college."

Isabella didn't really understand. But she decided not to ask.

"People just don't really understand what is going on," she said, "what soldiers have to do, what kinds of things are really happening." She dropped her voice down to a murmur. "What really happens in those bombings and those air-raids on Iraq – surely you know what I mean?"

He looked at her. "The thing is, I'm not going back into the army, Isabella. I have been honourably discharged. I can't fly a plane or drive no more now, and I need a lot more surgery. But I wouldn't have gone back anyway. Even if I was in perfect shape, I wouldn't have spent another day in active service. I went over to Iraq believing that we needed to. I believed that the invasion would be short and sweet; a quick success. Operation Shock and Awe, remember."

Isbella nodded. Of course she could remember. Harry had been glued to it for months. Sope carried on.

"We thought that we were doing the right thing by

going out there; we wanted to take out Saddam, bring some freedom to Iraq. But we learnt the hard way that there was a lot of stuff they were not telling us. We were killing kids and babies out there too, you know. I went out because it was the right thing to do for my country. I signed up for that. But I had to learn a lot the hard way."

He gazed out the window again, his voice dwindling to a mumble in the rattle of the train. Isabella strained to listen. He spoke so softly it was almost as if he were speaking to himself.

"People killing people – I volunteered for all that shit. I didn't even think about it. It's just an enemy force you're dealing with. A kind of abstract enemy. You're scared all the time, and homesick. You've got to see your buddies die; people that you love."

Isabella nodded. She just stayed quiet, listening to him speak. It was as if he was rolling out the words from memory.

"Liberation, that's the word they use," Sope looked at her. "But it's become like the American word for death now, liberation. You can't tell the difference when you just go on a raid. We just killed whatever enemy we thought we had found."

He seemed to sense the shock she felt.

"You blow up a building, or a suspect car," he explained more quietly, "and if there's a family inside, the family dies. End of story. It's all pretty random, war, you know." He turned away from her and looked out of the window again. "They say the weaponry is smart, that the intelligence is smart – but they tell a lot of lies. Bomb scares, intelligence, weapons of mass destruction, and so much more bullshit."

Sope shook his head and laughed a small, humourless laugh.

"Have you killed someone?" Isabella asked him quietly. In the rattle of the train and the emptiness of their carriage, she knew that nobody would hear.

Sope nodded and looked at her with a pained expression.

"I killed a few people in my life. But I'm not going to kill any more. I don't want that ever to happen again, and whatever I can do to stop it now, I will."

"What do you mean – what you can do to stop it?" Isabella whispered. Although they were alone at one end of a very empty carriage, she still felt that what Sope was saying sounded somehow very private.

Sope shrugged. "I don't know yet. Join with other military families. The mothers of servicemen who were lost in Iraq are forming a support group. There are conscientious objectors here too, and in Canada, who've gone AWOL from the army. People need to know the truth. The President is gonna change, but America needs to change too."

"Won't you get into trouble?"

Sope pointed at his missing eye. "Do you think I look like the kind of guy who's afraid of trouble?" he smiled at her.

"You think Kerry will win the election?"

"There's no doubt. There's no way, after what that war has done to the American nation, that Bush could get back into the White House one more time. But the Democrats won't stop the war, you know."

Isabella nodded. Then she remembered something important.

"There was a long story about . . . soap?" she asked.

He grinned at her. "Over lunch."

The subway opened up onto a dismal street. Hot and filthy, shops and businesses on the opposite side were peeling and half-painted. There was an overall feeling of mild decay at the junction where they paused to cross the road. Unlike Manhattan, there were very few people walking here. And those who did were old, or seemed to Isabella to be ill, or disabled, or feeble in some way. Old women hobbling along with shopping trolleys and old trainers; bone-thin ankles underneath a flowered skirt.

But they could catch the scent of the sea. Sope strode happily across a busy street towards the opposite corner from the subway, and Isabella chased after him.

Nathan's was a large yellow and green-painted seaside hot-dog restaurant, and she liked the look of it. It was jolly; clean looking, and what Eddie would have called *retro*, with a long queue at every counter. Isabella read the menu carefully while Sope got into line, but the queue moved much quicker than she expected and so she had to make her mind up suddenly. Sope ordered a large chilli dog with fries. And so Isabella ordered shrimp. It seemed somehow to be slightly more sea-sidey than a *dog*. They took their meals over to a picnic bench outside the cafe, in an area of wooden deck and outdoor seating and sat down opposite each other.

"Now that we are eating – and this is, I take it, officially lunch – why were you nicknamed *Sope?* You have to tell me now."

Sope wiped his mouth, and offered her some ketchup. Isabella shook her head.

"I grew up near Austin, Texas, went to a pretty much all-white grade school. My mother's idea. She didn't care a bit if we were the only black kids there – she just wanted us well-educated. And I got on fine. I was smart enough and I knew how to stay out of trouble. But I felt under pressure from day one to really prove myself. I was smart *enough*. But always scared of not being *seen* to be smart enough." He took a big firm bite from his hot-dog, and Isabella watched him as he chewed. "So," he carried on, "I used to borrow books. I borrowed tons of library books, and read as much as possible. My mom took us to the library every Tuesday, and we brought home books to read. And when I was eight, I borrowed this great book called *Theban Plays*, by an ancient Greek writer called Sophocles."

Isabella guffawed and almost spat out shrimp. "When you were *eight*? That's outrageous! What was wrong with *Huckleberry Finn*?" She laughed out loud again.

"Ah. I thought *The Theban Plays* might be a book about heroes. Macho stuff. Turns out, I was right. I didn't understand a lot about the plays. Only then we had to bring a book into school and tell the class about our favourite story. So, I told them that my favourite story was King Oedipus, by Sophocles. Only *I* thought that he was called Sope-Hercules. And the teacher tried to tell me that I'd got his name wrong, and so everyone laughed, and they called me Sope from then on. But after a few years, I kind of got to like it. It was like a link with this Greek guy, who wrote the plays, and with all the heroes of the ancient world. I suppose I kind of liked the idea that even though you could be a mythological character in classical Greece, you still had all that personal shit to deal with. It had really stuck with me. And there it is."

Sope returned to munching his fries and grinned at her as he sipped his coke. In the shade of afternoon sunshine they smelt the sea behind them. Isabella felt, for some unknown reason, extremely comfortable here. She had no idea how far they were from the East Village, or SoHo, or Broadway and Fourteenth. How far Coney Island was from the island of Manhattan, she couldn't even hazard a guess. But she felt happy and at ease, with this strange, rather *intellectual* one-eyed vet. For a man who has spent a lot of time killing people, Isabella thought, he seems to be as gentle as could be. She had got used to the strange one-eyed face, and was finding it quite beautiful to look at now. Sope was very confident and very proud. She felt secure with him.

She suddenly noticed that a homeless man, a tramp, was hovering around their picnic table, keeping a very beady eye on their food. Isabella felt uncomfortable again, and wished that he would go away. Sope was unperturbed and carried on chattering, asking her about Ireland, about the play, unaware of the presence of the homeless man who was on his blind side.

Isabella coughed, and tried to point the homeless man out to Sope, without actually appearing to point. She rolled her eyes around madly in her head and gesticulated with her shoulders.

But the man immediately sat down on the picnic bench beside them and Isabella stiffened up, not sure how to proceed.

Sope was still oblivious. The homeless man carried on staring at the food that Isabella was nibbling. She had always been a slow and troubled eater, and the shrimp, although delicious, were far too many. And she had been picking away at a handful of Sope's fries at the same time.

The man continued to stare at her, and at each mouthful of food as she lifted it to her mouth with her fingers. Isabella felt like a laboratory experiment. It was hideously uncomfortable. She tried to motion one more time to Sope with her eyes, to ask the man to leave, but Sope just chatted on and on, and didn't seem to mind the man sitting beside them, scrutinising their food as if he had never seen people eat before, whatsoever.

Perhaps he simply couldn't see enough of the man with his one seeing eye.

But then the man spoke, and Sope could not be unaware of him by now.

"Hurry up and finish that!" the man hissed at Isabella.

She looked up, shocked, and stopped her nibbling. She wasn't sure what to do. Should she offer him some food? Or walk away? Or shoo him away? The hobo continued to grumble at her.

"You are too slow. Too slow. Hurry up. Finish it up now. Hurry up. Too slow. Too slow."

He wore a shabby winter coat, despite the hot September day, and he smelt just like a dustbin. His hands were filthy, black underneath the fingernails, and cracked with dirt. Unshaven, he had long grey hair like wire, underneath a crumpled baseball cap.

Isabella wasn't sure whether or not to feel afraid. He seemed to be so powerless, if not entirely harmless. But he was really pestering her now. The smell of him was unbearable. His dirt was nauseating.

261

Sope, grinning over at Isabella, asked the man. "You want me to get you some food today, buddy?"

"*Hurry up and finish that!*" the old man insisted again, poking a finger into Isabella's fries.

"Here!" She pushed them over to him, enraged. "That's it. You can have them all! We're leaving now!"

"Okay, let's go." Sope, who had finished eating earlier, got up with her. He seemed surprised at her lack of patience.

She walked away, ashamed, taking just her drink with her.

"You were scared of him?"

"I don't know. It was so intrusive. I didn't want him to be hungry, but I felt so intimidated by him staring at my food. And he was *complaining* that I was eating it too slowly, that was what I found really odd. It was as if he was expecting me to leave some scraps for him, and he was worried that I was eating so slowly that I would let it all go cold."

"That's probably right!" Sope laughed. "That's probably what he was afraid of. But my question is; why were you so scared of him?"

"Yes. I suppose I was." She turned to look at him. "How ridiculous is that? To be afraid of someone as humble as that man; a poor old man who has absolutely nothing to threaten me at all with, except his hunger?"

Sope shrugged. "I guess that's the reason everybody gets scared. The hungrier other people get, the more they terrify us with their hunger."

The old man was still muttering to himself at their table.

America is such a crazy place, thought Isabella. Crazy, terrible, wonderful.

"Sope, how did you lose your eye?" she finally asked, as they strolled along the boardwalk.

He walked beside her with his true eye on her side. "It sort of was my fault."

"How? What happened to you?"

"We were in the middle of a sandstorm and we were ordered to go into Fallujah, north of Baghdad, to take the city out. There was a strong enemy insurgence there, and the US army wanted to get it under their control. There were ambushes and fire-fights. A free fire zone was ordered. We knew the people would try to get back out. They had no food. Their gunmen had to get supplies. Plenty of our men got hurt. And the dead Iraqis were lying on the streets for days. We were shooting everything that moved. There was a burnt-out car that people had been hiding in. We didn't know they were there, but we had it in our sites. They were hiding in it for days. And when they thought all the shooting had stopped, they came out and they tried to get away. It was a woman and her child, maybe eight years old. When you look down the barrel of a gun, you can make out their eyes. I just went crazy then, I guess. When we got back to camp I took a car out into the desert and I just drove and drove away: to get away from all that patriotism stuff you mentioned. It was just a nightmare. People killing people. That's when I knew that what was happening in Iraq had gone all wrong. And so I drove into the desert, on my own, and the car hit a pothole. Some blast hole that a US bomber had left there for me, and, well, the car took a tumble off the road, I guess. I went into a spin, off the track, car spun upside down. I though that I would probably die and I guess I didn't really care that much about it too. But then I didn't die, because in the morning two Iraqi women driving by in their car found me lying out there, unconscious and my leg was broke and blood all over, and the windscreen smashed." He pointed to his missing eye. "And they called for help, they got the US military to come out and get me back to base, to the hospital. Two Iraqi women. Two days earlier I had been killing the Iraqis but what do those two women do when they find a blacked-out American covered in blood coming out of a car wreck in the middle of the desert? They could have laughed and drove away, but they called for help. So here I am."

Isabella put her hand up to his face, and placed it gently where his eye was meant to be.

"So now I know I'll never look down the barrel of a gun at another human face and pull the trigger. And maybe that's okay."

They talked very little on the the journey back into Manhattan, quietly punctuating the silence here and there. She felt at ease. More so than ever she could have imagined that she might have felt only just a few days before an opening night.

"This has been a brilliant idea, coming out to the seaside today," she smiled at him. "Thank you so much, Sope, for such a lovely day. I needed to relax. The show is opening in three days time, and I've been such a bag of nerves."

"Yeah, the show. That'll be a big night, huh? And I'll be leaving New York City too this week."

Sope spoke dreamily, and her breath caught in her chest.

"I . . . " Isabella closed her mouth again.

I what?

 I wish you didn't have to go?

You can't say that kind of thing to a complete stranger. But.

She opened up her mouth to speak again.

"What?" he asked her.

She turned to look out of the window at the brown apartment blocks that flocked the railway line.

"Sope, before you go, I wonder if there is any chance you might be able to come to the opening night? Of the play. On Thursday. It's just that I don't really have anybody else here in New York who is going to be there for me." She swallowed, and then met his eyes. "And it's bad luck not to have someone in the audience opening night," she added.

Sope's mouth began to curl into a slow lazy smile. "Well, I sure don't want to bring the play bad luck." His mouth broke into a grin, white white teeth that teased her solemness.

"Then you'll come?" she said, trying hard to hide her anxiety.

"To the theatre? To see your play? *The Non-Pornographic Playboy of Western Patriarchy*?"

Isabella giggled. "I do know other people here, you know, but they are all Eddie or Rob's friends. And so there won't be anybody in the audience on opening night who's just *my* friend. Someone who's just there for me. And that, well, that could ruin the whole show. We could get terrible reviews. We might have to close after just four nights, you know."

Sope was chuckling.

"So, if you're still in New York, well, then that would be great," she finished.

"Well, then I'll come," he said.

"You'll come?" She couldn't help beaming at him now.

"I'll be there."

"Well! Sope, that's just great! I can leave a ticket at the door for you!" In sudden excitement she had clasped his hand. The sudden intimacy of strangers. A warm male hand in hers. Steel tendons and smooth fingernails. Her heartbeat and the rattle of the train. He kissed her fingers.

Isbella felt her face slowly and conspicuously become a fire of purple, but then the train plunged suddenly under-ground and the intermediate yellowing of light disguised her.

"Hey, you know, I can buy my own ticket!"

In the sudden clatter of the underground she just about heard him speak.

"Oh. I didn't mean . . . it's just that we get a free one each for the opening night to give to someone. It helps pad out the audience, to be honest. People often don't want to pay for an opening night – they wait for the reviews before they book a show like ours. So I can leave my free ticket at the box office for you!"

Sope nodded, smiling at her excitement.

"It would be so nice" she added, "to be able to tell that dragon at the box office that I've got someone that I'm leaving a ticket out for."

"Well. In that case," Sope replied, "I couldn't possibly refuse. There's no way I'm going to waste an opportunity to slay a dragon."

"And you'll get to meet Eddie. You'll love him. He's my best friend."

"We have to change trains at the next stop" he replied.

Isabella looked at the plan of the railway line, and at Sope again, and hoped he knew exactly where they were going. The map of the trains made very little sense to her. They seemed to be incapable of intersecting lines; the lines crossed but there was no joining up, as far as she could make out. But Sope seemed pretty confident. She would simply have to trust him to lead the way.

Manhattan trains were just a jumble, she decided, and put her hand out to his as their train squealed into the station.

Sope took her by the hand and skipped off the train, marching her at a jaunty pace through the elbows and briefcases towards their uptown train. Isabella didn't even know which station she was supposed to get off at to get back to Eddie's, but Sope weaved her confidently along the misery of platforms, in and out of corridors, as happy as a dog on a scent.

Despite the overheated tunnel and the shriek and wheeze of trains, Isabella followed Sope contentedly towards their train, wherever that might be. She battled through the crowded platforms with him, happily letting him lead, her small white hand in his. And then suddenly, he took a staircase at a sprint, and turned sharply to their right.

Leaping two steps at a time Sope flew down the steps

to the approaching train at a hare's pace, towing Isabella behind him. But the station was a throng of hot agresssive commuters, fighting all their way against their direction. And she had to let his hand go, very briefly, because a very tall man with a large paunch burst in between them, breaking their hand-hold, whirling by them down the staircase.

And she ran after him, in the direction that she thought he'd taken, shouting "*Sope!* Please wait for me! Wait!"

And then she saw his head, or was it him? Yes! That was him, just inside the doors of the first carriage of the first train, but there was a giant woman in her way, breasts swaying like sandbags and she had to dodge around her to the train and Sope's carriage doors were closing. And she tried to stop them. And her hand was trapped.

"Hey, lady!" came a sharp voice behind her.

The doors swept open once again. A carriage packed with knees and briefcases and suits but she could not see Sope at all and only her foot would fit onto the floor of the train just before the two doors closed again for the last time. She got her foot out just in time. And he was gone. She couldn't even see him leave; his head, or the head that she had thought was his head had just become a mystery now among a cheerless army of black and white and brown and beige faces in slow motion, still as corpses gliding by.

Isabella wept.

Perhaps it had all been too good to be true after all.

"Do you have any idea how I might get from here to Fourteenth St?" she sniffed to a smooth-looking businessman.

"You *are* on Fourteenth," he told her.

Isabella looked around her. "Oh. So, um, if I go outside of this station, can I find Fourteenth? Because that's my street." She checked his face again to see if he had heard her.

"That's what I said." He took out his newspaper.

So where on earth had Sope gone?

"Sir, I'm sorry to bother you, but do you know where that train that has just left is going?"

"That train is going to Brooklyn. Because it says so *on the sign*," he said carefully, before turning away in what Isabella assumed to be pity.

Oh God, Isabella sobbed to herself again. Sope *has* got on the wrong train after all. He probably can't *see properly*. He's going back to bloody Brooklyn!

Let me out of this hell-hole of an underground maze.

Eventually she found the exit, and discovered herself to be on Sixth Avenue, at the junction of Fourteenth.

With her head bent deep in a whirlwind of the afternoon's memory, she walked the remaining seven cross-town blocks home.

Chapter 23

On the last day before the opening night Isabella sat with Eddie in the kitchen eating pizza from a box and drinking root beer. Isabella had been feeling nervous during the dress rehearsal earlier that day, but Eddie was all giggly and relaxed, and so she couldn't see the point of worrying any more. Isabella knew that Eddie was normally a bag of nerves just before a show. He would be petrified of a bad review, or a dud performance from a leading role. But tonight he was really having fun. Isabella had noticed that his impetuous behaviour, which normally drove Rob into a seething sulk when he had had enough of it, was much easier to handle now if she could tease him out of it. And Rob was less likely to feel exasperated by Eddie's neurotic ranting before an opening night if Isabella was there to giggle with him and yell at Eddie to shut up, and slap the two of them across the wrists with rolled-up newspaper when they couldn't stop.

The dress rehearsal had been a dream. Eddie's

directions included as much opportunity for humour as possible. He had decided to cast a man as Widow Quinn, much to Isabella's initial doubt as she felt that it was turning the whole play into a send-up. But Gabriel from Offaly, the actor who was playing Widow Quinn with a strong midlands accent, had brought a rather sexy ambiguity to the part that was working brilliantly. And the cast adored him.

"Gabriel plays the part like a Manhattan Meatpacking drag queen who's been left in the bog too long," Eddie had giggled at the beginning of rehearsals, and Isabella could sense from the shocked snorts of laughter in the tiny audience at the dress-rehearsal, just how good the idea of cross-dressing Widow Quinn had been.

"I met a man, the other day," she told Eddie, chewing on a mouthful of extra low-fat crust.

"Oh my God! You didn't! Fantastic, Iz. What kind of man? Who are his *people*?" Eddie asked, dropping his tone to a growl for the word *people*.

"I don't know if he has any people." Isabella grinned, wiping mozzarella off her lips. "He's a soldier."

"Action Man!" Eddie yelped, visualising his taut, green-uniformed childhood doll, complete with gleaming plastic pecs. "Darling, how erotic!" He twirled around the kitchen in delight. "But where on earth did you meet this *soldier*? What have you been doing? Hanging around the queue to join the US Army in Times Square trying to pick up men?"

Isabella whacked him with a newspaper.

"There is no queue to join the US army in Times Square. There is hardly a handful. It's not that popular any more, believe it or not. Something about the bodies coming home that's putting people off. No, I met him at the 9/11."

"You mean the Seven Eleven, Pegeen. Sure, it's true for you, Pegeen Mike – there's never been the like of you in all of Ireland! And you beyond in *Amerrrica* now!" he mocked her, Synge-style.

"No! I mean the – the Ground Zero. The site of the bombing of the Twin Towers. I went to have a look. I wanted to see what it was like. And he was there, looking at it too. And so we started talking. And – well, that's all really, Eddie . . . " She let her voice trail off, and began to pick the olives off another slice of pizza. "Actually, you know," she carried on, "it's nothing at all, really, Eddie. I met a stranger, standing around watching the Ground Zero being dug up and rebuilt, and we started talking, and we had a conversation, and he bought me a hot dog, and then I lost him in the subway, and that was it. Nothing really. Only, he was very interesting. He has just come back from Iraq." She looked up at him. "He was in the war."

Eddie's eyebrows shot up.

She carried on. "And now he's lost his eye. That was an accident. But he was honourably discharged. So he's come to New York now to say goodbye to America, and he's going to live in Canada. Because he can't go back to the army, or the war."

Eddie was standing silently now, while she rattled on. He watched her as she spoke. *Holy crap,* Eddie thought. This is heavy stuff she's getting into just before the opening night.

Isabella had stopped talking and was sitting quietly on her stool, cradling a beer in her hands. She stared at the remaining pizza, saying nothing.

"What's his name?" Eddie eventually asked her.

"Sope," Isabella smiled.

Eddie coughed. "I won't ask," he said.

"It's short for Sophocles."

"Like I said – Sophocles? Hey, what a fantastic name." Eddie became dreamy for a minute.

Isabella watched him drift off into another fantasy. She knew that he was picturing Greek statues.

"Can you write to him?" he eventually asked.

She shook her head. "I think that everything he told me is probably a secret. You wouldn't speak out about the US army like that, would you? I mean, Sophocles isn't even his real name, you know," she added.

"No kidding," Eddie replied.

It did seem almost like a crazy dream now, she realised, when one considered the possibility that she didn't even know the man's real name. He had told her, but she had altogether forgotten. It was all a bit like a bizarre, unreal, but beautiful dream.

"It sounds like a nightmare." Eddie sat down on the other stool, and stared at Isabella.

"What does?"

"The story. Of the soldier. How very odd, that he told you all that, just a stranger on the street. Do you think it's true?"

"Yes. Actually I do. Why on earth would anyone make something like that up? We talked a long time. Ages and ages. We went to Coney Island. He likes this hot–dog restaurant there, and we walked along the boardwalk, and on the beach, and we talked for hours. Perhaps he needed to tell somebody who wouldn't mind. A stranger. From another land. Perhaps he needed to be able to tell the truth to someone who would actually believe in him."

"It's all we ever want, darling, isn't it?" Eddie sighed. "To have something to believe in."

"But Eddie, I've invited him to the opening tomorrow night . . . except then I lost him on the train. And now I'm not sure if he'll even come . . . I guess the truth is that I'll probably never see him again." She picked up the cold flabby pizza slice again, and nibbled at it.

Eddie sat silently for a moment.

"Stage left or stage right?" he suddenly said.

"What?"

"The missing eye," said Eddie, in all solemnity.

"Oh!" Isabella smiled a tiny smile. "Stage left, I think."

"Good." Eddie nodded sagely at her. "Because all your action is stage right, so at least he'll get to see you."

Chapter 24

The opening night had finally arrived.

Isabella sat calmly in front of her dressing mirror which was like a daisy with light bulbs for petals, painting on her face. She had a dark-stain lipstick for Pegeen Mike.

"Tight, hard West of Ireland lips," Eddie had told her, and she pouted her small mouth into a meaner shape to pencil it.

It was the first time in her life that she had done such a big part and she still didn't know if *anybody* would be there in the audience just for her.

"So toughen up, big girl. Showbusiness is full of cruelty," Eddie had said to her, giving her a little hug when she had mentioned it earlier.

And he was right of course, Isabella thought. Big deal if I'm out there speaking to a house of strangers. Rob will be here, rooting for us anyway. The worst thing that will happen is that we won't make ticket sales — not that I won't be able to shine for someone. It's not the flipping school show any more. Here I am, off Broadway, a leading role in one of the most important dramas in literary history. This *rules*! Isabella pulled a mean face at herself again, and giggled at her reflection.

She decided to practise her *stare* again, and then frowned and looked surprised and frowned again to make sure her make-up couldn't crease.

Eddie had wanted her to leave her wild hair loose around her shoulders like a banshee, but Costume had advised otherwise and so she began to twist her long coils of hair up into the loose long plait that she would secure with pins and half a can of hairspray. Just outside the dressing room the uileann piper who was going to play intermezzo music was noisily tuning up.

Isabella loved this moment – the last half hour of quiet introspection before a drama burst onto stage. She loved the jangling nerves, the fiddling with zips that wouldn't budge, the hems that had suddenly come down, shoes that had seemed to fit at dress rehearsal now causing corns. She breathed in slowly through her nostrils, soaking up the smell of grease and make-up, dust and mould and hairspray while she practiced her Alexander Technique, and rested her hair slowly to one side, then the other, gently easing out her neck.

Eddie knocked and stuck his head around the door. The auditorium was half-full already, and there were another fifteen minutes to go before curtain. He gave her a confident thumbs-up and she went to high-five him, missing his hand completely because her palms were all slippery with make-up and almost slapped him on the nose.

"It's break a leg, Pegeen, not break my nose!" Eddie backed away from her in fright and winked before he closed the door. "Don't forget the group hug before curtain. Meet you in the corridor in five."

Whether or not Sope turned up, she was going to cherish the memory of this play forever.

Isabella's lines were the first the audience would hear. She wanted them to be perfect. At first, her voice sounded stranger than she could have imagined in her head, all muffled out into the packed theatre, and so she spoke her lines even more slowly to make sure she could project.

"Six yards of stuff for to make a yellow gown. A pair of lace boots with lengthy heels on them and brassy eyes. A hat suited for a wedding-day."

The theatre had two parts to the arrangement of the audience, one larger main body in front of the stage, and the other smaller wing of audience at right angles. "Like a half-arsed Irish version of an amphitheatre," Eddie had explained. But Isabella felt this made things easier as she could speak with her back turned to one half of the audience and still be seen by the other.

Eddie had worked hard to coordinate the choreography of the to-and-fro moving about stage that the actors needed to do to get the most out of the space, and now with real live people sitting in every single seat it was an absolute joy to pace about the stage. She spoke out her lines at Christy, relishing the intimacy of the theatre even though, in her concentration, she couldn't see the expressions on the audience's faces. But she knew from the still atmosphere in the theatre that the action was being lapped up.

The scene between Widow Quinn and Christy at the end of Act II was almost homoerotic, Isabella thought.

"I am your like!" The Widow twirled around and teased Christy. *"And it's for that I'm taking a fancy to you, and I with my little houseen above where there'd be myself to tend you, and none to ask were you a murderer or what at all!"*

Even though Isabella had been worried that it would irritate theatre purists, there was no doubt in her mind as she sneaked a peek from the wings before the interval, that the naked suggestiveness of Eddie's idea for cross-dressing Widow Quinn had added intrigue to the scene and it was exhilarating.

During the interval Eddie was trying to remain cool. He was snowed under with clipboards and problems: the uileann piper had come in at the wrong time, cutting into Christy's most important soliloquy and poor Gabriel from Offaly was now furiously smoking a cigarette outside the stage door convinced that the piper had ruined the entire night. Eddie snapped at Gabriel to calm the fuck down and stop ruining his voice with bloody smoke, and so Gabriel gave Eddie the fingers.

Isabella sat in the dressing room and fixed the thick plait of her mass of hair just one more time and drank some warm water with lemon and ginger, sucking on an orange from the bowl that Rob had sent for them. There was a tiny bunch of lilacs and a card from Rob on the fruit bowl that said: *"Break both of your legs, both at the same time, both of you!"*

Suddenly, more than anything in the world, she wanted to ring Harry.

Now, with just ten minutes to curtain for the second half of opening night, for the first time in over two months she most desperately wanted to speak to him. To tell him that she was actually okay. That the show was going really well. That she wasn't angry with him any more. That everything was going to be all right now. She didn't even know what time it was in Ireland. Sometime in the past. *America is West, so we are in the future, Ireland's in the past*, was how Eddie had explained it to her.

She jumped up and started hunting frantically round the backstage area, looking for Gabriel who she knew would have a mobile phone on him.

"Gabriel, have you got your cell phone?" she asked the Widow Quinn.

"In my man-bag, honey, but don't be long. Stagehand's just called ten minutes to curtain."

Eddie was gathering them around in the corridor for the group hug; she would have to wait. They stood with their arms around each other while Ed gave them their pep talk, and Isabella burned with impatience. Before the first half, she had loved Eddie for doing this. *But now, for God's sakes, get on with it!* she thought.

"You've all worked incredibly hard."

Eddie was bloody rambling!

"And I'm incredibly proud of all of you. I love you all. Gabriel, I love the fact that you haven't been upset about the music and your acting is superb. The show is wonderful; and you are all brilliant. Now let's go back on stage and give it socks. Group hug!"

And they hugged each other dutifully.

Gabriel went outside to light another fag.

It took her half a minute to remember how long the code was for Ireland. She prodded furiously at the keypad, got the sequence wrong two times, and then at last the call was through. The phone rang. Eight rings she let it ring, and all the time she held her breath. And then she let it ring until she heard the answering machine click on with her own voice on it.

He had never changed it.

He wanted it to feel as though she still lived there.

Isabella switched off Gabriel's mobile phone and stared at her reflection.

"Two minutes to curtain, Isabella."

She heard the brisk knock on the door, but it sounded miles away.

She patted her weave of thick black hair one more time, and breathed her shoulders out before her final scene. In the dressing mirror, her eyes were absolutely wild.

The last act of the *Playboy* is where the climax has everybody out on stage. In a theatre suddenly full of noise, Isabella whirled around the others like a dervish, barking out her lines as if she was speaking them for the first time with completely unrehearsed emotions. Christy, one of Eddie's longterm side-dishes, looked positively terrified as Isabella squealed and roared at him.

"It's there your treachery is spurring me, till I'm hard set to think you're the one I'm after lacing in my heart-strings half-an-hour gone by!"

But she couldn't help herself. The anger that she acted for Pegeen and Christy, for the Widow Quinn and Shawn Keogh had become real. Eddie had always directed her to the back of the stage for her final lines so that she would come forward, letting the onstage crowd part as Shawn Keogh approaches her. Shawn Keogh would nudge her slyly, with a sarcastic reminder of their promised marriage, and she would push his face away from her and then pull a shawl over her head. Frustration followed by humility, Eddie had instructed. Her lament is like a prayer up to heaven, he'd decided.

But tonight she did no such thing.

To Eddie's horror Isabella slapped Shawn Keogh wildly across the mouth, sending him into a complete spin, and marched out to the centre of the stage where she stood like a mad thing. She waited for what seemed like ages, terrifying Eddie into wondering if she'd suddenly blanked. *She's in the wrong place! She must have frozen . . .* but he knew *that* was impossible. There was only one line left in the entire play.

Eddie steadied himself, and waited for her to speak.

Isabella covered her face with her hands briefly, just long enough for the rest of the cast to begin to look embarrassed at the sudden silence.

But the audience were on the edges of their seats to see what she would say.

And then she burst into tears.

"*Oh my grief!*" Isabella sobbed.

Real wet tears bucketed down her face and she covered her tear-soaked face with her hands. The outburst appeared to be so spontaneous that Eddie, from his astonished hiding place in the wings could actually see some of the audience looking around themselves in discomfort. *The leading lady has broken down on stage,* he could almost hear them thinking.

Eddie's face suddenly broke into the broadest grin that he could manage without actually bursting into laughter.

"*I've lost him surely!*" Isabella's howls filled the theatre.

And another ten blocks of Manhattan! Eddie thought to himself in amazement, his mouth open in sheer delight.

The reviews are going to be brilliant now!

Eddie stood open-mouthed while Isabella bawled. Her sorrow filled the theatre like a ghost. He watched the theatre-weary reviewers' faces in the front row crease in fascination. Eddie hugged himself with happiness. Oh, poor Iz, he thought, very slightly guiltily. But what a performance!

"*I've lost the only Playboy –*" Isabella shed more tears, sobbing heartily, and the first two rows of audience dabbed their eyes –"*of the Western World!*"

She didn't stop crying even when the standing ovation had begun. Like a wave the audience rose to their feet, and she could hear the voices, "Bravo!" and all the whistles, but it was all like being in a dream, the audience meant nothing to her now. Her eyes were swimming with fresh tears and although she held hands with Christy and Widow Quinn on either side while they took their bows and curtain calls, she had to keep wiping her eyes with her grubby sleeves.

"Isabella, knock it off, you are spreading snot everywhere!" Gabriel giggled as their heads went down to bow for what they thought would be the very last time. But no. The audience were still on their feet, stamping in applause, whistling for more.

"I'm sorry, Gaybo," Isabella sniffed, and squeezed his hand.

"What the fuck was that about? You sent me flying!"
Shawn Keogh hissed at her from behind Christy.

"I'm sorry too!" Isabella offered him a guilty smile.

"You mad lunatic!" Gabriel giggled, and raised her
hand up high for the audience to cheer her more.

Eddie was standing clapping quietly from the wings,
and Isabella looked over at his face while they stooped
down into their very final bow, and he held her eyes with
his.

"Well, done, sweetie!" Isabella saw him mouth.

The backstage was a cacophany of noise and laughter,
scraping of chairs and furniture, dismantling of props.
Isabella blew her nose long and hard on Gabriel's Aloe
Vera facial wipes and sniffed and laughed all at the same
time, while Eddie hugged her tightly and then scolded
her for ignoring her stage directions.

"Are you going to burst into tears like that every night,
sweetheart? Because my nerves won't stand it for thirteen
weeks running."

"Nah. I'm good, Eds. Thanks for being so sweet. I'll
do it the old way tomorrow and from now on."

"Oh ho, no no no you don't!" Eddie opened his eyes
wide in horror. "The reviewers will be promising real live
tears; you'd better bring 'em on now every single night
for the full run, or there'll be war!"

Rob planted a kiss on the top of her head, and she
laughed at the face he pulled when his lips were met with
sticky spun-glass hair.

"Fantastic show! And well done, honey." He kissed
Eddie on the lips.

And somehow in the middle of all that commotion and the howls of laughter, the giddy jumping up and down of Eddie who was giving an interview to the *Village Voice* and kissing Rob and Isabella at the same time, the rattling of props being taken down, the shouting and her tears, she noticed a familiar face in dark sunglasses standing back from the crowd around the mirrors, waiting in the corridor with a small pink bouquet in his hand.

It was the sort of bouquet that a bride carries at a wedding, all wrapped up in tissue paper with a little stalk to carry underneath.

Isabella rose from the seat where she was removing make-up and turned around to the face that she had seen in the mirror.

"You came! You found the place! It's so great to see you!"

Sope smiled cautiously, looking rather awkward with the flowers.

"Thank you, Sope! Thank you so much!" Isabella took them off him and sniffed the flowers. They smelt of nothing, but she kissed him on the cheek.

"The show was great," he nodded.

"Did you understand all of it? With the Irish accents and everything?" she asked him anxiously.

Sope nodded again and grinned. "It was fun. But I liked the widow best."

Isabella laughed. "Everybody does. Eddie's idea, the drag thing. But I think it really worked somehow."

She stood there in the fluster of the emptying corridor for a moment with him, wondering if she should invite him to the bar with them. But he wouldn't know anybody there except her and Isabella remembered the way Harry would complain about how boring it was to have to go drinking with a bunch of actors who were high as kites on their own show. They wouldn't be able to talk about anything else tonight, and Sope would probably be miserable. On the other hand, Eddie and Rob might actually like to meet *him*.

She glanced about her to see what the others were doing next, but Eddie was still deep in conversation with the *Village Voice,* and Rob was comforting the uileann pipes player with stories about musical clangers he'd experienced in the orchestra at the Met.

And then she looked at Sope. Despite his dark sunglasses and his solid pose, there was suddenly unsuredness. The way his mouth twitched slightly, as if he were saying something silently to himself.

"What about you Sope? Have you got plans; would you like to come with us to the bar or do you . . .?" Isabella cocked her head.

Soped nodded slowly. "Well, maybe I'll just be going on my way."

For the first time, surrounded by the flutter of Eddie's New York friends and the demi-Irish *Playboy* cast she heard his Southern accent.

"Well then, maybe I'll come with you," she replied. She lifted her bouquet to him as if to say cheers, and tapped him on the chin with it. "Come on!" and she took him by the arm.

It was hard to believe that the man who had seemed so coolly confident the day she'd met him now was now so uncomfortable that he couldn't wait to leave the party.

It must be his damaged eye, Isabella thought, and remembered the subway experience.

He's fine when he's on his own with someone, but doesn't want to have to get into a crowd because he can't properly see.

She felt a sudden tenderness towards him. Perhaps that day he *had* been comfortable with her, another stranger on her own, a foreigner in New York trying to figure out the way. But now, Isabella wanted to take his hands, just to reassure him that everything would be all right.

This man isn't used to frailty or imperfection, she thought. He is used to giving orders, taking command, being in control.

"Sope, let's go to a different bar; somewhere we can get a bit of peace from all the show-offs." She gave him her most reassuring smile.

They went to Peter Mc Manus' on 19th.

Isabella drank several beers and ate peanuts while Sope flipped through the juke box. She watched him, happily choosing sixties pop hits and seventies country ballads. They talked very little, content in one another's company. Sope studiously selecting records, Isabella dreaming through each and every line she had spoken that night, playing through the evening over and over again in a blissful retrospection.

Maybe it was the Kris Kristoffersen that did it. Or maybe it was the five and a half, well, almost six beers that she drank. Maybe it was the full moon that sank down over Manhattan, grinning wildly at them out of a cloudless sky while they walked the seventeen-and-a-half blocks home. Or maybe it was the sudden swell of confidence she felt now that the play had finally begun, and she had had someone in the audience who *had* been there for her. But that night for the first time in over thirteen years, Isabella slept with a man who wasn't Harry.

For the first time since she was a teenager, Isabella kissed a mouth that was unknown to her. She smelt new sweat, tasted new skin and touched hair that was insatiably unfamiliar.

"Please, let's leave the light on," she whispered to him, when he reached out to switch it off.

She wanted to see the zebra stripe of her marble white legs and his black ones entwined together like the strange branches of a tree.

His cautious, well-thought-out lovemaking was a complete surprise to her. She was intrigued by his rather gentlemanly dispassion, his almost scientific chivalry. But she was more than made content by it.

For the first time since she had arrived in New York, and for many months before, Isabella slept that night. An incredible deep, deep sleep.

And she knew that in the morning when she heavily awoke to a feeling of great restfulness, Sope Jordan would definitely have gone.

Chapter 25

Isabella had tried not to, but she found that she was spending a considerable amount of time thinking about Sope Jordan. She thought about him every day. As late summer melted into autumn, and a quick chill in the air made her shiver in the evenings, she though of Sope in the far Canadian north, all alone and getting colder.

She seemed to remember that he had told her that he was from Alabama, which she assumed was a very hot place, even in the wintertime.

Or perhaps it was Arkansas he'd said. She couldn't really remember which it was. How infuriating. She tried to hear him say the words, "Alabama" and "Arkansas", but nothing came up. Perhaps she had merely imagined that he had come from Alabama or from Arkansas. Perhaps she had imagined it all. There was no frame of reference. She couldn't ask anyone else. There were no other soldiers coming back from Afghanistan and Iraq walking around talking about it. He had come into her life and left it again just like a ghost.

Isabella shook her dark mop of hair to see if she could shake the memory up again, and quickened her pace, her stare glued to the pavement as she walked. She spent many hours walking, as the evenings came much nearer now, as if to try to hold onto the last possible breath of outdoors before the long icy New York winter fell. She walked seventeen blocks to work, to the theatre, and seventeen blocks home again. On her days off she walked in the evening after supper, usually alone, striding purposefully with her head bent down to keep the pavement always in her view. Isabella bumped into people, trees and lampposts when she walked, but at least she never missed her step along the way.

She saw Sope's face everywhere, and although she tried to make it go away, it was there in every black man she saw. The face was gritty, hard-eyed, almost sad. Most of all it was anxious. She looked and looked at all the other faces that were Sope, and saw the steeled anxiety, the lack of confidence, the being on edge. It was a face that was always having to look over its shoulder. A face that needed eyes in the back of its head. A face that needed to keep secrets. But it was a face that told the truth.

"Is it weird to meet a stranger and feel immediately close to them?" she asked Eddie after the performance one night in a sushi restaurant, and then immediately regretted the question because Eddie was bound to use it as an opportunity to drop a clatter of flip remarks about fabulous sex with strangers in lewd places.

Eddie raised one eyebrow, but was otherwise restrained.

"The sudden intimacy of strangers," he replied. He

picked some pickled ginger up with chopsticks and dipped it into soya sauce. "I think sometimes you just meet someone and you share something with them. It's not a real closeness – it's just that you are in the mood to be friendly and warm, and the day is just right for it, and the situation is set up for it, and they are in the mood too. Like the other night when we met that couple in the jazz club?"

"No, I didn't feel in the slightest bit close to *them,*" she replied.

Isabella had found the middle-aged lesbian couple to be embarrassingly boring. Eddie and Rob less so, because they had each snorted a line of coke and so were tickled pink by the couple's clumsy attempts at a quasi-maternal flirtation with two glamorous younger men.

"No, I mean Sope Jordan." Isabella cut a nori roll in two and handed half to Eddie.

"Ah. GI Soap."

She scowled at him. He patted her hand.

"It's just that I keep thinking about him, every day in fact. Because of the Iraq war. Every newspaper headline, every TV news bulletin, it's Sope Jordan. Why? It used to be Harry. And I do think about Harry too, only in a different, distant, trying-to-forget-about-him way. I suppose I just can't bear to think about Harry any more because he's in another country now, and with another woman: probably. And, I don't know when I'll ever see him again, or what it will be like, and so I want to keep on trying to forget. But there isn't very much *to* think about Sope. I didn't know him. I only met him twice. And now I'll never ever see him again."

"I think that this war is having a strange affect on all of

us. We know so much about it all and so very little too," Eddie said sadly.

Isabella was surprised at Eddie's observation. She stopped eating her noodles, and put her chopsticks down to sip her beer from the neck of the bottle, so that she could watch him properly. Eddie was very unpredictable. Up one minute, deeply solemn the next. His mind seemed to be plugged directly into the mains, she thought. His attention span could be close to zero most of the time, and yet he directed her and the other actors in the theatre with the concentration of a brain surgeon. Mad as a brush, Isabella thought, looking at Eddie's serious expression. He's my best friend ever.

"Did I ever tell you about the day when we had the blizzard, in Manhattan, and everyone was all snowed in, and I went to see *The Hours*?" he asked.

"That book you made me read at the Cape that time? The one with all the suicides?"

"The film based on the story of that book, yes. It's wonderful. Do you want to hear about it?"

So Eddie told her about the day of the snow that shut down Manhattan and forced him into the microcosm of a theatre audience.

"What I think about all of that, is that the film and the afternoon in the theatre became a common purpose. It was a mission that we had – those of us who were in the theatre watching that particular show. We were all there with one desire, one passion, one love for literature and art, and one desire to be out of our houses despite the snow that was trying to imprison us. And I felt an overwhelming feeling of togetherness with those other people. I didn't know any of them." Eddie slugged down a mouthful of green tea. "On the one hand they meant nothing to me, but on the other they meant just about everything. We shared the same feelings, all of us, at the same time. We were sharing the same moment in history."

"Go on." Isabella was intrigued.

"History was being made that week." Eddie prodded the air with his chopsticks. "The war was just about to begin. Manhattan, which is where the war really did begin, was underneath a cover of snow. Nobody could move. And so what did we do? We went to the theatre. Because art and theatre is what makes us human."

Isabella thought about this for a while. It seemed obvious, that people share the same feelings at the same moment in history; and yet, she reminded herself, history is full of people who have opposite and divided feelings. That division of feeling is what becomes politics.

"Are there no politics in art?" she asked.

"Of course there are, sweetie: art is full of politics. Look at Synge for God's sake. But talk about cryptology – I guess that art can't exactly transcend politics; but it can explain them. And bad art can certainly make politics worse." Eddie gagged on a too-large piece of horseradish and took a giant swig of beer.

"There is truth in art. Most of the time, there is," said Isabella, "but now I feel as though we live our lives knowing somehow that there's truth inside of us somewhere, but nobody will ever hear it because we have to go around all day underneath a cloud of lies."

The cloud of lies was puffed up and shaped and reshaped every night on TV that fall. Isabella watched as little American news as possible, but when she did, she felt bewildered by the Alice in Wonderland effect it had on her. Heroic soldiers home from war were cheerfully interviewed. Donald Rumsfeld was upbeat. Condoleezza Rice was coquettish. George W Bush, preparing for re-election, was inspired by God. Isabella felt as though, every time she switched the TV on, there was a parallel universe being played out. It felt as though the TV station was being run by children, who had no idea what was happening in the world, and so were making it all up as they went along. A female soldier was proud of her husband, still out keeping the peace in Afghanistan while she was expecting their third child. The female soldier was due to deliver on Thanksgiving. Sope Jordan would be eating turkey in Canada. The widows of Baghdad would be having another power cut.

As darkness fell earlier in the evenings and the wind became sharper and the rain fell colder, Isabella took her longest walks on Sundays when the theatre was closed. She walked along the river where the joggers bobbed, arms folded and hugged tightly to her chest, eyes down to watch her feet along the sidewalk. She could not get used to the New York City cold. Indoors like a sauna, outdoors like a deep freeze. She bought woolly hats, and mittens, and earmuffs, and scarves and gloves, and thicker socks, and eventually fur-lined boots.

Isabella walked faster, and further, as the winter deepened, and her pace quickened to a military goose-step. She bought thermal underwear and fleece pyjamas. And then as November sharply turned into December, she sat in front of the television with Rob and Eddie and watched in horror as the news unfolded that George W Bush had been re-elected.

Eddie threw a pizza box at the television, and howled that life was not worth living any more. Rob sat and stared in disbelief, unmoving, and then eventually said, "You know, Kissinger was right; this election was much too important for the American voters to decide for themselves."

Thanksgiving came and went, and Isabella realised that she was not going to go back to Ireland for Christmas.

Chapter 26

In Dublin that November, in the days following another major assault on Fallujah, Harry had organised a protest at the American Embassy, with a march to the Dáil. Christmas time was everywhere. In the fairy lights on the streets, and the adverts on TV. The frantic shopping and the office parties were in full swing. Harry rang his mother and asked if he could come home to Dunmallow for the Christmas. He would have to tell her now that Isabella hadn't come back, and that he didn't know when or if she ever would.

As November slid into December, and the coughs and colds formed a steady parade to the surgery every day, Sinead watched the skies darken earlier and earlier each night. She finished up her surgeries in the afternoons now, and welcomed the damp blanket of darkness that covered up life's sharpest edges. She had started tidying in the evenings, letting Dorinda go home early to catch the traffic earlier.

These days, Sinead enjoyed slowly filing documents and putting charts away, quite contented in the empty office. She drew the blinds to shut out the street noise, and made a cup of tea. Sinead could no longer stand the taste of coffee at all. She drank her tea with three sugars in it. It was a change in taste that made no sense to her; she hadn't drunk sugar in her tea since she was a child. But she nevertheless was relishing her new tastes and sensations, and enjoying her body as it spread and grew around her. She read a few medical articles in the evenings, or flicked through websites, enjoying the solitude of the surgery after hours, waiting for the traffic to fizzle out before she drove on home.

Sinead sent an email to Moussa almost every day, but she received increasingly distressed replies. Fallujah was under another terrible assault; far, far worse than the one in spring, and Moussa was still in Baghdad.

Fallujah is a horror story now. Most of the buildings bombed to the ground. 70% of the city is destroyed. No water, no electricity, no jobs. When people go back into the city they have to get a retina scan and get finger-printed so that they can have an ID card. The military are in total control of the town. There are snipers everywhere. The ambulances are not able to run. Fallujah General Hospital can barely function, because you have to go through checkpoints to get there. I am preparing for a convoy of medical and humanitarian aid to the people of Fallujah with the support of UK charity. I think a lot of work here needs to be done. No senior doctors are staying in the country now.

Sinead was worrying about him all the time. She worried that he wouldn't have enough to eat, or that the power cuts would be driving him insane. She spent a lot of time thinking up warm thoughts to send him and tried to make him feel as loved and needed as she possibly could, even from afar. She told him all about the demonstration at the American embassy after the assault, and about the numbers who were signing up to the petition against refuelling in Shannon.

She felt that she would have to balance Moussa's life with something of her own. Moussa must believe that his life would become normal once again, that he would practise medicine in a normal way, with drugs and anaesthetics and sterile operating theatres. She emailed him articles from the *British Medical Journal*, and the *New England Journal of Medicine*, and told him about websites that she had read. But she didn't mention yet to him her biggest news of all.

As the evenings drifted on, Sinead would rub her rounding belly and stretch out her spine, arching her head and neck to ease the cramp out of her back. She would switch off the computer and swivel round in her office chair. It would be getting late, late enough to finish up and lock the doors and drive away into the night across the city to the long apartment that overlooked a river and the park. On a clear night she could watch the stars before she went to sleep.

Moussa read the articles that Sinead sent and he surfed the web, but his only academic interest now was in depleted uranium. He was convinced that it was causing cancer in the children's bones. He sat up late into the night, as often as power cuts permitted, reading articles from Finland and Japan, trying to see if similar oncological patterns had existed in places that had been bombed or where nuclear power plants had suffered accidents.

The research was quite exhausting but Moussa felt overpowered by his desire to keep on going. He was losing weight and he felt very tired in the afternoons. He found he often had to take a nap that lasted almost two hours after lunch. The team he worked with were sympathetic, but there was so much work to be done.

Moussa worked quietly now, and said very little during operations, because there was very little any more to joke about in a children's operating theatre. He felt defeated by it all, and tended to remain quite silent most of the time at work, chatting very little to the nurses and anaesthetic staff.

As often as he could, whenever the electricity was working and he had the time, he sent a brief email to Sinead. He didn't want to make her miserable with his tales of woe. Yet he could think of very little cheerfulness to write to her.

When his closest colleague, Dr Ali, finally persuaded him that he ought to have a biopsy done, he didn't say a thing about that to Sinead. It was a private matter. There was no need to upset anyone. Moussa had been passing blood for several weeks, and Dr Ali was the only person that he had told: and that was only because he needed his opinion.

"God damn it man, you must investigate yourself!" Dr Ali had been exasperated.

But Moussa wouldn't stop working, though it was clear now that he needed to slow down.

By November, Moussa was preparing to publish the

first in a series of studies that he and Dr Ali had conducted at the hospital. They worked late into the night, at the computer and over x-rays and piles of charts, Ali watching Moussa's increasingly pale face with concern.

The biopsy had not been good news.

Moussa sat in the doctors' mess now, with a glass of sweet sweet tea in one hand, and read the brief pathology report again as he and Ali watched the lunchtime news on Al Jazeera. Moussa sat and read, and read again, for the fiftieth time, the pathologist's account of how his cells had changed, changed utterly, and were dividing and dividing now, and how the mitotic lesion divided and divided still, cell upon cell each one recognising nothing but itself and its divine and individual right to take up space and to divide.

"Divide and conquer." Moussa thought desperately of all the further cell divisions that were to come. "They have certainly conquered me now."

On a cold and foggy day in the last week before Christmas day, Isabella and Eddie took the Staten Island Ferry in the morning just to feel the icy breeze off the Atlantic and to smell the sea and to be away from the bleak shadows of Manhattan for an hour or two.

Eddie paced up and down the deck, slapping his hands together in grey woollen mittens grinning to himself. The *Playboy* was winding up at the end of the week. The reviews had been fantastic. There was another project in the pipeline after February, if the budget could be secured in time. He and Rob were going to spend the month of January in Florida with Rob's brother and his wife, and Isabella could look after the apartment. There was everything to look forward to. Christmas in the sun. New Year's on the beach. Eddie mentally ticked off the list of tasks he would have to get Isabella to do. Plants to be watered, and sprayed, and moved out of the cold if it became too icy near the big front window. Don't forget to put out the recycling. Clean the glass on all the mirrors and wipe them down after you take a shower. Keep all the mail on the top shelf near the clock.

Isabella sat on a bench on the side of the Staten Island Ferry, nursing a paper cup of coffee in her mittened hands, and watched the Statue of Liberty slip by like a ghost. The sea plopped up and down, black ink against the orange buoys. In the distance, Manhattan stood as solid as a fortress. She felt alone again, but more contentedly so. Eddie and Rob were off for a month, and she would have to brave the New York winter by herself. But she wasn't going back. She would stick it out, and get up every day, and go to work in the restaurant across the street where she had got herself a job until she had decided what to do.

Eddie would get her more theatre work in spring, she was sure of that. But she wasn't sure how much longer she should stay in America now. Her visa would expire in June, but that left another six months to live in Manhattan. Isabella felt alone, but she also needed solitude. She needed to see what kind of person she could become in the world. The money in the restaurant was all right, and she had enrolled for a couple of courses at Columbia: African American Poetry, and Political Literature. In her solitary future, excitement had finally succeeded dread.

The Staten Island Ferry was almost empty of

passengers, on that late December morning, so Isabella couldn't help noticing the couple on the bench beside her. The young man with the pale, chubby girl kissed and groped one another through their layers of winter clothes, giggling and mumbling in each other's hair. Their desire was palpable, even to someone sitting a whole bench away. Despite the fact that Isabella was desperate to absorb herself in the movement of the sea, and trying hard to listen to the gulls and the noise of the ferry engine grinding underneath, the gasps and sucking kisses of the couple were all that she could hear.

She pulled her arms around her own slender body in her grey duffle coat, and realised suddenly and in a gut-wrenching shock, how desperately she was longing for someone else to grasp his arms around her body now. She realised for the first time in months how much she longed for sex. For hot hands around her thighs, and wet breath heavy on her mouth. Isabella found herself remembering the way Sope Jordan had looked at her, when she had touched his face. His one beautiful eye had blinked for just one tiny second. He had glanced down while she looked away from his face, just to look at her shape, to *see* her body. Isabella recognised the feeling she had felt, as she had unbuttoned her Batik shirt for Sope that night, and shivered. She had thought that she just missed being in love. But she had utterly convinced herself that she did not miss any of the pain, or the invisibility she had felt in Harry's life. But what Isabella realised as she walked away from the kissing lovers on the Staten Island Ferry and went to look for Eddie, was that what she longed for now was *desire*. She ached now just to feel the clumsy desperate lust of a man, who didn't already know what she looked like without her clothes on.

"Oh my grief," Isabella smiled at Eddie as he came towards her slapping his suede mittens together, grinning in the cold, *"I've lost him surely!"*

Eddie wrapped his arms around her, making her warm again, and they swung to and fro and she hugged him to her in a child's hug.

"I've lost the only playboy of the Western World!" they sang.

Eddie laughed, and held her tight against his woollen coat, and then lifted up her face towards his.

"Hey! What's this? You're not even on stage, Pegeen, and you're at it already!"

"Eddie, why *am* I such a loser?" she sniffed into him.

Eddie held her back from him. "Do you really want to know?"

She nodded and walked over to the side, to watch the sea again, face in hands. He leaned against the barrier beside her.

"It's because you couldn't tell Harry that you were leaving him, and so you made him find out *after* you had gone. You will hum and haw over fifteen T-shirts in a shop, and then decide that you only want the one they *don't* have in your size. You want the only thing on the menu that you *can't* have. The only decisions that you make are compromises. And you don't negotiate."

Isabella stared at him.

"It's true, Iz, you know it is. You *give* other people all the control over all the decisions in your life, and then you blame them when you don't get what you planned. Nobody can care about you, Iz, as much as you can care about yourself." He looked at her, and turned about, and leaned his back towards the sea.

"I think," said Isabella, "that Sope Jordan is the only other person that I've met who really knows what it is like to be on the wrong side in a war."

"Isabella, you have got to make your own decisions in this world, and live with them. You can *change* things if you've made a huge mistake. But if you keep on hoping that someone else will fix it for you, you will always be unhappy."

"Ruth thinks I kept Harry on a pedestal, but that I didn't really love him," Isabella said, looking at him from under dark eyelashes.

"The thing is," Eddie swept her wild black hair off her forehead, "other people *don't* do things perfectly all the time. Some time you just have to be the one who does the stuff."

"That's harsh, Ed."

He kissed her cold red nose. "It's because I love you, babes."

Harry bought an espresso machine for his parents, and then took the last train to Campile on Christmas Eve. He helped his mum cook turkey and peeled sprouts, and chatted to his father about the Celtic Tiger, but it was a quiet holiday. They ate their Christmas dinner in front of the telly watching *Titanic*, which was fun enough, and in the evening they played cards in the warmth of the kitchen. Nobody bothered lighting a fire in the dining room any more, Tony said.

When he got back up to Dublin, Harry's basement flat had got mice.

Chapter 27

Spring and Summer 2005

In the spring, rain came to County Mayo like a monsoon. Ursula Skellig's garden was a flood of daffodils and red sodden tulips. And then as the days warmed up the slugs made a belligerent march across her lawn. Ursula rose early every day, and the brighter damper mornings thick with mist were like a magnet to her now. She set about clearing out the newborn weeds and picking snails and insects from her vegetable patch, humming gently as she observed new buds that burst on apple trees, and noticed birds picking worms from under grass.

It was great that Sinead was staying for a while. She looked forward to bringing her daughter a pot of tea in bed now every morning and taking up the baby for a feed. The baby was angelic, not a whisper out of him. Ursula couldn't believe Sinead's luck to have such a quiet, un-crying baby. She would gaze adoringly into the cot, for as long as Sinead would let her without laughing at her and then shooing her away. But Ursula simply couldn't get enough of her grandson.

He had thick brown hair, and deep, deep chocolate-brown eyes that were just too beautiful to watch. And his eyelashes were as long as a girl's.

Ursula gazed at Sinead in amazement, as she nursed the infant to her breast, and wondered what his father must have been like that the child was so thick-haired and brown-eyed and so placid in his nature.

Sinead said very little, but she said enough. There would be a father, but not yet. This is all I need for now, she told her mother, and she stroked the baby's hair.

Thank God the women have it better nowadays to raise a child alone, Ursula said to herself.

The early days of summer in Castlebar passed quietly and with few events. The baby fed and slept, and Sinead sat in the lush garden and bathed her face in morning sun. She rested in the afternoons, and wrote to Moussa in the evenings. His emails were much shorter now.

Sinead

The weather is like hell. And hot at night. Can't sleep, nobody can sleep. And electricity is terrible all the time. Four hours without electricity, then two hours with, then off again. It is so hard to wash clothes, and get the water going, and cook. So you will excuse me when I do not write. When we have the air conditioner on it's fine, but at night without electricity, what a hell to sleep.

I send you warm regards and fondest affection

Your dear friend Moussa

PS my research is almost complete and we hope to send to the Lancet to publish in the fall. Three cheers!

Sinead wrote back with as much news as she could manage, that might keep him entertained, but she did not tell him about her biggest news of all.

She wanted to wait just a little longer, for some unsure reason, before she let Moussa know about her son. She asked herself if she was even slightly afraid that Moussa might in some way not approve? It wasn't that she had anything that she felt she needed to hide. But Moussa had a lot to handle now, she told herself. He was clearly suffering heavily in the heat, with very few resources to keep going, and she didn't quite know how to broach the subject; not by email anyway. What she really wanted more than anything was to be able to tell him to his face.

She typed a few lines every night, telling him what she had seen on TV, or a book she had been reading, and commented on his replies about the situation in Baghdad. She would tell him about her news, quite soon, she thought. It was just a question of finding the right words.

Towards the end of June, Sinead noticed that Moussa had not written for three weeks. She sent a couple of quick emails, but her throat grew tight whenever she checked the in-box, and found no reply from him. If only Moussa had left and stayed away all those years ago! If only he had come to live in Ireland, or to London, or to anywhere that there was no war, and no depleted uranium, sanctions, bombings, cancers and power cuts. He had stayed there to be *with* the war. He stayed out of courage, and he never turned away. He had stayed there for the children.

She closed the lid of her laptop, and let her head rest on the top of it.

"He probably is busy," Ursula tried to reassure her.

"He writes no matter what, even when he's busy," Sinead unhappily replied.

There is a smell in a hospital that is universal no matter what part of the globe you are in: a thick, sweltering infecticide, full of germs, and soured by bleach and disinfectants. It pervades everything, penetrates your clothes, and sinks deep into your skin, underneath your nails and hair. It smells of coughs, phlegm, urine, soiled linen, bandages and vomitus, combing in and out of every room, in long pale corridors and bed-lined wards. The smell lingers in between machines, and wafts around the oxygen tanks like a dense and acrid ghost.

Moussa found the smell particularly unpalatable now that nausea was a permanent flavour of his every day. The corridors and wards were full of wheelchairs banging, trolleys clanging, bedpans chiming in the sluice, and phones rang over and over and over again. He found it impossible to sleep, even though he lay in a small single room away from the rest of the patients in the long overheated ward. The nurses spoke in short sharp yelps to one another, up and down the corridor in their rubber shoes, and there was a distant radio just off battery that tinkled all day long.

As Moussa lay in bed recovering from what would be his final operation, he broke in and out of fevered sleep. He dreamt that he was with Sinead again. They were driving in his old pale blue Mercedes, together through the suburbs of Baghdad on a dark, hot, windless summer night. He was trying to get the air conditioner to work, because there was a baby in the back seat with a temperature that they were both trying to cool down. Sinead was laughing in a pale green theatre gown, her golden hair thrown back, and he was telling her the same joke over and over again.

"Where did Sadaam Hussein hide his weapons of mass destruction?

Why, do you want to get them back from him again?"

The baby cried and cried, and Sinead laughed louder and drove faster and faster, and then Moussa said to her, *Why don't you make him stop?*

And then they both looked at the child in the back seat and saw that it had no legs or arms.

It looked exactly like a doll that Moussa had once seen after a car bomb, thrown out from a window by a roadside, covered in some dead child's splattered blood.

Moussa awoke in horror, sweating heavily from the dream. He lay exhausted, and watched the wind blow the blinds around like dancers in the open window frame. Moussa realised then that he was missing something that had been lost to him many years ago.

He missed having someone who could make him laugh.

He would go home at the end of the week, and write to her before then. He would tell her now about his cancer, and that some lymph nodes were removed, but there was hopefully no risk of bony spread. Sinead would know what to say to make it right. He was quite sure of that. She would be able to give him some good thoughts to think, some sort of promise for the future.

He closed his eyes again and welcomed sleep.

When Moussa's email finally arrived, she read it over and over and over again. While her son slept, she wept and rubbed her fingers through his hair. And then she stopped, and sat, and watched the baby in his silent cot. She touched her son's soft sleeping head, and knew exactly what she had to do.

There was only one more chance now, in this life, to take apart all of the mistakes that she had made and shred them into dust. She would go to Moussa now, no matter what it took, and be with him. And she would take him by the hand and make him leave Iraq, and all the death behind him. And he would come away with her to Ireland.

She would have to sleep now, as she was very tired. And in the morning she would tell her mother what she had decided.

And so when Ursula came into Sinead's pink and sunny childhood room with a tray of tea and toast, Sinead sat up in bed, and while the baby slept she took her mother's hands, and told her the long story of Baghdad, that she never had been able to tell.

"We were in a very protected, isolated and separate community. Most Westerners didn't have Iraqi friends. It wasn't that we didn't want them, but most of the Iraqis were afraid to socialise with us." She looked at her mother carefully.

"Go on," Ursula replied.

"People were afraid that even their own neighbours were spies. It wasn't forbidden to have a friend who was a Westerner, but you would have been afraid that you were being watched. A relationship between an Iraqi man and a Western woman would have attracted attention, and most Iraqis would have been afraid. Moussa was quite westernised himself – he had trained abroad of course. And he was quite open-minded and good-humoured, although he was very modest. But most Westerners didn't go into Iraqi homes – mainly because it would have made the Iraqis nervous. I suppose that's why Moussa was so different."

"Is he in trouble now – Moussa?" Ursula's quick eyes searched her daughter's face.

Sinead nodded. "He is very sick. And," she looked at her mother's anxious face, "I can't bear it if he dies out there. I have to see him again before . . . " but she couldn't finish it.

Ursula reached out to stroke her daughter's cheek and Sinead's eyes filled with tears.

Ursula turned to lift the baby who was stirring in his cot now, his soft head against her aging face. She will take care of Tariq, Sinead thought, putting down her tea to take him up. I'll only have to go there for a day or two. A week, max. And then I'll be back.

Her mother lifted the baby out of his cot and sat down on the bed beside her.

"Sinead, what is it that you are going to do?"

"I just want Moussa to live," Sinead told her. She tried to speak evenly. It was important not to upset Ursula any more. "But I don't know how sick he really is. I think that when I left Iraq I closed my eyes as soon as I could snap myself into the safety belt on the plane, and I didn't open them again until we stopped in Shannon. The broken bones and burns and kids that died and all the nights that we had never slept: I just closed my eyes to all of that and made it go away, and I feel like I put Moussa right behind me too. But he was there with me on those two long terrible days that never ended because the bombs kept coming and the hospital would never stop. We went through all that together." She shivered and then looked solidly at Ursula again. "But I'm not going to let him die out there now. There is something that I'm going to have to do." She stopped momentarily, and looked at the sleeping child, then turned back to face her mother. "And I know that I can do it."

Ursula's gentle face was creased with worry. Sinead reached out her hand to hold onto her mother's gnarled gardening fingers in hers. She stroked the chipped broken clay-worn nails.

All her life her mother had been gardening without gloves. Sinead had even tried to get her to use latex rubber surgical gloves, thinking that the lightness and dexterity might please her, but Ursula gardened on barehanded. She touched the black cracks in her mother's thumb-pad with her thumb now, thinking of the earth that had been absorbed by her mother's body. They sat side by side a moment, while Tariq yawned and gurgled on the bed beside her while he woke up.

"If there's anyone who has her mind made up and that there is no talking to, it's you," Ursula finally said. "But for God's sake, be careful, Sinead. Travel there with someone that you know. Because I won't stop worrying until you're back."

Ursula took her fiercely in her arms, and they held each other, and she smiled.

Chapter 28

Dublin, Summer 2005

The hardest thing, for Harry, was when pieces of mail fell through the hall door addressed to Isabella. Every now and then, a brochure for a theatre company, or one of the catalogues she subscribed to.

He had felt so angry with her for leaving him at first. Guilty for a day; and then overwhelmed with rage. Her curtly worded goodbye note. Her stiff instruction not to contact. She was travelling, Ruth had told him on the phone; and the euphemism of it all had infuriated him further.

Travelling.

He seemed to remember that he and Isabella were supposed to have gone travelling together; although there had been no exact plans. But Harry also knew deep inside that perhaps there was a reason why he and Isabella had never made those plans together. He was going to Venezuela, but he had only mentioned it to her just before she'd left.

Venezuela had been solely his idea; and although he had presumed she'd come, half of him had known that she could not or would not, or that work would not permit, or that it simply wasn't in her schedule: and mostly what he now realised was that he had never really thought to ask.

"She needs the freedom to get over you," Ruth had told him firmly on the phone when she rang him, and he had opened up his mouth to disagree, ready for an argument. But he knew that it was meaningless to argue with Ruth. She was just the messenger, and although her messages were cryptic, Harry could see right through them.

Freedom to get over you. Ruth's words were like a bomb. So Isabella was free. And he was *over* now, to Isabella.

He had never for a tiny instant seen it coming, he now realised as he sat staring at the summer schedule from the Project Theatre. There were two plays coming up that she would have loved; that he would have loved to bring her to. *Measure For Measure* was one of her favourite Shakespeares. But Harry knew that if he and Isabella had been sitting here now, on the battered yellow sofa opening up the mail, that he would never in a million years have thought to suggest a night out at the theatre. And when Harry tried to picture her asking him if he would have liked to go to see the play with her, he could almost hear his own predictable reply.

Yeah, I dunno. I'll see. I've got a lot on this week. I'll get back to you. Oh, I forgot that we were supposed to go to that. Can't somebody else use my ticket?

The truth was that it was pointless being angry with

Isabella any more. Anyone could see why she had gone; and at this stage, even Harry knew how he must have made her feel for all those years. All those rows about his work, his commitments, his plans to change the world.

He had felt such responsibility for other peoples lives, but he had utterly ignored the life that he would give anything to have back again.

Everything in both their lives had revolved around him, and he could see that now. He had never even asked her about her plans and dreams.

She had clearly dreamed about this journey she was on; and yet he couldn't even remember her having asked him if he'd like to come. Could it be possible that they had drifted so far apart in ten short years? (Or was it more? He had just lost count.) It simply felt to Harry as though he had been with Isabella forever. And he had assumed that she'd always be there with him.

He wondered often if she could have known about Sinead, and then he tried to figure how. Could one of his friends have told her something? But none of his friends *were* friends with Isabella: and that was not a reassuring thought.

Just who were his friends, anyway, now that Iz was gone? He had political relationships. Plenty of people to sit in pubs with, plenty of meetings, phone calls to make, hundreds of people who wanted to listen to him speak. But friends? Like Iz had Ruth? Like Eddie, who had adored her right through college and whom she had missed dreadfully when he had gone – even Harry had known just how much Iz missed Eddie. And yet he had behaved as though it didn't matter. Belated guilt swept through him like a wave. He thought about the night she'd left, the same night that he'd slept with Sinead.

His friendship with Sinead was something that he'd really needed. And then he had gone and screwed that up by sleeping with her.

"What about *our* plans, Harry?" Isabella had screamed at him, only days before she had left.

But Harry had always hated having to *talk things through*: feelings, emotions, the imbalance of the relationship. Maybe that was why he had always just escaped into another woman, when Isabella had picked a fight with him. He had always more or less believed that if you had to *work* at a relationship, then it wasn't a relationship worth having. *We must be free to love, in order for love to become a force for good,* he remembered saying once in college long ago.

But he would have given all the world now for a second chance just to do the work with Isabella that was desperately needed.

Nothing worthwhile comes easily, thought Harry, tearing up the theatre brochure and throwing it into the cold and empty fireplace. Love has got to be worth fighting for.

Chapter 29

Everywhere was dust. Thin brown dust, in the air, on the trucks, on the palm trees, on the windscreen of the battered two-door white Toyota car. Doctor Ali drove at a haphazard speed, jerking the stick shift with a rallying staccato while he kept up a running commentary for Sinead. Sinead stared wordlessly through the dust-covered window at the flat-roofed suburbs of Baghdad unfolding in a pockmarked landscape of potholes and half-tumbled walls like toothless smiles.

She stared at the giant hoardings, at shop fronts, and at gardens along streets that were blistered with blast holes. Doctor Ali chattered on. There was so much to tell her, about everything that had happened to Moussa since the last time Sinead had seen him. The state of the hospital – Sinead would be horrified at how pathetic it had become. He swept through brick-scattered suburban streets trying to avoid the traffic jams, and swung round roundabouts, all the time keeping his lyrical monologue alive.

"Oh, yes, poor Moussa *has* been in tremendous pain, Sinead, but thank God he has some relief now, *Inshallah*. But you know, Sinead, that damned man had been working every night on his research until he had to drop from exhaustion in the end!"

Through the dust-speckled windscreen Baghdad spread out like whitened boxes.

"Moussa was researching the very same carcinogens that are now rotting in his own glands! He thinks that the depleted uranium has caused all the children's bone cancer in Baghdad and North Iraq. But the same carcinogen has him in a wheelchair now, for God's sake!" Dr Ali thumped the steering wheel.

Sinead turned her head away to see out of the side window. "I suppose there are a lot of disabled people in Iraq by now."

"Oh yes, a lot of things have changed. You will hardly recognise the place."

She shook her head. "I don't. It's been fifteen years since I was last here. It's very difficult to see that anything is the same."

The blue sky was just the same though. Hot, screamingly blue sky that fifteen years ago had meant evening drinks of sweet iced tea in long cool alleyways, and starlit rooftop nights. She was accustomed to the way of avoiding an electrically blue midday sky, and so she avoided it now, keeping her gaze low, eyes right down to the empty tea-shops, the familiar rounded windows on apartment buildings, the children running by, the pavements and the prams.

"Rationing – always rationing now, and shortages!" Dr

Ali pointed as they slowed down at traffic lights. At the junction, a huge queue was trailing out onto the road beside a petrol station that was closed. Sinead took in the long line of drivers sitting in their cars, miserable in the heat.

"Do you get a special petrol ration, being a doctor?"

Ali laughed. "Oh, all that depends on what you know, and who you know!"

Sinead smiled. Ali revved the car furiously again as the traffic lights turned green.

"Sorry about my car!" He shook his head, laughing as the engine blustered and then roared, and they twitched back out onto the road. "We don't drive nice cars about in Iraq nowadays. You don't want to take a good car out in case there is a hijacking!"

Sinead shook her head and laughed. "Your car is absolutely fine, Ali. You are very kind to drive me here."

"You see, the city is now full of gangs. Most of them are from the slums. You know Saddam City? They call it Al Sadir City now."

"I'm not sure. I remember other things, I think."

"It's a notorious slum with well over one million people. That whole city is a terrifying place. If someone goes missing now, or your car is hijacked, that is where you would find them. Each of the gangs controls a different alley, and they are selling weapons openly on the streets. The Americans don't even go there." He rolled his eyes.

The car swung around a bend and onto another narrow road out of the traffic jam.

"Aren't you terribly afraid, then? To go out like this? Or is it safer in the day?"

"We don't go out much in the night, but that's mostly because of curfews too. But that makes it hard to see our friends and family now of course. So, you have to be well organised."

"Oh my God! Look at that!" Sinead gasped in horror, as the ghostly black skeleton of a bank loomed up at them out of a vast roadside concrete mess. "I remember that bank being there! The damage from the bombs is awful, Ali. They seem to have rebuilt almost nothing yet."

"Most of the damage in this area is from looting. But when the tanks and Apaches invaded Baghdad, they shot out all around them, at any vehicle that was in their way. The people who lived in these areas didn't know what to do with the bodies they found in burnt-out cars. They needed to be buried and honoured, and so the local people asked the troops to help them to find the families and to remove the dead bodies from the areas."

"Moussa told me: you had a terrible time at the hospital."

Ali nodded, frowning at the memory. "The bodies were decomposing in the heat: you couldn't have identified most of them. But the troops refused. Not our job, they said. So eventually the people started to make home-made roadside graves, near the burnt-out cars. You would see the little notices sometimes, beside the roadside graves that were all over Baghdad at that time on this kind of highway leading out of the city – hand-made cardboard signs with a little notice: *One adult female, adult male, three children, red Volkswagen.*"

Sinead gazed out at the market street in silence. They were at a shopping area now, with blocks of flats straddling both sides of a wide multi-laned street, and there were a series of traffic lights and stops. Sinead watched the women come and go, in black abayas, carrying shopping bags, just as always. But she noticed that there were fewer women walking to the market now, and none of them were walking alone. At traffic lights she stared at their long folded faces, and at their mouths turned down.

"I just don't recognise any of these streets at all, you know," she told him, as he swung around another corner. "It all looks terrible. So much worse than I'd imagined."

They were back out on the main road again.

"That's because so many buildings have been pulled down now. All the landmarks that you know are changed. We have to figure it out all the time too. Sometimes a whole street has disappeared, and so you have to think up another way of getting to where you want to go. And sometimes they block off roads, with tanks and barricades, so it's a bit of a mystery tour whenever you go out nowadays! You have to keep figuring out new routes every day!"

Sinead smiled. He was keeping a very good sense of humour up for her. She busied herself in gazing at the streets again and the passers-by, and stopped trying to figure out where they were going until they had almost run right into a military checkpoint that had appeared as if out of nowhere, round a corner past a mosque.

Sinead grabbed the steering wheel as Ali slammed the breaks and the tyres squealed. There were a large number of bulky white-brown uniformed soldiers on the road in front of them, and a block of several tanks and armoured cars. The soldiers' dark sunglasses flashed like mirrors in the sun; and they were very heavily armed.

There was only one other car in front, but there were shouts coming from both sides, and terrified replies in Arabic and English. Ali began muttering very nervously, and drummed his fingers on the steering wheel.

"This is not good for us, not good at all. *These* kinds of soldiers are very difficult to speak to. We must be very polite and co-operative and they will let us go. If they try to search us that could take forever. But we must be very careful now!"

"But I'm a Westerner. We will be all right."

"Oh yes, of course," he nodded. "Yes, you will be safe. But we will have to explain what you are doing in Iraq. You will have to show your papers and ID. They might start to think that I am kidnapping you, or that you are an unofficial aid worker. Or an undercover journalist. There are a lot of misunderstandings nowadays, you see."

Sinead saw Ali's face becoming creased with fear. She had not anticipated this. Surely nothing would go wrong. She was on official business, visiting a friend. The driver of the car was a respected medical practitioner and a surgeon – nothing could be more benign. The only thing to do would be to try to remain as calm as possible. It was going to be difficult enough sitting still in the midday heat waiting to be searched, and Dr Ali was doing enough panicking for both of them.

The soldiers in helmets and sunglasses were barking out incomprehensible orders at the driver of the car in front. Ali was mumbling something in Arabic, and Sinead half heard some familiar words from the Koran.

"Will you please stop worrying, Ali?" He was beginning to make her feel uneasy now. She fingered the black headscarf that was hot and tight around her head and neck. "We are going to be fine. There is only one car in front of us. And then us, and then we can go, and we will be all right." She turned away again.

Ali merely continued to pray.

A small man in the front was prodded with the guns and forced out of his car.

"*SIR! PUT YOUR HANDS ON YOUR HEAD AND STAND IN THE DIRT! GET OUT OF THE CAR! PUT YOUR HANDS ON YOUR HEAD AND STAND IN THE DIRT!*"

The small man had a thick black moustache and was shaking his head, and he seemed to be in tears now. Sinead felt her throat beginning to close over, and she tried to swallow, to make it moist again. The moustached man was backing away from the soldiers now, stumbling as he tried to walk, trembling arms clinging to his head. Ali gripped the steering wheel of the car with knuckles that were growing whiter by the second.

"Oh this is very bad now, Sinead, a very bad situation to be in." His voice had shrunk down to a whisper.

Sinead steeled herself to be calm. More tension in the tiny car was not an option now.

"Ali," she said, with as much control as she could manage, "please, stay quiet now. I'm telling you to stay calm. We are going to be all right."

They were screaming orders at the small moustached man in front, and he was pinned at gunpoint now, prostrate on the bonnet of his car. Sinead watched them for a moment, ignoring Dr Ali's prayers. She craned her neck to see exactly what was happening out there. It was all getting very confusing. The shouting was much louder now. The moustached man appeared to be under arrest, and was being handcuffed fiercely. The atmosphere of agitation thickened.

Their two-door white Toyota car seemed all at once to be very small, and powerless and alone.

All the guns, and the constant sound of soldiers shouting were making her feel very dizzy and afraid. Sinead reached down to the floor of the car, trying to find her handbag at her feet. She began to rummage in it for her phone, thinking that she needed to make a call. Her hands shook, and so she held her mobile phone in both of them, staring at the screen to concentrate. She could call Moussa to tell him what was happening to them now. He would know what they should do. What exactly they should say about her situation in Baghdad. And so, distracted by this need, she didn't quite react in time to Dr Ali's scream, that told her *"No!"*

Nor did she see the shadows of the snipers that Dr Ali had just spied, who had their sights on the windows of the small two-door white Toyota car. And so, when the glass of the four windows smashed into a thousand pieces, and the blood burst out of Dr Ali's mouth and drowned Sinead's blonde hair and soaked her clothing in a flood of clotted black, she did not see any of it at all.

Sinead died with her handbag open on her knees, her head resting softly on one side, her splattered mobile phone clasped tightly in her hands. Her chest ripped apart with a gunshot wound that ruptured her heart, tearing it completely in two.

Ursula Skellig would say to people, as they came in hundreds to the small graveyard at the rainy foot of Croke

Patrick Hill, that her only daughter Sinead had gone to
Baghdad to be with a man she loved, and had died of a
broken heart.

She would rock Sinead's ten-week-old son tightly in
her arms, praying as hard as she could when the coffin
lowered in the grave, and hold his tiny sleeping face into
her neck and stroke his hair, until it was sticky with her
tears.

The official report into the deaths of Dr Sinead Skellig
and Dr Ali Abu Ra'ad would state that both had died as
a result of a suicide bombing at a military checkpoint just
outside the Green Zone in Baghdad.

Exactly one week following the shooting of Sinead and
Ali Abu Ra'ad, Harry Waters would discover that an
unnamed Irish doctor on a humanitarian mission in Iraq
had been killed by a terrorist attack. But he would not
link the unnamed Irish volunteer with Sinead Skellig,
peace activist and medical practitioner, because he would
hear it on the BBC World Service while sitting in a cafe
in Caracas. Harry would hear the news briefly, and
process it as another terrible Iraqi death, along with
twenty-five other civilians killed that day on the roadside
in Baghdad.

The only person known to Harry who would know
enough about what exactly had happened in Baghdad,
and who the unnamed Irish doctor was, would be
Maggie Hennelly. Maggie would learn through a BBC
embedded journalist whom she had met in Northern
Ireland, that the name of the doctor was Sinead Skellig,

and that she was from Mayo, and was, in fact, visiting friends and colleagues in Baghdad. Maggie would read in Bob Simon's blog that it wasn't clear why the small white 1985 Toyota had been targeted by gunfire, killing both the occupants instantly. But, as far as he could make out from contacts in the Green Zone, there was an understanding that the woman involved, who was wearing dark glasses and a headscarf, had been rummaging in a bag as the car approached the checkpoint at high speed. Her corpse had been found clutching a mobile phone. A mobile phone could have been mistaken by military personnel to be a detonator for a car bomb, said the correspondent from the BBC.

Maggie read the email slowly, several times, before she took her own mobile phone out of her handbag. Her hands trembled while she desperately scrolled the contact list for Harry. She found his name, and stared at it for a while, *H Waters*, while she summoned up all the courage that she could, to say what she had to say.

She had thought the world of Sinead.

Her death is like the death of a part of all of us, thought Maggie. *What are people to do now,* she wondered hopelessly. *How can there be any solution to this kind of chaos in the world?*

Maggie lifted the receiver to her ear, and tucked her red curls out of the way, as the tone rang and rang. There was no reply. She hung up first, not knowing what to say to Harry. What kind of message could she leave? She would have to have a think. She stared at the screen again for a moment, and then dialled him up for a second time. This time, she spoke in a low and careful voice.

"Harry. It's Maggie Hennelly here. I hope you are okay. Harry, I am ringing you to tell you that I've had some news today that came in from the BBC. And it's about Sinead. I think the best thing would be if we could meet. Ring me back as soon as you get this, and I'll meet you straight away."

Maggie sat with Harry in the corner of the Chaplins on D'Olier St, exactly where he had once sat with Sinead, for almost five hours that day. She had simply left the office, switched her phone to voicemail and cancelled all her bookings for tomorrow. She took a copy of Bob's email with her, so that Harry could have a small memento of Sinead; it was a death notice of sorts.

Harry read it slowly too, taking in all the small political details about the numbers who had died, the suspicion of a bombing, and the lack of evidence to support a bomb, the identity of Sinead's driver Dr Ali Abu Ra'ad whose family had been subsequently arrested. Maggie bought him several pints, which he drank in quick succession, and she let him use her scarf to wipe his tears. She stroked his knees and held his hands while Harry wept, and they talked for hours and hours; about the war and politics; about occupation and resistance; and most of all about Sinead.

What Maggie didn't mention at that stage, because she didn't know how to, was what she also knew from local news reporters in Mayo.

That Sinead had left behind a son.

Chapter 30

In the months that followed, Harry hardened his resolve, and set about organising another demonstration for the autumn. On the anniversary of 9/11, a group of Irish Americans in Dublin wanted to protest outside the embassy, to commemorate the American dead and demand an end to war. Harry threw himself into phone calls and public meetings, and collected street petitions with Alan and Fiona. The Stop The War campaign had grown larger too, since the Shannon demonstration, and there were plenty of students around that summer who were helping out. And, there were loads of other things to do.

There was a campaign to support striking Latvian Workers who were being paid one quarter of the national minimum wage. There was a big campaign developing in North Mayo, where farmers had been put in jail for trying to block an oil pipe going through their land. Harry spent his days deep in a variety of activities, and tried not to think about Isabella, or Sinead, at all.

In the evenings he returned as late as possible to the basement flat, which had become colder and more empty as the sun climbed higher in the sky, and the days outside became more blue and yellow, gold and green. By mid-July, when the tree-lined avenue outside was dappled with a sparkling light, Harry's flat had all the atmosphere of a grave.

He stood in the middle of the living room, now a chaos of books and newspapers and empty plates of half-eaten food, and he knew that it was time to move. Living here with Isabella had once been fun. There was something decrepit and bohemian about the squalor that had appealed to both of them. But, since last year, when she had disappeared one morning and he had to face his life alone, there was very little about this flat that could appeal to him any more.

Harry opened up the back door to the yard, where a small shaft of sunlight hit the step for just about an hour each day, and sat down on the step to smoke his last cigarette. He would move out of here tonight, he decided. Alan had a place, he knew, because Alan's roommate had gone back to Australia at short notice and there was a large empty room at the back of Alan's redbrick terrace in Rialto where Harry could have privacy and good company at the same time. He smoked his cigarette happily, visualising the warm sun-filled double room, and he could almost smell the fresh summer breeze blow the curtains from the window, and feel the comfort of a newly-made bed.

A new start, Harry thought excitedly. Alan would cook good meals; like all overweight people, he loved to feed others. Harry would have Internet access, and a well-fitted kitchen to come home to, and easy but intelligent company in the evenings. He would find household chores much less tiresome when he could share them with another man. And Alan would be pleased too, to have the rent, and pleased that a new tenant could be organised so quickly. It was altogether an excellent idea.

As Harry sat smoking at the back door of his flat, Isabella and Eddie stood in an interminable queue at Newark Airport, waiting to board their evening flight to Dublin. Isabella was infinitely more patient than Eddie could possibly be, and she spoke to him gently every now and then to tell him to calm down because he was going to cause a scene if he didn't stop hopping up and down and calling the security staff rude names.

Eddie hadn't flown inside or outside America since 9/11, and he was in a state of fury over all the waiting and intrusive checks. Isabella was simply more prepared, having flown out to New York just over a year ago, and she also felt that one of them would have to remain on the right side of the law or they would never get to board the plane.

The queue wound around and around the departure hall, and Eddie snapped and moaned, and made horrendously insulting remarks about the size and shape of every member of the security personnel.

"Christ, Isabella, this woman coming up with the walkie-talkie, face like a boxer hound," he muttered as a grim-faced black woman waddled over to them, her body squeezed into a pale brown uniform that was several sizes too tight.

"Ma'am, are you carrying any luggage that you have not packed yourself?" asked the boxer-faced woman.

"Jeeesus fucking Christ, who do they think we are?" grumbled Eddie, far too loudly for Isabella's nerves. "Who the fuck gets on a plane and gets somebody else to pack their luggage? Oh, excuse me, sir, I just thought you might like me to pack your luggage for you. Here, let me give you this small incendiary device, I seem to have so many of them, I just haven't got the room to pack them all in my Louis Vuitton!"

"Shut the fuck up, Eddie!" hissed Isabella, smiling at the boxer-faced lady, who stared blankly back.

She lost Eddie briefly in the Duty Free, while he galloped off to seize handfuls of cosmetics that he was convinced would be much cheaper in America than in Ireland. Isabella welcomed the chance to sit down and have a think in peace and quiet for half an hour. She found a table and a seat outside a mock-pavement cafe, and bought a large and watery American cappuccino and a muffin.

She hadn't been in touch with Harry at all – not in over a year, since she left Dublin on a cool midsummer's morning to fly to this same airport. She hadn't called him either, to tell him that she was coming back. She would call him on arrival – or, maybe not. Perhaps it would be better to leave it for a week or two, and get her bearings first. She wasn't going to go back to the flat, of course. She had walked away from all that, and even though there were dozens of her books still there and several kitchen things, and some linen and even clothes, she didn't want all that stuff now. Her suitcases were on the plane, filled with all her new American things, and she would start from scratch when she got home.

She and Eddie were going to stay with Ruth and Bernard in Blackrock until she settled in. Eddie only had a fortnight in Ireland on vacation and would be busy networking like mad at the Dublin Gay Theatre Festival, but he was going to jangle the phone and charm some people that he knew and get her something in a new television station that was putting out all kinds of stuff. He was quite confident about that. Isabella was not quite as confident as he was, but she felt that luck was going to go her way.

When Harry had torn her heart in two last summer, she had felt that everything in her life was out of her control. Nothing she could have done could make Harry love her more, or want to share his life completely with her. But now, she realised for the first time that she was strong enough to hold her life in her own small hands, and decide that she didn't want, or need, to share it with anyone.

Eddie held a substantial part of her life now, which she let him try on and borrow, and twirl around in just to make her happy, but he handed it back to her respectfully again so that she could keep it safe. It was an ideal relationship; but it was not romance. She would meet Harry, and spend some time with him. She was quite sure of that. But whether or not she would take him by the hand and let him lead her down his road again, she felt, was a most uncertain thing. Harry had no doubt moved on too.

He might indeed be with someone else. Isabella knew that even if Harry was deeply ensconced in a new relationship by now, he would still believe himself to love

Isabella first. They had shared too much of a life together for him to want to walk away. And in fact she felt that when he would meet her for the first time, after more than a year away, that he would quite probably long to have her back, and would gaze at her with childlike eyes, and speak hoarsely to her, and beg her once again to be his love.

But she was convinced that it would take a lot more than begging and soft eyes to return to Harry's side again.

Everything was different now. She felt that she had grown inside. She looked different, and she felt different. Isabella turned around to inspect her reflection in the glass of the window that was behind the little table where she sat, and liked what she now saw. Her hair bounced healthily around her chin, and her face was more visible now, more uplifted, than the old face that she had hidden behind a cloud of thick black hair.

"*And I the fright of seven townlands with my biting tongue!*" she said out loud to her reflection and caught the eye of an elderly man at the next table, scowling at her.

Poor old thing, she thought, beaming at him. How horribly miserable some people are.

She felt immensely pleased with herself today, and looked down to admire her legs in her neat new navy jeans and platform heels. It was good to be going back to Ireland now. Isabella looked up and spotted Eddie who bounded across the concourse towards her now flapping his bags of purchases by his sides as he walked. She waved happily at him as he made a swift bee-line for her.

"Eddie, you look just like a demented bag-lady with a Mastercard account!"

Her freshly washed hair smelt really good, she thought, and she sniffed a strand of it as it swung across her face. Her nails were clean and shapely, polished to a well-buffed shine that drew attention to her dainty hands.

Eddie threw himself down on a chair across from her, and began to rattle off his purchases to her like a stock report.

"Five hundred dollars on *Lancome for Men*. Two hundred dollars on perfume. Sweetie, am I mad or what?" He sighed, and grabbed the last biteful of her muffin and rammed in into his mouth just in time before a disgruntled bus girl could swipe it away. Isabella stroked his boyish face and laughed.

"For such beautiful skin as yours, Eddie? Totally worth it, darling. Every penny of it!" And she kissed her index finger, and placed it gently on his mouth.

Chapter 31

One year later

Ursula Skellig sat in her sunny yellow kitchen and made her first cup of tea of the day, while Sinead's son gurgled in his high chair. Ursula listened to the morning radio while she stirred a small teapot and popped some toast into her mouth, cutting another piece in soldiers for the baby.

The garden was full of moist mid-summer now. Ursula stood at the sink to munch her toast, and admired the bed of dahlias that she had nursed through a recent plague of slugs, the fuchsia by the old shed door, blowing in the cool wet morning breeze, the dog roses nodding around the dry stone wall.

She rubbed her hands together, and then wiped them on a tea towel to get rid of crumbs, and decided it was time to make her call.

Getting Harry Water's phone number had not been too easy. But at Christmas time, a glittered snowman card had arrived from Alan Steadman, the nice schoolteacher who had come up for Sinead's funeral mass, with Harry Waters' phone number and address.

Alan told Ursula in his brief note on the card that he had not discussed it yet with Harry. He thought that Ursula should be the one to tell him everything that had happened. And in fact, that arrangement had suited Ursula very well.

She had needed as much time as possible before she could make up her mind what to do about Harry Waters, a man about whom she knew a lot, but whom she had never met. They had a whole world in common now, she and this young man, none of which he could yet know. Ursula was quite unsure for many months how long she would be able to keep the truth from him.

But the truth was that she did not quite want to share Sinead's son yet, with anyone. Not even with the man who was his father. The baby was her only living link with her only daughter, and his presence in her life was a gift that was far too precious yet to share.

And yet, she had become increasingly aware, as winter days grew shorter and her bones began to hurt, that the work she had to do around the house and garden had become a chore. And she knew that for a tiny baby to be raised solely by a seventy-two-year-old grandmother was not the most desirable long-term situation for any of them now.

All her friends admired her greatly, as she strode up and down the town with her smiling grandson in a brand new navy-blue stroller. And she was never short of offers from her friends to baby-sit, nor of visitors to coo and tickle the baby and bring toys and bricks, nor of other toddlers to come around to play. But the truth was that she really was far too old for it all by now. Her bladder was not as strong as she needed it to be, in order to lift a growing chubby boy in and out of a pram all day. Her eyesight was not really up to reading stories every night, or doing homework in the kitchen, and she did not relish the thought of being the eighty-five-year-old mother to a strapping teenage boy.

Ursula felt that she knew what Sinead would have wanted her to do for baby Tariq now. It was quite clear. The Christmas card from Alan still lay on the kitchen table, where it had lain for several months while Ursula chewed her thoughts over in her mind and thought about what it was that she must say. She glanced up at the clock, and saw that it was almost ten. On a Saturday morning, in the summertime, that was a very reasonable and yet sufficiently unsociable time in which to make a salient phone call to a stranger.

Harry Waters didn't lie in long on Saturdays. There was always something big in town to do. Today he had been up at eight to buy the *Guardian* and have some cornflakes in the tidy kitchen that he shared with Alan Steadman. Alan was busy cooking rashers and black puddings, and stirring scrambled eggs, so Harry reached across him to the phone when it began to ring.

He answered with his mouth full.

"Hrrmmmmmouuuu?"

There was a low cough on the other end.

"May I speak please with Harry Waters, please?"

Harry swallowed, and there was a pause. "This is me," he replied.

The lady on the other end spoke in a low-toned, almost masculine voice. West of Ireland accent. Possibly quite old, he thought, and she seemed nervous in her speech. But she was very clear about what she had to say.

He listened carefully at first, and as she spoke he understood the words that she was saying. But the more she spoke about what she needed to say to him, the more his mind began to spin, and his concentration slipped and wobbled and became a blur. A thousand images had begun to flash around his head.

Sinead.

A shooting dead. A bomb. Images he had pushed away from his mind a year ago, and hoped would never again return. The old lady was her mother. *Oh, God!* It was all coming horribly back now. Sinead was dead. Her body gone. Buried in a cold cold grave. His eyes began to sting with tears again.

He hadn't been to Sinead's funeral. He was still ashamed of that. But he had been away. He couldn't have gone anyway. He hadn't known until it was all too late.

But Ursula wasn't bothered that Harry had missed Sinead's funeral. That wasn't why she had phoned at all.

"There is something very important that you have to know *now* about Sinead." Ursula spoke her well-rehearsed words carefully. "Something that you clearly haven't heard before. This thing that I have to tell you is something that I will have to tell you in person, I'm afraid. It really is something very important, and I think that it will change your life forever. And so, I am phoning, Harry, to ask if you and I can meet. In Dublin. Or in Castlebar. Or wherever you prefer. As soon as you are ready, son."

There was a silence. Harry felt very ill at ease. There was obviously something terrible about Sinead's death that he was going to have to know. He wondered if perhaps she hadn't died in Iraq after all. Perhaps she had killed herself. Or, worse still, perhaps she had gone to Iraq and she really had detonated a car bomb like the Americans had said.

No – that would be ridiculous.

But he had a dreadful feeling that what Ursula wanted to tell him so badly was something that he really didn't want to know at all.

On the day that Ursula travelled up to Dublin on the train, with Tariq on her lap, and off her lap, and crawling all over the seats and other strangers that she met, Harry had been doing a radio debate with someone from the American Embassy. The question was about the ongoing refuelling at Shannon Airport. Paul Cranny probed and fooled around with the ideas, Harry thought, and was just trying to turn a non-sequitur into a debate.

The trajectory in the media had turned completely against the war by now. Opinion polls in America had slid right away from Bush. But Cranny who had hotly supported the war from the very beginning was simply trying to wave his willy round again, thought Harry.

Harry was becoming bored with the debate, and the lack of analysis that the media was indulging in now. George Galloway had been elected in the UK, solely on an anti-war ticket, Harry reminded Cranny. Even in America, opinion polls were turning rapidly away from the Washington agenda of more troops and less domestic spending.

Hurricane Katrina had put a huge dent in the Bush consensus, argued Harry methodically, but he was finding it difficult to concentrate today. The representative from the Embassy seemed to be feeling awkward too, and the arguments about weapons of mass destruction and regime change were not the issue any more. It was fairly easy to convince people that more money should have been spent on the victims of New Orleans than on sending Americans to their deaths in Iraq.

The representative from the Embassy was being sanguine, Harry thought, and he started to almost feel quite sorry for the guy. It can't be easy trying to defend the indefensible any more, he thought, and so he let the American representative talk on about responsibilities of NATO, and the special relationship with the United States.

Harry's words came out as always, as he was accustomed to the same arguments over and over again. Lies about weapons of mass destruction. Deaths of American troops. Loss of civilian lives in Iraq. Kidnappings and torture in the jails. Harry trotted through the arguments mechanically, but he felt a strange fuzziness in his head because every mention of every car bomb and every shooting was a shooting of Sinead.

Harry desperately wanted this war to end. He was being pulled into it all the time, and he felt it was his task to keep debate alive for peace campaigners everywhere. But he found it quite impossible to concentrate on this debate today. The questions seemed so futile now. There was no question that the refuelling in Shannon was disgraceful – so why continue to debate it even? There was no way that even the most belligerent neo-con could expect to get away with wanting new troops sent into Iran, or to fund an Israeli assault on Lebanon when the people of New Orleans were still without their homes. So why are we still talking about these things?

Public and political opinion had changed utterly now, but here was Cranny still waffling on, as if these were ideas that were still worthy of debate. Harry, if he had not been so passionate about what he wanted for the world, would almost have walked out. He smiled at the Embassy man as the debate wound up, and said goodbye with a friendly grace. Cranny ignored Harry as he left the building, but Harry didn't care at all. He had a more important person to meet right now, and his mind was set on that. He swung his canvas satchel across his shoulder, and strode away from the radio building and into town.

Ursula had decided to meet Harry on the top floor of Bewleys café on Grafton Street, because it was the only place she knew in Dublin that she was sure was going to be still there. She wasn't terribly confident about travelling around the city nowadays. It was all one-way systems and she didn't recognise the route the bus took into town along the wrong side of the quays, and then down a side street into a sudden crush of traffic. She watched the city nervously through the windows, holding tightly onto Tariq who was by now fast asleep. His buggy was folded down, and Ursula was worried about unfolding it quickly enough again while not waking the baby at the same time and not getting in the other people's way.

She suddenly recognised the street that they were on

and Trinity College and the Bank, and then she knew exactly where they were. Good. Tariq was heavier by the day, she thought, as she stood up awkwardly with the baby in her arms. He woke, and squealed, and Ursula hauled her handbag over one arm, and grasped him on her hip with the other.

The buggy was insoluble. She left it where it was and approached the driver at the front of the bus to ask him if there was any way that he could possibly help.

The tall black African bus driver stepped gracefully from his seat, and lifted the huge pram up as if it were a feather, landing it skilfully at Ursula's feet on the pavement outside. He snapped it open like a light umbrella. She beamed at him, and settled Tariq inside his seat.

"Thank you – you have no idea how grateful I am for all your help!"

"My pleasure, Madame. Have a good day now." The beautiful tall African spoke with a throaty French accent.

Ursula was delighted, and waved bye-bye to the bus with Tariq. It was an exotic and very promising start to the day.

She crossed the wide streets with what felt like a million other people. All around her there were youths; sucking drinks out of straws, yapping incessantly into mobile phones, shouting at each other across the roar of cars.

What would it be like to raise a small child in this town, she wondered as she wheeled Tariq across the road and round the corner into Grafton Street.

Where do children in the city go to play? Would he have a nice suburban garden to run around? Would he spend his teenage years in a hoodie and a set of headphones, hanging round a mall?

She nosed the pram up Grafton Street, past the jugglers and electric guitars to get to Bewleys. Ursula realised as she approached it that Bewleys Café was probably a big mistake as the part that she liked was up the stairs. She stood in the lobby of the café, looking up at the huge staircase that wound around the restaurant to the top, and felt exhausted just looking at it. Tariq was getting very wriggly, kicking to be let out of his pram.

Ursula looked around her to see if there was a lift, or anyone who could help her with the buggy.

"You are a desperate job for an old lady to manage!" She pulled a funny face at Tariq, who squealed at her in delight.

Eventually she found the lift and ploughed the pram inside, alighting on the top floor that she liked. She settled herself and Tariq at a cosy table in the window, overlooking crowded Grafton Street. The street was very busy really, for a Monday morning at half past eleven, and she wondered if she would be able to see Harry Waters as he approached.

Ursula knew what *he* looked like, of course, although she was conscious that he would have no idea what to expect of her. She felt quite sorry for Harry now, having to face into all of this, she thought, wiping orange baby food off Tariq's chin, and giving him back his rattle toy to play with. If only she could have met him when he was *with* Sinead.

This was going to be so hard; so hard for all of them.

Harry climbed the big staircase of Bewley's cafe slowly with a cautious step. He was on edge, seeking out the image he imagined of an elderly woman who might look like Sinead, or maybe not. Ursula hadn't really said what she looked like on the phone, and he had no idea what to expect. He quickly glanced around the mezzanine when he reached the top of the stairs, and checked for a single elderly lady at every table.

But she clearly wasn't there. The cafe was very quiet, with only five of the tables occupied, and these had couples, and a group of tourists, and there was one woman by the window but she was with a child.

Harry wondered if he should go back downstairs and have a look down there again. But Ursula had definitely said to meet her on the top floor because she liked the waiter service there. He wondered if he should simply get a seat and wait for her. She knew what *he* looked like, she had said. So, he had an *Irish Times*. He would get a coffee and just see what happened next.

The woman with the jolly laughing child was coming over to him now and smiling, reaching out a hand to touch his arm. Harry stood back slightly, not sure if this lady was begging, or just going around being a bit odd. He smiled politely at her and then stepped away again, looking around him for a vacant seat.

But she was following him. She said nothing but she was gazing into his eyes, with tears in hers. Harry decided that she most probably was a small bit mad and so he looked about him to see if there was someone else with her, and tried to get away again.

"I'm sorry, but I've got to meet someone," he told her gently, backing away towards an empty table.

But Ursula grabbed his hand in hers, and pulled him back towards her.

"Harry," she growled, "I'm Ursula Skellig. Sinead's mother. It's *me* that you have to meet."

But she was smaller than she had sounded on the phone, and younger-looking with silver grey hair in a chignon bun swept off a lined but merry face. Her eyes were a vivid blue despite her years, and she dressed in a casual, sporty style; an older version of Sinead. Jeans and runners with a zipped cardigan on top, and an ethnic-looking blouse and coloured beads. The hand that clutched on to his was thick-fingered and loose-skinned. Her fingernails were broken; cracked and full of dirt. But she wore several glamorous rings, giant jewels of turquoise, amber, and black stones. And she had an open and a generous face. Harry stared at her and wondered if he should now take her in his arms. An embrace would be appropriate enough. They'd had a death in common.

But, on the other hand . . . he rested his hand in hers for a while, and let her gaze into his face, and then he kissed her on one cheek. It was soft and powdery. She brushed a tear away.

"You are very good to come. I'm afraid it's all a bit emotional for me. It brings things back, you know, this meeting, Harry."

"It must be very difficult for you." He watched her dab her eyes.

Harry let her steer him to the table where she had been sitting with the child. The baby was absorbed in chewing on a Rusk, and not bothered in the slightest by the arrival of a stranger at the table. Harry sat down, and nodded to the waiter. He ordered a cappuccino, some more tea for Ursula and two *pains au chocolat*.

He turned to smile at Ursula again.

"I thought that you would be alone," he said.

"Yes. I suppose you would have thought so," she replied. "But I'm not."

She looked at the chubby brown-haired baby in the pushchair, and at Harry, and then back again.

Harry wasn't sure what he should say to her and so he thought he'd let her speak. She had organised the meeting after all. It was an awkward enough thing to have to do, for him. He felt incredibly guilty about Sinead, and he had absolutely no idea how he could even begin to be a comfort to this kind, elderly lady, who had lost her only daughter just a year ago. He waited for his order to arrive, and he let her look at him, and then they both looked at the baby together.

The waiter with the drinks arrived, then left.

She took a breath.

"Harry, this is Sinead's son."

Harry nodded. He did not know what to say. So Sinead had had a son. He had never known. Poor child. He smiled again at Ursula, and sipped his coffee. Ursula took his hand, and looking very steadily into his eyes, said "And he's your son, too."

The baby had chewed his Rusk away completely, and it was smeared all over his face like a brown war paint. He squawked at Harry from his pram.

Harry put his cup down and stared at the smeary-faced babbling baby in a state of absolute shock.

Ursula's words were still hovering in the air − "*He's your son, too*" − and the baby squealed at him to be unleashed. His head began to buzz. This child, this strange, and yet suddenly utterly familiar, chubby face. The thick brown hair. The chocolate dark-brown eyes.

The baby kicked his heels in fury, and tugged frantically at the strap that held him in. He reached his fat creased hands up to Harry's face, pleading with him to lift him up. Ursula reacted. She reached across to try to undo Tariq's straps, and let him out of his restraint. But Harry stopped her.

"Please?" His voice was choked. He looked at Ursula's gentle face, and allowed himself to see Sinead's face in it, to see Tariq's face in it, to see a whole new world opening up that he would step into like a marvellous adventure.

Ursula nodded, and she backed away. He carefully unclasped the strap that held his son in place, and let his hands slide around the chubby body, lifting him underneath his armpits, and raising him out of the pram.

The baby swung his legs in glee, and laughed and pulled at Harry's hair, babbling at him.

"Daaadaaadaaadaaa!"

Ursula laughed and tut-tutted at the child.

"Oh, he's really pulling on your heart strings now, isn't he, Harry? But don't be too impressed. He calls me Dada all the time as well. But, hasn't he got your eyes, boy?"

Harry ran his fingers through the floppy fringe to see the baby's eyes properly, and stroked them down his cheek again. He held the baby on his lap, and placed a finger in his palm, and let him tug his shirt, and place his sticky hands around his face.

How this all had happened, he could not begin to know. A girl that he had loved, once loved, for a brief summer's moment, and then left, had died in a country that the world had blown apart.

But there was this. This child. His son. He had a son, and he held him in his arms and watched his face, loving him right back.

Everything was perfect now to Harry Waters at that moment that he held his son Tariq for that first time, and he understood that out of all that tragedy, out of all the misery in the world, something beautiful had been born.

Chapter 32

Isabella studied the small pasted notice on the lamppost carefully, to make sure she'd got the details right.

FREE THE ROSSPORT FIVE!
Shell-To-Sea Campaign.
Five county Mayo farmers have been
Jailed for their legitimate protest
Against the multinational Shell Oil
Running an illegal pipeline through
Their lands.
Stop this government from giving away
Our national resources
Join the demonstration and Send Shell To Sea!
Free The Rossport Five
March and Rally to the GPO
Thursday 26th July 6 pm
THE WEST'S AWAKE!

It was a campaign; it was a protest; it was anti-globalisation in the West of Ireland. And that meant only one thing, as far as Isabella was concerned. Harry Waters would be there.

She had gone about all day with a sense of mounting anticipation, excitement growing like a flower in her belly. She dropped things. She spent what seemed like hours fiddling around with her underwear, folding her T-shirts, trying to decide what to wear. "It isn't the bloody Prom night," Isabella scolded herself. But she didn't really feel ridiculous. She felt happy, confident, and alive.

Isabella selected from her new wardrobe of New York American clothes a crisp white shirt that fitted neatly over her small breasts and tiny waist, to wear with dark navy-blue stretch jeans with boot-leg flares and a pair of low wedge strappy sandals. She stood in front of her bedroom mirror, slowly fastening a thick rope of beads around her neck, and shook her neatly cropped mop of shiny thick black hair.

"And I with my gowns bought ready, the way that I can wed you and not wait at all!" she giggled happily to herself.

She chose a lipstick called Honey Blush from her newly acquired New York make-up bag, and smeared it over her full pale lips until they gleamed like a ripe sliced peach.

Isabella had finally succumbed to Eddie's pestering about her appearance and had allowed him to frog-march her up and down Madison Avenue forcing her to try on smoking jackets and cropped trousers, and pencil skirts, low-slung jeans and killer heels. She had done exactly as Eddie instructed and thrown her horrible, hideous, ghastly sweatshirts in the bin.

"Easy on the tautology, Eddie,'" Isabella had warned him as he whipped one faded garment after another out of her suitcase, and flung it across the bedroom in disgust.

"*Nobody* wears purple and orange any more, Isabella – nobody! What on earth do you think this is, Woodstock?" Eddie had screamed at her.

But she hadn't minded. She was only too happy to dump the whole lot, the whole screaming purple and orange kaleidoscope of mistakes from her past right into a fiery furnace and let them all go to hell, while she slipped coolly into her new collection of Gap, DKNY and Calvin Klein.

"Black. It simply has to be black. Or white. Or grey." Eddie had piled things up in armfuls and steered her into dressing rooms. And Isabella stood in front of her new reflection in the mirrors of the Fifth Avenue stores and saw a sleek figure looking back. She had had her long, messy, tangled mop of Pegeen Mike hair cropped as soon as the theatre run was over.

"And good riddance to Pegeen Mike and the Rodent-nest of the Western World!" Eddie had clapped his hands with joy, as Rob's ex-boyfriend Dino clipped and snipped and let the clouds of black fall away to the floor revealing her smooth, nape-length Park Avenue bob.

She had switched the long, batik-dyed fringed scarves that had previously draped her neck and doubled up as hair bands and bandanas, for a new collection of earrings, pendants and necklaces. "Accessorise, accessorise, accessorise!" Rob and Eddie had chimed. They had selected smart and coolly monochrome outfits, dozens of them. She begged them for a little more colour. And so they had chosen ornaments and beads in reds, blues, browns, taupe, magenta, rose, teal, gold, silver.

"*Six yards of stuff to make a gown, Shawn Keogh, and a pair of lace boots with lengthy heels on them with brassy eyes!*" Isabella quoted.

"Anything but purple, darling," Eddie sighed, and he twirled her around and around, and clapped his hands with glee because she looked so beautiful, confident, and chic.

She had learned eventually to stop despising make-up off-stage, and was happily using mascara under the instruction of two very well-rehearsed gay men to whip her eyelashes up into a beautiful frame for her pale grey almond eyes, so much paler now that she shadowed their lids and let their smokiness captivate. She made her lips seem full and sensuous, with pale flesh-toned colours, browns and plums, and she loved herself. For the first time in thirty-five years, Isabella Somerfield felt she might be something almost like attractive.

Harry will probably prefer the way I used to look, she thought happily to herself as she smoothed the white shirt down over her slender hips and selected a wide black belt to wrap around them. He probably would prefer the hippy long skirt and the scruffy T-shirt look, and Doc Martins over striped socks that I used to wear. But I don't care. I want to look like this. I want to look like me.

Isabella took a bus into the city centre and decided to get off at the beginning of Ormond Quay and walk the rest of the way to the GPO. She was really a little bit too early. That was just the excitement, the anticipation, she reminded herself. But it was a beautiful warm late summer's evening.

The sun was just beginning to melt down behind the buildings on the south quays, but its long rays warmed the boardwalk on the north side where it sent sparkles on the river, bouncing off the chrome chairs and tables where people sat and smoked and drank coffee and ate ice cream after work.

I'll walk along there, Isabella decided. And then if I'm much too early I can have a cup of coffee and sit beside the river and have a think. And if I'm just in time, I can go on up to the GPO straightaway.

She did arrive much too early and so she bought a Mocha and a chocolate muffin and found a seat beside the river where the sun was just beginning to shrink. Imagine me, thought Isabella, eating a muffin like this instead of proper meal. I would never have done this in the old days. I would have had brown rice and vegetables for lunch and a small salad then for tea. And no cakes. And no fattening Mocha coffees, or chocolates or scones. Nothing like the treats that Ruth constantly pops into her mouth whenever she feels like it.

She realised that it was getting slightly colder now, as the sun finally slid behind the buildings to the south and the water was becoming black and darker, and the shadows were becoming cold.

It was time to go and see if he was there.

Isabella walked slowly up O'Connell St, scanning all the people she could see on either side of the road. It was busy. Thursday evening, late night shopping. She glanced from one face to the next as she passed the groups of people, just in case Harry was among them. But then she quickly spotted her goal – the large gathering outside the

GPO, where there was a lorry parked as a platform for speakers, and a group of people were lined up to address the crowd. There was music playing.

The rally must be either just beginning, or just about to end.

She walked more quickly now, trying to estimate the size of the crowd. There were probably well over five thousand people there. It was difficult to see. Some of the crowd were on the island in the middle of the street, and some were even gathered on the pavement on the opposite side of the large boulevard.

Needle in a haystack, thought Isabella anxiously as she realised that Harry could be absolutely anywhere buried in that crowd of happy, cheering farmers. It's really just the story of our lives, she smiled to herself. Me, and Harry, and several thousand people, and he's buried right into the heart of them and my task is simply to find him again.

She stopped walking and stood back from the crowd of people who were now singing along with the guitar player on a lorry stage.

When all beside
A vigil keep
The west's asleep
The west's asleep
Alas and well
May Erin weep
When Connaught lies
In slumber deep

Five thousand Christy Mahons all singing on O'Connell Street!

Isabella giggled to herself as she watched the farmers solemnly sing their hearts out. She decided to join in the last beautiful verse. It reminded her of Eddie and the New York *Playboy* cast, and their drunken closing night at a tuneless piano in a Midtown bar.

Sing HO! Let man learn liberty
From crashing rocks
And lashing sea!

And then she saw him.

Harry was at the back of the crowd, on the island in the middle of the boulevard. He was dressed just as usual; same clothes on for fifteen years, she noticed with a fond smile. Wearing an off-white cotton hooded vest with faded jeans and chunky brown laced-up battered shoes. His hair was still too long: curling brown around his ears and neck, and long in the fringe over his eyes. The beard was gone – his face was smooth and child-like again, although he did look very slightly older. He was crouching down on his heels, only ten meters away from her now, and he was peering into the push-chair pram of a large, chubby baby.

How very odd, thought Isabella. Seeing Harry with a baby. And she smiled at the image. Harry had never been remotely interested in children. Ruth's son Roly had been a mystery to him, and he had never been able to see the fascination other people held in procreation.

Isabella stood and watched Harry now, as he seemed to be fixing on the shoes of this particular baby, and wondered whose it was. As she walked closer towards him she noticed that Harry did seem to be in some way in charge of the baby. There was no-one else with him.

Isabella couldn't think of Harry *choosing* to baby-sit, on a day when there was a big public demonstration on in town.

She stood apart from them for a moment, and watched as Harry fiddled with the baby's shoes, and the baby kicked and giggled, and Harry grinned foolishly back. Harry couldn't see her, and as she watched him she began to notice a certain look about Harry, that she had seen before. A look that she had seen come over the faces of Ruth and Bernard, when Roly was a baby. A sort of besotted grin that transfixed the faces of parents when they gazed into the faces of their offspring, and were rewarded with a smile. She saw the same, parent-baby interaction of gooing and mimicry, and open-mouthed mock surprise.

Harry was exasperated in trying to get the kicking baby to retain his shoe, but Tariq wriggled and kicked and giggled all the more each time Harry tried to get the shoe back on his chubby foot.

"You silly bean, you silly silly bean, you silly bean, you silly silly bean, who's a silly bean? *You're* a silly bean!" Harry repeated over and over again, with an open-mouthed surprised look into the baby's eyes, and Tariq squealed over and over and shrieked with joy as Harry poked him full of tickles every time the shoe kicked off.

"A-a-a-a-a!" mouthed Harry, and Tariq gurgled again, and then Harry noticed that there was someone standing over him who was watching everything.

He cocked his head, squinting against the last piercing rays of the evening sun in his eyes, and shook his mop of brown hair out of his way so that he could see who it was. A woman. She was petite, and slender. Dressed smartly, he noticed, in pointed soft leather shoes, with slim brown feet inside them. Her feet were familiar. Her body was familiar. Her face was even more familiar. She was glamorous – and her hair had changed.

But it was Isabella.

"Iz!" Harry breathed out in delight. "It is you! Oh my God, you're back!"

He stood up and reached out to embrace her. But Isabella stepped away. And turned.

And ran, and ran, and ran.

Chapter 33

Summer swept away on a storm of autumn, and Harry spent the evenings miserably trying to come to terms with what had finally happened to him and Isabella. She was back in Dublin, possibly for good. She had tried to meet him, probably to surprise him, he realised now. And he had let her down with all his powerlessness.

She had looked so beautiful, so vulnerable that day. Her short hair made her look really young again, just as if nothing about her had changed at all since Mrs Glynn's class in primary school, twenty years ago, when he had watched her tuck her curls behind her ears, and circle in the i's for him in *history*.

She had looked so small and lost when the realisation had struck her that Harry was not alone in the world any more. He had shouted, as loudly as he possibly could, across the roar of buses and the clang of trams to her to please come back. *Please. Isabella, please!* But his voice was hoarse and far too weak. He had watched her run away, into the crowds, along the street and down towards the quays again; and he hadn't seen her since.

He spent the days writing political opinion articles now, and preparing for a probable election in the spring. Maggie Hennelly had been very useful in putting him in touch with editors who commissioned his work regularly enough to put a rent on the table for Alan in the small Rialto house.

He dropped Tariq off every morning at the noisy day-care centre in the community hall and took the tram into town, or wrote at home, and in the evenings he met with other leftist groups to think about a strategy for a forthcoming election campaign. There was a new Socialist Alliance emerging now, from the remnants of the peace campaign and the addition of several prominent trade unionists and feminist groups. Harry was being pushed by many of them to put himself forward for election next time round.

He needed far more people around him now than he had ever done before, because Tariq came first, no matter what. But Alan was often free to baby-sit, and Fiona often let him bring Tariq around to play with her two older kids, while Harry sat in darkened pubs and meeting halls and planned fundraising. But Harry didn't like to be apart from Tariq that much, even when he was deep in polemic and strategic debate.

He went to sleep at night beside the child, in the double bed, and Tariq's fat laughing face was the first thing that he saw on waking every morning. They would giggle and tickle and play together for a while, before Harry rose to dress and wash his son and made him Ready Brek to eat. He walked everywhere with Tariq, pushing him onto buses in his pram. He took him into meetings with him, shushing him up with bags of crisps and lollipops and rubber books to read.

He had visited Ursula several times during the past six months, and they had been fun trips that he regularly looked forward to now. An early morning Westport train, with a newspaper and a cappuccino and a piece of cake to share with Tariq. Ursula was quite good company, too. She was sharp and witty, and intelligent, and they talked deep into the night about the situation in America, in Ireland, and Iraq.

She had shown him photographs of Sinead as a child. A freckled jolly child with Tariq's face, under thick blond hair that was sun-bleached almost white. There was her graduation photograph too. Sinead posing happily in a mortar board, her black cape blowing round her in a West of Ireland summer wind.

There were photographs of her first time in Iraq in 1991 too, and Harry traced his finger over these, taking in the hot white walls of buildings, the sharp sunshine, and the dark-skinned faces of Sinead and all her friends. Sinead smiling by a swimming pool. Laughing, wearing sunglasses in a coffee bar. He touched the images of a different, long-ago Sinead, and rubbed his hand through Tariq's over-growing mop of hair.

They sat in silences as well. Ursula reading library books of South American magic realism, and Harry a biography of Hugo Chavez. On Sunday nights she put them on the train again, with a loaf of soda bread wrapped in a striped tea towel, and a large still-warm apple-pie. Alan would seize the apple-pie as soon as they arrived and wolf it down almost in one go.

But despite the many distractions that he threw himself into now, Harry could not keep Isabella from his mind. She was in Dublin, and that was all he needed to know to prevent him from being able to stop thinking about her every day. He looked in every crowd and on every bus that passed, just in case her face might travel by. He often took detours along streets that she might have walked – around cinemas where they used to go as students, or along lanes that led to cafes where they once had been. He didn't even know where she lived in Dublin, and the basement flat in Rathmines was home to a large Romanian family now.

Walking past the flat had brought back all the memories of the past fifteen years. He and Isabella aged eighteen, at college in the spring, falling wonderfully in love.

The unmade lumpy bed. The endless cups and plates and half-eaten rolls of bread. The endless lovemaking in the mornings, in the afternoons, and the endless silences too. The sulking rows. The flinging of the plates. The days when he had walked away in thick despair, and vowed never to go back again, only to slip inside late at night again, when she was quite asleep, and pull her tight towards him only to be pushed away.

He thought about the last time he had seen her there – the morning before the night that he had gone on the TV, and spent that one night afterwards with Sinead. Isabella had waited all alone for him, and then in the morning left a small, neatly written note that meant absolutely nothing at all.

Harry, I have gone. Don't follow me, or write or phone. I want to be away forever now.

Love with Isabella had been sometimes hard. But she

was a part of him that he simply could not let go. She was the only person that had known him all his life, with whom he felt that he could still live the rest of his life. Though he had Tariq now, of course, and nothing would ever replace that love, which overwhelmed him like a wave.

But Isabella ate away at his heart, her small face present to him always, her low voice a constant echo in his mind.

He had rung her old department at the university, but the secretary was vague. Isabella Somerfield was off the payroll now. No, didn't know if she was in Dublin. Couldn't remember where she had said she was going to work next. Didn't she go to America a year or two ago? Yes, but he was sure that she was back now. Uhuh. No, can't say I have heard from her. Did you try Personnel?

As Christmas time approached, Harry bought a toy fire engine for Tariq, and thought about the fact that he had a family now himself for Christmas, small though it might be. There would be a Santa Claus to arrange, he thought happily, as he paid for the noisy toy (that he would, on a dark hungover New Year's early morning, deeply regret).

He would have to go to County Wexford to the parents' house for Christmas – and that might be fun. Harry and Tariq, and his mum and dad. He wondered what Tariq's other granny Ursula would like to do for Christmas. He hadn't spoken to her yet about it and he didn't want to presume too much. She might have other plans – and then again, she just might not. In his new extended family, there were several very welcome combinations.

Harry pushed the pram out through the doors of the overheated toyshop, and onto the damp cold of Henry

Street, which was darkened now at five o'clock. The shops were full of Christmas queues, and in the cold air people walked by quickly with overloaded bags. Tariq was fast asleep in his buggy and Harry bent to make sure that his face was not too cold, and to fasten his fleece hat around his chin.

He tucked the baby's long fringe into his pale blue little hat and checked that his safety belt was fastened. He would have a think about what sort of presents to get for Ursula and his mum next week. But there was still plenty of time for all that.

Harry stood for a moment watching Henry Street go by, and tried to decide what was the best way to get home now. The tram would just be vacuum-packed. He could go back up to O'Connell Street for a bus. The bus was slower, but infinitely more pleasant, and he had a fascinating book to read.

He turned to walk towards the main street, when something on a newly-pasted billboard poster caught his eye.

Pinter At The Gate

Harry stood to read the text underneath the giant photo of the playwright. Harold Pinter was going to be in Dublin that weekend, to open a performance of *Old Times* at the Gate Theatre on Parnell Square. Harry stood there reading it for several minutes. He checked off all the small print of the notice – but it was all quite clear.

Pinter At The Gate.

The Nobel Laureate would be reading from his poetry, and then opening a performance of the play!

Harry's search was over.

If there was *anywhere* that Isabella Somerfield would

choose to be that night, in all the world, it was at a poetry reading by Harold Pinter in her own home town.

He felt his body sink into the ground with relief.

He knew where he would find her now.

At a quarter to eight, Harry stood outside the theatre doors, and waited in the cold. It was pitch dark, and with what felt like an early frost, the night was getting very nippy now indeed. Harry stamped his feet and clapped his woollen gloves together, searching every face that approached the theatre doors, in despair.

Everyone was walking by so quickly now because of the cold, and he had to really concentrate to try to pick her face out of all the possible faces in the crowds that milled around the doorways of the theatre. And none of them were her. It was freezing here outside, and there was no sign of her. No sign of her at all.

But she would have to come. He was so utterly sure of that. He had rehearsed it over and over again in his head before tonight. He had imagined what she would wear, how her new short hair would look. He had seen her face turn to look at his, in his new black three-quarter-length wool coat and scarf, and she would smile, and they would take each other's hands . . . or possibly not of course, he knew, but it was worth a daydream.

She would ask him why he had come, and he would say, 'I came to find you again': and they would go and eat, or have a drink, and talk about all the things that had gone by in the two years since they were apart, and they would laugh and hold each other's hands again, and promise that they would love each other now forever.

Harry knew that this imaginary scene was quite ridiculous, but he kept on playing it over and over again regardless in his mind. It made him happy just to think about it.

Of course, she might have changed, he realised. Changed completely, and be quite disinterested in him. But he wanted to tell her all about Tariq. She might have been quite shocked that day. But she would be so pleased when he could finally arrange for them to meet. He wanted her to love Tariq, and find him special, in the way that all parents believe that their children are the special ones.

Half an hour had gone by, and she still had not appeared. They were beginning to close the theatre doors. He had to do something to find out if she was already in the theatre. He opened the outside door, and stood in front of the box-office window, wondering what to say.

He couldn't ask if Isabella had gone in – because they wouldn't know. But he couldn't get in to find her there without a ticket.

The box-office woman looked up at him. "All tickets are sold out, sir," she said.

"Er, no. I didn't want . . . I mean, I thought perhaps that I could collect my ticket here? The name is Somerfield. I just thought that you might have it?"

The woman glanced down, rummaging through a pile of envelopes.

"No, sorry, no Somerfield in here. Are you sure that you arranged for box-office collection?"

"What other kind of collections are there?"

"Well, you could have had them sent out to you by post," she smiled.

"Yes. Oh yes, perhaps I did. Yes, that's it! By post! To my house! And, if I had requested for them to be sent out by post, to my house, where I live, then what address would they have been sent to?" he asked, excited.

"The address you gave us, most probably." She gave him a curious look.

"Ah yes, of course. The address that I gave you. You see, that is what the problem is. It's just that we have moved, several times, recently, and I can't be sure which address we *might* have said to you." Harry tried to put on an expression of innocence.

The woman glanced down again, and tapped her keyboard for a moment.

"Well, those two tickets for Somerfield, Isabella, were sent out to 27 Oak Court Lawn, Blackrock – and they were sent out to you two weeks ago, so they were."

"Oh great! Oh, thank you! Thank you so so much!" Harry almost sobbed with relief.

"So, have you received them?" she asked him, quite puzzled now.

"Oh, yes. I mean no. I mean, thank you. Oh, that's fantastic news. Yes. I know where to go to look for them now. Thank you!" He lifted his hands to her in prayer position. "Thank you so much for everything!" and he turned to walk away.

"You're going to miss the first half of the play . . . "

But the strange, distracted, rather emotional man had already gone.

Chapter 34

Isabella found the Pinter play to be rather dull. The acting was just wooden. The stage set uninspired. And the theatre was overcrowded and uncomfortable. But Pinter's own poetry reading had been wonderful – there was absolutely no doubt in her mind about that. In a painful, cracked dry voice, Harold Pinter had read words that were simply too beautiful to believe. The audience sat like statues while he spoke.

"There are no hard distinctions between what is real and what is unreal, nor between what is true and what is false. A thing is not necessarily either true or false; it can be both true and false. I believe that these assertions still make sense and do still apply to the exploration of reality through art. So as a writer I stand by them but as a citizen I cannot. As a citizen I must ask: What is true? What is false? Truth in drama is forever elusive. You never quite find it but the search for it is compulsive. The search is clearly what drives the endeavour. The search is your task.

More often than not you stumble upon the truth in the dark, colliding with it or just glimpsing an image or a shape which seems to correspond to the truth, often without realising that you have done so. But the real truth is that there never is any such thing as one truth to be found in dramatic art. There are many. These truths challenge each other, recoil from each other, reflect each other, ignore each other, tease each other, are blind to each other. Sometimes you feel you have the truth of a moment in your hand, then it slips through your fingers and is lost."

Isabella felt the tears swell her eyes, as she listened to Pinter's words. There were many truths that she knew she had failed to discover, questions she'd ignored. The truth about the war was becoming clearer now, to everyone; and she felt incredibly proud of Harry and all the work that he had done two years ago when it had been so much harder, standing in a hurricane of easily believed lies, to say and keep on saying what was truth.

Harry had trusted her implicitly, and yet he had so easily let her go. The truth of the moment, of so many of the moments of their past, was something that she had certainly let slip away; not just once, not twice, but all the time.

If only she had had the strength to ask him truthfully where he had been, and who he had been with that night, a whole year of suffering and crying alone could have been spared her. But asking for the truth was just too hard. Perhaps she had just preferred not to know; but there was no freedom in that choice either. It was the choice of self-deception and deliberate self-harm, over an eternity of pain. And she had hidden painful truths from Harry too.

Harry had always argued that a thorough understanding

of the facts, no matter how unpleasant, would lead to better things.

Unless we know how slavery works, how can we understand racism? Harry used to say. Unless we know what causes war, how can we fight for peace?

Does the same apply to love? Isabella wondered. If we can understand an infidelity, can we then be better organised to make love work? If we know *why* it is that we are jealous, can our jealousy be defeated?

Isabella wasn't sure. The emotions of the heart might well be based in logic. Love and jealousy might well make sense, when one analysed their origins in terms of the balances of power, desire, and fear of being alone. But the feelings that she had for Harry now, and the truths that they had held from one another, were far more complex than before.

There was a complete situation now, the exploration of which would possibly lead to a series of new truths. But she was not sure if those were the kind of truths that she would want to bear.

She had walked away, because Harry's life had been so utterly absorbed by his love for everyone else, rather than for her. But to realise that as well as Harry's undeniable love for all the world, that he had loved another woman too while sleeping every night with Isabella in her bed, was far too painful to bear.

She hadn't always been completely honest with Harry. But now there was a situation for Harry, which he must have created through a lie. Either she knew Harry well, or she did not. And if she did not know the man with whom she had spent fifteen years of her life, what could she know? Nothing could be true any more.

Isabella tried not to return to Harry in her thoughts now, as she went about her days, working on her daytime TV show, and returning to her room-share with Ruth and Bernard every night. She went out to parties, and had drinks after work, and ate Chinese in front of DVDs. She went on several dates and enjoyed every one of them. Harry didn't matter any more, she told herself. He had outlived his sell-by date.

It was a great love that had lived with her for fifteen years, but leaving it had almost destroyed her. She was not going back there now. Harry was no more.

After cocktails in the Clarence Hotel bar, she said goodbye to the colleague she had gone to see the Pinter with in town, and caught the late bus home.

In the darkness of the tree-lined street, the lamplight cast mysterious shadows. Isabella thought she saw someone passing up and down in front of her house as she approached it from the bus stop on the main road, but she wasn't sure. And then she saw him move again.

There seemed to be someone skulking around outside the house. He must be a neighbour who was locked out. She hoped he wasn't someone checking out the house, with a view to a robbery. It wasn't very late, just past twelve o'clock. But she wasn't sure she liked the look of the nervous-looking man, pacing up and down in front of the terraced house wearing a black coat.

She quickened her pace to get to the front door as quickly as possible and lock herself in, and then he spoke, and called her by her name.

"Isabella!"

She turned and looked at him.

"Harry."

He stood there, very still.

She had left the key in the lock when she turned to face him and the front door yawned open.

"I was waiting for you to get home. I hope you don't mind me coming out here."

"I . . . "

She didn't know what to say. Of course she minded. This was not what she wanted now, not what she wanted at all. It was after midnight now. She had been out and she was tired and now Harry Waters was here, at her house, with no clear way of getting home again. And obviously hoping to be invited in.

"I need to talk to you. Just for a moment. I want to tell you about everything that's happened to me. There's been a lot of stuff, and I really, really want for you to know."

She put a hand up to stop him. "No, Harry. Please stop. I can't. I can't do this for you. I let you go, and you found your way in the world. Please don't come back into mine now, and turn it all around again. I had to fight so hard to let you go. Please don't make me have to go through all that again. Please," she ended in a whisper.

"Oh, darling Iz!" He moved towards her.

"No, don't! Don't try, Harry, please don't even try. It's been too hard. You have someone now, who loves you, and whom you love. So let me find someone else now too. I've been away for so long, and it was the bravest, hardest thing I had to do. I lived alone, in New York City, Harry, without you, and it was the loneliest time I have ever spent in all my life; but you know what? It was the biggest thing that I've ever done too. I grew up, and I got smart and proud of what I can do. And that's been a fight worth fighting. It was worth losing you to get to be myself. And this is what I want now. I don't want to be your shadow, Harry. Your mini-me. Your childhood sweetheart. Your lover. I don't even want to be your friend. Our lives were long ago – in school, in college, those times with Ruth and Eddie, and the politics, and all the days of you and me together loving one another. That's all just a dream now, Harry. I was afraid that it was becoming a nightmare. I was afraid that loving you was making me a lesser person; turning me into a nobody. I thought that I was going to have to live all of my life through yours, and not do any living of my own. But I was wrong. I only needed to walk away to see the difference. And walking away from you was just the hardest thing that I will ever want to do. And so don't, don't, don't make me have to do it all again!" She was sobbing now.

"Isabella, I came to tell you that I have a son."

"And what, exactly, do you think that has to do with me?" she screamed at him.

"Let's go inside," he begged.

"*No!*" she roared. "I live here in this street. This is my life now, Harry Waters. If you choose to march up here and disrupt it all for me, I'll scream and yell as loudly as I want!"

A light went on in the house across the road.

"I have a son, but it isn't what you think."

"Oh, indeed, is that so? And what exactly do you

suppose I *do* think it is, Harry, that I might wonder how you came to have a son, just by the way? 'Oh, Isabella, hello, and here's my son.' We were a *couple,* Harry!" She was hysterical now. "We lived together. We planned a life together. I know we weren't planning much, but by Jesus, we planned to buy more tea bags, and to get the bins out in time on Thursdays, and we paid the bills together, and bought milk, and fed the cat."

"We never had a cat."

"Well, we could have had a cat. But, oh, you had to go ahead and have a *baby*!"

"I didn't have a baby!"

"Oh? And is that so? And so, who had the baby for you? Who did you donate your sperm to, Harry? Is she a surrogate mom, some – some lesbian who wanted your offspring or some politically-correct single mum like that? Or, perhaps you felt like adopting that baby. Did you find him on a convent wall? Or, did one of your ships that passed in the night leave him on your doorstep one morning, with a note? 'Please find one baby, he's all yours'!"

Harry opened up his mouth to answer, but she cut him off. Several of the neighbours were twitching curtains now as Isabella shouted on the street.

"You know, don't even bother to try to tell me, Harry. I think that at this stage, I really don't want to have to know. So you have a child – well, big swinging Mickey! I had an abortion. Bet you never knew that, did you? So, there's two kids you could have had by now. Only I wasn't smart enough to keep mine. I put it all aside for you and me, so we could have each other. And look at what a big fat mistake that turned out to be. So take your baby, in his lovely shiny new pram, with all his Early Learning Centre toys, and go away and live your life, Harry. And let me just live mine. Because you may have a baby, but I've got me. And I'm still very very precious to myself, so I am, and you'd better get used to that!"

"The baby's mother died." Harry finally spoke.

Silence filled the air. In the distance a dog howled, and several others barked, and the bus pulling up at the end of the road squealed – but Isabella heard nothing except the still cold night, and hers and Harry's rapid breathing now.

"What?" she asked, in a choked small voice.

He stepped towards her.

"I'd really like it if we could go in."

They talked until the morning light. Side by side on a faded floral sofa, Harry told Isabella the long unhappy story of how he had met Sinead. He left nothing out.

There was nothing left to hide from Isabella now. He and Isabella were not a couple any more – their love was in the past. She had been furious with him, and said she never wanted to see him ever again, but he owed her an explanation for everything that had happened.

His life was with Tariq, he told her now, and he knew it would always be. But he still wanted Isabella, the first and the most precious love of all his life, to know what it was that his life was going to be all about from now on. And most of all, he wanted to reassure her that he had never meant to hurt her.

He never would have left her for Sinead, he told her, as they drank cup after cup of hot strong midnight tea. He had wanted very much, for a very brief amount of time, to be with Sinead, and she with him. But he hadn't wanted to lose Isabella either. If only he had had that choice.

And Isabella had done the right thing, walking out on him that morning. He realised that now. She had become a different person. A person that she now wanted herself to be. And he had found Tariq.

Harry told the story of how Sinead had died, without his knowing, and Isabella sat beside him holding both his hands. She stroked his hair, and listened to his account of his first meeting with Ursula Skellig, and his finding out the truth about Sinead, and that he had a boy.

She tried to picture him putting a little boy to bed, and reading him a story, giving him a bath. "What kind of stories does Tariq like? Do you bring him to a crèche? What are his friends called?" she asked cautiously. "Does he look like you? Or like his mum?"

That was the hardest question that she'd had to ask him. But she asked it anyway, because she knew that it was the sort of thing one asks a parent. And there was a part of her that really needed to find out, before she got to know Tariq.

She had to know that she had the courage now to look at Harry's son, and not feel upset that he had belonged to someone else.

"Why didn't you tell me that you'd had an abortion?" he asked her quietly.

She closed her eyes. "Because we were too young," she opened them again. "And all I wanted at that time was for us to be together, and for everything just to be the same."

"Didn't you trust me to be a good enough dad, back

then? Because I don't blame you if you did. I made a lot of mistakes about us, back then."

She shook her head. "That wasn't really it. The truth is that I didn't trust myself to be a good enough mum either, in those days, and maybe that's the real reason I couldn't tell you." She looked at him sadly, and then touched his face. "Harry, let's not talk about the past any more. All the secrets and the lies are over now. Everything will be different from now on."

Harry leaned his head onto her shoulder and eventually they fell asleep, in one another's arms.

Chapter 35

On Christmas day it snowed in County Wexford for the first time in over fifteen years.

Tony Waters stood at the big bay window in the dining room jangling the coins in his pockets and watched the snow fall thickly on the grass below, and over fallen leaves and hard brown flower beds.

He hummed a little Christmas song:

On the twelfth day of Christmas my true love gave to me
Five gold rings!
Four calling birds
Three French hens
Two turtledoves
And a partridge in a pear tree!

Tata tum ta ta tum, Tony continued tunefully, and smiled to himself as he surveyed his whitening garden. He watched a solitary robin perched in a barren rosebush, beadily staking out the soil beneath where Marion had scattered crumbs. The robin suddenly took courage and bounced down onto the hard brown soil, briskly pecking up a crumb up from underneath his bush hideout and then fluttered away back up into the trees again in triumph.

It was going to be a wonderful Christmas day.

They had all been up early for a change, but it was good to be awake after dawn in the cold bright morning just to see the first snowfall. Marion had gone to Mass, just to have a bit of a sing she told him, and he had helped her to defrost the car, revving it up for her before she drove it off and away and down the slippery hill.

Ursula Skellig, who had arrived yesterday morning on the train at Campile, was proving to be a fantastic help with new ideas for his garden. Tony was delighted. Ursula and Tony had spent most of the morning talking about plants, manure, and compost heaps, while Harry and Isabella had got the fire going in the sitting room and opened presents from Santa Claus. Tariq had squealed with pleasure when his new red fire engine emerged from its plastic box.

Tony thought Ursula to be a surprisingly likable woman. She was a good bit older than himself and Marion, he decided. But she was clearly very fit and active for her years. And her knowledge of the land and of gardening and horticulture was superb. She was laughing there with Marion at the kitchen table now, and they both sat opposite each other peeling carrots and potatoes.

The best thing was that Ursula was fitting right in despite Isabella being here, thought Tony to himself. He was very glad to see that Ursula was a solid and determined help for Harry, without being interfering or granny-ish, or telling him what to do. It must be so hard for Ursula trying to cope with Sinead's death and everything. But she seemed to be a strong and solid kind of woman, who took things as they came.

Marion Waters, on the other hand, was still quite timid with the baby. It had taken her much more effort to come to terms with the situation, of Harry, and Isabella, and Harry and Sinead's son. But Marion couldn't help but warm to Ursula as she made herself at home in the kitchen, doing all the washing up and peeling sprouts, and taking white wine out of the fridge to breathe.

Her presence was really quite *serene*, thought Tony. Quite serene it is.

Sinead must have been a lovely person though, he thought, as he carefully selected some logs from the pile to stoke the fire so that the room would be nice and cosy for their lunch. Through the door of the dining room to the sitting room floor next door, he could see Harry, Isabella and Tariq playing on the floor in front of another bright log fire, curled up near the heat. The baby crawled up and down, back and over with the red fire engine, and Harry patiently wound it's clanger up for him, over and over and over again.

The noise of the fire engine was appalling, but there was so much going on in the big house that morning with the Christmas carols on the radio and the two women laughing like a pair of drains in the kitchen over the sprouts, and the telly in the other room with a silly Christmas movie on it that Isabella was half watching. Despite the racket, it was just lovely to have the house this full again.

And there it would be getting fuller later on that day.

Isabella's two friends were over from America for the holidays and they were on their way down from Dublin now, to spend the night in Dunmallow too.

Tony was very pleased indeed that Isabella was now back in their lives again. And he had always liked Eddie Mannion – what a ticket he had been when Harry had been friends with him in college. Eddie had a *partner* now too – a violin player, Isabella told him, who had a beautiful baritone voice. Tony hoped that they might play the piano later on and that he and Rob could get the others going, and they would sing a few carols, and maybe some songs from one of the old Broadway shows.

The conversation in the kitchen had descended to a lower murmuring pitch now, and so Tony thought it might be a good time to get a bit of peace all to himself before the commotion would begin for lunch. He sat down in an armchair just beside the fireplace in the dining room and closed his eyes and let his thoughts drift over the events that had unfolded in the Waters family over the last two years.

Tony had worried terribly about Marion, when Harry had told her that Isabella had left him and gone somewhere he didn't know. Marion had been shocked. And that first Christmas that Harry had been down without Isabella had been so difficult for Marion to understand. Isabella had been working in America of course, they all knew now, and so Marion approved of that. And now Isabella was back, but there was such an unexpected situation for them all to get used to now.

What Marion had always wanted more than anything for Harry was for him to be settled, happy, and with the possibility of a family in his future.

The family that Tony watched now, as he settled down into an armchair across from Harry and Isabella on the floor, was not exactly what Marion had always had in mind. Harry with Isabella, with someone else's child. But they were happy, clearly. Anyone could see that now. And that was as much as Marion could ever really want.

The baby was like a clone of their own baby, Harry, as a child. It was uncanny to see the two of them pull the fire engine together, and to see baby Tariq squeal with joy, just the way his father had done over thirty years ago. Tony felt quite emotional now, with *privilege*, to be able to have had a grandchild, albeit not in the circumstances of his own choosing.

Outside the snow had stopped, and the white gardens threw midday sun light back into the house through wide French windows. Tony closed his eyes in the growing heat of the crackling log fire, and dozed off into a light, pre-lunch sleep, looking forward to his turkey and ham and stuffing, and some more of that nice red wine.

Marion was showing Ursula some of Harry's photographs.

Harry as a small brown-eyed solemn boy, slightly older than Tariq was now. Harry as a teenager in a grey uniform and striped school tie. The student graduation day. Isabella too, as she was then, underneath a long thick tangle of black hair with a tiny pointed face, smiling, holding onto his hand, a green and purple bandana round her hair.

And there were later photographs of Harry too. Harry in a Palestinian scarf, outside the American Embassy on a march. Some news clippings. Photos of his time in

Venezuela. And then their conversations inevitably lead back to Sinead.

Ursula talked about Sinead's graduation in Galway. Her time spent in Iraq. About the time that she had bravely stayed back in Baghdad in 1991. She talked about how many international friends she had had. Ursula told Marion how much Harry had meant to Sinead, encouraging her to protest against the war, and about how much Harry and his friends had meant to Moussa and the other doctors. Marion listened carefully to Ursula, her head bent low to listen, and held her hand while she talked and talked. They sat in silence for a while. Ursula patted Marion's hand.

They had another sherry, and then put the roast potatoes on.

Isabella lolled along the floor, half reading a book that Tony had given her for Christmas about the life of Oscar Wilde, and half watching *Charlie And The Chocolate Factory* on the television with Tariq. They had had a late, coffee-ish breakfast, of hot sweet cranberry muffins that Ursula had baked as soon as she had woken up. The thick Christmas marmaladey smell had woken everybody with excitement; along with Tariq's peals of surprise on finding that Santa Claus had come.

Isabella wasn't too hungry yet, but the growing smell of turkey and of roast potatoes spitting in the Rayburn was becoming rather wonderful. She closed her book for another while, as it was impossible to fully concentrate with the television on at the same time, and decided to play with Tariq's bricks instead that Tony and Marion had rescued from the attic box of toys from Harry's baby days.

The Waters, ever practical, had given Harry money to buy a Christmas present for Tariq rather than have to try themselves to choose some unnecessary toy. Ursula had knitted a rather shapeless and unsuitably prickly jumper that Isabella knew no baby would tolerate to wear. But she loved her for it anyway.

Isabella had given Harry a book; a copy of some of Harold Pinter's poetry, which she was sure that he was going to love. And he had given her a scarf. It was not the most imaginative present ever, but it was a big improvement as a gift compared to *The State And Revolution* by Lenin, which was a gift that Harry had once thought suitable to place into her hands, and she had thrown into the bin in tears. This year's scarf was long, and wound several times around her neck, and was a multi-coloured orange, red and pink – the old Isabella colours, but it looked surprisingly nice on her, with small sparkly sequins sewn through the silk that glimmered in the firelight now.

She had written an inscription in the Pinter book – *Happy Christmas Harry, Lots of Love from Izzy and Tariq.* There were no circles, only dots above the i's.

Isabella looked over at Harry to see if he was watching telly, or watching Tariq, who was crawling round across the floor and making a hot trek into the kitchen, possibly following the good smell of cooking food. Harry, lying on the floor in front of the fire, called his mother to attend to Tariq, and from the kitchen he heard Marion call back, "It's okay, love, I've got him here. I'll give him a bit of a carrot stick to chew on while he waits for his Christmas dinner."

Harry opened his mouth to tell his mother not to give

the baby a carrot stick in case he shoved the carrot up his nose: and then he remembered that she had raised a son herself, and so he closed his mouth again. He looked at Isabella, who was grinning at him, watching him being a dad, fussing over his child, being over-protective all the time.

"Happy New Year, Isabella," he said to her.

"Happy New Year, Harry."

And she kissed him.

THE END